David Lakeman spent [barcode: GW01454553] :a, particularly Libya w[...] in the oil fields and later with the military ... :gic radio communications systems including encoding and encryption methods. During this time he travelled extensively throughout the Sahara desert and experienced it's many facets and weather including severe sand storms. He is also a qualified pilot and Marine Coastguard Agency (MCA) certified yacht master and navigator. In his earlier career he trained as a marine radio officer and is familiar with all forms of communications from low frequency (LF) wireless telegraphy (WT) to high frequency (HF) single side band (SSB) transmission as well as marine and aviation radio navigation equipment.

During his career he has accumulated 1500 hours of flying various aircraft throughout Europe and North Africa. In Africa he has spent time in Libya, Tunisia, Algeria, Morocco, Belgian Congo, Gabon, Angola and South Africa. In South America he has visited and spent time in Brazil, Argentina, Paraguay and Chile.

Flight of the *Swastika*

David Lakeman

For my sister Yvonne for her help and encouragement
For my sister Sandra for her advice and encouragement
For my brother Dennis for his support and encouragement
For my best friend Mervyn, my sister Yvonne and my wife
Maggie for their proof reading and helpful suggestions.

Contents

❖

Chapter 1

❖

J ames St Clair awoke that morning to the hum of an air conditioner, a mild headache and a dry mouth and throat. Perhaps he should not have had that last beer and chaser the previous evening in the mess with the hard-drinking drillers and tool pushers; he really was not in the same league as those tough Texan oilmen when it came to alcohol.

His accommodation was one of a number of single berth units within portable containers set out around the mess hall and common room for the personnel who worked at the oil camp known by its radio call sign, King One. With its own shower and toilet, it was by any standards quite comfortable considering it was in the middle of the Sahara Desert.

Since most of the personnel spent periods of many months and some even up to a year at the camp before getting leave to go back to civilization, a reasonable standard of comfort was a necessity.

James, known as Jaime to his friends, was a pilot with Air Libya, a company which flew stores and workers to and from the desert oil camps to either Tripoli or Benghazi. He was not one of the permanent personnel but had been forced to stay overnight due to a very severe sandstorm the previous day.

It was still quite early in the morning when he struggled out of bed but there were already sounds of activity outside. Camp life started early in the desert to take advantage of the cool before the dawn. By mid-morning the temperature was into the nineties and by midday much higher so activity ceased until the sun had descended to a lower altitude.

Jaime took a luxurious shower and could not but wonder how so much water was available in the desert. It was previously largely unexplored until the Second World War during which forces had only reconnoitred mostly within a hundred miles from the coast in the need for intelligence on enemy movements and not with any geological intent. Since the discovery of oil in the early sixties, however, much geological survey work had been undertaken and, together with the discovery of considerable oil reserves areas of the desert as far south as the Khufra oasis, vast water reserves had been found not far below the surface. The first thing that was done when a site was established to build a camp, either as a wellhead or as a construction site for building the ever-expanding pipeline network, was to drill for water, which could be argued as being a more valuable commodity than oil in that most hostile environment.

Having showered and dressed, Jaime, who was a little over six feet tall, of athletic build and with fair hair which tended towards a more blondish hue due to the exposure to the strong sunlight in the desert, opened the door to his unit. It was still dark but the sky to the east was gradually brightening as the dawn approached. It was the time of day he liked the most. The sandstorm had blown itself out during the night and it was breathlessly calm and cool. As Jaime watched the eastern sky, a tiny orange red spot appeared on the horizon and slowly grew from a spot to an ever-expanding arc growing with intensity and power as it gradually began to take the form of a fiery orb. It reminded Jaime of the pictures he had seen of atomic explosions in slow motion which in fact it really was except what he was witnessing was millions of such explosions on the sun's surface which was the source of all such energy in the universe and the bringer of life to the planet Earth.

Sunlight spread across the desert surface from the horizon banishing the shadows, revealing the other trailers and equipment of the camp. Just beyond the outer trailers was the outline of an aircraft parked at the end of a rough runway levelled and graded in the sand. The surface here was largely flat which made it ideal for constructing a runway. From where the aircraft was parked, two lines of black painted fifty-gallon oil drums stretched out into the distance marking the landing area.

The centre of the camp was the living area set out with two rows of accommodation trailers facing each other with the mess hall and recreation trailers between them forming a U-shape. In front of the mess hall, there were a number of rough wooden tables with benches just like those found in picnic areas all over the world. This was the barbecue area much favoured by the oilmen after a hard day's work where they could enjoy enormous steaks that Americans seemed to thrive on. The barbecues consisted of the two halves of a fifty-gallon oil drum with metal legs welded on. Cleaning these from the sand which had deposited itself everywhere and worked its way into every nook and cranny from the sandstorm was Hakim, the camp boss. Although not in charge of the camp as the title implied, he was in charge of providing the creature comforts for all the personnel without which the camp could not function. He was in fact, for all intents and purposes, the camp housekeeper. The person in overall charge was the camp superintendent, responsible for the construction and efficient operation and management when the camp started production.

Jaime said hello to Hakim as he approached the mess hall.

"Good morning, Captain," said Hakim, "Weather looks good for flying today. What time will you be off?"

"Not sure exactly. I have to check the aircraft thoroughly for sand just like you with the barbecues."

The mess hall was already busy when Jaime entered with oilmen fuelling up with enormous breakfasts ready for a strenuous day's work. Since coming to Libya and flying all over the desert to the oil camps, the thing that impressed him the most was the size of some of these oilmen and the size of their appetites. Down one side of the mess hall was a buffet-style area with hot metal trays loaded with eggs, bacon, sausages, fried potatoes waffles, pancakes and tomatoes. Next to it was a refrigerated open display of fruit pies and every type of ice cream. The Americans loved ice cream and apple pie even for breakfast.

Helping himself to a modest portion of bacon and eggs, Jaime carried his tray over to a table occupied by the camp superintendent Joe Osborne. Sitting down, Joe poured him a cup of coffee from a steaming jug on the table.

"Sorry we don't have any tea," he said.

"Don't worry, I've got used to coffee with breakfast now when I'm out here. Do I have any passengers on this return trip?"

"No, no one is due any leave and those you brought out were new men or replacements. What time will you be leaving?"

"I just need to check all the sand covers and filters did their job last night and I'll be away. When are you due back in Tripoli?"

"A week from now. I hope we can get together for a drink."

"I look forward to it," said Jaime.

Joe had a company apartment in Tripoli which he managed to get back to for one week every month and during the last year that Jaime had been flying out to King One, he and Joe had become friends. Their mutual bond stemmed from the fact Joe had been a wartime pilot just like Jaime so they had much in common.

Jaime had been just sixteen at the outbreak of the war. Like all schoolboys of that time, he became inspired by the exploits of the RAF pilots and was determined to join up as soon as possible and learn to fly. In 1941, he was accepted into the RAF and, following flying lessons in Canada, he qualified for his wings. He immediately applied for twin engine training determined to fly the incredible new Mosquito wooden wonder fighter bomber that was creating havoc with the Luftwaffe in all sorts of daring exploits. After qualifying, he was posted to a Beaufighter bomber squadron flying the sturdier but equally devastating long-range aircraft.

By the end of 1942, he was flying with the Desert Air Force and took part in the rout of the Afrika Korps pursuing the retreating German forces all the way from El Alamein to Tripoli. With its heavy 20 mm cannons and under wing rockets, the Beaufighter took a heavy toll on the fleeing tanks and armoured cars.

Following the war in the desert, Jaime finally got his wish to fly the Mosquito and was posted to a squadron based in England. He flew night intruder missions into Germany attacking fighters returning home to their bases after attacking the Lancaster bomber streams which nightly were destroying the enemy's industrial capacity to continue the war. He continued in this until the end of the war destroying ten enemy aircraft and, in the process, becoming a double ace and earning a DFC and bar.

With the war's end, Jaime was offered a permanent commission to stay on but after the excitement of wartime flying, he thought the peacetime RAF would be something of an anti-climax. With the expanding new commercial aviation world and the possibilities of seeing much more of the actual world, pioneering new routes was more appealing. Declining the offer of the permanent commission, he gained his commercial licence and applied for a position with the new British airline BOAC, successor to Imperial Airlines. Although created in 1939, BOAC had limited opportunities during wartime but now with the peace, the recreation of the European and empire network was a priority. Limited to the use of modified wartime bombers, such as the Lancastrian: a civil conversion of the Lancaster initially for long-range routes, they were eventually replaced by the many new designs on the drawing board for pressurized aircraft of both American and English design. Jaime felt he would like to be part of this new aviation world.

After a successful interview, he was offered a position as first officer on the ubiquitous and famous Douglas DC-3. The DC-3 was built in enormous numbers during the war under its military designation C47, primarily as a troop transport and for dropping paratroopers. Civilian conversions were flooding the airline market and it formed the backbone of the world's short-range airlines. Although un-pressurized, it filled the need in the immediate post-war years.

Within two years, Jaime was promoted to captain and continued to fly the new pressurized aircraft such as the

Douglas DC-4 and its bigger brothers the DC-6, DC-7 and Stratocruiser. His heart, however, was set upon the new Comet Jet liner which was coming into service in early 1952. Following type training on the Comet, Jaime was appointed a first officer on one of the first Comets to enter service. During this period, he met and married a beautiful woman called Cecilia, who was a stewardess on the Comet fleet. In 1954, disaster destroyed his life and happiness when a Comet broke up in mid-air killing his wife who was part of the crew.

After struggling with this tragedy for a few months, he was unable to continue his association with BOAC. He couldn't deal with the sympathy from staff and crew who were close to Cecilia and himself on a daily basis and he resigned. To get away from it all, he took a much less prestigious position working as a bush pilot for an airline in Africa flying medical supplies and passengers to remote areas in the wilderness. Although being a big step down from jets to the venerable DC-3, he found the work adventurous and satisfying. After ten years, he found himself in Libya flying the same old DC-3s and an occasional twin Beech, or C45 as the military version was known.

It was precisely this type of aircraft he walked out to parked on the end of the runway to do his pre-flight inspection ready to return to Tripoli. The twin Beech was a ten passenger seat tail wheel aircraft powered by two 450 horsepower Pratt and Whitney radial engines. The previous evening, he had secured canvas covers over the cowlings of the radial engines in order to prevent the sand getting into the engine inlets. Sand was one of the biggest problems flying in a desert environment which was why the engines were fitted with extra-large intake filters to minimize the sand getting into the engines and causing wear and damage.

Removing the covers and satisfying himself they had done their job, he completed the walk round pre-flight inspection. He walked back over to the office to check out and notify the regional Flight Information Service (FIS) in Tripoli of his flight plan and ETA.

On entering the office, Joe looked up and asked, "Almost ready to go, Jaime?"

"I'll just check in with FIS in Tripoli and then I'll be off."

"I'm a bit worried about a couple of supply trucks that were due in yesterday evening. Could you keep a look out for them and radio me if you see them? They must have holed up somewhere during the storm."

"Will do. I'll call you on your HF SSB frequency if I spot them so keep the frequency open."

"Roger wilco," replied Joe using a wartime cliche.

Jaime called Tripoli with his flight plan and told them he would deviate off his normal direct track to Tripoli in search of the missing trucks and report in when back on track.

Directly between the camp site and the road to Tripoli and the coast was an extensive area of sand dunes. The road deviated around the southernmost part as the shifting sand made it impossible to construct any sort of permanent road or track.

Settling into the pilot's seat, Jaime went through his pre start-up checklist. Having completed this, he pressed the starter for the number one port engine. After a couple of revolutions, it coughed and emitted a cloud of white smoke, coughed again and fired up gradually increasing in revolutions and settling down to a steady rumble. Repeating the process with the starboard number two engine, this also, after a couple of coughs, caught and joined its twin in a steady satisfying rumble.

No matter how long he had been flying, the start-up was always a source of satisfaction to Jaime as he witnessed the aircraft coming to life. He truly believed they had lives of their own as well as individual idiosyncrasies. A good pilot always took note of these and always listened carefully to the engine noise and kept a constant watch on the engine instruments.

Allowing the engines to warm up to the working temperature and watching temperature and pressure gauges was like watching a sleeping creature come to life. Checking the instruments were all in the green and no warning lights showed, Jaime gradually opened the throttles to manoeuvre the aircraft to the centre of the runway. He then ran through the engine checks on both engines to ensure both magnetos were working and that the propeller feathering mechanisms were both operative. He reduced the throttles to a steady tick over. He then set the fuel mixtures to rich, switched on the fuel pumps, and set fifteen degrees of flap and neutral trim for take-off.

Fortunately, the wind was blowing down the runway from the far end so he had no need to taxi all the way to the far end to turn around for take-off. Waving to one of the locals who had stood by during start-up with a fire extinguisher in case of fire, he opened the throttles fully. With no passengers or cargo, the aircraft was light and rapidly built up speed as Jaime kept the aircraft on the centre line, or in this case between the two rows of barrels, with a sensitive touch on the rudder pedals. As the speed built up, Jaime felt the tail wheel begin to lift from the runway as he eased the control column gently forwards and then held it in the neutral position as the aircraft approached take-off speed. This was always preceded by a couple of light bumps as the lift increased over the wings and the aircraft became airborne. Keeping the nose down to increase flying speed, Jaime raised the undercarriage reducing the drag and as the aircraft exceeded minimum control speed, he gradually eased back on the control column in a gentle climb with a slight turn to the left.

Climbing to five hundred feet, he continued his gradual left turn until he had made a one-hundred-and-eighty-degree turn and was back over the far end of the runway looking down towards the office. He spotted Joe outside waiting to wave him off. Lowering the nose, he aimed for the camp to do a flyby over it.

Looking up, Joe could see Jaime's intention and readied himself to wave goodbye. With a grin on his face, Joe watched the aircraft approach and thought, *there he goes, thinks he's back at El Alamein strafing tanks.*

As the plane roared overhead, Joe caught sight of Jaime's face in the cockpit window and gave him a vigorous wave.

Chapter 2

❖

Pulling up, Jaime climbed to a thousand feet; the best height to search for the missing trucks. He throttled back to the cruise and trimmed the aircraft for minimum control input so he could look outside the cockpit without having to concentrate too much on flying. Satisfied with the trim, he altered course off the direct track to Tripoli to fly around the sand sea.

Thirty minutes after take-off, he spotted the dust trail of two trucks on the road to the camp. Descending to five hundred feet, he circled the trucks and waggled his wings which brought a wave from the drivers. Climbing back to a thousand feet, he called King One on their frequency and confirmed the trucks were safe and sound and a couple of hours away from the camp.

Having done this, he set course for Tripoli across the sand sea. Since he had no passengers, he decided to descend to a hundred feet to indulge in a little low flying. He always did this when he had the opportunity as the sensation of speed one got with low flying was extremely exhilarating especially with the two roaring radial engines on either side reminding him of his wartime days flying the Beaufighter.

11

With the sun high over his right shoulder, Jaime could see the shadow of the aircraft racing ahead down to his left side as he looked out from the cabin window; always just ahead keeping pace as if in formation. The terrain below varied from small dunes to areas of relatively flat sand.

Suddenly, an object came into view almost too quickly for Jaime to recognise it as a vehicle half-buried in the sand. Pulling up, he made a wide turn whilst trying to keep the object in view. Widening the turn, he slowed down as much as he dared and pulled out a pair of binoculars and focused on the vehicle which leapt into view in greater detail. It was, without doubt, a military vehicle of some sort but what grabbed his attention was the insignia painted on the side. It was one he had seen many times before during his wartime flying here in Libya. With its swastika below the palm tree, it was impossible to mistake it as anything other than the insignia of Rommel's Afrika Korps.

Whilst he continued his wide circle overhead, he scanned the ground for a possible landing site. About a quarter of a mile from the vehicle, there appeared to be a flat area suitable for landing albeit a little on the short side. Confident of his ability as a pilot, he decided to attempt a landing; something he would not have done had he passengers on board. Having first overflown the site, he made his approach with full flaps just above the stall and touched down almost exactly at the start of the flat area and, with judicious application of the brakes, he easily stopped with distance to spare.

The surface appeared to be hard packed sand so there was no danger of becoming bogged down but nevertheless he exercised extreme care as he turned the aircraft around and cautiously taxied back towards the truck. Having got as close as he felt safe to do so, he shut down both engines and, pulling on his cap to protect him from the heat of the sun, he walked down the sloping interior towards the rear passenger door. Even though it was still mid-morning, after the coolness of the aircraft interior, the heat hit him as he stepped out onto the ground; the temperature was already high and would get higher as midday approached.

Just as during the war here in the desert, aircraft kept the same equipment on board as the LRDG, the long-range desert group. This consisted of spades and matting to put under the wheels in case they got bogged down in soft sand. Taking one of the spades, Jaime set off towards the truck. As always in the desert, distances were deceptive and it turned out to be farther than it looked.

As he got nearer, he could make out the detail. It appeared to be a medium sized truck of German design which was quite common in Libya even today as Libya had been colonised by Italy since 1911. In the years before the Second World War, Mussolini had poured enormous amounts of military equipment into the country. As the war progressed, the Germans supplied equal numbers of trucks to Rommel's Afrika Korps. It was not uncommon, therefore, in the chaos of advances and retreats of the desert campaign that all sides used a variety of each other's equipment.

After the Italians' first attempt to invade Egypt, they were soundly beaten by the British and forced all the way back to Benghazi. Sadly, they did not push on to Tripoli and finish the job but other demands of war rightly or wrongly intervened and half of the troops were transferred to Greece in a vain attempt to prevent the German advance. This mistake gave the Italians the time to regroup and for Hitler to pour in German troops under Rommel through the port of Tripoli to assist his ally.

The rear half of the truck was still buried in soft sand but the front open cabin was clear and looked in good condition except for a row of what appeared to be bullet holes stitched up across the bonnet and the windscreen. The radiator, however, had obviously taken some severe hits, probably from cannon shells. Lifting up the bonnet a little, Jaime could see a shattered engine. Easing the bonnet down, he stared at the scene before him.

Two sightless skeletons in tattered uniforms looked back at him. In the passenger's seat, the skeleton appeared to be dressed in a Luftwaffe uniform which Jaime recognized from his wartime service as that of a *Hauptmann*, the equivalent of a captain or flight lieutenant in the RAF. The other in the driving seat was wearing the uniform with the insignia of a colonel or group captain.

The wind had cleared most of the sand in the cabin down to the waist level of the occupants so Jaime pulled the handle of the cab firstly on the driver's side which, to his surprise, unlatched easily. Without too much force, it came open a little more allowing the soft sand to pour out. Repeating the process on the passenger side lowered the level of sand in the cabin even more.

He then commenced to examine the remains more closely. Although tattered, the uniforms were largely intact and he managed to extract from the breast pocket of the driver the *Soldbuch*, or paybook as they were most commonly referred to, which all German military personnel carried. This identified him as Hauptmann Johann Steinberg. Tucked inside the book was a faded photograph of a dark-haired smiling man with his arm around the shoulders of a pretty blonde-haired woman, no doubt his wife or sweetheart. It was strange to reconcile the image of what he looked like in real life with the skeleton before him.

From around his neck, he recovered an aluminium identification disc on a chain similar to those worn by US personnel except there was only one disc, designed to be broken in half along a perforation across the middle. Each half contained the same information: the wearer's number and blood type. In the event of death, one half was collected and handed in to the appropriate authority responsible for identification and burial and the other half remained with the body.

Turning his attention to the other in the colonel's uniform, he did not find a Soldbuch but there was a letter addressed to Oberst Walter von Lutzdorf. He did recover, however, the same type of identification disc as that on the Hauptmann. Putting both the letter and the paybook together with the discs in his breast pocket, Jaime continued his search. On the colonel's wrist was a gold watch with an inscription on the back bearing the same name as on the letter. The only other thing of interest was a Luger pistol in a leather holster around the waist. Undoing the belt buckle, he removed the pistol and holster and after hesitating for a moment, he decided to leave it in the vehicle so he wedged it under the passenger seat as best he could because of the amount of sand still remaining in the cab.

Disinclined to disturb the dead further, he decided it was best to leave them where they were as he would report his find to both the British and German Embassies in Tripoli on his return. They could decide what to do about notifying family and recovering the remains.

Closing both cabin doors to prevent any further disturbance, Jaime made his way back to the aircraft. As soon as he returned to the cabin, he pulled out his chart of the area and tried to estimate his position. Since there were no navigation aids this deep in the desert, he could only calculate a rough dead reckoning position based on his known point of departure and various tracks and time he had flown. He knew his rough track to Tripoli and he could correct this when he came in range of the Tripoli VOR and NDB navigation beacons.

The aircraft had now been on the ground for nearly an hour and the interior was becoming increasingly hot and uncomfortable. Quickly running through his checklist, Jaime started both engines and opened the cabin window to get a little cooling draft from the propellers. Since there was no wind to speak of, he back tracked to the point where he landed to start his take-off. Making a one-hundred-and-eighty-degree turn, he selected take-off flap and ran the engines up to full throttle whilst holding the aircraft on the brakes. Satisfied everything was in the green and ready to go, he released the brakes and the aircraft lurched forwards and quickly accelerated to flying speed. After a couple of small bounces, he was airborne well within the length of the makeshift landing site.

As he climbed away, Jaime made another wide circle over the area to imprint on his mind any particular features which would help him to recognise the location again in order to lead a team to recover the remains and any other items which may be in the back of the truck.

Setting course back to Tripoli, he selected the HF frequency for the longer range communication and called up the Flight Information Service, FIS, operated by International Aeradio who monitored all the desert operations and kept track of aircraft movements in case of loss or emergency. He confirmed he was back on track, gave his ETA, signed off and settled down to what would be approximately a three-hour flight.

The landing at Tripoli airport, located twenty miles south of the city, was routine and having parked the aircraft on the company apron in front of the hanger, Jaime reported to the office. He checked the roster and was pleased to see he was not down to fly again for two days. A company driver then took him into Tripoli to his apartment situated in a block on the avenue called the Adrian Pelt which ran along the harbour front from the old Turkish castle eastwards towards the big American Air Force base. Established after the war at the former Italian air base of Mellaha, Wheelus Air Base was America's largest facility of its type outside of the USA.

Chapter 3

❖

Jaime had visited the base several times with Joe Osborne who, as a former Air Force pilot, was permitted access to the officers' club and to enjoy all its amenities. Jaime, having been introduced by Joe and having been made aware of his wartime rank and status, was given honorary membership at the club to visit any time he wished.

As with all American overseas bases, the recreational facilities were extensive especially access to the PX, or Post Exchange, where all sorts of tax-free luxuries, unavailable outside, were to be found.

Libya, a former Italian colony, now, since 1951, the Independent Kingdom of Libya, still had a very great Italian influence and atmosphere. Since following independence, the government had granted residential status to all those Italians colonist who had been born there. They still owned many farms and businesses and were the mainstay of the economy. They provided the vast bulk of the craftsmen such as plumbers, carpenters and tradesmen of every sort of essential for the everyday efficient running of society.

It was now 1963 and Jaime, at 39, was still unmarried. Following the tragic death of his first wife, he had not felt the need to become involved in any similar relationship. Not that he did not enjoy the company of women and all that went with it but his lifestyle, working in different countries and irregular hours, was not conducive with a permanent relationship and the opportunities of meeting someone were few and far between.

Except he had recently met someone at an embassy party to which he had been invited. He was first attracted to her because she reminded him greatly of his long dead wife. Although similar in looks with the same long auburn hair and hazel green eyes, it was the mannerisms that had the most impact on him. Her smile and the way she tossed her head were just like Cecilia which left him feeling a little confused at the effect she had on him. It turned out she worked at the embassy in some sort of information post. As with all titles of embassy employees, they were very ambiguous and uninformative about what duties they actually performed. It turned out her name was Mary and she had the most wonderful and appealing surname of Loveday.

During the course of their conversation, it became apparent to him she did not find him unattractive and they exchanged contact details with the objective of perhaps having a drink or lunch together sometime. As difficult as it was for him to meet suitable company, it was equally difficult for someone like her as Tripoli was not London and although cosmopolitan to some extent, her circles were largely limited to the diplomatic set.

Entering his apartment, Jaime went first to his bedroom and stripped off his somewhat grimy and sweaty uniform and took a long relaxing shower. Wearing only a light dressing gown, he walked out through the French windows onto his terrace overlooking the harbour and traffic along the Adrian Pelt. It was late afternoon and he decided it was time for a relaxing cocktail. In the corner of the sitting room, he had set up a little bar with a selection of spirits and mixes. From his refrigerator in the small kitchen, he returned with a bowl of ice cubes and a lemon.

Filling the cocktail shaker with ice, he poured in a generous amount of gin and using a sharp vegetable peeler, he sliced off several thin pieces of the outer skin of the lemon which he added to the shaker. Then, opening a bottle of dry vermouth, he added the equivalent of about quarter of the amount of gin as he liked his dry martinis dry. Taking the shaker and a cocktail glass with him, he went back out to the terrace and poured himself his first drink of the day.

It was nearly two weeks since he had first met Mary so he decided, since he now had two days off, he would call her and invite her out to dinner this evening at his favourite Italian restaurant at the Uaddan Hotel further along the Adrian Pelt between his apartment and the embassy. She did not live in the embassy compound like a number of the personnel but as he knew from their last meeting, she lived in an apartment close by. She had given him both her personal number and that of the embassy so on the chance that she was still at work, he first phoned the embassy and to his delight he was put straight through to her.

"Well, Jaime, this is a nice surprise. What can I do for you?"

"I'm sorry it's short notice but would you like to have dinner with me tonight?"

"That would be lovely," she exclaimed. "My social calendar is not exactly full at the moment and you have brightened up my day. What time and where?"

"How about the terrace restaurant at the Uaddan? Have you been there before?"

"Yes, several times. It's lovely and sometimes they have music and dancing."

"I shall book it right away and insist on the music and dancing. Shall we say 7:30?"

"Yes, wonderful. I'm looking forward to it. Bye for now."

"See you then."

With that, Jaime rang off and sat there with a pleased look on his face. "Well, that was easier than expected," he said to himself, "Better not drink any more after this. Don't want to make a bad impression."

Sitting there relaxing with his drink, Jaime suddenly remembered the letter he had taken from the Luftwaffe colonel's pocket. Retrieving it from his bedroom where he had put it together with the watch and the paybook, he carefully opened the envelope and spread two pages out on the table. Naturally it was written in German and although he had studied German in school, he could not make out much of what was written other than it was obviously a love letter. Folding the pages and returning them to the envelope, he replaced them with the other items he intended to take to the German Embassy in the morning.

Having enjoyed his sundowner, he looked through his limited wardrobe to choose something suitable to wear for his first dinner date in a very long time. Most of his days were spent in uniform so he was rather limited in choice to a couple of pairs of light tropical trousers and an assortment of short-sleeve shirts which closely resembled his uniform shirts with large breast pockets. Choosing a pair of light tan trousers and a white shirt, he looked in the mirror. *I really must do something about my wardrobe*, he thought as he looked in the mirror, *I still look like I'm in uniform.*

As the time approached for him to leave, he decided to walk to the Uaddan which was no more than a fifteen-minute walk along the front. Leaving at 7:00 p.m., he was confident he would be there before her and made sure they had a good table on the terrace overlooking the sea and harbour. On a whim, he had decided to take the items he had found in the desert and show them to Mary as they would make an interesting topic for conversation during dinner.

The maître d', Pasquale, was a tall, handsome Italian with dark wavy hair greying at the temples and a dazzling white smile. He greeted Jaime as a familiar and regular customer and showed him to a secluded corner table on the raised section of the terrace. He declined an offer of a drink deciding to await his guest before choosing an appropriate bottle of champagne.

Precisely on time, Mary arrived and, as the maître d' brought her to the table, Jaime rose to greet her. Taking her outstretched hand gently in his, he bowed towards her and lightly kissed her hand.

"Oh, Captain St Clair, how gallant," said Mary, responding to the moment with mock surprise.

"The occasion demands it," said Jaime, "First impressions are important."

They both looked at each other and laughed breaking the ice and relaxing as if they were old friends instead of new acquaintances.

The maître d' seated Mary, and Jaime resumed his seat, looking at the wine list. "What would you like to drink, Mary?"

"Oh, for this occasion I think a champagne cocktail would be in order."

"Two Kia Royals if you please, Pasquale," he said to the waiting maître d'.

Now feeling at ease with each other, they started a normal exchange of conventional conversation.

"How have you been since we last met?" asked Jaime by way of an opener, "Have you done anything interesting or exciting?"

"Not much opportunity for anything exciting in the embassy."

"How so? You must be privy to all sorts of secrets and interesting things. What exactly do you do at the embassy?"

"Well, I'm an analyst. I spend my days compiling statistics on all aspects of the economy and life in Libya for an obscure civil service department who file it all away in the deepest depths of Whitehall for civil servants to ponder over and write obscure reports on that no one ever reads. How interesting is that?"

"Sorry I asked."

"Anything exciting happen to you? At least you get to fly out over the desert and visit interesting places."

"As a matter of fact, I've had a most interesting two days," said Jaime.

"Are you going to tell me or keep it a secret?"

"I'm not sure you're cleared for information at this level," said Jaime teasingly.

"Suit yourself," said Mary with a toss of her head exactly like Cecilia.

The emotional impact on Jaime of this mannerism took him unawares and for a moment, he was lost for words. The effect was not lost on Mary.

"What's the matter, Jaime? Did I say something wrong?"

"Not at all. You just remind me of someone, that's all."

"Well, come on. Tell me about your interesting day."

"Let's order first. It's a long story and best told after dinner."

After dinner was over, they relaxed over coffee and liqueurs and having finished with the small talk, Mary said, "Come on, Jaime. It's time to tell me about your interesting day."

Without saying anything, Jaime produced the three items he had recovered from the truck placing first the paybook on the table, then the letter and lastly the gold watch.

"What is this?" asked Mary with a smile, "Some sort of parlour guessing game?"

"First of all, what do you make of this?" said Jaime picking up the paybook.

Mary examined it and the photograph and said, "It's a form of military identification used by the Germans in the last war."

"Correct. All German troops carried what was known as a paybook for identification."

"Where on earth did you get this?"

"I took it off a corpse, or more precisely the remains of a corpse, this morning out in the desert."

"It certainly sounds like you had a much more interesting day than mine. Go on."

Jaime proceeded to tell her about his flight that morning and how he had discovered the Afrika Korps vehicle after searching for the missing supply trucks.

"Fascinating. What do you think happened to them?" she asked.

"I didn't think much about that at the time because I assumed they were just casualties of war as were so many. But now I think about it, they were way down in the desert far away from the main fighting which was mostly limited to within a hundred miles from the coast."

"The watch is interesting, especially the name on the back."

"Yes, I took it off the wrist of what was the Luftwaffe colonel and also this letter which I could not make much of with my schoolboy German."

"Let me have a look at it. I'll see what I can do."

Jaime looked at Mary with a new interest. "You speak German?" he asked with a hint of admiration in his voice.

"I'm not just a pretty face," she said with a laugh. "My father was in the Diplomatic Corps and we spent a number of years in Bonn where I went to school and later studied languages. German being my speciality."

Jaime opened the letter and passed the pages to her.

As Mary concentrated on the writing, he watched her face which showed various emotions as she continued reading. At one point, she let out a little gasp of surprise as her eyes widened in amazement.

"What is it? Anything interesting?"

Mary raised her hand and said, "Shush, let me finish."

Intrigued, Jaime waited until she finished, impatient to know what she had discovered.

Finally, Mary looked up and Jaime could see surprise and excitement in her eyes.

"Well? Out with it. Don't keep me in suspense. What does it say?"

Mary sat there looking at Jaime enjoying the moment of suspense. Finally with a smile, she said, "This is a remarkable find. I don't know where to start."

"The beginning is a good place," said Jaime impatiently.

"This letter was written by a woman who was obviously the fiancée of the colonel but it is who she was that is fascinating. She refers to Uncle Hermann who is very pleased with him and has a special mission for him when he returns. Uncle Hermann, I have no doubt, was Reichsmarschall Hermann Goering, head of the Luftwaffe. She also goes on to say he will be there to attend their marriage, as will Hitler. Heady stuff. Your boy, it appears, was quite a celebrity."

"I thought the name rang a bell. Now I remember. Walter von Lutzdorf was a famous German aviator. He was a pioneer of long-range flying and held a number of pre-war records."

"You realize this discovery will make the headlines considering who he was and his relationship to the Nazi hierarchy."

"Yes, for one thing it will clear up the mystery of what happened to him. It was probably assumed he was a normal casualty of war but this will open up all sorts of conspiracy theories once it gets out where he's been all this time."

"What's your next move? Are you taking these items to the German Embassy tomorrow?"

"That was my plan, yes."

"Before you do that, would you mind if I took a copy of this letter? It would make a very interesting souvenir."

"Of course, I don't see why not. Can you do it at the embassy tomorrow?"

"Thank you, Jaime. Yes, we have the facilities there to do it. Why don't you come to the embassy in the morning and ask for me and then you can go on to the German Embassy afterwards?"

"Sounds good to me. Now, what about a nightcap? And then I'll walk you home."

"Why don't you walk me home first and have a nightcap at my place?"

"Even better. I'll just ask for the bill." Jaime signaled to the waiter for the bill which he quickly settled and, taking Mary by the arm, he guided her down the steps from the terrace restaurant and on to the Adrian Pelt.

Mary turned to the right and set off in the direction of the British Embassy. "It's just a couple of minutes from here. Very handy for the embassy with a good view over the harbour."

Jaime had released his grip on Mary's arm and was pleased when she tucked her hand into the crook of his arm as they strolled along the front like a pair of intimate friends heading home after an evening out.

The effect of the champagne and liqueurs, together with the warm gentle breeze of the semitropical climate, gave Jaime a feeling of happy contentment he had not experienced for a very long time and which held the promise of even more to come.

Within a few minutes, they arrived in front of an elegant block of apartments of Italian design.

"Here we are," she said, "I'm on the top floor but don't worry we have a lift."

They walked up a couple of steps through double doors to the foyer where they were met by the concierge, an elderly Italian woman dressed in the customary long black dress with the greying hair tied in a bun, who greeted Mary with a friendly, "Buona sera, signora," whilst looking at Jaime with a suspicious frown.

"Hello Anna. This is my good friend Captain St Clair from England," said Mary.

The frown changed to a smile as she acknowledged him with, "Buona sera, signore," as she opened the gates of an old-fashioned lift.

"She's very protective of me and always looks at visitors she does not recognize that way."

"Good to know. I thought for a minute she was going to refuse to let me in," said Jaime with a laugh.

Mary pressed four for the top floor and they slowly ascended watching the stairs as they passed each floor through the open-caged lift. When the lift stopped, Jaime slid the safety cage door open and they entered a small lobby which led to two apartments both facing the sea. Turning left, Mary produced a key from her purse and opened the door to her apartment.

"Please come in and make yourself comfortable. What sort of nightcap would you like?"

"What are you having?"

"Well, alcohol will make me go to sleep and coffee will keep me awake. What do you suggest?"

"It's still not late. Perhaps a small liqueur balanced by a large coffee. What do you say?"

"A very good compromise. No doubt you're used to weighing up the options and consequences. Must be a result of your flying background where decisions have to be quick and decisive."

"I wouldn't go that far," said Jaime with a laugh. "You seem to know a lot about me on such a limited acquaintance."

"Put that down to a woman's natural curiosity and my analytical training. I have to admit that I did a background check on you after we first met, so I know your wartime service and achievements."

Jaime blushed a little and replied. "That was a long time ago. Now, where is that nightcap? Do you want me to pour the liqueur while you make the coffee or shall I sit out on the terrace and let you wait on me?"

"Please take a seat, sir, I won't be a minute."

"At your command," he said as he walked out on to the terrace and made himself comfortable in one of the wicker armchairs.

Whilst he sat there looking out at the lights of the outer harbour, he could hear Mary busying herself in what was no doubt the kitchen and after what seemed a rather long time to make a coffee, she reappeared in bare feet wearing a loose flowing dressing gown and carrying a tray with a small jug of coffee, sugar and cream and two liqueur glasses containing an amber liquid.

"Grand Marnier okay for you? It's one of my favourites."

"Perfect, my favourite also."

"Please excuse me for changing but it's been a long day at the office and my feet were killing me in those new shoes."

Jaime laughed as he said, "Personally it amazes me how you all manage to squeeze your feet into those tiny high heeled shoes and can walk on your toes all day long even though the effect is very attractive to the male eye."

"Put it down to a woman's vanity."

Jaime passed a very pleasant further hour with Mary as they continued to speculate over the mystery of why the former German aviator was found so far down in the Sahara away from the main battle areas. It also begged the question that if he was so far away from the main battle area, how was it he had obviously been a victim of an aerial strafing attack? It was something they had to leave for future speculation and perhaps some research into the military archives to determine if there had been any allied air activity in the area at that time.

All evening since they returned to Mary's apartment, Jaime was thinking of the turn of events and how attracted he was beginning to feel towards Mary especially as she made him feel so relaxed and it was obvious she had mutual feelings towards him. As much as he would have liked to take things further, he knew this evening was not the right time so looking at his watch he stood up.

"It's getting late. I really must be off. I have lots to do tomorrow and need an early night."

As Mary rose, she looked at Jaime with a smile and said, "Always the gentleman and you're right, a girl needs her beauty sleep."

Taking her by the hand, he walked her towards the door and put his hand on the handle. At the same time, he felt her hand on his shoulder as she gently kissed him on the cheek. "Goodnight, Jaime. Thank you for a wonderful evening."

"It is I who should thank you. I cannot remember when I last had such a memorable evening. See you tomorrow."

With that, he gently returned her kiss on the cheek and walked the few yards to the lift and pressed the button to call it up to the fourth floor.

When it arrived, he slid open the safety gate and turned towards Mary who was waiting in the doorway. With a wave, she said, "Don't forget, nine o'clock tomorrow at the embassy."

Jaime returned her wave and pressed the button for the ground floor.

When he exited the lift, Anna was still there and he was greeted this time with a warm smile. "Buona notte, signore."

"Buona notte, Anna," he replied as he walked out into the night.

Chapter 4

❖

At ten minutes to nine the next morning, Jaime entered the reception area of the British Embassy, gave his name to the receptionist and asked to see Mary saying he had an appointment with her.

"Just a minute, sir. I'll tell her you're here."

Thanking her, he took a seat in the waiting area. Five minutes later, the lift opened and Mary emerged dressed in a cream-coloured skirt just above the knee with matching semi high heeled shoes and a white short-sleeve blouse with a string of small pearls at her neck with matching earrings. Wearing her hair pulled back on top with a ponytail behind, she looked stunning. She immediately caught sight of Jaime, and with a smile on her face, she walked over to him as he rose from his seat.

"Right on time, I see. How do you feel this morning?" she said as she took his hand in hers.

"All the better for seeing you. You look wonderful."

"It's my efficient office look. I'm glad you like it. Come, let's go to my office." She turned back towards the lift as Jaime followed.

"I've arranged for you to see the ambassador after we've finished," she said as they emerged on the second floor.

"That's an unexpected honour. What have I done to deserve that?"

"Oh, I just happened to mention your discovery to him this morning and he was intrigued and said he would like to meet you while you're here."

Mary's office, although relatively small, was large enough to contain her desk with a bookcase and filing cabinet down one side and a sitting area with a small settee and chair. It had, however, the advantage of an air conditioner and a large window providing a view out to the sea. Mary had brightened it up with a few tasteful pictures and photographs of whom Jaime supposed were her parents.

"Take the comfortable chair over there whilst I take the letter to be copied and I'll organize some coffee."

Handing over the letter, he said, "Do you also want to copy the paybook?"

"Might as well," she said as she took both items from Jaime, "Make yourself comfortable. I won't be long."

Whilst she was gone, Jaime studied the books in the bookcase and was surprised at the content. A large section was taken up with the history of Libya from the Ottoman Empire right up to the Italian occupation and including the war in the desert.

He was leafing through one on the battle of El Alamein when she returned.

"Quite a collection you have here. Not what I would have thought would be your choice of reading."

"On the contrary, even a boring analyst must have some knowledge of the history of the country to fully appreciate its culture and potential."

"You're quite right, of course. I stand corrected."

Right behind Mary, a steward, who Jaime took to be an embassy servant, entered with a small trolley bearing coffee for the two of them. Setting the tray down on the coffee table in the sitting area, he quietly withdrew.

"Thank you, Ahmed," Mary said as he closed the door.

She poured two cups of coffee and handed one to Jaime. "I took the liberty this morning and phoned the German Embassy and have arranged for you to see the military attaché, Hugo von Oppersdorf who I have met on several occasions at embassy cocktail parties. I thought it would save you the trouble of trying to explain why you needed to see someone at the reception. It can sometimes be quite a rigmarole to get to the right person."

"Thank you, that was very thoughtful and helpful. Is there no end to your talents and efficiency?"

"One tries to please," said Mary with a smile and a laugh.

"Did you explain what it concerned?"

"Naturally he asked me what it was all about. I just said I wasn't sure but that it was better if you explained to him personally."

"Did he state a specific time?"

"No, he said just ask for him when you get there."

They had finished their coffee when a messenger knocked and entered the office with the paybook, letter and copies. Picking up her desk phone, she called the ambassador's secretary and asked if he was free to see Jaime.

"He can see you now. Let's go."

Mary took Jaime up to the third floor where they entered the secretary's outer office.

"Hello Jean. This is James St Clair," said Mary as a woman of about fifty years of age walked around from behind her desk and shook Jaime's hand. She was dressed in a smart skirt and white blouse combination similar to that of Mary's with greying short cut hair.

"Nice to meet you, Mr St Clair. The ambassador is waiting for you. Please, come with me." She knocked and opened the door to the ambassador's office and, standing to one side, she allowed Jaime to enter followed by Mary.

The ambassador was already walking towards them as they entered and offered his hand to Jaime which he took and felt the firm grip. He responded in a similar manner.

"Welcome to the embassy, Captain. It's good to meet you."

"Thank you, Mr Ambassador. Please call me Jaime. Thank you for inviting me."

Mary made a move towards the door to leave but the ambassador said, "Don't go, Mary. This was of your making. Please stay. I may need your expertise. I understand you did some translation for our friend."

Jaime pondered that statement for a moment as he had understood Mary had only mentioned the find to the ambassador in passing and had not given him any details.

The ambassador led them to the sitting area and they made themselves comfortable.

"I understand you found something of extreme interest in the desert and I know you have an appointment later with the German Embassy. Please forgive my curiosity if I ask you to first tell me all about it. Mary only mentioned the find had the potential for creating headlines back home and in Germany."

Jaime went on to explain how he had discovered the wrecked Afrika Korps vehicle and what he had found in it.

"Fascinating. It seems you have discovered both a World War Two story and also a mystery. How do you account for where you found them?"

"Difficult to say at the moment. It may need a little research. I think, however, the most important course of action is to see that the next of kin are informed of the find so the missing in action report can be cleared up and they can be given a Christian burial."

"Quite right. I understand the colonel was something of a well-known aviator and celebrity with connections to the Nazi hierarchy which is sure to make the headlines."

At this comment, Jaime realized Mary had given much more information to the ambassador than just a brief summary and probably right now there was not only a copy of the letter sitting on the ambassador's desk but also a translation in the making.

Looking at the ambassador, he noticed a quick glance pass between him and Mary and he was about to say something when the ambassador continued.

"Jaime, I must confess to you that it isn't just idle curiosity that prompted me to ask you here. What I have to tell you now is confidential and probably will become classified under the Official Secrets Act. As a wartime flyer, especially with experience here in the Libyan desert, you will know that many clandestine activities happen in wartime. I want to ask you something before you go to see the German military attaché and to be careful what you disclose to him."

"Mr Ambassador, please tell me what is going on. If you know something that I should know, please tell me. You can rely on my cooperation."

"I know it's a long time since the war but many questions from that time remain unanswered and there are still some issues to be cleared up."

"What particularly do you want to tell me?" asked Jaime.

"It was the reference to Goering and the mission that alerted us to the fact that there may be more to this situation than just a wartime incident. As I'm sure you can understand, embassies are a source of information to the intelligence services around the world. The letter not only refers to a mission that was in the process but that another mission was planned. And not only did the central figure in it never return to Germany but the planner behind it and a future mission was Goering, Hitler's deputy."

"Yes, I can see that is an interesting fact of history but the war's been over for nearly twenty years, how can it be of interest to the intelligence services now?"

"The Second World War left Europe in a shambles. The Nazis raped the occupied countries of assets, money and other valuables and caused the displacement of whole populations. The allies organized the Nuremberg war crimes trials where the most senior Nazis were tried and sentenced but many Nazis equally guilty disappeared and slipped the net. There were just too many to round up. They changed their names and appearances and either fled or merged back into the population. Many of them infiltrated themselves back into the government protected by secret organizations that still exist today, funded by the spoils of war and intent on re-emerging one day."

"I'm intrigued. Please go on. How does this affect me?"

"Let me first ask you something," said the ambassador, "How certain are you of the location of the vehicle and could you find it again? I understand you were flying off your normal route over a very remote part of the desert."

"Yes, that's true but I kept a note of my track, course changes and flight times on my flight back from there. I'm sure with a little calculation I could get within a few miles of it. Then it would be a case of doing a square search from that point until I recognized the area."

"In view of what I've told you, it is important that we find the vehicle first and search it for any items or documentary evidence that would help us discover more about the mission. I would ask you therefore to be very vague about its location when you speak to von Oppersdorf at the German Embassy this morning. Once this find is published in the German newspapers, it will alert certain parties there who will have as much interest as us, if not more, in finding the vehicle."

"I understand, of course, and I'll be vague about the location but the publicity will demand that an expedition and search is organized to bring back the bodies for a proper burial. I cannot refuse a request to help in that recovery."

"No, of course not, but we will have time to organize something ourselves before that, so go to your meeting with von Oppersdorf, come back afterwards and tell us how you got on. We can then discuss the matter further."

"This has turned out to be a more interesting day than yesterday and looks like it's becoming even more interesting."

"Thank you for coming in, Jaime, I'm sure we can rely on you to use your judgement in dealing with this matter." Looking at Mary, the ambassador said, "Please show Jaime out and then come back here." To Jaime, he added, "I don't expect you'll be more than an hour with von Oppersdorf. When you're finished, would you care to come back to the embassy for lunch and we can talk more?"

"I would enjoy that, thank you very much," said Jaime as he stood up.

Mary escorted him out of the office and back down to the embassy foyer. Looking at Mary with a smile on his face, he said, "Analyst, my foot. Why do I feel I have been in the hands of Mata Hari?"

"Analysis is the heart of all intelligence work. It's true, I spend my days going through reports, publications, statistics and even rumours, compiling reports for others to investigate. Every now and again, something interesting pops up that needs further investigation. Your desert find is the most excitement I've had since I've been here and it also led to me meeting you which is a most definite plus as far as I'm concerned, so don't blame me for doing my job."

"You can use me as much as you like. I think I'll enjoy being in the hands of a femme fatale spy," said Jaime with a grin.

With a squeeze of her hand and a light kiss on her cheek, Jaime left for his appointment at the German Embassy.

Chapter 5

❖

The German Embassy in Tripoli was not as large or as grand as the British Embassy since Britain was much more involved with the affairs of Libya. Following the Second World War, Britain was granted a United Nations' mandate to govern the country for five years pending the transition to its status as the Independent Kingdom of Libya. It had been agreed, during the war in the desert with the then religious leader of the Senussi, that in return for assisting the allies, the country would be granted independence under the rule of King Idris of the Senussi following the cessation of hostilities.

Formerly, since 1911, it had been an Italian colony and the main commercial second language was Italian. Following the war, however, Britain had established strong commercial and military links with Libya and the commercial language now almost universally spoken by the younger Libyans was English.

Jaime introduced himself at the security desk in the entrance of the embassy and was quickly escorted to the office of von Oppersdorf who had obviously alerted them to his appointment. Knocking on the door of the office, the messenger opened it and permitted Jaime to enter.

"Good morning, Captain St Clair. Or should I say, Wing Commander? My name is Hugo von Oppersdorf. Please come in and take a seat," said the military attaché rising from his seat behind his desk and indicating one of the two seats in front.

"Good morning and thank you," said Jaime as he reached across the desk and shook the outstretched hand.

Von Oppersdorf was a little older in appearance than Jaime, his blond hair showing a few flecks of grey. He was dressed in a pair of light tropical slacks and a matching short-sleeved uniform shirt with double breast pockets and epaulets. He had the unmistakable bearing of a military man.

"Mary at the British Embassy, who I have been fortunate to meet on several occasions, said you had something interesting to show me. Other than that, she was most mysterious which naturally aroused my curiosity. Please don't keep me in suspense too much longer," he said with a friendly smile.

Having taken his seat, Jaime produced the letter, paybook, watch and discs and put them on the desk in front of von Oppersdorf.

"I think you might be interested in these," said Jaime, "Especially the letter."

Von Oppersdorf first picked up the paybook and examined it. "A standard World War Two identification document. Where did you get it?"

"I found it in the desert yesterday."

Von Oppersdorf then picked up the watch and examined it closely and looked at Jaime with a serious expression on his face. Lastly, he opened the letter and started to read it.

Jaime watched him closely as he read, observing the same expressions of surprise and disbelief Mary had shown.

"Well, Wing Commander, you are right. These are extremely interesting finds. Being an aviator, you obviously know who Walter von Lutzdorf was."

"Yes, it took me a while to recognise the name but then when I did, I realized this would be of great interest to the German authorities."

"Please tell me how you managed to find these out in the desert."

Jaime then related his story of how he came to find the Afrika Korps vehicle and its contents whilst searching for the missing supply trucks.

"A chance in a million in that remote part of the Sahara. That sandstorm must have cleared some of the sand from the vehicle to reveal it for the first time in years. Do you think you could find it again?" asked von Oppersdorf.

"Well, I was flying off my normal track and spent some time crisscrossing the area and there are no navigation aids down there to get a good position fix so I could only estimate the position to within a ten- to fifteen-mile radius."

"That's unfortunate. That could cover about five hundred square miles. Can you not be a little more precise?"

"Not at this stage but I will go over my flight plan and see if I can narrow it down a bit."

"Thank you for that. Please let me know how you get on. I will let my government know of this find and no doubt they will want to mount a recovery expedition. Sorry for my bad manners, would you like a cup of coffee? I would like to talk to you some more."

Looking at his watch, Jaime said, "Yes, that would be good."

Von Oppersdorf lifted the telephone and ordered some coffee and then turned back to Jaime.

"I think we have some things in common. Like you, I was a wartime flyer but I have only a brief knowledge of your wartime career. I understand you flew here during the desert campaign and then in Europe until the end of the war."

Jaime did not normally like to talk about his wartime experiences but here was a flyer who was after all one of the enemy and he had never had the chance to talk to someone from the other side and from the enemy's point of view.

"Yes, I was here from 1942 flying Beaufighters and then in Europe flying Mosquitos."

"Ah, the Mosquito, the wooden wonder. You gave us a lot of problems with that aircraft."

"Yes, it was an inspired design and quite an aircraft. I enjoyed flying it. What about you?"

"I was on fighters throughout the war. First on the Messerschmitt 109 and then the FW190 and lastly the Junkers 88 night fighter."

"That's interesting. We must have shared the same airspace from time to time. I also was on night fighters with the Mosquito on night intruder missions. You were exactly the targets we were after, returning to your base after attacking our Lancaster bomber streams."

"Amazing. Fate is a chancy thing. We might have shot each other down and would never have met here under these circumstances."

In spite of them being former enemies, Jaime felt himself warming to this charismatic man and his charm and felt no animosity to him for the past.

"A lot of bad things happened during that time. It was not a good war from the German side and many of us in the armed forces regret being involved. However, I was a professional soldier and had to do my duty and obey orders."

Jaime was surprised at this admission from von Oppersdorf but from the tone of his voice, he believed his sentiments were genuine and felt a little sorry for him.

"Wing Commander, I hope we can meet again and chat. Please let me have your contact details as we shall need to keep in touch over this matter and I shall make sure you are on our cocktail party and social list for future functions, if you would do me the honour."

"It would be a pleasure. Now I must be off. I have much to do during my brief respite from flying."

Jaime shook hands and von Oppersdorf escorted him back down to the entrance. "I hope to see you again soon."

Chapter 6

❖

Jaime looked at his watch as he walked away from the embassy and saw that it was 12:30 so he made his way back to the British Embassy and asked for Mary. This time he was escorted without delay back to her office where she was looking through some files.

"Good timing. How did you get on with von Oppersdorf?"

"Fine. He's not what I expected."

"Yes, you're right. He has a certain charm but he is quite astute and intelligent. He doesn't miss much."

"Well, you'll be pleased to know that we've become buddies and I'm on their cocktail party list from now on."

"He's not going to let you get away until he finds the answers to this mystery."

"I'm aware of his motives but that does not stop me liking him and maybe I'll learn something in return."

"Spoken like a true intelligence agent. You may have missed your calling. You know what they say, keep your friends close and your enemies closer."

"What are we? Friends or enemies? And how close will we be?" he asked with a grin.

"That remains to be seen but for the moment, let's settle for close friends."

"I'd like that. What time's lunch?"

"You've been honoured. The ambassador has arranged for the three of us to have lunch on his private terrace."

"It's enough to turn a poor humble pilot's head. My social life is suddenly expanding at an alarming rate. I shall have to get a new wardrobe to be up to it."

"Nothing humble about you, Jaime. I think you'll fit right in."

"Well, my new close friend, I hope it'll be a light lunch because can we have dinner together this evening?"

"Already organized and it's my treat. You're having dinner at my apartment and I'm cooking."

"What's this? The ambassador's orders to keep an eye on me?"

"Out of office hours, I have my own life."

"Okay, but how's your cooking?"

"Wait and see. But to put your mind at rest, after university, I took a Cordon Bleu cookery course."

"I think I must be dreaming. I've died and gone to heaven. Not only am I having dinner with the most beautiful girl in Libya but she is also a Cordon Bleu cook."

Before she could reply, the telephone rang and smiling, she picked it up.

"We've been summoned to lunch. Let's go."

Lunch had been prepared in the pleasant cool setting on the ambassador's private terrace which afforded an unrestricted view over the garden to the side of the embassy.

After the normal pleasantries, the ambassador asked how Jaime got on at the German Embassy and Jaime related much the same as he had explained to Mary.

"Well, I have a little more news for you. I sent a translation of the letter together with a report back to the foreign office by secure telex and within the hour received a reply. Apparently, it has perked up someone's interest in MI6 and they are sending someone out to speak with you in the next day or two. I will send the copy of the original by courier as there is a BOAC flight from London tomorrow and I expect that their man will be on it. No doubt I will get a signal later today confirming that. What is your schedule for the next few days?"

"I'm off tomorrow but return to flying the following day. Most days, depending on the weather, I'm off early and unless it's one of the longer flights, I am normally back in Tripoli by 4:30 at the latest. I'll call the office later and check my schedule and can then be more precise."

"Good. Let's enjoy our lunch. How do you like the local wine? The Italians have some very good vineyards here, quite comparable with the best of any French vintages."

Lunch passed off with mostly small talk on how they liked Libya and what they found of interest.

"Have you ever been out to Leptis Magna, Jaime?" asked Mary.

"No, but I've heard that it's one of the most amazingly well-preserved Roman cities in North Africa and well worth a visit."

"It's marvellous. I'll drive you out there one day when you have a day off. It's only about thirty miles east of Tripoli."

"That would be very kind of you. I hope we can arrange that when I next get a couple of days off."

Chapter 7

❖

After lunch, Jaime said goodbye to the ambassador and thanked him for lunch, then Mary saw him out of the embassy and said, "See you at seven o'clock," and kissed him on the cheek.

As he walked back towards his apartment, he detoured from the Adrian Pelt up through the centre of town to Cathedral Square so called because of the magnificent Catholic cathedral which dominated the square. He then strolled down the wide avenue called the Istaklal which led back down to the square and the old Turkish castle next to the entrance to the souk and Gold Market. which was part of the old city or medina.

The Italian influence was everywhere with every sort of shop selling fashionable Italian clothing and goods and numerous little cafes with outside tables where people congregated to gossip and drink coffee.

At the bottom of the Istaklal on the left-hand side just before the square was a shop selling men's clothing which Jaime had noticed before. Making a decision, he entered and, having looked around, he decided to start his new wardrobe. Aided by an enthusiastic assistant, he soon picked out a couple of pairs of fashionable slacks and as a complete change from his normal style, he also bought a couple of coloured summer shirts.

It was still just early afternoon so instead of going straight back to his apartment, Jaime carried on down the avenue into the main square. Each time he visited the square, he had visions of the wartime newsreel showing General Montgomery reviewing the Eighth Army's triumphant entry into Tripoli after Rommel and the Afrika Korps deserted the city in January 1943 after being chased all the way from El Alamein in Egypt.

Jaime continued on across the square towards where the castle met with the corner of the harbour and carried on around the castle wall which led to the Tripoli Sailing Club where he decided to pass the time having a beer until it was time to go back to get changed for dinner.

At seven o'clock, Jaime entered the lobby of Mary's apartment building and this time he was greeted by Anna with a friendly smile.

"Buona sera, signore."

"Good evening, Anna," he replied as she opened the lift gate for him. "Grazie," he added in his limited Italian.

"Prego, signore," she replied and then surprised him by adding in English with a smile, "Have a nice evening."

"Thank you, Anna," he responded with a grin.

Exiting from the lift on the fourth floor, he rang Mary's bell and the door opened almost before he took his finger off the button.

"My, that was quick. Were you hiding behind the door in anticipation?"

"Don't flatter yourself. I heard the lift coming up. Being on the top floor I can hear the lift motor quite clearly. I must say, you do look nice. I approve of your new wardrobe especially the shirt, very stylish."

"Thank you and you look wonderful."

Mary was dressed in an off-the-shoulder black evening cocktail dress that was obviously a product of one of the better design houses with a simple small gold crucifix at her neck. She had changed her hairstyle from when he had last seen her at lunch. Her long auburn hair now hung down over her shoulders freshly washed and glistening in the reflected lighting.

"Enough of the compliments, please do come in," said Mary as she offered her cheek to Jaime who responded by lightly gripping her shoulders as he brushed her cheek with his lips.

"You smell lovely," said Jaime as he caught the aroma of her delicate perfume.

Gripping his wrists in her hands, she lowered his arms and led him into the sitting room where an overhead fan whirred gently above.

The lighting was subdued creating a warm welcoming atmosphere and through the open French windows, the harbour lights were twinkling in the fading light.

As he entered the room, he was greeted by the aroma of cooking coming from the kitchen. "That smells delicious. What's on the menu?"

"A surprise. Something I've learned since coming here to Tripoli."

"Not something from your Cordon Bleu repertoire then?"

"No, not the first course but I think you'll enjoy it as a starter. After that, it's all my own creation. Help yourself to an aperitif and pour me a gin and tonic please. I must go back to the kitchen."

Mary had set out some bottles and mixes together with a bowl of ice on a drinks trolley in the sitting room. After making the gin and tonic for Mary, which he took to her in the kitchen, he poured himself a small whiskey with ice and lots of water, not wanting to spoil the evening with too much to drink. He was not a heavy drinker because he was always conscious that flying and alcohol were not a good mix. He normally limited himself to a martini in the evening when he returned home and occasionally a glass of wine or two with his evening meal. However, he was aware how social drinking could catch up with you if one was not careful. He had limited himself to just two glasses of white wine at lunch which the ambassador had insisted he try with the fish they had eaten. He had taken care to drink several glasses of water at the same time to help dilute the effect. His one beer at the sailing club had been several hours before so he felt he could manage a glass of wine with dinner without too much trouble.

"Do you need any help in there?" he called to Mary.

"No, go and sit on the terrace and enjoy your drink. I shan't be too long."

Mary had set out a table for two with a candle lit inside a large glass container, to prevent the breeze from blowing it out, set in the centre giving it an intimate atmosphere. Leaning on the terrace balustrade, Jaime sipped his drink while he watched the traffic on the Adrian Pelt and the people strolling along the pavement either returning home or out for an evening meal at one of the several restaurants that overlooked the harbour.

In the night sky to the north, he caught sight of the lights of an approaching aircraft. He watched the flashing anti-collision beacon mounted on top of the vertical tail plane and made out the red port navigation light visible from his angle of view. At that moment, the pilot switched on the landing lights indicating he was starting an approach to land. From this, Jaime knew it would be an aircraft inbound to Wheelus, the USAF base five miles to the east of the city. Civil aircraft from Europe inbound to Tripoli airport made their approach further to the west of the city. As it grew nearer, the pilot made a left turn to line up with the runway and the red port light disappeared and was replaced by the green of the starboard light. The distant drone of a large multi-engine aircraft broke through the hum of the traffic below and the chirruping sound of the crickets.

Most likely a piston engine Globemaster bringing in supplies from Europe, thought Jaime as he watched the lights disappear to the east as it sank lower out of sight below the buildings.

Catching the waft of her perfume, he turned as Mary came towards him and took him by the hand. "Come and sit down. It's nearly ready."

Jaime took his seat as she returned to the kitchen and came back carrying a tureen with a covered lid in her gloved hands which she set on the table between them. The table was already laid with cutlery and soup bowls. Producing a ladle, she removed the tureen lid and served Jaime a generous portion of the contents and then, after serving herself, she sat down.

"It smells delicious. What is it?"

"It's a local dish called *shorba*. It's really just a lamb soup with herbs and spices. I love it."

Jaime took a spoonful raised it to his lips.

"Careful, it's hot," she added.

Sipping it gently, he said, "You're right. It is delicious. What's in it?"

"Lamb, onions, garlic, tomato, either puree or passata, cumin, chickpeas, mint and lemon juice. And if you like it a little spicier, add a dash of harissa which has chili pepper in it."

Jaime was now enjoying with relish as he tasted the various ingredients.

"If you want it in a more substantial form, you just add more lamb, chickpeas and potato so it's more like a stew."

"You must show me how to make it. Just knowing the ingredients is like having the list of parts for an engine but it takes a mechanic to put them all together."

Mary poured them both a glass of red wine which was in a raffia wrapped chianti style bottle with an Italian label. "It's from a local vineyard, recommended by the ambassador. He's really into the local wines which you no doubt realized at lunch."

After the soup, Jaime helped Mary take the tureen and bowls to the kitchen and returned to the table, shortly followed by Mary bearing a tray with a dish of lamb cutlets, a bowl with sauté potatoes, another of courgettes which had been sliced and coated with a mixture of flour and salt, briefly deep-fried to retain a crispness, and a soup jug filled with a savoury cream sauce.

Over dinner, they indulged in small talk exchanging personal details and talking about their background and family history. Jaime learnt Mary's family were from Hampshire where she spent her early years before joining her parents in Germany where her father was first secretary at the embassy in Bonn. Further education there gave her the skill in German and other languages which she studied, determined to make a career following her father in the diplomatic service.

For his part, Jaime revealed his parents had died and his elder brother had inherited a minor title of the laird as head of the clan and a draughty castle in Scotland. He had been educated in England at Winchester but instead of going on to Oxford like his father and brother, the war had intervened and afterwards he felt no desire to return to the academic world having decided that flying was his life.

"That was a wonderful dinner," said Jaime as they settled down in the sitting room with coffee.

"I've got something for you," said Mary as she produced an envelope. "I made an extra copy of the letter for you and have typed out the translation to go with it. I thought we might study it a bit more to see if we can learn what he was doing in the desert. It's dated December 1942 and it's addressed to Major von Lutzdorf so obviously he had been promoted some time shortly after the letter had been written and before you found him. I think we must assume he had returned from his first mission to Germany, been promoted and was returning from the second mission mentioned in the letter when he was killed on his way back."

"What else can we assume from the letter?" asked Jaime.

"Well, the writer is called Magda and presumably she married von Lutzdorf on his leave so she'll be his next of kin and the one most likely to know more about his second mission as she was also related to Goering."

"Yes, I think you're right. I'm sure MI6 will come to the same conclusion, don't you?"

"I think that's inevitable and they have the resources to find her if anyone can."

"We should know something more after speaking to this MI6 man who's coming out to interview me."

"Oh yes, of course. Sorry, Jaime, I forgot to tell you. The ambassador told me he received a signal confirming the man from MI6 will be on the BOAC flight tomorrow."

"That's quick. This must be more important than we thought."

"I'm sure it is. MI6 don't waste time and resources sending people about unless there's something of special interest behind it."

"Tomorrow is going to be a very interesting day."

Chapter 8

❖

OCTOBER 1942
BERLIN, GERMANY

Major Walter von Lutzdorf walked into the entrance of the Air Ministry's impressive building on Wilhelmstrasse on his way to a meeting with his commander-in-chief, Reichsmarschall Hermann Goering. He had received the summons to the meeting completely out of the blue whilst on leave recuperating from a wound he had received flying a Heinkel 111 bomber on the Eastern Front.

One of Goering's aides quickly rushed him through security and accompanied him to the chief's office.

One of the guards outside the office, who had obviously been alerted of his arrival, saluted and having knocked on the door, opened it to allow von Lutzdorf to enter the large opulent office. Goering, resplendent in his impressive uniform covered with gold braid and medals especially the Pour le Mérite, the highest award for valour at that time at his neck, rose from behind his desk, gave a casual slight semblance of a Nazi salute and said, "Ah, Major von Lutzdorf, come in, come in. That will be all, Freiberg," he added to his aide who saluted and left the room.

Von Lutzdorf returned the salute and remained standing at attention whilst the aide left.

"At ease, at ease. Relax and take a seat," said Goering indicating one of the seats in front of his large desk.

Von Lutzdorf did as he was ordered and sat down as Goering eased his corpulent figure back down onto his own chair. "How is your wound coming along?" he inquired.

"Healing nicely, thank you, Herr Reichsmarschall. I shall soon be fit to return to active duty."

"Excellent. That's good to hear as I have something of importance to discuss with you. By the way, how is my niece Magda? I understand you see each other socially occasionally."

Von Lutzdorf was a little surprised at the question but then again, as a former chief of police, Goering had an extensive network of informers so there was probably nothing much that escaped his attention.

"Very well when last I saw her. She has been very kind visiting me in the hospital and the convalescent home. We met before the war but my duties and postings since did not give us many opportunities to meet that often," said von Lutzdorf. "I suppose my being wounded can be viewed as a lucky break as my convalescence in Berlin gave us the opportunity to meet again," he added with a smile.

"Quite so," said Goering. Privately he was quite pleased with the budding relationship between his niece, of whom he was very fond, and von Lutzdorf as not only was he a fellow aviator with an excellent record but also something of a celebrity and he came from one of the oldest families in Germany so

Goering had made a point of keeping well informed of his career and wellbeing.

"I expect you are wondering why I have sent for you, Major."

"If it is anything that I can do to help with the war effort then I am pleased and honoured to be asked and am ready to help in any way I can."

"I'm sure you're the right man for what I have in mind. I am particularly interested in your pre-war career and experience pioneering the long-distance flights to Africa and South America."

"They were interesting times, Herr Reichsmarschall, especially as the aircraft and equipment were not as reliable and advanced as today."

"Nevertheless, you were very successful and contributed greatly to the advance of aviation and international flying."

"How can I be of service now?"

"You are an intelligent man, Major, and have a more than passing knowledge of the international stage outside Germany being fluent in English and having visited many countries including England and America."

"I was indeed fortunate in that respect," agreed von Lutzdorf.

"Whilst we are masters of Europe in this conflict, Britain still has great influence and control over many parts of its pre-war empire and now that America has entered the war that influence and control will become even greater in the hands of our enemies."

"I understand that. America's entry is of great concern as their industrial capacity is unrivalled and now there will be no restrictions on the aid and equipment it can give to Britain," said von Lutzdorf, who was no Nazi but he was a patriot and knew his duty.

"Europe may be the centre of the civilized world," said Goering, "And whilst we have an abundance of coal and now oil in Romania and iron ore from Norway, there is a lack of other natural resources especially rare metals and other products essential for industrial development and research. We particularly need industrial diamonds for machine tools and precision engineering."

"And these come mostly from Africa. Primarily South Africa, part of the British Empire and an ally to Britain," said von Lutzdorf beginning to see where the conversation was heading.

"Quite so. I see you understand our position. However, whilst we ourselves no longer have any colonies in Africa, we still have friends in our former colonies of Cameroon and South West Africa. I believe you are familiar with these countries having flown there before the war."

"Yes, I made several flights there in 1936 and 1937. There are still many former German citizens living there. German is widely spoken and I received very warm welcomes in both countries."

"Excellent. That will be of great help. We obviously have agents in both countries and we are assured of help in procuring all the industrial diamonds we need. The allies, particularly the British, control much of the air space and the Royal Navy is in command of the sea routes. What I need from you, Major, is to make a plan for a safe air route to South West Africa avoiding any contact with the RAF patrols, and deciding what type of aircraft would be appropriate and have sufficient range for the missions. You will have full cooperation from the aircraft manufacturers and the Luftwaffe under my personal orders."

"What about my present duties, Herr Reichsmarschall?"

"Naturally you will be transferred and attached to my ministry under special duties."

"I take it you would like me to start the planning as soon as possible. Where will I be based?"

"You will be provided with offices and staff here at the ministry in Berlin."

"Thank you, Herr Reichsmarschall. I understand the need for flights to Africa but what about South America? They have no natural resources that would be of use to us and certainly not in any quantity that could be usefully transported by aircraft."

"Very astute of you, Major. Let me just say for the moment that there are certain plans in motion essential to the survival of the Third Reich which will require these flights to be undertaken. For the moment, they will remain top secret and when the time comes, we will have a further discussion. I expect you to exercise extreme discretion on your oath as an officer to discuss this with no one."

"You can rely on me, Herr Reichsmarschall."

"I will inform you when your offices are ready and I expect you may like to choose some of your own assistants and staff so I will not detain you any further. Enjoy the rest of your leave and we will meet each other again very soon."

Goering pressed a button on his desk for his aide to escort von Lutzdorf out of the building and as he did so, he eased his bulk up from his chair and came around to shake his hand. Whatever else he was Goering was always extremely genial and polite to those he liked. This together with his strong personality always engendered a feeling of loyalty towards him from by those within his circle.

"Thank you for your confidence, Herr Reichsmarschall. I shall look forward to working here at the ministry and planning the flights."

"Give my regards to Magda," said Goering with a parting smile.

"It will be my pleasure, Herr Reichsmarschall."

"No doubt it will, Major."

Chapter 9

❖

Von Lutzdorf left the Air Ministry with a spring in his step pleased with the new turn of events and the prospect of staying in Berlin instead of returning to the uncertainty of the Eastern Front where prospects of survival were not in his favour. The aide, Hauptmann Freiberg, had organized the services of an official car and as he shook hands with von Lutzdorf, he handed him a card on which was written his name Hauptmann Klaus Freiberg and a telephone number.

"If you need anything in the meantime, Major, please call this number and ask for me. I am at your service for anything you may need until you are fully established at the Air Ministry."

Thanking the aide, von Lutzdorf entered the car and ordered the driver to take him to the address of an apartment in the suburbs of Berlin owned by his family which he used from time to time instead of his military quarters. The apartment was one of just two situated in a grand building dating from the 1800s. It was extensive consisting of three floors with servants' quarters on the lower floor and a luxurious three bed apartment on the second and third. His parents rarely stayed in Berlin these days due to the bombing, preferring to stay at their country estate.

Since he would now be based in Berlin for the foreseeable future, von Lutzdorf would have his servant pack up his belongings and bring them from his quarters to the apartment which he would make his base. The bombing had had little or no effect in the fashionable suburb where the apartment building was located and there was no discernible damage to be seen so he felt confident in staying there.

In spite of the bombing, the Berlin telephone system was surprisingly efficient and in good order. Any damage was quickly repaired as communications between ministries and high-ranking officials was imperative. His meeting had been early; it was just midday when he entered the apartment. He took a chance that Magda was at home as he called her number. After a couple of rings, he was rewarded with a click as Magda picked up the phone.

"Hello?" was the firm answer at the other end of the line. "Who's calling?"

"It's your favourite aviator," responded von Lutzdorf.

"Really? I know quite a few aviators what with my uncle being Hermann Goering. I wonder which one it could be."

"Perhaps if you could think of your favourite of all your admirers, you might be able to guess," said von Lutzdorf responding to her sense of humour.

"Could that be Johann or perhaps Willi? I just can't think for the moment, I have so many admirers."

"Try Walter."

"Walter… Walter…" she teased, "Oh, now I recognise who it is. How nice to hear from you. How are you?"

"You mustn't tease me like that. I'm still convalescing and may have a relapse then you would be sorry."

"I'm sorry, darling, but I haven't heard from you for three days and I'm missing you and you are so easy to tease. Forgive me."

"Nothing to forgive and I miss you too."

"Where are you? I'll come to you right away, if that's all right."

"I've just come from a meeting with your uncle and have lots to tell you. I'm in my parents' apartment. Do you remember where it is?"

"Yes, of course. What are you doing there?"

"I'll tell you when you get here. Can you get a car?"

"Yes, Uncle Hermann has provided me with a car and driver. He's very sweet."

Von Lutzdorf laughed to himself. He had heard Goering described as many things but never sweet.

"Why don't you come over here about six o'clock and I can tell you about my day and we can then have dinner at that restaurant by the lake that you like."

"I'll be there at six then. Bye, darling."

Von Lutzdorf passed the rest of the day making some phone calls to friends and thinking about who he would like to have on his staff to help him plan the mission.

He had already decided that a modified Heinkel 111 would be the most suitable aircraft for the job as it already had a reasonable range. Stripped of its armaments and bomb load, it could carry a further five thousand litres of fuel giving it a range of more than three thousand miles sufficient to reach the former German colony of South West Africa from Tripoli in Libya. He would need a good co-pilot and navigator on such long flights so he immediately thought of his long-time friend and crew member Johann Steinberg who had been his co-pilot since they joined the Luftwaffe together and who was currently still serving on the Eastern Front. Picking up the telephone, he dialled the number on the card that the aide had given him and was put through to Hauptmann Freiberg without delay.

Giving his friend's name, rank and other details, he asked Freiberg to have him transferred immediately from Russia to Berlin as a matter of priority. Freiberg assured him he would ensure a signal would be sent that day with Goering's authority and Steinberg would be back in Berlin by the quickest means possible. Von Lutzdorf smiled as he thought how Johann would react to receiving such an order as he realized how gratifying it was to have the ability to order things to be done with the unlimited power of the commander-in-chief of the Luftwaffe behind him. The coming days and months were going to be very satisfying indeed.

***

Magda arrived at six o'clock as arranged and they embraced each other as she entered the apartment.

"This is a pleasant surprise," she said. "Tell me all about your meeting. How long will you be staying in Berlin?"

"You will be pleased to know that I have been relieved of my normal duties and been transferred to the Air Ministry under the direct orders of your dear sweet uncle," he said with a smile. "By the way, he knows we've been seeing each other."

"Well, I never told him but that just goes to show you how concerned he is for my feelings. He obviously doesn't want you in any danger. He really is sweet to me."

Allowing Magda to score the point, he did not explain the real reason for his transfer to the Air Ministry except to say he had been given an assignment in the planning department.

"So, you will now be based permanently in Berlin? That's wonderful."

"Well, I'll have to make some test flights that will take me away from Berlin occasionally but not into the combat zone, at least not intentionally."

Von Lutzdorf opened a bottle of champagne and they toasted his good fortune as they caught up with each other's news.

Finishing their drinks, they went down to the waiting car and driver and drove the short distance to a fashionable restaurant by the shores of a small lake and enjoyed an intimate dinner. Even though it was wartime, there was no shortage of quality food or wines, as the occupied countries were systematically stripped of produce which was sent back to Germany whilst the citizens of those countries suffered severe shortages and even starvation.

Chapter 10

❖

Early the following morning, von Lutzdorf telephoned Hauptmann Freiberg and asked him if he had organized an office for him at the ministry.

"We have allocated you an office but as yet we have not arranged for your support staff. That will take us a few days more."

"That's not a problem. As long as I have a place to work, I can get started with my planning. Please send a car for me right away."

"Yes, Herr Major. I shall be waiting for you when you arrive."

"Thank you, Hauptmann."

As before when he entered the Air Ministry, Goering's aide was waiting for him and escorted him to a large well-furnished office with an adjoining secretary's office which was occupied by a middle-aged woman wearing the Luftwaffe uniform of a signals auxiliary with the insignia of a Haupthelferin, the civil service equivalent of a Feldwebel (*Sergeant*).

"This is Hanna Braun who will be your secretary and will help you to settle in and assist you with understanding how the system works here at the ministry."

Thanking them both, von Lutzdorf walked over to the window overlooking Wilhelmstrasse and turned to Freiberg. As he was leaving, he asked, "Hauptmann, do you have any news on when Steinberg will be arriving in Berlin?"

"I had a signal acknowledging the order but I have no other news at present. I will check with the communications department right way and see if any further signals have been received," he said as he left the room.

A little later, von Lutzdorf was sitting at his desk making some notes when his telephone rang. It was Freiberg.

"Herr Major, I have just received a signal which says that Steinberg is on a flight to Berlin which left two hours ago so he should be here this afternoon about two o'clock. I shall arrange to have him met at the airport and brought here directly to the ministry."

"Thank you, Freiberg. That's good news," said von Lutzdorf and, having put the telephone down, he continued adding to his list of things to do and people to see.

One of his first meetings would be with the Heinkel company to discuss the modifications he would like done to the Heinkel 111. Apart from stripping out the armaments and modifying the bomb bay to carry the extra fuel, he wanted to have the latest automatic pilot technology fitted to the aircraft as flights of up to twelve hours duration were extremely tiring even with two pilots, and autopilots could keep an aircraft more accurately on track over long distances than was possible by hand flying.

Apart from extra fuel, the engines would have to have larger oil tanks than normal as oil was consumed as well as petrol during flight.

He continued making notes about the necessary modifications but his thoughts also strayed to the flights he had undertaken to Africa before the war. He would not be able to fly the same routes as then because much of that air space was now no longer available to him as it was controlled by the enemy. Fortunately, most of Libya was in the hands of Germany and Italy and south of the Sahara was sparsely populated and not occupied by the allies until one approached the west African coast where Sierra Leone and Nigeria were controlled by Britain. There was, however, the Vichy-controlled area of the Ivory Coast which could be used as a staging post for refuelling if necessary. He did not expect there to be much air activity in these areas as it was not involved in any major fighting. He was also sure there was no radar coverage to speak of so combat patrols would be few and far between and flying mostly over largely uninhabited areas would make their detection unlikely.

He continued making notes and thinking about the best route to plan until midday when he decided to take a stroll along Wilhelmstrasse and find a cafe for lunch.

Wilhelmstrasse was largely occupied by government buildings but there were a few social areas where office workers gathered during their lunch breaks. Von Lutzdorf took a seat at one of the outside tables and ordered a drink and a light snack.

In spite of the occasional night time bombing, life appeared little changed from the pre-war bustle and activity apart from the fact there were far more uniforms in evidence.

Having enjoyed a pleasant hour, he walked back to the Air Ministry and, showing his security pass which Freiberg had given him that morning, he was admitted to the building without undue scrutiny as they now recognised him from being with Freiberg who had obviously told them he was attached to the personal staff of the commander-in-chief.

Von Lutzdorf had no trouble finding his way back to his office on the second floor and as he passed through his secretary's office, she said, "Major, we have received a message that your colleague Hauptmann Steinberg's plane has landed and he will be here within the hour."

"Thank you. Please show him straight in when he arrives."

"Yes, Major."

When he sat down at his desk, he was pleased to see a large scale map of North Africa which he had ordered that morning had been placed on his desk. The area covered was from the Mediterranean coastline down as far as northern Nigeria showing the countries of Chad, Mali, Niger and part of Algeria.

He was still studying the map and considering various possible routes, taking into account the changed circumstances and dangers imposed in wartime as opposed to the trouble-free pre-war flying, when there was knock on the door. His secretary opened it and entered ushering in the visitor as she announced, "Hauptmann Steinberg is here, Major."

Von Lutzdorf rose from his chair and approached his visitor exclaiming, "Johann, my dear friend, it's so good to see you. Come in."

Thanking his secretary as she closed the adjoining door, he clasped Steinberg by the shoulders as his friend did the same and they looked at each other in obvious delight.

"You're looking well, Walter. Have you fully recovered?"

"Yes, fit again and ready to get back in the cockpit. Come, sit down and let's talk."

"I'm highly intrigued, Walter. One minute I'm getting ready to fly a combat mission only to be told it's cancelled and I'm to report to you at the Air Ministry on the express orders of Goering himself. What goes?"

"We're attached to the personal staff of Goering for special duties and I can do pretty much as I like carrying out those duties and have all the authority of Goering behind me. It's a pretty heady feeling. The first thing I did was to get you back here out of that hell hole of the Eastern Front. Just one word from me and the order was issued in Goering's name."

"Very impressive and I thank you for that. Now, tell me what it's all about."

Von Lutzdorf explained to Steinberg what Goering had told him about the shortage of industrial diamonds and how critical they were to future research and industrial development for the Third Reich and what Goering had ordered him to do to try to get them from South Africa. Bound as he was by his oath as an officer to not disclose anything concerning the flights to South America, he made a decision and decided to disclose what Goering had said to him regarding these flights and their importance to the future of the Third Reich. Since he would be involved eventually in them and the pre-planning, he felt his friend should be aware of everything from the start, stressing, however, that at that point he knew nothing of the details and swore him to secrecy on that subject. He then told Steinberg what he had decided so far concerning the type of aircraft and modifications he felt were necessary.

"Now, let's look at this map and see if we can work out the most suitable route," said von Lutzdorf as he spread it out on his desk.

"It's a very long way from Tripoli to the Ivory Coast and over some very inhospitable territory," observed Steinberg. "We should see if we can arrange some sort of staging post in case of emergency. It would have to be in an area where we can have security and control. I think it must be in Libya where we still have a military presence."

"That would mean as far south as the border with Chad or Niger," said von Lutzdorf.

"Why don't we speak to the Italians? They've been there since 1911. They must have explored that area and may have some suggestions," said Steinberg.

"Good idea. I'll have a word with their air attaché. He must be here somewhere in Berlin."

Picking up the telephone, he put a call through to Goering's aide Freiberg and asked him if he knew the whereabouts of the Italian air attaché.

"Well, that's a bit of luck, he's got an office here in the ministry," said von Lutzdorf as he put down the handset and pressed a button on his desk for his secretary who entered and said, "Yes, Herr Major, what do you need?"

"Could you please contact the Italian air attaché who I understand has an office here and arrange a meeting with him for me?"

"Do you want him to come here or do you wish to go to him?"

"Please ask him when it would be convenient to see him." Turning to Steinberg, he said, "We'll play it diplomatically and leave the decision to him. These Italian Embassy appointees can sometimes be a bit self-important."

Five minutes later, the secretary returned and said, "Maggiore Gratziani will be pleased to see you and said he will come here to you shortly."

"He must be bored with nothing to do to come right away," observed Steinberg, "At least he doesn't outrank you."

"Yes, that's something. At least we won't have to observe protocol too much."

Chapter 11

❖

Shortly after his secretary had given him the information regarding the air attaché, there was a knock at the adjoining door which opened and an Italian Air Force officer with a chest full of medals entered. He gave a casual salute and introduced himself.

"Major Mario Gratziani at your service, Major."

"Major, thank you for coming to see me so promptly," von Lutzdorf replied and indicating Steinberg, he continued. "This is my friend and assistant Hauptmann Johann Steinberg. Please take a seat."

"Thank you, Major," he said as he took the other seat in front of the desk after shaking hands with both von Lutzdorf and Steinberg. "How can I be of help? Naturally when your secretary informed me who you were I was happy of the opportunity to meet you. As a pre-war flyer myself, I knew of your reputation and exploits."

"Well, that was some time ago and we're in to a different type of flying these days except that what I would like to discuss with you relates to long-distance flying."

"Anything to do with active participation with flying would greatly please me. Since my wound, I am no longer operational and am bound to a desk which, I must confess, bores me to death."

Von Lutzdorf and Steinberg exchanged smiles at this confession.

"Major, what we would like to know from you is whether the Italian Air Force ever built any airfields in the interior of Libya especially down near the southern border with Chad or Niger?"

"Luckily, you are speaking to the right man," said Gratziani. "Before the war, I was stationed in Libya and am familiar with most of the airfields there and know of several in the south of the country. I was stationed for most of my service near Benghazi in Cyrenaica flying Fiat G50 fighters that was where I lost these," he said, holding up his left hand showing the missing third and fourth fingers. "An encounter with a British Hurricane. Fortunately, I was able to bail out over our own territory but it put an end to my combat career," he added with a rueful smile.

"It would be very helpful if you could get us some charts showing the exact location of these airfields," said von Lutzdorf.

"That won't be a problem. I'll send a signal to the Air Force headquarters in Rome and ask them to be sent by courier on the next flight. In the meantime, if you have a map of Africa, I can show you the location of one near the Tibesti mountain range that I know of and visited once. It's about as far south in Libya as you can go, close to the border with Chad."

"That would be splendid, Major," said Steinberg.

"May I ask why you need to know about these airfields or is that a state secret?"

"Well, naturally anything to do with military flying in wartime is secret but in this case, I can tell you that we are looking at establishing flying links with some of the Vichy-controlled territories in Africa and need some staging posts in case of emergencies. No secret there between allies," he added.

"Quite so."

"You say you once visited this airfield close to the Chad border and the Tibesti Mountains. What can you tell us about the area?"

"I think you will be very pleased with this particular airstrip. Whilst it is only hard packed sand, it is sufficient length for most aircraft and is very well-equipped and also very secure, situated as it is in a most remote and desolate part of the Libyan desert."

"Are there any settlements in the surrounding area?"

"The area is very remote and quite uninhabited which is good for security reasons. The mountains are the highest in the Sahara and are mostly located in Chad with just the lower slopes extending across the border into Libya. The higher regions in the centre are up to about three thousand metres and do get some rainfall forming some lakes and rivers that eventually run off into the desert. But in the meantime, it forms fertile areas where the native people, the Toubous, have settled for centuries but they stay well within Chad. The Libyan region has some dramatic scenery of smaller mountains and rock formations which are quite beautiful but it is very arid and without vegetation of any sort."

"Sounds ideal for what we have in mind," said Steinberg.

"I agree," added von Lutzdorf. "We must visit the place soon to do a survey. Do you know if it is occupied at the moment, Major?"

"I am afraid I don't know about that but I will inquire when I send the signal to Rome later today," said Gratziani.

"You have been a great help, Major. We are most grateful."

"It's a pleasure and in return I would like to ask you a great favour."

"If I can grant it, I would be pleased to do so. What is it that I can do for you?"

"When you go to survey the airfield, would you take me along? It would get me out from behind my desk and back into flying, at least for a while."

"You would be most welcome, Major."

"Excellent. I have enjoyed our meeting. Now I will return to my office and prepare the signal to Rome."

"Thank you for coming and being so helpful," said von Lutzdorf as he stood and shook Gratziani's outstretched hand.

After he had departed, von Lutzdorf and Steinberg relaxed and discussed more immediate issues.

"Have you been allocated any quarters here in Berlin?" asked von Lutzdorf.

"Yes, I have a room at the officers' quarters at Luftwaffe headquarters, quite a luxury after the Eastern Front. What about you, Walter?"

"I'll be staying at my parents' apartment in the suburbs. It's more comfortable than the officers' quarters and my fiancée Magda can visit me there."

"Will I get the opportunity to meet this woman who has captured you?"

"Of course, but be careful what you say, she is Goering's favourite niece."

"You certainly are mixing in heady circles these days. Does he approve of the liaison?"

"He appears to, so far. So, I suppose I'll have to marry her or be sent back to the Eastern Front."

"I don't recommend that. It's got worse since you were last there so let's make a success of these new missions and enjoy the high life in Berlin for a while," said Steinberg with a laugh.

Von Lutzdorf picked up the telephone and called Hauptmann Freiberg who answered after the second ring.

"Von Lutzdorf here. I would like to requisition a Heinkel 111 from the Luftwaffe to do some initial survey work in regard to the planning for the mission. Can you arrange that or should I approach the Luftwaffe with Goering's authority? What is the protocol for this? Do I place all requests through you or make my approaches directly?"

"You may safely leave all requirements for this mission to my department, Herr Major. Please give me a list of everything you need and I will see that you have everything necessary."

"I have spoken to the Italian air attaché about needing to survey certain aspects of their facilities in Libya. Is there any diplomatic protocol I must observe in that respect or do I have enough authority to act on my own in these matters?"

"You have the full authority of the Reichsmarschall behind you so please do as you see fit but keep me informed at all stages so that I can deal with the formalities. Even in wartime we are still bound by a certain amount of bureaucracy."

"Thank you, Freiberg. I will provide you with a preliminary list of requirements shortly." Putting down the telephone, von Lutzdorf looked at his friend and said, "I think we're off to a good start. That was a bit of luck finding Gratziani here. I think he'll be very useful." Looking at his watch, he added, "We've done enough for today so I'll drop you off at headquarters on my way back to my apartment."

"That'll suit me. I haven't had the chance to get cleaned up since I got here and I would like to get showered and changed before this evening."

"That's quick. Do you have a date already?"

"Nothing so exciting but my mother and sister who I have not seen for a long time are here in Berlin so I'll have a little family reunion which I'm looking forward to."

Von Lutzdorf pressed the button on the intercom for his secretary, who answered immediately, and asked her to have his car and driver meet them outside.

As they got up to leave, he handed his friend a piece of notepaper with Freiberg's number on it and said, "Call this number in the morning and ask Hauptmann Freiberg to organise a car for you."

Chapter 12

❖

When von Lutzdorf arrived back at his apartment, he was pleased to find his orderly had arrived with all his kit and spare uniforms and was busy putting his bedroom and more generally the house in order for his comfort.

"Good afternoon, Albert," he said using his Christian name in a friendly greeting. Feldwebel Wachtmeister (*Staff Sergeant*) Albert Schmitt had been Von Lutzdorf's orderly for almost four years. In private, they had developed a friendly informal relationship during that time as they shared both moments of danger and intimate moments together. When others were present, the relationship was formal and respectful from both sides.

"Good afternoon, Major. I'm just getting the household organised and getting to know the staff. Will you be in this evening or do you have a social engagement?"

The staff consisted of a cook, housekeeper and a maid which his parents had employed for a number of years.

"Yes, I do have an engagement this evening. And good luck with Frau Hoffmann, she's quite formidable."

"No problem there," replied Albert. "I think she is quite relieved to have some male company in the house at times like this," he added with a smile.

"I'll leave her in your capable hands then and please set out my best uniform."

Von Lutzdorf went into the sitting room, picked up the telephone and called Magda.

At this time, before the bombing reached its later more destructive phase, nightlife in wartime Berlin was surprisingly active and lively. The authorities encouraged all the arts including the opera, theatres, nightclubs and cabarets not only to keep up morale but to show the outside world that life was normal in the capital.

Von Lutzdorf had arranged to meet Magda at her apartment at seven o'clock and then go on to the famous Adlon Hotel where there was music and dancing.

***

Arriving promptly at Magda's apartment at seven o'clock, she greeted him at the door wearing a shimmering silver evening dress fitted to show off her tall athletic figure with her long blonde hair piled high on top in an elegant style. She wore a pair of long silver earrings to match her dress and accentuate her long graceful neck. In her high heels, her eyes were almost on the same level as von Lutzdorf's.

"You look amazing," he said.

"And you look very handsome and gallant in your uniform. I think we will be the best-looking couple at the Adlon this evening. Now, open that champagne and let's start the evening.

I've booked a table for nine o'clock and I feel like dancing all night."

"In that case, I hope I can keep up with you. I had better fuel up with champagne," he said as he deftly removed the cork with a loud pop and quickly poured the champagne into the glasses to avoid losing any as it fizzed furiously out of the bottle.

Giving one glass to Magda, he took the other and they toasted each other with a chink as the two glasses touched gently together. Setting the glasses down, von Lutzdorf gently pulled Magda to him in an embrace and kissed her lightly on the lips. Magda responded by pressing herself firmly to him and boldly pressing her lips to his as the tip of her tongue explored his. Reacting to this ardent and sensuous response, he pulled her strongly into an even tighter embrace as his hands explored the contours of her body beneath the tightly fitting dress.

Placing the palms of her hands on his chest, Magda pushed them gently apart and kissed him lightly on the cheek and said, "The evening is still young, darling. Let's enjoy a little champagne and dancing before we get to the finale."

Von Lutzdorf reluctantly released her and said with a smile, "I forgot, I'm wearing my gallant uniform and mustn't disgrace it."

They spent the next couple of hours talking about their immediate plans and finishing the champagne. Then Magda picked up a silver fox fur wrap and gave it to von Lutzdorf who draped it over her shoulders ready to depart.

Downstairs, their car was waiting for them for the short journey to the Adlon Hotel.

The elderly door keeper, obviously a former Luftwaffe member, gave von Lutzdorf a pre-Nazi salute which he acknowledged in the same manner and, nodding to Magda, said, "Good evening, Fraulein. It's good to see you again," as he opened the door for them.

***

Crossing the grand lobby of the Adlon Hotel with its massive square marble columns, they entered the lift and were taken to the restaurant floor where they were greeted by the maître d' who, after taking Magda's fur wrap and von Lutzdorf's uniform cap, showed them to a table close to the dance floor where a quartet was softly playing a popular dance tune of the time. All heads turned to watch them, the men obviously focused on Magda who, having discarded her fur wrap, showed off her tall elegant figure to great effect as she strode confidently through the tables. Her silvery evening dress glistened in the restaurant lighting whilst Walter drew some admiring looks from the women. Obviously well-known in German society, Magda exchanged smiles and greetings with various clientele as she passed through.

Walking behind her, Walter nodded occasionally to some of those in uniform recognising their envious glances secretly feeling proud to be escorting the most beautiful woman in the room.

After being seated, Magda leant over towards von Lutzdorf and whispered in his ear, "There, what did I tell you? Aren't you the lucky man?"

Smiling at her whilst gently squeezing her hand, he whispered back. "If I didn't know how modest you really are, I would think you were fishing for compliments but then you know how much I love you." He kissed her gently on the cheek.

"And I love you too."

They were interrupted by the waiter arriving at the table, so releasing hands, von Lutzdorf ordered champagne as Magda said, "Let's order now. I'm starving."

"Good idea, so am I."

The waiter handed them each a copy of the menu and hurried off to get the champagne. The menu was extensive with little sign of wartime shortages especially for the elite of Berlin. Having ordered their meal, they alternated courses with dances and passed a very pleasant and intimate dinner largely unaware of others around them until they were enjoying their after dinner liqueurs. A man in the uniform of an SS Gruppenfuehrer approached their table. As they looked up at him, he said, "Good evening, Magda. May I join you for a moment?"

"Good evening, Herr Mueller. May I introduce my fiancé, Major Walter von Lutzdorf." Turning to von Lutzdorf, she said, "Walter, this is Herr Heinrich Mueller."

As the Gruppenfuehrer turned his attention to him, von Lutzdorf was immediately struck by a pair of piercing grey eyes which seemed to bore right into him. Looking him straight back eye to eye and trying not to appear in any way disconcerted, he took his outstretched hand and noting the Bavarian Pilot's Badge on his uniform said, "Good evening, Herr Gruppenfuehrer. Please do join us."

Shaking his hand, Mueller replied, "Good evening, Major. Congratulations, you are indeed a lucky man but please forgive this intrusion."

Von Lutzdorf signalled to a waiter who quickly produced another chair and seated Mueller at the table with Magda between them.

Von Lutzdorf knew who Mueller was and although not himself a Nazi, protocol and circumstances decreed a certain degree of formal politeness. "No intrusion at all. Can I tempt you to join us in a liqueur?"

"No, thank you, Major. I shall not keep you long. As much as I was tempted by the beauty of your fiancée, it was you I wanted to speak to."

As modesty required, Magda inclined her head with a demure smile at what she knew was an insincere comment and said, "Why, thank you, Herr Mueller. How kind of you." She did not refer to his rank or official title, which she knew would irritate him.

"I'm flattered, Herr Gruppenfuehrer," von Lutzdorf said, "How may I help you?"

"It's nothing like that. It's just that as a fellow aviator albeit my service is from a long time ago, the first war in fact, I am aware of your pre-war exploits and wanted to shake your hand."

"That's very kind of you and it's my pleasure."

"No, mine, I assure you, Major," Mueller continued. "I understand you are now attached to the personal staff of our illustrious Reichsmarschall Goering for special duties. If there is anything I can do to help you in these, please feel free to call me."

Not sure of how to respond to this and amazed that word of his so recent appointment had reached the ears of the chief of the Gestapo so soon, von Lutzdorf replied, "It's very early days yet. I'm only just settling in but I will keep your offer in mind."

Just at that moment, they were startled by the pop and sudden flash of light from a camera flash bulb. A professional photographer employed by the hotel to take souvenir photographs for the clientele, no doubt attracted by the combination of the most beautiful woman in the room with two military uniforms on either side, had taken the opportunity to snap them together.

Looking up in annoyance at this sudden intrusion, Mueller scowled at the photographer who retreated before he could say anything.

Recovering his composure, Mueller said, "Please do. Now, I won't disturb you any longer as I must be off."

Standing up, he took Magda's outstretched hand, bowed his head towards her and kissed the back of her hand as he clicked his heels together. "Good night, my dear Magda," he said and turning to von Lutzdorf, he continued. "Good night, Major. I hope we will meet again."

After bidding Mueller goodnight, von Lutzdorf sat down and looked at Magda.

"Well, what do you make of that? And how do you know the chief of the Gestapo?"

"I've met him a number of times at functions with Uncle Hermann and he always makes a point of cornering me and asking questions. Frankly, he makes my skin crawl. He has such a cold ruthless air about him. That display of politeness was just for show. He never does anything without some ulterior motive behind it."

"How on earth did he know of my new appointment? I only learnt about it yesterday myself."

"Don't underestimate him. There is nothing that goes on in Germany, especially here in Berlin, that he doesn't know about. He has spies and informers everywhere."

"Did you notice his annoyance at that photographer?"

"Yes. I'm not surprised at all. He's a very secretive man and there are very few photographs of him in circulation. He likes to keep his identity out of the limelight unlike all the other prominent Nazis who like nothing better than strutting before the cameras."

"What does your Uncle Hermann think of him?"

"Well, even though he's my uncle and I owe him a lot, I have to say he's like all the rest. None of them trust each other as they're all jealous of their positions and constantly on guard of any infringement of their authority or access to Hitler. It's his way of keeping them all under control. It's the old story of divide and conquer."

"I think I shall be very cautious in any dealings with Mueller. In fact, I shall try to have no dealings with him whatsoever. He must have some devious agenda in mind."

"Good idea, darling. Now, I think it's time we left. We still have a finale to think about."

Von Lutzdorf smiled as he said, "I thought you had forgotten all about that. I'll get the bill and we can leave."

"Don't worry, darling. I have an account here. They'll send the bill to me."

"Things just keep getting better and better. I think I will enjoy being a kept man."

"Just because I have an account doesn't mean you won't eventually pay, especially when we're married."

As they were about to rise from the table, the photographer reappeared and handed them a card with his details on it. "I'm sorry I had to rush off but here is my business card. If you would like a copy of the photograph I took this evening, I'll arrange for it to be delivered here to the hotel for you to collect at your convenience or to your address if you write it on the back of the card."

"Yes, we would like two copies but send them to the hotel. They have my address and will settle the bill with you," said Magda.

"Thank you, Fraulein."

After the photographer left, von Lutzdorf said with a grin, "Do you think we should order a copy for the Gruppenfuehrer?"

Magda laughed and said, "I think this will be our secret, don't you?"

Chapter 13

❖

Von Lutzdorf arrived at his office in the Air Ministry promptly at eight o'clock the next morning to find Hauptmann Steinberg already there sitting at his desk making notes.

For convenience, von Lutzdorf had ordered that another desk be placed in his spacious office for Steinberg as this would make it easier for them to work together on the project.

"Good morning, Johann. How did your evening go? Did you see your mother and sister?"

"Yes, we had a very long overdue reunion. I'm very grateful that you requested me to be on your team back here in Berlin. Had it not been for that I don't know when, if ever, I would have seen them again. My mother asked me to express her gratitude to you."

"Think nothing of it, Johann. You would have done the same for me."

"What about your evening? I take it that you took your bride-to-be out to somewhere expensive."

"Yes, and it turned out to be more interesting than I expected. We went to the Adlon Hotel for dinner and I was introduced to none other than Heinrich Mueller, the chief of the Gestapo. It appears that my bride-to-be knows everyone of influence in Berlin."

"What's he like? I hear he's very secretive and doesn't mix much socially. I don't think I've ever even seen a photograph of him."

"You're quite right about that. He doesn't like to have his photograph taken," said von Lutzdorf as he described the incident with the photographer and went on to tell Steinberg about the meeting with Mueller and how he was convinced Mueller did not introduce himself merely to shake his hand and congratulate him for his past flying exploits.

"I think he has a hidden agenda and likes to keep tabs on everything and everyone of interest especially if they have links with the rest of the Nazi hierarchy. How else would he know about my appointment to the Air Ministry so quickly? Magda said he has spies and informers everywhere, so we must be very careful what we say and do here in Berlin."

"I must say that I didn't think there could be a more dangerous place than the Eastern Front but listening to you I think perhaps Berlin could be just as dangerous but from a different aspect."

"I agree, but let's concentrate on the planning for the mission. I will call Gratziani and see if he has any information from Rome."

Just as he was about to pick up the telephone, it rang. Quickly putting the receiver to his ear, von Lutzdorf was greeted with a, "Good morning, Major. This is Gratziani. I have some news from Rome. If you are free, I will come to your office right away."

"Please do, Major. I was about to call you when you rang."

Five minutes later, there was a knock on the door and Gratziani entered with a smile on his face. "Good news, Major. I received a signal this morning to my query regarding our airfields in the south of Libya. I am pleased to tell you that the one I had in mind near the Chad border and Tibesti Mountains, although not occupied, has been maintained and kept operational if required by a small unit that visits every three months. As soon as you decide to make a survey flight, they will ensure that the maintenance unit is dispatched to meet us there."

"Excellent. That is good news. Now let's see if Hauptmann Freiberg has managed to get us that Heinkel 111 so we can plan our next move."

In response, Steinberg picked up the telephone and called Freiberg who five minutes later arrived at their office.

"Rather than getting you one on loan for the survey flight, I have arranged with Heinkel that you will be allocated one straight from the assembly line for the project. You should visit them directly and ensure that it is fitted out with whatever equipment you need for the mission."

"We'll need transport," said von Lutzdorf. "Can you get us the use of a Junker 52? The plant is at Warnemuende on the Baltic coast. I've been there before. It's less than a one-hour flight from Berlin."

"I shall arrange that at once. The Herr Reichsmarschall has one on standby here in Berlin at all times, Major."

"Very convenient," said Gratziani. "Do you mind if I come along with you, Major?"

"You're more than welcome. I consider you now part of our team, Major. Did the signal say anything about charts or other information concerning the airfield?"

"They will send all available information by courier, hopefully arriving later today as I did stress the urgency of the matter."

"Hauptmann Freiberg, can you please alert the crew of the Junker 52 to be ready for a flight to Warnemuende at midday?"

"I will deal with it right away, Major," said Freiberg as he left the office.

"Major Gratziani, when you last visited the airfield, do you remember if it had any radio navigational aids?"

"Not when I was last there but that was a few years ago."

"We must obtain a short-range transmitter on the Lorenz beam frequency which we can install there. We can then use the Lorenz beam receiver fitted in all of our bombers to help locate the airfield when we are in range. This will be essential when we're returning from our first mission as it's a long distance from West Africa and the Ivory Coast. Although we may not need to land there except in an emergency, it will enable us to get a good fix to correct our dead reckoning navigation."

They spent the rest of the morning going over their plans and deciding what other equipment would be useful in the aircraft for the long-distance mission.

Chapter 14

❖

At eleven o'clock, von Lutzdorf, Steinberg and Gratziani left the Air Ministry and were taken to the Berlin Templehof Airport where a Ju 52 aircraft was waiting for them. They were taken to the aircraft by a Luftwaffe airman who was part of the crew and acted as an orderly steward to take care of VIP passengers. The pilot, a Luftwaffe captain, was waiting outside the aircraft and greeted von Lutzdorf with a salute and said, "I have submitted my flight plan for Warnemuende and they will be expecting us, Major."

"Very good," said von Lutzdorf as all three followed the pilot into the aircraft with the orderly following up behind. The pilot made his way forwards to the cockpit as the orderly secured the passenger door and then ensured his passengers were comfortably seated for the flight.

Since this aircraft was used for VIPs, it was more comfortably upholstered than those normally fitted for transporting troops or paratroopers.

"Well, I must say," said Steinberg with a grin, "I could get used to this comfort. It's much better than sitting on a parachute."

When the aircraft had reached its cruising altitude and settled on its course to their destination, the orderly came back and served them all with coffee.

"First time I've had coffee on an aircraft served in a cup," said Steinberg.

"Make the most of it," laughed von Lutzdorf, "The best you can hope for in the future will be in a tin mug from a thermos flask."

As predicted, the flight time was just under an hour and they landed without incident at the Heinkel factory airfield and taxied up to the apron to the waiting welcoming committee.

As the aircraft came to a stop and the engines were shut down, a ground crew approached the aircraft with a set of steps which they placed in front of the passenger door as it was opened from inside by the orderly.

Alighting from the aircraft, von Lutzdorf, Steinberg and Gratziani were approached by the party from the factory which consisted of two civilians and two in uniform. To von Lutzdorf's surprise, one was dressed as an SS Hauptsturmfuehrer. The other was a regular Luftwaffe officer.

One of the civilians introduced himself as the works manager and the other as the chief engineer. After shaking hands with both, the manager indicated the two in uniform who stepped forwards. The Luftwaffe officer saluted von Lutzdorf and introduced himself saying, "Hauptmann Eric Weber, Luftwaffe liaison officer, at your service, Major."

The SS officer stepped forwards and gave a Nazi salute, which von Lutzdorf did not acknowledge, and said, "Hauptsturmfuehrer Hans Heidrich, state security, Major."

"Thank you, gentlemen," said von Lutzdorf as he introduced Steinberg and Gratziani.

Taking the lead, the manager led the party towards the hangar entrance inside of which von Lutzdorf could see, stretching deep into the interior, rows of Heinkel 111 bombers in final assembly lines. Passing through the hangar to the rear, they arrived at a set of stairs which led up to the works offices overlooking the factory floor.

They were shown into what looked like a conference room with a number of chairs around a long table.

"Well, gentlemen," the chief engineer said, "We have received orders from the Air Ministry to give you every cooperation with your requirements regarding some modifications to the normal specifications of our 111 bomber. Please explain what those might be and we can get our design department working on them and see if they are possible or practical."

Von Lutzdorf, who had been sworn to secrecy by Goering regarding the real reason for the aircraft, had not expected the presence of the Gestapo officer, who he was sure was there on the express orders of Heinrich Mueller to learn everything he could and keep his master informed. However, he already had a cover story worked out to explain the reason for the required modifications so he launched into this before discussing their requirements. Steinberg was already privy to this strategy and Gratziani had no reason to speculate or comment.

"As you know, gentlemen," he began, "We are well entrenched in Libya and Rommel is, in fact, in Egypt at the gates of Alexandria poised to take the Suez Canal. There is no reason to suppose that based on his performance to date against the British forces in the Western Desert that he will not soon be successful in that endeavour.

"When that happens, we shall need to extend our reconnaissance flights deeper into the Middle East and Africa to consolidate our control of the Suez Canal. This will force the allies to use the longer route around the tip of South Africa to supply their forces in the Far East. If we can then link up with our main armies in the Crimea, we will be able to take control of the oil fields in Iraq and Iran giving us access to this valuable asset and thus denying this source to the enemy."

This brought nods of approval and agreement from those other than Steinberg and Gratziani, who kept a respectful silence while their leader continued.

"Based on my experience of pre-war long-distance flying, the commander-in-chief, Reichsmarschall Goering, has done me the honour of appointing me to head up this effort and to pioneer some routes which will be necessary as the Third Reich expands its influence."

Throughout this explanation, von Lutzdorf was not at all convinced himself that what he had expounded as the aims and expectations of the Third Reich would come about.

Unlike many in the German military and Nazi Party, he had travelled outside of the country to the United States and England. He was aware of their character and determination and especially of the latent industrial capacity of America now gearing up to full production turning out aircraft, ships, tanks and every other type of armament Germany could never hope to compete with. With their combined navies, Britain and America controlled the oceans of the world to a degree that Germany could never aspire to, cutting off Germany from ever-diminishing supplies of essential natural resources, especially rare metals.

However, for the expediency of the moment, von Lutzdorf did his best to appear convinced of his own argument. Steinberg, who, like his friend, was no Nazi and had also spent time abroad, was firmly of the same mind. Gratziani, being Italian and no fascist, well-educated and of good family was no fan of Mussolini and had never been comfortable with the alliance with Germany. With Italy's extensive family ties to much of the immigrant population in America, he had been astonished and appalled at Hitler's declaration of war against America following the Pearl Harbour attack by the Japanese thinking it extreme folly on his part. Up until then, America was neutral in the war against Germany. This decision of Hitler's, no doubt driven by his ego and fanatical belief in his own military tactical and strategic ability, often led to him to interfere with the conduct of the war, much to the frustration of his professional generals. This declaration of war against America gave President Roosevelt the excuse he needed to circumvent those isolationists in Congress, who had constantly opposed any involvement in the European war, and come out openly and join Britain in the war against Germany.

Having set out his reasons for the specification changes to the Heinkel bomber that he needed to pursue these requirements, he looked to Steinberg and said, "Steinberg, you have the file with the list of modifications we need. Perhaps if you give that to the chief engineer for his department to study, we can dispense with any further discussion at this stage whilst we have a tour of the factory which I am sure would be informative."

The chief engineer agreed and said, "You are quite right, Major. We cannot discuss anything in detail until my department have seen your file so I agree. Let me give you a guided tour and you can ask questions and I will do my best to answer as to the feasibility of the changes you need."

Von Lutzdorf was anxious to move the meeting on and get rid of the presence of the Gestapo representative and move on to safer ground.

Having agreed, they all stood. The Gestapo and Luftwaffe officers excused themselves while von Lutzdorf and the Heinkel staff went down to the factory floor to begin their tour.

"I was surprised to see the SS Hauptsturmfuehrer here. Has he been with you long?" asked von Lutzdorf.

"As a matter of fact, Major, he just arrived this morning. I thought it was on the orders of the Air Ministry," replied the manager.

Not wishing to make an issue of it realising Mueller must have an informer in the heart of the Air Ministry, von Lutzdorf said, "I expect you're right. Security is necessary at times like these."

As they stood looking at one of the bombers in the assembly line, the chief engineer asked, "What are your main requirements, Major?"

"Well, for long-distance reconnaissance we will obviously need much more fuel so I would like you modify the bomb bay to accommodate more fuel tanks. Enough to give at least another two thousand miles to its normal range, say a total of three thousand five hundred miles. It will also require larger oil tanks for the engines and you can dispense with the ventral gun emplacements to reduce the drag. We intend to use stealth and speed whenever necessary to avoid the enemy.

"Can you perhaps fit a methanol or water injection system to the engines to give us a speed boost in an emergency? And perhaps a two-stage compressor to enable us to fly at a greater altitude, which will also improve our fuel efficiency. We will also need to have the bombardier's position changed for that of a second pilot and dual controls fitted."

"The air frame changes are relatively easy. The engine modifications may be a bit more difficult but I shall speak to the manufacturers to see what they can do."

"You have our file so I will leave everything to you. I would appreciate hearing from you by tomorrow on what you can do and with a time scale as we would like to carry out some trial flights as soon as possible."

"We shall do our best."

With that, von Lutzdorf turned to his companions and said, "I think that's enough for the moment. We should get back to Berlin."

Turning down an invitation to lunch, von Lutzdorf led Steinberg and Gratziani back to the waiting Ju 52 and, thanking their hosts, they boarded the aircraft for the return journey.

Once the aircraft was on course for Berlin, Steinberg turned to his chief and asked, "I know it's not for me to question your decision, Walter, but why did you turn down the invitation for lunch?"

"Sorry about that, Johann, but I didn't want to take the risk that Hauptsturmfuehrer Heidrich would be there as he's in Heinrich Mueller's camp and reports everything back to him. The less contact we have with him, the better." Turning to Gratziani, he said, "Sorry about this, Mario. I know you're not involved in this in the way we are, but I'm grateful for your help."

"Frankly, Major, the less contact I have with the Gestapo and the SS, the better. I never feel comfortable in their company at any time," said Gratziani.

"That's something on which I think we can all agree," said von Lutzdorf, "I don't think there's much more we can do until we receive the documentation from Rome and hear back from Heinkel. I suggest we make use of what leisure time we have before we start on the serious planning."

After landing, the Italian Embassy car picked up Gratziani, and von Lutzdorf dropped off Steinberg at his quarters and then continued on to his apartment.

Chapter 15

❖

The first thing von Lutzdorf did on arrival at his office the following morning was to call Goering's aide Hauptmann Freiberg to his office and report on his visit to the Heinkel works. He made a point of telling Freiberg of the presence of the Gestapo officer Hauptsturmfuehrer Heidrich which he was sure would be reported in turn to Goering, certain this would infuriate the Reichsmarschall. By reporting this to Freiberg, he had cleared himself from any controversy and he was sure Goering would take Mueller to account over his intrusion into what was after all the Reichsmarschall's exclusive domain.

He would, however, be careful what was said in his office as he was sure the only persons to have been privy to their trip to Heinkel other than himself, Steinberg and Gratziani were Freiberg and his secretary. Of Freiberg's discretion and loyalty to Goering, he had little doubt but his secretary was another matter. Mueller's ability to reach out and coerce somebody like Hanna Braun with threats or blackmail to do his bidding was routine for the Gestapo who terrified everyone in Germany, military and civilians alike.

Steinberg arrived shortly after he had finished with Freiberg. They were discussing the events of the day when the telephone rang and it was Gratziani with the news that the courier had brought the documents from Rome. He would bring them to von Lutzdorf shortly. Von Lutzdorf suggested he delay his arrival for half an hour whilst he dealt with some other matters and cleared his desk to which Gratziani agreed.

Von Lutzdorf took this opportunity to suggest to Steinberg that they take a short walk outside to take a coffee on Wilhelmstrasse. Looking askance at his friend, Steinberg agreed and followed him out through his secretary's office and out of the building.

Once clear of the building, von Lutzdorf said, "Sorry about that little bit of subterfuge but I didn't want to say anything whilst in my office."

He then went on to explain his suspicions of a leak in the office and in particular about his secretary and how they must not in future ever mention anything about flights to South America in the office where they might be in danger of being overheard.

"The flights to Africa are logical and easily explained as a strategic necessity for Germany but the South American flights, which I stress I know nothing about, could be misconstrued and I have given my oath to Goering not to disclose even the prospect of them."

"I understand completely, Walter. My lips are sealed. Let's get back now. I want to see what Gratziani has for us," said Steinberg.

***

They were just back in von Lutzdorf's office when there was a knock on the door and Gratziani entered carrying a large leather satchel.

"Good morning, Major," he said with a broad grin. "I've had a brief look at the contents and I think you will be pleased with what we have."

Taking the seat in front of the desk, Gratziani opened the satchel and began taking out a number of different documents from lists of equipment to charts of the area and some aerial photographs as well as photographs of the cliff face into which had been built the hangar. The camouflaged sliding doors blended cleverly with the strata and surface of the surrounding rock face, making it almost undetectable other than from close scrutiny.

The contents list of equipment at the base was impressive. There were two diesel generators, and an air compressor for filling the compressed air bottles used for starting them. Tanks for diesel, petrol and water. A tractor for towing the aircraft, two trucks and one half-track and a special vehicle with large towed brushes for clearing any truck or aircraft tracks from the sand to aid in their security from discovery either from the air or land. Most important was the fact there was a water supply from a nearby spring.

"It seems that your Air Force people have thought of everything," said von Lutzdorf. "What reason is there for having such a secret and clandestine base so far south in the desert?"

"I'm not sure of the thinking at the time but it's in a most arid and inhospitable part of the Sahara and was only intended to be manned from time to time. It is well off the traditional historic trade routes with no endemic tribes or people living in the area so I suppose it was decided to make it as difficult to find by accident as possible but could be made operational quickly in any emergency."

"Whatever the reason, it suits our purpose admirably. I shall look forward to paying a visit of inspection as soon as our aircraft is ready for its test flight. Let's hope we hear something from Heinkel this morning regarding the modifications and the time schedule."

***

Later than morning, the Heinkel chief engineer called from Warnemuende and was put through to von Lutzdorf.

"The preliminary report from my department is good, Major. They can definitely accommodate sufficient fuel in the bomb bay area to comfortably give the aircraft an extra two thousand miles of range. Also, combined with removing the ventral gun emplacements and removing all other armaments and fuselage blisters except for the star sight navigation blister on top and with only two crew as specified, they expect the normal top speed will be increased to two hundred and ninety miles per hour at fifteen thousand feet.

"I have spoken to the engine manufacturers and they have a model available which will not only incorporate the two-stage compressor but also, they have developed a new system of methanol and water injection which for short periods will give twenty percent increase in power which should result in a speed at thirty thousand feet of in excess of three hundred and twenty miles per hour."

"Excellent news. When do you think the aircraft will be available for a test flight?"

"One week from now, Major. That will also give us time to fit the new automatic pilot and the HF radio equipment you specified."

"Please keep me informed of progress," said von Lutzdorf as he thanked the chief engineer and rang off.

Relaying this information to Steinberg, he asked him if he had had any luck with the Lorenz company in Berlin regarding the supply of a portable transmitter to act as a locator beacon on the frequency of 33.33 megacycles, the standard blind landing beam frequency.

"As a matter of fact, they've been very helpful. When I explained what we needed it for, they came up with an ingenious solution for us."

"What did they suggest?"

"When I explained that the transmitter will be located at a remote, largely unmanned site for periods of up to a week or more, they were concerned about the battery life being on constant transmit for such a long period. So, they proposed placing a receiver on site tuned to the frequency of an onboard transmitter in the aircraft. When in range on the approach to the airfield a signal from the aircraft to the ground receiver will switch on the the locator beacon and give the pilot a course to steer. This will greatly extend the battery life as on receive, the current drain is quite small."

"Sounds like a good solution. How long will it take them to fit the transmitter in the aircraft?"

"Only the matter of one day, at most."

"Tell them to get their equipment to Heinkel right away. Get it installed in couple of days and put their portable transmitter and batteries in a crate and place it in the aircraft."

Steinberg did as he was bid and confirmed the Lorenz company would comply with their request as a matter of urgency and would contact Heinkel and inform them of the facilities they would need so they would not conflict with the current work being carried out on the aircraft.

They then spent the rest of the morning going over the charts and the aerial photographs of the airfield Gratziani had supplied.

"This photograph is very useful. See this unusual rock formation of three large rocks which are in alignment with the approach to the runway?"

The landing strip was not discernible from the air being an area of flat sand. On the photograph, an arrow pointed in the direction of the runway from the last rock in the formation with the distance of five hundred metres marked from the rock to the threshold of the landing strip.

"Yes, that's a very helpful approach guide. We should not have any difficulty lining up to land."

Chapter 16

❖

Impatient to get on with their plans, von Lutzdorf telephoned the chief engineer every day pressing him to complete the work as soon as possible with the result that Heinkel put on a double shift of workers to comply with his urging. He was rewarded with a telephone call after the fifth day telling him the aircraft was ready for inspection.

Putting the Junker 52 crew on standby to leave within the hour, von Lutzdorf called Gratziani, who together with Steinberg and himself were taken to Templehof Airport once again.

This time it was only the works manager and chief engineer who were there to greet them and they were taken to a cordoned-off section of the hangar where the aircraft awaited them resplendent in its new colour scheme. The top wings' surfaces and the top half of the fuselage were painted in a desert sand colour whilst the wing undersides and lower half of the fuselage were a very pale blue. There were no black crosses or any other markings on the aircraft except for a large black swastika inside a white circle on the background of a broad red stripe on each side of the vertical tail fin and in small letters and numbers a Lufthansa commercial registration and manufacturer's number on the rear section of the fuselage.

With no defensive armaments, the clean lines of the aircraft were in stark contrast to those of the standard 111 bombers on the assembly line. The commercial Lufthansa registration and lack of armaments had been von Lutzdorf's suggestion since it would not have been appropriate for an armed German military aircraft to be seen flying over neutral countries.

"An admirable job," said von Lutzdorf. "I hope she flies as well as she looks."

"I think you can be assured of that, Major," said the chief engineer, obviously pleased with his creation. He added, "All the systems and equipment have been thoroughly tested including engine ground runs, taxi trials and brakes so other than your normal take-off checks, the aircraft is all ready for you to go."

"In that case, would you have the aircraft towed out to the apron where we can do our inspection? And perhaps you will point out anything we need to know in the cockpit."

"Of course, Major." He then waved to the ground crew who were standing by to move the aircraft from the hanger.

Following a normal pre-flight walk around ground inspection, von Lutzdorf noted that where the ventral bath tub gun position had been Heinkel had built in the new combined crew and cargo hatch which he had specified. He then, together with Steinberg and Gratziani, entered the aircraft followed by the chief engineer. Gratziani settled himself in the navigator's position behind the pilots while the chief engineer placed himself between the two pilots and said, "Apart from the standard controls and switches which you will be familiar with, the only additions are the controls for the engine boost injection and the control switches for the Lorenz beam transmitter that you asked for."

After pointing these out and explaining how they worked, he said, "If you're satisfied there is nothing else you need, I shall leave you now and wish you a good flight back to Berlin."

"I think we can manage from here," said von Lutzdorf. "Thank you for all your help."

After the engineer had left the aircraft, von Lutzdorf turned to his companions and said with a smile, "Let's see if this beauty can fly."

They then went through the engine start-up procedures and pre-flight checks and then asked permission from the control tower to taxi from the apron to the runway.

Having received permission to proceed, von Lutzdorf, by use of the throttles, rudder and brakes, manoeuvred the aircraft to the holding point at the runway threshold and satisfied with the propeller pitch and engine power checks, he asked for permission to take off.

Receiving this, he entered the runway, ran the engines up to take-off power and released the brakes. Accelerating down the runway, first the tail lifted and as they reached flying speed, he eased back on the control column and the aircraft took to the air in a steady climb to five thousand feet: the altitude he had requested in his flight plan. Since the 111 was much faster than the Ju 52 which had left some time before them, they soon caught up with it and as they passed, von Lutzdorf gave the other pilot a wave which was returned.

Instead of returning to Berlin Templehof Airport, it had been arranged for them to land at a Luftwaffe base near to Berlin for reasons of security, not wanting this unusually marked aircraft to be seen in public more than necessary.

Hauptmann Freiberg had arranged with the Luftwaffe base commander for the aircraft to be kept apart from other aircraft in a separate hangar in a more isolated part of the airfield. On landing, they were instructed to follow a vehicle to the hangar which had been opened ready to receive them. Stopping in front of it, von Lutzdorf and Steinberg shut down the engines and left the aircraft to a ground crew to move it inside.

As well as making all the arrangements, Freiberg was on hand to meet them with transport back to the Air Ministry where Gratziani took his leave and was taken on to the Italian Embassy.

Chapter 17

❖

Back in the office, von Lutzdorf prepared a report for Goering on the state of progress to date, recommending they leave the following day on the test and survey flight to Libya. Having completed this, he called Hauptmann Freiberg and requested a meeting with Reichsmarschall Goering.

To Steinberg, he said, "I suggest you see your mother and sister this evening as we'll be off tomorrow. It may be your last chance for some time with them. I'm going to have an evening with Magda and tell her our plans. In the meantime, work out a flight plan. I've looked at the charts and think we're best to fly direct from here to Rome then Palermo in Sicily and then via Tripoli avoiding Maltese air space. There is too much activity there at the moment and we don't want to run into any of the Spitfires they have based there. We can then fly on south via Sebha which puts us on track very nearly for the airfield. Then we'll have to look for the three rock formation to locate the airstrip."

"I'll work on it before I leave the office today. What time do you want to depart in the morning?"

"Early enough to get us there before we lose the daylight. Otherwise, we'll have to stop over in Tripoli for the night."

Before leaving the Air Ministry, von Lutzdorf placed a call to Magda who picked up after a few rings.

"It's me, darling," he said, "I'm ringing to tell you we'll be leaving tomorrow for a few days and when we return, I won't have the opportunity to see you again for a while. We're going off on an extended trip to Africa and I'm not sure when I'll be back, so let's make an evening of it to remember."

"Your apartment or mine?" she asked.

"Yours is better. With no staff, it's less crowded than mine and cosier. Do you have somewhere in mind that we could go to for a nice intimate dinner?"

"I'll give it some thought. What time shall I expect you?"

"Seven o'clock. Let's make the most of it."

He rang off and told Steinberg he would see him in the morning at eight o'clock and left the building ordering the driver to take him to his apartment.

Chapter 18

❖

As usual, his orderly was on hand ready to see to his needs as von Lutzdorf told him of his planned departure the next day for the test and survey flight.

"Just pack my flying gear, Albert, and enough for four days for this trip but for my next one, I shall be away for perhaps two weeks."

"Yes, Major. Will you be in for dinner this evening or should I set out your clean uniform?"

"I shall be dining out tonight, Albert, so you may take the evening off."

"Very well, Major."

Whilst he was getting ready to go to Magda's, von Lutzdorf was thinking about what gear he needed for the trip which prompted him to call Hauptmann Freiberg's number. He was surprised when he answered expecting him to have already left the office.

"Freiberg, sorry to call you so late."

"Not at all, Major. I am always available to you."

"Can you please contact the base commander and ensure he supplies us with three electrically heated flying suits and sufficient oxygen for ten hours for tomorrow."

"Of course, Major. Is there anything else you may need for this flight?"

"Nothing I can think of right now, Hauptmann. Good night."

Even though they would be flying south to the Sahara, he wanted to test the aircraft to its maximum altitude to check the new engines' performance fitted with the two-stage compressors and if, as he expected, they reached thirty thousand feet, the temperature at that height could be as low as minus forty-five degrees centigrade and even lower if they exceeded that height.

Satisfied he had done all he could for the moment, von Lutzdorf finished dressing, told Albert to order his driver to be ready and left for the evening.

Now the concierge knew von Lutzdorf was Magda's fiancé, he was greeted with a welcoming smile as he entered the lobby and pressed the button for the lift.

As Magda opened the door to her apartment, von Lutzdorf looked at her and marvelled to himself how she always appeared more beautiful each time he saw her and how each time she set his pulse racing. This evening, instead of a sophisticated glamorous evening dress, she was wearing a flowered summer dress with no jewellery other than some small diamond stud earrings with her hair loose and flowing around her shoulders and semi high heels so he looked down on her slightly. Her appearance was girlish rather than sophisticated elegance but nonetheless breath-taking.

"You look as beautiful as ever, darling. I take it that we're not going to the Adlon or another nightclub."

She laughed as she said, "You noticed. No, for an intimate evening I know of a charming little Italian restaurant with a secluded garden where we can eat outside as the evening is beautiful and warm."

"Sounds like an excellent choice. I must mention it to my new Italian friend I've just met."

"You have an Italian friend? That's interesting. How did you meet him? You've only been in Berlin for a few days."

"Quite by chance really. He's the air attaché at the Italian Embassy, Major Gratziani."

"Oh, you mean Conte Mario Gratziani? The charming Count Mario Leonardo of the Italian noble house of Gratziani?"

Startled by her remark, von Lutzdorf exclaimed with a tinge of jealousy, "How on earth do you know him? Is there anyone in Berlin you don't know?"

"I do get a lot of invitations to embassy functions, darling, and you know what Italians are like when it comes to flirting with women."

Feeling his jealousy more, he said, "I hope you don't reciprocate those flirtations."

"Of course not, darling. As charming a flirt as he is, Mario is an absolute gentleman and very modest. He never uses his title and, in any case, it's only a little harmless fun." With a mischievous smile, she added, "Why, I do believe you are jealous, Walter."

Recovering his dignity, he replied, "Not at all. It's just that you surprised me, that's all."

"Rest assured, darling. You are the only man for me," said Magda as she threw her arms around his neck and planted a passionate kiss on his lips.

Clasping his arms around her waist, he held her tightly to him as he responded to her passion with equal warmth and let the moment linger until they eventually leant back and looked into each other's eyes and laughed.

"I must admit, darling, that I did feel a little tinge of jealousy when you spoke so warmly of Mario."

"That's lovely to know but you have no need to ever be jealous. I love only you."

"Well, I'm glad we've settled that," said von Lutzdorf with a grin. "What about a drink to celebrate before we go out?"

"There's champagne in the ice bucket on the terrace. Let's have a glass before we go to dinner."

***

The restaurant turned out to be located in a small back street off the fashionable Kurfuerstendamm. It was a family-run business specialising in food from the Tuscany region of Italy and very popular with those residents from the Italian community.

The rear of the restaurant opened into a medium sized courtyard whose trellised walls were covered with climbing plants and bougainvillea. The seating was divided off by potted shrubs and trimmed lemon trees providing secluded tables, giving the whole area a feeling of intimacy. The owner, Antonio, who knew Magda as a frequent client, led them to a table in the corner with dimmed lighting and with a flourish, he lit the candle in the centre of the table. Whilst he knew Magda was related in some way to Goering and was no fan of Mussolini, fascists or Nazis, she was always welcome as he knew her to be non-political. Von Lutzdorf dressed in Luftwaffe uniform was equally welcome. What he and most of the Italian community disliked and resented were the SS who strutted and threw their weight about and were generally rude and discourteous to the staff and other customers.

"I've never eaten much Italian food before," said von Lutzdorf, "Is there anything you can recommend?"

"I love Italian food," said Magda, "In fact, I think their cuisine is far better than the French. However, I always leave the choice to Antonio. He knows exactly what combination to produce especially at this time because some things are difficult to find. Believe me, you will not be disappointed." Turning to Antonio, who had returned to the table, she said, "Antonio, this is my friend's first experience of Italian food especially from the Tuscany region. Can I leave the choice to you?"

Antonio smiled as he poured them a welcoming aperitif and said, "Of course. We have some very nice specials tonight which I'm sure you will enjoy."

"Please choose the wines to go with them too."

"It will be my pleasure, signora. You can leave everything to me."

As he left the table, von Lutzdorf, who had been looking at the menu which was all in Italian, said, "That's a relief. My Italian isn't very good."

The evening passed in an atmosphere that to von Lutzdorf was almost like a dream. From time to time, an elderly violinist passed amongst the tables stopping occasionally to serenade the diners with nostalgic romantic Italian melodies. He couldn't help contrasting this with the real world outside, especially the horrors of the Eastern Front and the night-time bombing of cities throughout the German Reich. Mercifully, there had been no air raid warning to spoil this evening so far.

His thoughts were interrupted by Magda squeezing his hand and saying, "Walter, darling, where are you? You look miles away."

"Sorry, darling. I was just thinking about the war and how lovely it is here, and how it's such a pity it can't last and that I must go off again tomorrow."

"All the more reason why we must make the most of what we have. Let's finish up and go home."

"Yours or mine?" he asked.

"Mine's nearer."

***

The evening was still young and the temperature still warm when they entered Magda's apartment.

"Go and sit on the terrace while I change," she said. "There's still some champagne in the ice bucket to finish off. It should still be good to drink with the stopper in it."

Slipping off his uniform jacket, von Lutzdorf walked out onto the terrace and took the champagne bottle out of the bucket. The ice had all melted but the bottle was still cool enough to enjoy the drink.

Replacing it in the cold water, he relaxed in one of the easy chairs thinking about his relationship with Magda. They had known each other barely four months but, in that time, his feelings for her had developed way beyond a casual attraction into a deep abiding love, which he felt was returned by Magda. During this whole time, due to the circumstances of his convalescence from his wounds and the lack of opportunity and also because of his feelings for her, they had never been intimate. Von Lutzdorf was not inexperienced in the act of sex or female relationships. As a student and later due to his celebrity status and travels abroad, he had had more than his share of female attention and opportunity for sexual liaisons.

With Magda, however, he wanted a deeper kind of relationship so he had refrained from attempting a casual seduction. Whilst he was not naive enough to suppose Magda was without admirers and had not experienced amorous relationships herself, to his great relief he felt she too wanted the same relationship and was prepared to wait until the moment was right.

As he sat there thinking, he knew tonight was the right moment, certain Magda had given him all the signs that she too was ready to consummate their engagement.

Suddenly and silently in her bare feet, she appeared before him like a phantom apparition dressed in a flimsy transparent dressing gown which, with the light behind her from the sitting room, it was obvious she was wearing nothing underneath.

Von Lutzdorf rose from the chair, all thoughts of champagne forgotten. He took her in his arms and kissed her tenderly but passionately as his hands felt the softness of her skin beneath the gossamer thin fabric.

Wordlessly, Magda took him by the hand and led him through the sitting room to her bedroom. He quickly undressed revealing his athletic body showing the scars from his wounds to his shoulder, upper left arm and side where the machine gun bullets from a Soviet fighter had smashed through the cockpit of his aircraft. Luckily, none of them had proved fatal and he had managed to regain control and land his aircraft safely back at his home base just as he was succumbing to the loss of blood. The wounds were serious enough for him to be transferred back to Berlin for surgery and an extensive period of recuperation.

Magda had slipped off her flimsy gown and lay down on the bed looking at him as he undressed. For the first time, he was able to see the full beauty of her body showing her full firm breasts and slim waist and legs; her beautiful long blonde hair fanned out on the pillow around her head. He lay down on his side to look at her and as she turned towards him and traced her finger along his scars, she said, "They look all nicely healed. Do you still have any pain?"

"Only a deep ache in my heart for you," he said with a smile.

"I'll have to see what I can do to heal that."

"The way I feel about you, it is a pain I can endure as long as we remain together forever."

Kissing her gently, his hands began to explore the more intimate parts of her body that had previously been hidden from him. Magda rolled on to her back as he began to feel roused and, raising himself, he lay between her legs as she opened them to receive him into her awaiting body.

As he entered her, she moaned and clasped her arms around him in a passionate embrace. Reliving his past experiences, he kept his movements to a slow steady rhythm to prolong the sensation and make the moment last as long as possible so they both experienced the moment of climax together. Responding to his love-making with equal ardour, she kissed him constantly on his lips and cheeks whilst her hands and fingers ruffled his hair and dug into his skin.

Finally, they climaxed and lay back exhausted. Clasping hands, Magda turned her head to him and said, "That was wonderful, darling. I do love you so much."

Turning to face her, von Lutzdorf replied, "Well, I suppose I really will have to marry you now, won't I?"

"You'd better or I shall get Uncle Hermann to send you back to the Russian front," she replied with a laugh.

During the night, they made love several more times each time better than before until sleep finally overcame them. Used to being a light sleeper, von Lutzdorf awoke as the sun was rising and slipped out of bed. It was not yet 6 a.m. so he made some coffee which he found in the kitchen pleased to see it was real coffee and not the artificial ersatz coffee that he, like most other Germans, was accustomed to. No doubt it came to her through her connection to Goering. He smiled to himself as he thought, *there's nothing like the privileges of rank and position.*

Completing his toilet, he quickly dressed and wrote a note which he placed on the pillow of the still sleeping Magda. Not wanting to wake her, he refrained from the urge to kiss her lightly on the forehead and quietly left the apartment. He walked down to the waiting car which he had organised with his orderly Albert the previous evening and ordered the driver to take him directly to the Luftwaffe air base.

Chapter 19

❖

It was still relatively early so von Lutzdorf went straight to the officers' mess and had breakfast and more coffee. Using the room the base commander had allocated to him, he changed out of his best uniform and into his normal flying gear from the bag Albert had packed for him and placed in the car that morning.

As he prepared to leave the room, there a knock on the door and the orderly entered with Steinberg and Gratziani close behind.

They were both already dressed in their flying gear and, after the usual greetings, von Lutzdorf said, "Johann, please go to operations and file the flight plan we decided on yesterday. I'm going to the aircraft to ensure everything we asked for is on board and it's refuelled ready for flight." To Gratziani, he said, "Major, you can come with me, if you please."

As Steinberg left to go to operations, Gratziani followed von Lutzdorf out to the waiting transport and they were driven across the airfield to the hangar housing the special Heinkel 111. The aircraft was standing on the apron outside the hangar with a number of ground crew attending to the various checks necessary when preparing an aircraft for flight. The crew from the fuel bowser were just completing the fuelling as von Lutzdorf arrived. The Feldwebel (*Sergeant*) in charge of the ground crew approached him with a clipboard in his hand as he stepped out of the vehicle.

"Fuel and oil tanks all topped up, Major. And the crate with some radio equipment is stowed in the aft cargo space and I have your three heated flying suits here ready for you, sir," he said.

Together with Gratziani, von Lutzdorf walked around the aircraft and, opening the newly fitted rear cargo door, he inspected the crate with the Lorenz transmitter to ensure it was securely tied down. He stowed both his and Gratziani's holdalls containing their spare clothing in the same space.

At that moment, Steinberg arrived and von Lutzdorf ordered him to put his holdall together with theirs and closed and locked the door.

"Flight plan has been submitted and will be passed on to all the military air operations commands on the planned route, Walter. They all have our call sign and identification procedure so we won't be confused with any enemy air activity which may occur."

"Very good, Johann. Wouldn't do to get shot down by our own people."

The chief engineer of Heinkel had assured von Lutzdorf that, in spite of the extra fuel load, the weight and balance calculations without a bomb load had confirmed little or no change to the centre of gravity. The aircraft would therefore not be out of trim.

Satisfied that everything was in order and that the aircraft was ready, he asked the Feldwebel for their heated flying suits which they were able to fit over their lighter flying overalls. They boarded the aircraft. First, Gratziani who made his way to the navigator's seat behind the pilot's, followed by Steinberg and von Lutzdorf last.

When they were all settled in their positions, von Lutzdorf opened the cockpit side window and signalled to the ground crew chief he was ready to start engines. The chief standing in front of the aircraft raised his hand in acknowledgement and confirmed all the ground crew were clear of the aircraft and propellers.

Having set the throttle and pitch controls, he pressed the starter for the number one port engine and the Junkers Jumo 211 inline liquid cooled engine started after two revolutions and settled down to a steady subdued roar. Repeating the procedure for the number two engine, it started and joined its companion balancing the sound on each side of the cockpit. Allowing time for the engines to reach their operating temperatures, he ran through the other cockpit checks with Steinberg and when satisfied, he signalled to the ground chief to remove the chocks from the wheels so they could taxi to the runway.

At the hold of the runway, they ran through the pre-flight engine checks and having received permission for departure, they entered the runway, lined up and opened the throttles to full take-off power. Climbing smoothly away, they headed out on a southerly track for their destination.

Since, at this time, most enemy air activity was confined to the west of Germany in the industrial area of the Ruhr valley, von Lutzdorf did not expect to encounter any enemy aircraft. From Berlin, their course ran directly in a line through Austria and over the Alps to Rome at an initial planned altitude of twenty thousand feet. The forecast was for clear weather all the way to Sicily and beyond so they would have a clear view of the terrain and be able to calculate their ground speed with ease.

At twenty thousand feet, they were able to attain close to two hundred and ninety miles per hour on a cruise setting of the engines. A little over two and a half hours into the flight, they were approaching Rome who they called and, after identifying themselves, they were cleared through that sector.

Halfway from Rome to Palermo in the west of Sicily, von Lutzdorf decided to see what altitude they could attain and began his climb. He called Gratziani on the intercom and asked him to stand in the astro-navigation dome and watch behind as they approached twenty-five thousand feet and report when they began to generate a contrail. He did not want to betray their position unnecessarily to any enemy aircraft which may be flying in the area from Malta. They reached twenty-five thousand feet and continued climbing. At twenty-six thousand feet, Gratziani reported intermittent contrails forming in the aircraft's wake. Levelling off, he settled at just below that altitude.

They continued flying steadily towards Sicily when Gratziani broke in on the intercom. "I don't want to worry you, Major, but I've just spotted a contrail behind us about five thousand feet above which is catching up with us."

"Keep an eye on it and let me know if you can identify it as it gets closer."

Steinberg passed a pair of binoculars back to Gratziani to help him see the other aircraft more clearly.

Deciding now was the time to test the new engine power boost injection system, von Lutzdorf pulled the operating knobs for both engines and immediately they all felt the acceleration as the extra twenty percent of engine power was applied to the propellers and the speed increased by a good thirty plus miles per hour.

Keeping his eyes on the other aircraft, Gratziani reported the overtaking speed had decreased considerably although it was still shortening the distance between them albeit slower than before.

Peering through the binoculars, Gratziani exclaimed, "By God, I do believe it's a British Mosquito and it has increased speed and is diving towards us."

"What a time to be unarmed," said Steinberg.

They were all aware of the infamous Mosquito and its amazing performance and there was little they could do as it could outperform them in every aspect of flying.

As they waited for it to make its firing pass, von Lutzdorf did his best to jink the aircraft from side to side as much as he dared not wanting to bend the air fame hoping to put the Mosquito pilot off his aim.

To their surprise, nothing happened. The aircraft slowed down and flew neatly into formation with them on their port side.

"It's a photo reconnaissance version and thankfully it's unarmed," said Steinberg.

They all peered out of the glazed nose of the 111 as it flew fifty feet, wing tip to wing tip, with them while its crew returned their stares and the navigator in the right-hand seat took photographs of them.

As suddenly as it appeared, the Mosquito crew gave them a cheery wave, peeled off to port, dived rapidly away and disappeared towards Malta at a speed they could never hope to match.

"That's the first time I've seen a Mosquito in the flesh, so to speak," said von Lutzdorf, "I must admit they're about one of the most beautiful aircraft I have ever seen. Their performance is astonishing and they are the bane of our illustrious leader's life."

They all agreed and thanked their lucky stars it was unarmed.

The De Havilland Mosquito, affectionately known as the "Wooden Wonder", both in the photo reconnaissance and bombing roles, had a speed of over four hundred miles per hour, range in excess of one thousand five hundred miles and an operational ceiling approaching forty thousand feet. It ranged freely over Germany, impervious to interception. Those few that were intercepted and destroyed were largely the result of luck or accident.

Unbeknownst to the three of them, the Mosquito pilot had reported them to his base in Malta remarking on the fact it was unarmed with a commercial registration number and particularly noting its high speed and altitude. He further suggested that it was probably a high-speed transport possibly carrying VIPs or high-ranking Afrika Korps officers to Tripoli and they should scramble Spitfires to intercept it and force it to land in Malta. The pilot, Flight Lieutenant David Lucas, was not to know this encounter would not be the last time he would see this unusual aircraft.

Anticipating that they would be reported to air operations in Malta, von Lutzdorf decided that prudence was the order of the day and altered course further to the west to Tunis and into Vichy France controlled air space.

Discontinuing the use of the engine power boost system now the Mosquito had left them, von Lutzdorf reduced the power to a more economic setting while maintaining an altitude of twenty-five thousand feet just below the contrail level. Now in the safety of Vichy and Italian air space, they flew on to the Regia Aeronautica base at Tripoli, Castel Benito airfield named after the Italian dictator Benito Mussolini, from where they set a course to the desert city of Sebha which was on a direct track to their destination.

Overflying Sebha at twenty-five thousand feet, von Lutzdorf began his descent as they continued on track for the remote airstrip, a distance of approximately three hundred miles which would mean a flying time of just over an hour.

After half an hour at a five hundred feet per minute descent rate, they were at ten thousand feet and one hundred and fifty miles from their destination. They could make out the beginnings of the Tibesti mountain range on the horizon. Continuing the descent to one thousand feet, they were close enough to clearly see the low-lying edge of the mountains where they extended across the border from Chad.

"It won't be long now," said Steinberg who had been marking off their course on the chart and was now studying the aerial photographs to pick out the landmarks to aid their approach for landing.

Suddenly, just off to starboard of their approach to a line of rock outcrops and an extended cliff face, a white smoke flare shot up and they could make out a vehicle and a group of people on the ground where it had come from.

"Well done, Major," said von Lutzdorf to Gratziani, "It seems that your instructions to Rome were duly passed on to the maintenance crew."

"So it appears," said Gratziani. He had sent a signal to Rome before they left instructing that, on detecting the approach of their aircraft, the crew should fire a signal flare to aid their location.

Overflying the spot, Steinberg had already located the three rock formation shown on the photograph and, giving instruction to his pilot, von Lutzdorf made a turn to port and flew back parallel towards the rock formation to prepare for his approach. Passing them and then completing his turn, he lined up with the formation and began his final approach from five hundred feet for the five hundred yards indicated on the photograph. The ground crew had moved their vehicle away from the touchdown area and watched as they prepared to land. The touchdown was smooth and, as they continued straight ahead, the tail wheel made contact as von Lutzdorf closed the throttles and kept the aircraft straight as they gradually slowed to a stop.

The maintenance crew vehicle had followed them down the strip and drove around them so von Lutzdorf could see them as they indicated he should follow them. Trusting them to keep him out of any soft sand, he did as instructed and followed them back towards the cliff face from where they had fired the flare. One of the crew jumped from the vehicle and gave taxi directions. When he finally gave them the signal to shut down engines, they were in front of the cliff face with their tail pointing towards it.

"It looks like we have arrived, my friends. Let's have a look at the facilities. Johann, open the hatch and let's get out and get these heavy flying suits off. It's getting very hot in here."

Steinberg was first down the boarding ladder followed by Gratziani, who was greeted enthusiastically by the Regia Aeronautica lieutenant in charge of the crew of three maintenance technicians: one with the warrant officer rank of a maggiore sergente and two caporales who were helping both Gratziani and Steinberg off with their heavy heated flying suits by the time von Lutzdorf descended the ladder. The lieutenant saluted von Lutzdorf and instructed his men to assist him with his heavy flying suit.

"The lieutenant just informed me that it was lucky we stopped where we did," said Gratziani. "The area at the end of the landing strip is extremely soft sand. They've had to dig aircraft out from there on several occasions when they've over run the landing area."

"Good to know for future operations," said von Lutzdorf to Gratziani. "What happens next?"

With a smile, Gratziani said, "Wait and see, Major," as he observed one of the technicians approaching the cliff face.

They all watched as two sections of the cliff face started to move apart accompanied by a hissing sound. As the gap between them widened, it began to reveal the interior of a huge cavern set back into the mountain. When finally the sections stopped moving, the gap had widened to one hundred and fifty feet and fifty feet high. One of the other technicians had already entered the cavern. Suddenly, the deeper part of the interior lit up as the lights came on to the sound of a diesel generator starting up, revealing the equipment and vehicles which had been listed in the documents from Rome.

"That's ingenious," declared von Lutzdorf. "Surely you don't rely on batteries and electric motors."

"Compressed air motors. We have a compressor and a reservoir of air bottles which we also use for starting the diesel generators. The compressed air lasts indefinitely and once the generators are started, we have all the electrical power for all our requirements and can charge batteries also if needed.

It makes the place pretty well self-sufficient and can be left unattended for very long periods. This area is very arid with little moisture all year round and once closed, the hangar doors are as air tight as a pharaoh's tomb and you know how well-preserved Tutankhamun's was after more than three thousand years. Not that I'm suggesting intervals as long as that between operations," said Gratziani with a laugh, "But you get the point. This installation can remain dormant for many years if necessary."

Whilst all this had been going on, the remaining technician had been busy fitting a towing bar to the tail wheel of the Heinkel and, shortly after the sound of another vehicle starting up inside, a tractor emerged and backed up to the tow bar to which it was attached. The driver then slowly towed the aircraft into the hangar.

"A very efficient operation. Is there accommodation here also?" asked von Lutzdorf.

"Yes, there are several dormitories in the back with washing and toilet facilities. Not very luxurious, I'm afraid, but perfectly satisfactory under the circumstances of where we are," said Gratziani.

"Better than the Russian front, I'll be bound," observed Steinberg.

"I can guarantee that," said Gratziani, "At least for our short stay."

All three had retrieved their holdalls from the cargo space and as Gratziani led them to the back of the hangar and the accommodation, he continued. "It seems we are in luck. One of the corporals, before being impressed into service, was a chef in his family's restaurant in Milan so we should be well catered for tonight."

Noted for enjoying their food, the Italian military, especially the officers, were preoccupied with ensuring they had all the creature comforts available. The lieutenant had made sure they brought with them an ample supply of fresh and cured meats and both vegetables and preserves to last them for the estimated two-week sojourn in the desert, together with an ample supply of wine, when they had left Tripoli. It was obvious that the officer and his men enjoyed a relaxed and informal bond that would naturally develop in a small unit as opposed to the stricter, more formal relationships that were normal in the German military.

"Perhaps you could give us a breakdown of what there is here and how it all works. If we use this place as a staging post, it's likely that we won't have the convenience of the maintenance crew on hand to assist us," said von Lutzdorf.

Gratziani obliged them with a tour of the interior where, right at the back next to the accommodations, there was a storeroom containing all kinds of dried and canned food, tins of olive oil, and other essential goods to sustain a considerable number of personnel for many months. Closer to the front of the hangar, fuel tanks containing diesel and aviation spirit had been installed whilst in a separate area, a large water tank had been built into the side wall.

"Where does the water come from?" asked Steinberg.

"There's a small spring about a hundred yards along the cliff face from here which tops this tank up from time to time. It's fed from somewhere deeper in the Tibesti Mountains where they have infrequent seasonal rainfall," said Gratziani.

He then showed them the compressed air facility and how to start the generators and the electrical system for charging batteries.

Taking them outside, he led them along the cliff face to a hidden cleft which concealed the lever for the door opening mechanism. Further along, they came to the spring which was dry.

"It's the dry season at the moment but hopefully it will freshen up the water tank when the rainy season starts. The water gets brackish after a while but it's usable for the other domestic needs and drinkable when boiled."

"That all seems pretty clear. Now we need to find a suitable spot to mount the aerial for the Lorenz transmitter," said von Lutzdorf.

"Let's speak to the electrical technician. He knows the layout here better than most. He's spent several years here on and off."

The corporal technician proved to be the right man and immediately identified a small concealed ledge above and to the left of the hangar doors. It was reachable by means of a not too difficult climb which the corporal assured them he had made before and was willing to do so again.

That being settled, they returned to the hangar accommodation area where a table had been set up for the evening meal. It was obvious the Italian crew all ate together as rank did not interfere with their domestic life. Von Lutzdorf and Steinberg, used to the more formal arrangement of officers and enlisted men eating in separate messes, had no problem in joining in with the less formal arrangement. They did not subscribe to the rigid discipline in the German military as a matter to be adhered to under all circumstances. They believed that, in small independent units, friendship took precedence over rank when off duty or on special detail when the need to work together was paramount. Gratziani was of the same mind and, being a sociable man of some sophistication, was pleased to be the means of interaction and social discourse. They sat down together to enjoy an unusually sumptuous meal in the most unlikely of settings, made more congenial by the liberal flow of wine. Gratziani translated some of the Italian conversation and jokes for von Lutzdorf and Steinberg whose Italian was minimal.

***

The following morning was spent setting up the Lorenz transmitter-receiver unit and charging sufficient of the batteries, setting them up in a block to ensure sufficient current capacity to keep the receiver unit operative for several weeks unattended.

In the meantime, Steinberg was working on their return flight plan with the intention of departing around midday. The plan called for a stop at Tripoli on the return to top up with fuel and leave the fuel in the storage tank available for emergency use on their Africa and South America flights. Even allowing for the stop at Tripoli, they should be back in Berlin well before dark as long as the flight was without incident. After take-off, they would fly in a wide circuit to test the Lorenz transmitter and then fly on to Tripoli.

Thanking the maintenance crew for their help and the chef for the great meal, they left them to clean up and secure the installation. Von Lutzdorf, Steinberg and Gratziani then boarded the aircraft which had been towed out of the hangar and positioned in such a way that the wash from the propellers, when they started the engines and taxied, would not cause clouds of sand to be blown into the hangar.

When everyone was securely strapped in, von Lutzdorf opened the cockpit side window and signalled to the sergeant major who gave him the thumbs up to start the engines. Von Lutzdorf taxied to the start of the take-off area and, with Steinberg, he ran through their checklist before opening up the throttles to take off.

After the check confirmed they were receiving the signal from the Lorenz transmitter, they overflew the watching ground crew, waggled their wings and set course for Tripoli where they landed, spent minimal time refuelling and resumed their flight back to Berlin. It proceeded without incident and they landed after a total flying time of just over seven hours.

They were met by Hauptmann Freiberg who congratulated them on a successful proving flight and transported them all back to the city. As they said their goodbyes, Freiberg told von Lutzdorf that Goering would like to see him first thing in the morning.

Chapter 20

❖

Goering was seated behind his desk in his office when his aide Hauptmann Freiberg knocked and entered with von Lutzdorf that morning. Not rising from his chair, he gave von Lutzdorf a casual air force salute which he returned albeit in a more formal manner. Nazi though he was, Goering was of the old school military and, amongst those he considered to be in his inner circle, he did not expound or practise the somewhat exaggerated Nazi salute as practised by those of a more subservient and ardent adherence to the party.

"Come in, my dear von Lutzdorf. Welcome back. I hear you had a successful test flight and are ready to start planning your first mission."

"Yes, Herr Reichsmarschall. Everything went better than expected and I am very pleased with the work carried out by Heinkel."

"Good. I shall see to it that their efforts are recognised. It always pays to pat these manufacturers on the back when they get things right. Keeps them on their toes."

"The Italian air attaché was particularly helpful in this matter. Perhaps you could acknowledge him in some way. I may need his assistance again."

"I'll send him a thank you note or something. It's a change to hear that they can get some things right occasionally."

Like most high-ranking Germans, they were not overly impressed with the Italian armed forces' abilities having had to rescue them in Libya and Greece from annihilation.

"Whilst you've been getting your side of things together, our intelligence services have been in contact with our supporters in our old colonies in Africa and will have several landing strips organised for you in Cameroon and Namibia."

"Where is the principal pick up location for the diamonds, Herr Reichsmarschall?"

"The information we have is that the best location is in the far north of Namibia where there are many former German settlers from the old colonial past and many sympathetic Boers who are anti-British. Our agents have contact with them and they will give us the location of several private landing strips suitable for our use. The industrial diamonds will be delivered once we are ready to collect."

"We will be ready whenever that time comes. If we use the airfield in Libya, we can make that distance from there in one flight. No need to land in Cameroon."

"That's good. Now, I must ask you this. Has Gruppenfuehrer Mueller tried to contact you since the last time you saw him in the Adlon Hotel?"

"No, Herr Reichsmarschall." Von Lutzdorf hesitated before asking his question, not wanting to appear insubordinate or offend his commander-in-chief. "Herr Reichsmarschall, is there any reason I should know about why the Herr Gruppenfuehrer would want to contact me?"

"No particular reason, Major. But, as you know, you are under my military command and the Gestapo have no business interfering in military matters especially secret special operations."

Having opened the subject, von Lutzdorf could not resist persisting a little more. "I understand the need for security, but what's so secret about the procurement of vital materials for the war effort amongst those in government and positions of authority?"

Goering smiled and, looking at von Lutzdorf as one would to an innocent child, he said, "Whilst I agree with you that the objective is vital and necessary, it is not always wise to reveal the ways and means of achieving that objective. Especially to those whose perspective on these matters may not be in accordance with one's own. Let us leave the subject there for the moment, Major. I'm sure you have things to do and I would like you to let me have a written report of your flight and recommendations."

Not really satisfied with the answer but realising the matter was closed, von Lutzdorf changed the subject and continued on a lighter note. "We did have an unusual experience during the flight, sir."

"Really? What was that?" asked Goering, happy to change the subject.

"Over the Mediterranean, near Sicily, we were intercepted by a British Mosquito."

"Those damned aircraft," exclaimed Goering, "You're still here. How did you survive the encounter?"

"Luckily, it was an unarmed photo reconnaissance version but the most extraordinary thing was it formatted on us while the crew took photographs, waved at us and flew off."

Shaking his head, Goering said, "I'll never understand those Britishers' sense of humour and that aircraft is well named as the British use it to irritate me like its namesake."

With its speed, range and considerable bomb load, the RAF used the Mosquito to bomb Berlin whenever they could on special occasions to cause disruption and embarrassment to the Nazi regime, especially to Goering exposing his vain boast that the RAF would never drop a bomb on Berlin saying they could call him "Meyer", a common Jewish name, if it ever happened.

Von Lutzdorf was familiar with this boast so he tried not to smile as he said, "It certainly is a very beautiful and sleek aeroplane. Made mostly of wood, I understand."

Not wanting to give any hint of praise to this comment, Goering said, "It appears that our U-boat blockade is causing them great problems with the lack of strategic materials."

After a few more comments and pleasantries, Goering thanked von Lutzdorf saying he would be in touch with him soon. He was shown out by Hauptmann Freiberg.

Chapter 21

❖

The Heinkel had proved very reliable with no faults developing on the test flight but even so, von Lutzdorf had left instructions at the Luftwaffe base for the aircraft to have a thorough check over and be fully serviced ready for the next operation.

Returning to his office from the meeting with Goering, von Lutzdorf found Steinberg reading a copy of Der Adler (*The eagle*), the official Luftwaffe publication distributed to all personnel.

"Anything interesting, Johann?"

"All the usual guff and propaganda. How did your meeting go with the big boss?"

"The same elusive and evasive answers. However, we have nothing special to do for a while and since I know we can be ready at twenty-four hours' notice, I think we should take the opportunity to indulge in a little leisure time while we can. Have you found yourself a lady friend yet?"

"My sister introduced me to a very attractive friend of hers who works in her family's business. Not sure what she does but she seems to have plenty of leisure time and also has access to a car so they must have means or some sort of influence. I was thinking of asking her out for a date but not being sure of our schedule I have refrained from doing so. But, if you're saying we have some time available, I'll take the chance and give her a call."

"I'm going off home now and will be seeing Magda later. Perhaps we could all meet up in the next few days."

"I'll look forward to it, Walter."

Von Lutzdorf left Steinberg reading his magazine and left the Air Ministry building and was driven back to his family's apartment.

Albert was on hand when he arrived. Surprised at his early return, he inquired if he had any special instructions for him and asked if they were being transferred again.

"No, Albert. I'm just taking a few days off after a rather strenuous trip, that's all. Rest assured we shall be billeted here for the foreseeable future now that I'm on official secondment to Goering's staff and the Air Ministry."

Albert was rather enjoying his officer's new duty away from the dangers and shortages at the front especially the comforts of his own accommodation and attentions of the housekeeper, a not altogether unattractive widow obviously missing the normal comforts that went with a married relationship. He smiled as he said with a silent sigh of relief, "That is good news, Major. Is there anything special I can get you for lunch? A glass of wine perhaps to give you an appetite?"

"Why not, Albert? We don't get many opportunities to indulge ourselves in these times so a glass of that white Riesling we have in the wine store would do nicely."

He knew Albert, who liked his comforts, would help himself to a glass or two also which he never begrudged him.

He never over-indulged and was always sober in front of him and available at any hour of the day or night such was their easy relationship with each other.

It was too early to telephone Magda as he knew she was not just a socialite who spent her time frivolously. She was very active in a private charity supporting disabled Luftwaffe personnel and their families so she would not be available until the evening. It had been through this activity that they had met when he was in hospital recuperating from his wounds. Though they knew each other from before the war, they had lost touch and it was completely by chance that she was visiting other disabled Luftwaffe personnel on the same ward that they recognised each other and rekindled their friendship.

The exigencies of wartime service left little time to cultivate many friendships and those friends he did have were either in the service on distant postings or dead so von Lutzdorf spent an impatient afternoon perusing books on the library bookshelves until six o'clock resisting the temptation to telephone before.

To his great relief and pleasure, Magda answered his call after the second ring.

"Hello darling," he said, "It's so good to hear your voice."

"Yours too. Where are you?"

"In my apartment, longing to see you."

"When did you get back?" she asked.

"Yesterday evening."

"Why didn't you phone me?"

"I did, darling, but no answer. Where were you?" he said in a slightly accusative tone.

"I do have a social life outside of our relationship," she said in a teasing manner.

"We'll have to see about that." As he said it, he knew he could never get the better of her in a teasing contest or make her do something she did not want to so he capitulated and said, "I have missed you so terribly, darling, and must see you this evening."

"That's better. Let me just check my diary and see if I'm free," she said, keeping the ball in her court.

"You are a heartless she-devil," he said, "Why do you torture me so?"

"You are fortunate, my darling. I have no commitments this evening so where are you taking me?"

"Why don't you come here for a change? You might like to consider it as our home when we get married."

"It belongs to your parents."

"Of course, but it will come to me eventually, so why don't you see if you'll like it?"

"That sounds very nice, darling. I shall be there at eight o'clock. Until then, darling."

Until he suggested them using the apartment as their marital home, it had not occurred to him he must begin to consider their situation and be serious about the future. At least, as much as one could do so in wartime. The more he thought about it, the better he liked the idea and he was determined to discuss a marriage date with Magda that evening.

The apartment had the benefit of an internal telephone system so he called Albert and asked him to come to him and explained Magda was coming for the evening and that they would need dinner. Albert assured him that, between the housekeeper and himself, there would be no problem as they had all that was necessary to produce a respectable meal.

True to his assurance, Albert and Hannelore, von Lutzdorf's housekeeper, produced a very acceptable dinner and waited on them with all the attention of a first-class establishment. The evening passed in a comfortable sense of mutual attraction and disclosure but always aware of each other's needs and first sexual encounter, waiting for the discreet withdrawal of Albert and his own female admirer before the evening's inevitable conclusion.

Their love-making this time was more relaxed as they accepted they had both found a person with whom they could always be honest and completely at one with each other. As they lay there with Magda's head resting on his chest with his arm around her, von Lutzdorf talked about marriage and how he had been reluctant to make a commitment before. Because of being on the Russian front, his future prospects were very uncertain as survival in combat was very unlikely due to the high attrition rate. He had been lucky this last time to survive but fate had recently changed his prospects. Now, his foreseeable future looked more secure with his transfer out of the combat zone to a permanent position at the Air Ministry.

He told her he would shortly be going on a trip which would take him away for perhaps a period of up to two weeks but when he returned, they could be married. Happy with the prospect, Magda agreed and said she would speak to her uncle to ask him to stand up with her during the ceremony as both her parents were dead.

He told her it would be difficult to speak to each other during the coming few weeks but if she had anything she wanted to say to him, she could write to him and give it to his orderly Albert who would see that he received it.

They continued discussing future plans until sleep overcame them and they slept in a lover's embrace until the morning sun lit up the room through the uncurtained window.

Having freshened themselves, put on their dressing gowns and now sitting up in bed, there was a discreet knock on the door followed by Albert bidding them good morning and inquiring if they were ready for coffee. Receiving an affirmative, the door opened and Albert entered followed by the housekeeper, both bearing trays which were placed before them on the bed.

They exchanged a few pleasantries and then Albert and the housekeeper withdrew smiling to each other.

"I think I should like living here after we are married," said Magda.

"I'm glad you agree," said von Lutzdorf relieved that had been settled. "What plans do you have for the day?"

"Nothing special. What about you?"

"I'm on standby waiting for orders. I'll have to check in with the office later this morning."

Later that morning, von Lutzdorf telephoned Hauptmann Freiberg to inquire if he had any orders from Goering to be told Goering was in conference and he would call him back.

Von Lutzdorf and Magda were sitting in the drawing room discussing wedding plans when Albert appeared saying Hauptmann Freiberg was on the telephone and urgently needed to speak to him.

Picking up the handset, he found Freiberg on the line who quickly explained he was needed back at the Air Ministry right away. Apparently, there was a major battle going on between the Afrika Korps and the British forces at a place called El Alamein just over the Libyan border in Egypt.

"Sorry, darling," von Lutzdorf said to Magda, "My orders have come sooner than I expected. I must go immediately to the Air Ministry."

He went to his bedroom where Albert was already setting out his uniform. Dressing quickly, he ordered Albert to tell his driver to get the car ready. He then returned to Magda and, holding her lightly by both shoulders, he kissed her and said, "I don't know how long I will be. Wait here and I'll telephone you when I have more news."

Agreeing with his suggestion, Magda saw him to his waiting car and returned to the drawing room to wait.

Chapter 22

❖

When he arrived at his office, von Lutzdorf found Steinberg already there who said, "That was the shortest break. What's all the fuss about?"

"Apparently, there's a major battle going on in Egypt between our Erwin Rommel and the British forces under a General called Montgomery at a place called El Alamein."

"That's thousands of miles away in the Egyptian desert. How does that affect us?"

"We'll soon find out, when I see Goering."

As he said it, the telephone rang. It was Freiberg requesting his presence in Goering's office immediately.

"Here we go. I'll be back as soon as I find out what he wants."

***

Having completed the usual formalities, von Lutzdorf was sitting facing Goering who said, "Early this morning, the British mounted a major attack on our forces in Egypt starting with a massive artillery bombardment. Our intelligence information is that the enemy has at least twice the men and materials available to Rommel with divisions from Australia, New Zealand, South Africa, India and some Free French and Polish divisions, as well as overwhelming superiority in air power.

"As much as we all rate Rommel's ability, I think there's a good chance that this time the British will succeed in breaking through to Tripoli. Therefore, we must consider the consequences should we and the Italians lose Libya and the effect it might have on our ability to overfly the area safely. For that reason, I think it would be prudent to fly the first mission to South Africa as soon as you are ready."

"We are ready now, Herr Reichsmarschall. I just need twenty-four hours to get the aircraft prepared."

"Excellent, Major. We will have to load you some cargo which I shall arrange."

"What would that be, sir?"

"We will need to pay for the diamonds naturally, so you will take a certain amount of gold with you for these and other costs."

"A great responsibility, Herr Reichsmarschall."

"Indeed. Now, do not let me detain you any further. Freiberg will see to all your needs."

Von Lutzdorf made his way back to the office and broke the news to Steinberg instructing him to liaise with Freiberg to get the navigational coordinates for the airstrips in West Africa and to put the agents on alert to receive them.

He alerted the Luftwaffe base commander to have the aircraft refuelled and ready to depart the following morning and then called Magda to break the news of his coming departure and said he was on his way back to the apartment.

As soon as he saw Magda, he said, "I'm sorry, darling. I had hoped for a little more time together before this trip but it can't be helped." He went on to explain to her what Goering had told him and the need to bring the flight forward.

"At least we got the matter of marriage sorted so we have something to look forward to when you return," said Magda.

Von Lutzdorf was deeply moved by her attitude and understanding and silently thanked his luck to have found someone like her who could rise to the occasion with such fortitude and equanimity.

"I'm glad you're not too upset. What would you like to do for the time we have?"

"I would really like to spend the time here with you."

"In that case, I shall ask Albert and Hannelore to put on something special for tonight."

"Hannelore?"

"Yes, that's the housekeeper's name. I forgot to tell you before."

"It's a very nice name. I think it means gracious."

"Well, she's certainly well named."

The evening went off well and Albert and Hannelore outperformed their previous effort of the night before.

***

Rising early, von Lutzdorf was driven to the airfield where he found the ground crew fussing around the aircraft being overseen by Steinberg.

"Everything in order?" he asked.

"Just received a signal from Hauptmann Freiberg. He's on his way with the cargo."

"Good. As soon as it's loaded, we'll be off. Do you have all the navigation information from him?"

"Yes. The first leg is nearly the same as we did before, only on a direct track to Tunis. This time I've planned direct from Tunis to the Chad border. I think we won't have any difficulty finding the field with the Lorenz transmitter in place and best to stay as far from Malta as possible, in case the next Mosquito we meet is armed. We'll top up fuel in Libya and fly direct to the pick-up field in northern Namibia."

The sound of truck motors alerted them to the sight of two trucks, one covered followed by an open one with armed troops, approaching them around the airfield perimeter roadway.

"Looks like our cargo has arrived," said von Lutzdorf.

The covered truck pulled up next to the aircraft and Hauptmann Freiberg emerged from the passenger door of the cabin.

"Good morning, Herr Major. I have some boxes here that need to be loaded. Can you direct these men on how to proceed?"

Several soldiers in Wehrmacht uniform descended from the back of the truck and were unloading four heavy boxes with rope handles from inside.

"How many of these boxes are there and what is the total weight?" asked von Lutzdorf of Freiberg who was holding a clipboard with some papers attached.

"Four boxes in total each weighing two hundred and seventy pounds. A little over a thousand pounds in total, say five hundred kilograms."

Von Lutzdorf did a quick weight and balance calculation in his head and determined that loaded in the rear cargo space it would still fall within the safety margin for the centre of gravity of the aircraft. He directed the boxes to be loaded and securely strapped down to rings built into the floor.

"A little bit of bureaucratic red tape to deal with, Major, I'm afraid. Can you please sign here for the boxes? I believe you know what's in them."

"Well, unless we open them, I shall have to take your word for it, and unless I'm much mistaken, there would not be much point in the flight if things are not what you say."

"Quite so, Major," said Freiberg with the hint of a smile.

Von Lutzdorf, who had got to know Freiberg quite well, believed him to be totally loyal to Goering and equally efficient and trustworthy, so he had no hesitation signing for the cargo.

"That's quite a responsibility you have just accepted, Major," said Freiberg as he handed von Lutzdorf an MP 40 Schmeisser machine pistol. "A little extra insurance never goes amiss."

"What am I to do with the contents? I know it's payment for what we're bringing back but I'm not privy to the payment details and have no idea of the values."

"I understand that the accepted payment is one kilo of diamonds for two kilos of gold depending on size and quality but that will be dealt with by our agent on the ground. He will calculate how much of the content you pass over. Bear in mind that these are industrial diamonds. They don't look anything like the cut and polished jewellery diamonds we're used to seeing so you have to rely on the agent's judgement. Anything surplus, you bring back."

"That's perfectly clear. Thank you, Freiberg. We will hopefully see you back here within ten days allowing for weather and any delays or complications at the destination or en route. We will keep you informed of progress by radio when we can and conditions permit."

"Very well. We shall keep a listening watch on your allocated Luftwaffe frequencies. Good luck."

Formalities completed, von Lutzdorf and Steinberg donned their heated flying suits, boarded the Heinkel 111 and prepared to depart.

Chapter 23

❖

After take-off, they climbed steadily to twelve thousand feet, their chosen altitude, while in German and Italian air space to avoid the need to wear oxygen masks for as long as possible. Their track took them down over Corsica and Sardinia whose military air command sectors were alerted to their flight. Approaching Tunis and Vichy-controlled air space, they climbed to twenty-five thousand feet as Steinberg observed from the astrodome blister to ensure they did not generate a contrail and to look for any other possible aircraft at a higher altitude.

From Tunis, they continued on track to their destination without encountering any other air activity at their altitude. At Sebha, as before, they started their descent until they once again made out the low-lying foothills of the Tibesti Mountains. As they continued, the direction indicator of their Lorenz beam approach system began to flicker and they could hear the faint Morse signal TBS1 which they had used to modulate the signal and identify the beacon. The needle was now firmly in the centre indicating they were on the correct heading. They were now down to one thousand feet and the signal was loud in their headsets when the three rock formation came into view.

"Spot on, Johann," said von Lutzdorf as he overflew them and came round to make his approach. The landing went smoothly and he taxied as before and positioned the aircraft with the tail pointing towards the cliff face hangar doors.

The maintenance crew had left the day after them so there was no one to greet them as they climbed down from the crew ladder, stretching to ease the cramps after being confined in one position for such a long journey.

Steinberg went over to the concealed cleft and operated the lever to open the doors as von Lutzdorf entered and made his way to the generators. Following the procedure he had been shown by Gratziani, he soon had one of the generators started and, throwing the main breaker switch on the electrical panel, the interior lights came on. By this time, Steinberg had started the towing tractor and was manoeuvring it out to the parked aircraft. With the tow bar attached, he then brought the Heinkel 111 into the hangar.

"Here we are again, Walter. Home sweet home."

In the accommodation area, they removed their heavy heated flying suits and began to relax. Steinberg came out from the stores with a bottle in one hand and, going into the kitchen, he emerged with two glasses. Setting them down on the table, he filled both with schnapps and, giving one to von Lutzdorf, he raised his glass and said, "Here's to a successful trip."

"So far," replied von Lutzdorf.

"What was all that about with Freiberg and the MP 40? And what's in the boxes?"

"Would you believe five hundred kilos of gold?"

"Really? What's that worth?"

"From what I remember and doing a rough calculation in my head, I think it's about six hundred thousand American dollars."

Steinberg was quiet for a while and then with a smile on his face, he said, "I always wanted to be rich and here we are in the middle of nowhere with all this money and our own personal transport. Why don't we just carry straight on to South America and buy ourselves a cattle ranch and retire?"

Von Lutzdorf laughed and said, "A nice idea but I've been giving the situation a great deal of serious thought and you may not be the only one with such ideas."

"What do you mean? I was only joking, Walter."

"I know you were, but what about the others?"

"What do you mean the others?"

"We're not the only ones who know about this gold. What about those we're going to meet in Namibia? What do we know about them?"

"I take your point. What have you been told?"

"Only that one of them is one of our agents and the others are pre-colonial German settlers sympathetic to our cause and some disaffected anti-British Boers."

"Plenty of room there for some avaricious thoughts and let's face it, the temptation will be very great especially with no possible repercussions from the law. What do you think we should do?"

"Not much we can do until we get there and assess the situation. But we must remain on guard at all times for any indications of treachery. We'll keep our sidearms concealed on us and the MP 40 out of sight in the aircraft. No one will enter it without us being present. That way they won't expect any resistance from us and may show their hand giving us the time and means to outwit them. If indeed there is any intent from someone amongst them."

It was still light outside so they spent the time refuelling and topping up the oil levels ready for an early take-off the next morning. Closing the hangar doors, they prepared themselves an evening meal and went over their flight plan for the next leg.

The flight they had calculated was approximately two thousand five hundred miles and would take between nine and ten hours depending on the winds. The first part of the flight would be over Chad which had declared allegiance to the Free French so they would need to cross that part at maximum altitude but below the contrail level to avoid detection. At that height, even without a contrail, they would be out of sight and sound from any observer on the ground. Their track would then take them over Leopoldville, the capital of the Belgian Congo, which, like Chad, had declared allegiance to the Belgian government in exile in London but since it was over territory with little or no radar coverage or patrols, they did not expect any problems.

Once past these two countries, they would be over Portuguese Angola which was neutral and the capital of Luanda on the coast would give them a very accurate navigation check, before their final leg to their destination.

Since they would be crossing the equator and flying into the southern hemisphere and their summer time, they expected there to be still enough daylight when they arrived if they left at six o'clock in the morning local time. Their destination was close to the Namibian town of Ruacana just on the border with Angola at an airstrip on some farmland belonging to a German settler. The area was chosen because of the prominent landmark of the Ruacana Falls on the Kunene River. It was a very remote area and any aircraft activity would be largely unnoticed. Smoke signal flares would be available to help locate the strip so von Lutzdorf and Steinberg were confident not only in their navigational abilities but also the facilities that had been arranged to help.

Such was their habit and discipline, they awoke before dawn and prepared to leave at the prescribed time. Whilst von Lutzdorf opened the doors, Steinberg started the tractor which was still attached by the tow bar to the tail wheel and skilfully turned the aircraft around and towed it to the take-off position. Detaching the tow bar from the aircraft, he returned to the hangar and parked the tractor in its normal place. Meanwhile, von Lutzdorf had shut down the generator and, after a final check to make sure all was secure, they closed the doors and walked out to the aircraft.

***

Climbing to twenty-five thousand feet, they settled on track and engaged the autopilot, preparing for the long flight ahead. The weather ahead, as far as they could see, looked clear and without a vestige of cloud. They were aware of an air raid mounted by the Luftwaffe Sonderkommando, an elite special operations unit, earlier that year against the capital of Chad, Fort Lamy. Deciding they may have increased the air defences around the capital, they kept well to the east of it, confident they would remain undetected. From their height, however, they could see it in the distance as they marked it off on the chart. Their next route check was Leopoldville, the capital of the Belgian Congo, which passed below them without incident and finally Luanda, the capital of Portuguese Angola, on the west coast of the continent: their final checkpoint.

From there, they flew on for a further four hundred miles on a track across the coastal mountains heading for Ruacana and the falls. Steinberg had monitored their track and the wind continuously and had compensated for drift using the autopilot to keep them on a very accurate heading at all times.

One hundred and fifty miles from their destination, they commenced their descent until they made out the Kunene River which led to the falls. Descending lower, they followed the river until the sparkling white cascading waterfall, glistening in the sunlight, came into view.

Clear of the mountains and down to three thousand feet, they turned onto the heading from the falls to the makeshift airstrip that was their destination. They were now over the inland plateau area of farmland and scrub when signs of habitation appeared in front of them. Descending lower still, they flew over a farmhouse surrounded by out buildings and cattle pens as a white smoke flare was fired into the sky. They could see a number of people and a white arrow set out on the ground at what was the beginning of the landing area. Keeping the arrow in sight, von Lutzdorf brought the aircraft around and lined up in the approach for landing. They taxied back to the farmhouse area where a group of men, some carrying rifles, waited to meet them.

Chapter 24

❖

A heavily built, medium height, dark-haired man with a bushy beard and moustache approached von Lutzdorf and Steinberg holding out his hand.

"Welcome to Namibia, Major. My name is Gerhart Hardbach. I'm the farmer and these men here are Dutch Boers from across the border in Angola," he said as he indicated his companions and shook hands.

"Thank you, Herr Hardbach. Where is our agent? I thought he would be here to meet us."

"Unfortunately, it seems he has been held up at the embassy in Luanda, but we should get news of his arrival any time soon. Please, come into the house. I'm sure you will need to eat and rest up after such a long flight."

"Thank you," said von Lutzdorf as he and Steinberg exchanged glances indicating to each other to be cautious.

They had taken the precaution of securing the crew entry hatch as well as the bulkhead door between the rear cargo space and the radio compartment before leaving the aircraft. This would deter anyone from anything other than a cursory search, even if they managed to open the crew escape hatch to gain entry, which was unlikely for the moment.

Von Lutzdorf, Steinberg, the three Boers and the farmer were all seated around a large wooden table in the kitchen dining area of the farmhouse where a meal had been prepared for them by the farmer's wife who had withdrawn discreetly once they were all seated.

"Do you have the diamonds here at the farm?" inquired von Lutzdorf.

"Our friends here have several boxes all packaged and ready to exchange. I take it you have the gold with you."

"Once I am satisfied as to the quantity and quality, which will be determined by our agent when here, we can exchange as agreed. You said that he had been delayed at the embassy in Luanda. How do you communicate with him?"

"There's a telegraph office in Ruacana where we can exchange telegrams," said the farmer.

"Then we must get word to him that we are here and it is urgent that he comes right away."

"I will send a telegram in the morning. In the meantime, rest up. It takes a whole day to drive from Luanda to here, sometimes more depending on the rains. The roads are often impassable in places."

Having to accept the situation for the moment, von Lutzdorf had to agree to the delay and rely on the farmer's argument and suggestion of a telegram. Privately, he was determined to try to get a wireless message through to Berlin first thing in the morning to report the situation and ask them to contact the embassy in Luanda to check up on the farmer's story. He could also ask them to give him the diplomatic frequencies so he could contact them directly. Both he and Steinberg were adept at communicating in Morse code and they had an enigma machine on board together with the daily code book.

Throughout the meal, the Boers conversed in Afrikaans amongst themselves which von Lutzdorf could understand in parts due to the similarity of it to German but when spoken to directly, they answered in German.

After the meal was finished, he and Steinberg professed tiredness after their long journey and the farmer showed them to a bedroom in a separate part of the farmhouse containing two single beds where he wished them goodnight.

"What did you think of the farmer's explanation about the agent?" asked von Lutzdorf.

"Sounded a bit too convenient for me. He had plenty of notice of our arrival and knew we were on a tight schedule. Something just doesn't feel right to me."

"We must get through to Berlin in the morning. Can you rig up that external aerial first thing? We can say, if asked, that we have to make a routine report on our safe arrival to allay any suspicions."

Locking the door to their room, they spent the night with their pistols under their pillows as a precaution.

***

Life on a farm starts early everywhere in the world and it was no different here in this remote part of Namibia. Farm animals did not look after themselves and were ready and noisy as soon as the sun came up.

As usual, von Lutzdorf and Steinberg woke with the dawn chorus and refreshed themselves with the bowls and jugs of water that had been placed in their room. They dressed and made their way to the kitchen where the farmer's wife was already preparing breakfast for the others seated around the table.

The air smelt of fresh bread rolls which she placed on the table with some home cured meats and cheeses and home churned butter. She then filled their mugs in turn with steaming hot coffee from a large pot straight from the stove.

"I trust you are both refreshed from a good night's sleep, Major," said the farmer.

"Yes, thank you." He turned to face the farmer's wife and said, "And thank you, madam, for dinner yesterday evening and for this breakfast we are about to enjoy."

Unused to compliments in this male-dominated company and old-fashioned German culture, she blushed slightly as she smiled and nodded her head in pleasure at this acknowledgement of her presence.

"Will you send off the telegram as soon as possible this morning, Herr Hardbach?"

"Yes, indeed. As soon as I am finished here, I shall drive into Ruacana."

"Will you wait for a reply?"

"I will stress the urgency of the matter and that I need an immediate response."

Satisfied they had done all they could for the moment, von Lutzdorf and Steinberg finished their breakfast and announced they were going to do some routine checks on the aircraft and left the kitchen.

The crew hatch and boarding ladder showed no signs of being opened or used as they entered the glazed cockpit section, and the bulkhead door was still securely locked.

Retrieving a bundle of aluminium tubes from the radio compartment, Steinberg unstrapped them and proceeded to screw them together to form a tapered whip aerial approximately seven metres long with a screw fixing on the lower end. Clambering on to the wing, he screwed this end into a special fitting in the fuselage over the radio cabin. This was one of the modifications they had asked for to enable them to more efficiently communicate with the Air Ministry when on the ground.

Being on almost the same longitude as Berlin, they were in the same time zone so, checking their schedule of times and frequencies for their communications with base, they switched on and allowed the equipment to warm up. Precisely on the hour of 0900 hours GMT, Steinberg began sending their call sign in Morse code. As aviators and navigators they syncronized their time to the BBC's GMT signals, a facility used by both allies and enemies alike. He was rewarded with a faint but clear acknowledgement signal and immediately started sending their prepared message. When he finished, both stations signed off until the next scheduled communications check.

"We should know something in a couple of hours. That should give them time to check with the embassy in Luanda."

During that time, they busied themselves making a show of checking the engines and undercarriage for the benefit of the watching Boers. When asked about the external aerial by one of the more outspoken of them, who was obviously their leader, Steinberg told him it was used for reporting their safe arrival and to receive orders when their business here was completed.

At 1100 hours GMT, after acknowledging their call sign, they received a coded message from base which von Lutzdorf decoded using the enigma machine.

Without saying anything, he passed the decoded message to Steinberg who, after reading it, looked at von Lutzdorf.

"According to this, the agent left the embassy two days ago and should have been here to meet us on time."

"Of course, he could have had an accident on the way but we have no way of knowing. We shall just have to wait it out for a while. If he doesn't show up by tomorrow, we'll radio for orders. Let's see what Hardbach has to say when he gets back from Ruacana."

The drive from the farm to the town was an hour each way so by midday the farmer had returned. Von Lutzdorf and Steinberg were still at the aircraft when his truck appeared and seeing them there, he drove straight over to them and parked nearby.

"What news do you have for us?"

"It's very strange, Major. They said that your agent left two days ago. I don't understand it. He should have been here by now."

"We'll wait another day and then we'll have to radio Berlin for orders. What do you know about industrial diamonds? Are you familiar with them and can you judge the quality?"

"I'm afraid not. I've seen some but I'm no expert. That's why I contacted these Boers. They were recommended to me as expert dealers in illicit diamond smuggling."

"Well, if the agent doesn't show up, we'll have to inspect them ourselves and see what we can do."

The farmer agreed and said if the agent did not show up today, he would send another telegram in the morning to see if the embassy had any more news of the agent and then they would ask to inspect the diamonds before making any decision. He then drove the truck back to the farmhouse leaving von Lutzdorf and Steinberg alone.

"What do you think, Johann?"

"At least his story coincides with the message we received, so I think he's on the straight and level. But I don't have the same confidence in these Boers," said Steinberg.

"Agreed. Let's play along with the farmer's plan to send another telegram tomorrow and be on our guard."

At the planned time of 1800 hours GMT, they received another coded message with the diplomatic frequencies and a time schedule to contact the embassy directly. The atmospheric conditions were not always good enough to communicate with Berlin, whereas Luanda was always reachable at any time of the day or night. They did not, however, reveal to the farmer they now had this ability which gave them the facility to check on the veracity of his claims.

There was no sign of the agent that day and the following morning, the farmer once more drove into Ruacana to exchange telegrams. At 0900 hours GMT, they made contact with the embassy and were told that through the Angolan Foreign Office, they had contacted the police who reported they had no reports of any accidents on the road from the capital to Ruacana that could in any way be connected to the disappearance of the agent who had accredited diplomatic status and was therefore of some concern to the authorities. When the farmer returned, he confirmed what they already knew from the embassy.

In the afternoon, von Lutzdorf decided it was time to take the initiative and confront the Boers to try to determine their intentions, honest or otherwise, whichever those turned out to be. Steinberg would remain in the aircraft, ostensibly working on their return flight plan, to act as his back up in case of duplicity. He would gather them all together in the house and ask them to show him the diamonds so he could confirm their availability by wireless to the authorities in Germany if the agent continued to fail to show up. This would at least give them some proof as to the authenticity, and force the Boers to show their hand.

The plan was for Steinberg to give sufficient time for him to get the dialogue started and then, armed with the MP 40, he would come via the back of the house out of sight and, if possible, spy on the assembled party either through one of the windows or by eavesdropping through the back kitchen door. If all was well, he would conceal the MP 40 and enter the kitchen.

Von Lutzdorf asked the farmer to get the Boers together as he had something to say. When all were seated around the kitchen table, he explained to the leader that in view of the absence of their agent, he had to report the situation to Germany. He asked if he could be shown the diamonds so he could at least confirm the quantity.

"What about the gold?" asked the leader.

"If you have the diamonds, we will show you the gold. After all, there wouldn't be much point in coming all this way if we don't have the means to complete the deal," said von Lutzdorf.

The leader of the Boers said something in Afrikaans to the others and they left the room, returning shortly with a heavy metal-bound box which they placed on the table. The leader took a key from his pocket and opened the padlock, swinging open the lid. The box was packed with individual canvas sacks all secured with tie strings at the neck.

Opening one of them, he poured some of the contents on to the table. To von Lutzdorf, they looked like dull glass pebbles of different colours and he picked one up the size of a cherry.

"They don't look like much, do they?" he said.

"They're not gemstones but just as hard and indestructible," said the Boer.

"How much in weight is there in the box?"

"Each bag weighs two kilograms and there are twenty-five bags in each of the five boxes. A total of two hundred and fifty kilograms."

"I would like you to open some more of the bags."

"When you show us the gold, you can open all of the bags."

"Not before we open the bags."

"Well, Major, then I am afraid I must insist on the gold first."

With that, the other two Boers raised their rifles and, with a click and a snap of the bolts, they each loaded a round into the chamber and pointed them at von Lutzdorf.

"What is the meaning of this?" asked the farmer with alarm staring from the leader to the raised rifles and back to the leader.

"No need to be alarmed, my dear Hardbach," said the Boer leader, "We're just negotiating a business deal. Be quiet and nobody will get hurt. Now, Major, what about the gold? Do we have to get forceful or will you cooperate as you are in no position to argue?"

"I suppose I would be right in assuming there are no more diamonds in this box or the others?"

"Yes, you would be right in that assumption. A collection of pebbles is all, similar in weight but not in quality, I'm afraid," said the leader with a smile.

"And the agent? I suppose you had something to do with his not showing up."

"Quite right again, Major. I'm afraid he met with an unfortunate accident just over the border in Angola. Now, Major, the gold, if you please."

"I think not," said Steinberg as he stepped into the kitchen holding the MP 40. "Drop your rifles, gentlemen. Please, don't force me to pull the trigger. This machine pistol will make a nasty mess of you at this range."

The leader of the Boers, startled at the intrusion, pulled a handgun from his pocket and turned towards Steinberg raising his pistol as he did so. There was a tearing sound as Steinberg pulled the trigger of the MP 40 sending a stream of 9 mm bullets smashing into the Boer's torso. The force of the impact of a dozen 9 mm lead bulletsflung his body backwards against the wall where he remained upright for a brief moment with his eyes and mouth wide open in a silent scream and then he slid slowly down the blood-streaked wall with the look of shock still on his face. His two companions immediately dropped their rifles which clattered onto the floor as they raised their hands and cried, "Nitch schiessen! Nitch schiessen! (*Don't shoot! Don't shoot!*

Von Lutzdorf, who had drawn his Luger pistol, pointed it at the two Boers who stood there apprehensively not knowing if they were shortly going to join their dead colleague. Motioning them with his pistol, he ordered them to stand either side of the dead Boer and keep their hands raised.

At the sound of the gunfire, unconcerned for her own safety, the farmer's wife came rushing into the kitchen fearful for her husband's life. All the while the farmer had stood there gaping, obviously in shock at the turn of events. Deciding that he posed no threat, von Lutzdorf told his wife to be calm and ordered her to join him and to sit down and remain quiet.

"Good timing, Johann. Well done."

While Steinberg covered the prisoners with the MP 40, von Lutzdorf searched them for any other concealed weapons and relieved each of them of a knife and one other handgun as well as their individual identity documents. Collecting all of these, he placed them together with the rifles and the other pistol on the dresser behind him and ordered the prisoners to sit at the table facing him with their hands flat on the table.

"Now, gentlemen, we are going to have a little question and answer session. How did you come to know of my government's quest for industrial diamonds in the first place?"

"We're not strangers to dealing in the illicit trade of diamond smuggling and when we were approached by some friends of Herr Hardbach here, we contacted him to see what quantities were involved and how much you were willing to pay for them. The rest was easy once we determined how inexperienced our friend the farmer was, so we convinced him we could supply any amount required," answered one of them.

"I take it you have no allegiance to either of the warring parties in this conflict?"

"We have little love for the British for reasons which I am sure you know but neither do we care for your Nazi government especially after they invaded our mother country and the way they persecute our former countrymen. We thought it would be a good chance to pluck your feathers, so to speak. And after all, I'm sure neither the British or the Portuguese would be bothered if we relieved you of a little gold."

"There is the question of the death of an accredited diplomat in a neutral country."

"Yes, that was most unfortunate but put that down to the fortunes of war, Major."

"I'm sure the Portuguese won't look at it in that light."

"Perhaps, but then without a body and no evidence, I think that will be lost in the greater conflict. More to the point, what do you intend to do with us?"

"Luckily for you, we are not ardent Nazis but we are serving officers and have our duty. We will relieve you of your weapons and the sack of diamonds and send you on your way. We will also inform the authorities, both here in Namibia and Angola, of the death of our agent so I should make sure you disappear well away from here and don't try to come back. Do I make myself clear?"

"Perfectly, Major. We will be on our way then."

"Not just yet. Johann, check their truck, remove all the boxes and search for any other valuables and weapons."

"We see you are a clever man, Major. Our leader was wrong to underestimate you. Never fear, we shall not come back or attempt to recover the diamonds."

Handing the MP 40 to von Lutzdorf, Johann did as he was bid returning shortly to confirm there were no more weapons or valuables in the truck.

All this time, the farmer had sat silently watching events not daring to speak until von Lutzdorf spoke. "A salutary lesson for you, Herr Hardbach. Be careful who you trust next time."

"I am very sorry about this, Major. I had no reason to suspect anything. They came highly recommended by friends. What are you going to do now?"

"First of all, we must dispose of the body. Can you suggest a remote spot where we can bury him?"

"Yes, of course, Major."

"Now, gentlemen, please pick up your colleague and carry him outside. You can have the honour of digging his grave."

With the farmer in the lead, the two Boers carried the body outside followed by Steinberg and von Lutzdorf. Loading it on the now empty Boer's truck together with two shovels, the farmer drove them to an area remote from the farm.

"The earth is quite soft here so we can bury him deep," said the farmer.

"Get started, gentlemen," said von Lutzdorf, indicating the spot with his pistol. "The sooner you finish, the sooner you can leave."

The two men set to digging and soon had a hole some six feet deep. Meanwhile, the farmer had produced a sheet of canvas in which they wrapped the body and lay it on the ground.

"Do either of you gentlemen wish to say anything over your comrade before we send him on his way?"

Neither of them answered other than to shake their heads at which he ordered them to lower the body into the grave and fill it with earth.

When they had finished and stood back from the site, von Lutzdorf's natural humanity prompted him to clasp his hands together and say aloud, "Lord, we commit this body to the earth and commend his soul into your keeping."

They all then uttered, "Amen."

They returned to the farmhouse and, collecting their personal belongings, the two Boers returned to the truck where von Lutzdorf was waiting.

"You have enough fuel and water to get you to the nearest town where you can get more supplies. Remember what I said. Don't attempt to come back and don't linger in the area as the British authorities will also have been informed of your presence and no doubt have other reasons to capture you. The farmer here was not responsible for your colleague's death. Just your own stupidity."

"Don't worry, Major. We know when we're better off."

With those words, they started the truck and drove off eastward towards the nearest habitation.

Back at the farm, von Lutzdorf and Steinberg discussed the turn of events deciding how best to proceed now that their mission was abortive.

To Steinberg, he said, "We will radio and report the situation and await new orders. Meanwhile we must refuel the aircraft." To the farmer, he asked, "Did you manage to obtain the petrol we requested?"

"Yes, Major. I have ten two-hundred-litre barrels stored in the barn. It was all I could get."

Von Lutzdorf did a calculation in his head and estimated with this amount, plus what he had remaining in the tanks, they could make it back to Libya with two hundred miles reserve, providing they did not encounter any strong headwinds.

"It will have to be enough. We will refuel first thing in the morning."

"Very good, Major," said the farmer, relieved von Lutzdorf had not been harsher.

"We must get a full report of this off at 1800 hours and also report the loss of their agent to the embassy. They will need to inform the Angolan authorities," said von Lutzdorf. "I'll write it out now and we can take it to the aircraft and encode and send it. We only have two thousand litres of petrol available for refuelling. Please dip the tanks and calculate exactly what we have remaining from the flight. It's going to be a tight margin getting back to base in Libya."

"Could we request a fuel stop in Cameroon? We have the coordinates of that temporary airstrip they had prepared."

"Do the calculation first and then we will decide."

"Very good, Walter."

It was late afternoon by the time they went out to the aircraft together with the farmer. To the west, the sky was dark as heavy clouds blocked out the setting sun.

"That sky looks a bit ominous," said Steinberg. "It looks like some rain on the way. What do you think, Herr Hardbach?"

"The rainy season is due soon. Those clouds are certainly rain bearing. Perhaps it's a little early this year."

"What's the ground like along the airstrip? Does it drain well?"

"I'm afraid it does get quite soggy depending on the amount of rainfall."

"Do you have any matting or boards we can use? I would like to put something under the wheels to stop getting bogged down if the rain is heavy."

"Yes, I will bring some from the barn."

"Let's start up and position the aircraft on the threshold ready for take-off, Johann. I don't like the look of those clouds."

Whilst the farmer went to the barn, they started the engines and taxied to the threshold, lined up with the runway and shut down.

Placing the matting and boards in front of the main wheels and the tail wheel, they restarted the engines and edged forwards until all three were squarely on the matting.

Von Lutzdorf then began encoding the messages for the Air Ministry and the embassy in Luanda as Steinberg, using a specially calibrated rod, dipped all four wing tanks and the additional ones fitted in the former bomb bay.

Von Lutzdorf had just finished sending when Steinberg entered the radio compartment. "I am pleased to report,

Walter, that we had a much more economical flight down here than I expected. The higher altitude must have made all the difference."

"That's good to hear. What do you estimate our range?"

"With the two thousand litres and what we have in the tanks, we can make Libya with a three-hundred-mile reserve."

"Let's hope we don't encounter any serious headwinds."

"I shall keep a constant check on those and let you know if it becomes a problem."

"Let's pack up here and get back to the house. It's starting to rain."

As they got back to the farmhouse, the rain had settled into a steady downpour which continued throughout the night and on into the morning.

"Doesn't look good out there," said the farmer coming into the kitchen after seeing to the livestock. He was dressed in waterproofs and a wide brimmed hat, which he took off and shook to get rid of the water. "I checked the ground around the aircraft. It's quite waterlogged but the wheels are well clear. I don't think you will be taking off anywhere today."

"How long do these rains normally last?" asked Steinberg.

"It's just the beginning of the rainy season so we might get a break after a few days but later, when we are well into it, it can go on for weeks."

"Do you have some waterproofs I could use?" asked von Lutzdorf. "I would like to take a look for myself."

The farmer produced two sets for him and Steinberg which they put on and proceeded to walk along the length of the take-off area. Trudging back with their boots squelching in the waterlogged surface, it was obvious that a take-off in these conditions was impossible and they returned despondent to the kitchen.

***

The steady rain continued for a further four days much to their frustration then finally, on the fifth day, it stopped and the sun came out.

The airstrip ran in an east-west direction with a slight downwards slope to the south side. After a further inspection of the waterlogged surface, von Lutzdorf made for the barn and after searching the interior, he said, "I have an idea. Let's go and speak to Hardbach."

After explaining his idea to the farmer, all three went back to the barn and pulled out a long metal girder, a leftover from the original construction. They also managed to extract several long lengths of chain which they attached to each end of the girder and then adjusted them and fitted the joined chains to the tow bar of the tractor. Positioning the tractor on the north side of the airstrip in front of the aircraft, they commenced to drag the girder along the waterlogged surface. At the far end, they reversed the girder and dragged it back along the way they had come. Going back and forth along the airstrip gradually working their way across to the south side, they managed to remove much of the surface water.

Meanwhile, the sun continued, causing the wet surface to steam in the heat. During this time, they cast nervous glances to the west praying for the sky above the distant horizon to remain clear of rain clouds. By the end of the day, von Lutzdorf was satisfied that they would be able to take off safely from the rapidly drying surface so they returned to the farmhouse for one last night.

Much to their relief, it did not rain during the night and the sun rose in a clear sky with no sign of any rain clouds to the west. After an early breakfast, they thanked the farmer and his wife as von Lutzdorf pressed a bundle of British five pound notes, that he had been given by Freiberg for just such a necessity, into Hardbach's hand.

"For the fuel and the hospitality."

Being under British administration, he knew the five pound notes would be acceptable anywhere in the country. After the unfortunate affair with the Boers, the farmer was not expecting to be paid for the fuel which had cost him a heavy price on the black market so he accepted the payment with gratitude.

A quick inspection of the airstrip showed the surface had dried even more during the night. Steinberg removed the external whip aerial from its mounting after sending a signal with their ETA at the base in Libya and restowed it in the radio cabin.

Referring to their checklist, they started both engines and allowed them to reach their operating temperatures. Then von Lutzdorf, with a wave to Hardbach, opened both throttles, accelerated down the runway and climbed away to the north.

Following their southward track in reverse, their heading took them past Luanda to the west but in sight from their altitude of twenty-five thousand feet. Their checkpoints of Leopoldville and Fort Lamy passed without incident all the while Steinberg monitored their track for possible headwinds and was pleased to report nothing of consequence. After Fort Lamy, they began a gradual descent towards TBS1.

Switching on the Lorenz frequency transmitter, they transmitted the signal to switch on the transmitter at their secret base and were surprised when they received the TBS1 signal in Morse coming in through their headphones.

"It seems those extra batteries we connected have done the trick, Johann."

"So it appears but, in any case, I can make out the Tibesti foothills in the distance and am sure we will recognise the rock formation when we get there."

And so it proved as they both recognised the landscape below as it unfolded and had no difficulty in lining up for the approach. After landing, they taxied and positioned themselves tail first to the cliff face hangar doors. Glad to stand on firm ground and relax their stiff and cramped bodies, they fitted the external aerial, confirmed their safe arrival and signed off before opening the doors and towing the aircraft inside.

"I think we deserve a glass of schnapps before we do anything else, Johann. Please get a bottle and glasses from the store."

"That's your best order of the day by far, Walter."

"Not an order, my dear Johann, rather a necessity, I think."

"Order, suggestion or necessity. Whichever, I shall comply immediately," said Johann with a contented sigh.

They relaxed in a couple of easy chairs enjoying their schnapps as von Lutzdorf remarked, "It's been twelve days since we left and the battle at El Alamein started. I wonder how it's going. Can we pick anything up on that wireless? Perhaps some world news from the BBC. They broadcast in German as well as English for the benefit of their worldwide audience and frankly I would believe them over our esteemed Herr Goebbels."

Johann switched to the short-wave band and spun the dial getting a kaleidoscope of signals of different languages when suddenly the clear tones of a male BBC announcer came through. Turning up the volume, they listened avidly as he announced the progress of the battle which was prime news in the English-speaking world. He described how, after a heavy artillery bombardment, the British forces had broken through in several places and had destroyed a large number of German and Italian tanks due largely to the introduction of the new medium US Sherman tank and its 75 mm gun which heavily outnumbered their enemy. Shortages of fuel had seriously hampered Rommel's ability to manoeuvre whereas Montgomery enjoyed unlimited supplies of fuel and ammunition and the allied air force enjoyed superiority over the enemy in both fighters and bombers.

"Looks bad. I don't see Rommel recovering himself from this without more men and equipment. With the Wehrmacht bogged down and bleeding to death in Russia, I don't see where those will come from," said von Lutzdorf. "We'll radio for the latest update tomorrow morning, 5th November, and ask for orders. We still have the gold so we need to know what to do with it in light of the situation. Let's at least see what we have in the store to make a decent meal and check the wine list. I think that Italian officer had good taste in wine and it would be a shame to waste it."

"I hope we can keep our private little air transport command as it certainly beats all the normal bullshit and the perks are quite good," said Steinberg topping up their glasses with schnapps.

"I'll drink to that, Johann."

***

The next morning at their scheduled time after exchanging call signals and security checks, they received a top secret coded signal signed by Goering himself ordering them to conceal the gold at TBS1 and return to Berlin at utmost haste. It warned that enemy air activity along the North African coast and around Malta was intensifying and that they should take the safest route possible through Vichy-controlled air space.

A search through the interior of the hangar for a place to conceal the gold proved fruitless as the walls were solid rock and, without the proper equipment, it would be difficult and take time. They decided, therefore, to bury it outside along the cliff face with a prominent feature to mark the place to facilitate its easy recovery. The nearest most prominent feature was the cleft in the rock face where the opening mechanism was concealed. At the foot of this, they dug a hole deep enough to contain the four boxes, into one of which they also placed the bag of industrial diamonds.

Refilling the hole, they brushed over the surface and placed a number of rocks over the spot to hide the recent activity sure that the first sandstorm would complete the job.

"Let's see what the BBC has to say this morning," said von Lutzdorf switching on the wireless and tuning it to the overseas station they had listened to the previous day. On the hour, following some marshal music, the announcer came on the air and even the normal phlegmatic tones of the BBC announcer could not conceal the hint of excitement as he read the latest bulletin from the correspondent at the battle front.

It revealed that the whole of Rommel's front was crumbling due to the massive loss of tanks and lack of fuel and supplies. Those tanks that had to be abandoned due to lack of fuel were systematically being destroyed by cannon and rocket firing aircraft. The British were poised for the breakthrough bringing up their massive armoured reserves of tanks and artillery. It was now only a matter of hours before the axis forces were in full flight. Without fuel, they had to abandon most of their equipment and give priority to their retreating troops.

"Looks like the end of Rommel in North Africa, Johann. The sooner we get back to Berlin, the better."

"Do you still think it'll be safe to go via Tripoli to refuel?"

"Yes, we still have time for that. Let's just top up with enough fuel to get there and get going."

Having completed the refuelling, they closed down everything and towed the aircraft outside. After disconnecting the towing tractor and returning it inside, they closed the hangar doors.

At Tripoli, they refuelled with enough to get them back to Berlin and also recharged their oxygen bottles which were almost exhausted. Thanking the Italian commandant, they asked him his opinion of the situation.

"I think the British will be here by Christmas. Now the Americans are in the war, they have limitless supplies of everything they need. We cannot even get anything from Europe. The Royal Navy and the RAF in Malta sink every tanker and supply ship they send. I curse that fool Mussolini for dragging us into this war."

Von Lutzdorf knew many Italians were reluctant partners of Germany and, with his anti-Nazi feelings, he felt a certain sympathy for him.

Leaving Tripoli, they flew along the coast to Tunis and then directly back to Berlin at high altitude encountering no other aircraft during the flight.

Chapter 25

❖

They were met at Berlin Templehof Airport by Hauptmann Freiberg who informed them that Goering would see them in the morning.

"An eventful mission, Major. I don't know all the details but I congratulate you on a safe return. The Reichsmarschall will expect a full report tomorrow."

"Unfortunately, we did not achieve what we set out to do but we did prove the feasibility of these long-distance flights. The aircraft and equipment were very reliable."

"No doubt largely due to your experience and ability, Major, in spite of the problem you encountered. I know the Reichsmarschall is pleased with your safe return and is anxious to discuss further matters with you. Now, I have transport here to take you both back to your quarters. Until tomorrow then."

Steinberg went off to his officers' quarters and von Lutzdorf settled comfortably in the back of the staff car and was taken to his apartment where he found Albert waiting for him.

"Welcome back, Major," said Albert obviously pleased to see him. "Hauptmann Freiberg was kind enough to inform me of your arrival."

"Thank you, Albert. Freiberg thinks of everything. He is the perfect aide. Please fetch me a drink to the study, I must telephone my fiancée."

"I have a letter here for you from her. I didn't know where to forward it to so I kept it here for you."

Von Lutzdorf took the letter with him into the study and sat down at his desk deciding to read it before he called Magda.

He quickly skimmed through the letter and smiled at the part where she mentioned Goering was pleased with him and she wouldn't be surprised if there was a promotion pending. She seemed to be privy to much of Goering's thinking. He did seem fond of her and perhaps he found her easy to talk to outside of his official position where one was always on duty.

Magda answered the telephone after the third ring and almost shrieked with pleasure at the sound of his voice. "Oh Walter, is it you? Where are you?"

"Calm down, darling. Yes, it's me. I'm here at my apartment, just arrived from the airport." Secretly he smiled, pleased at her exclamation of pleasure.

"I shall come over there right away, darling. Are you well? Are you hurt? Oh darling, I've been so worried while you've been away not hearing anything from you."

"I'm perfectly well, and I'm counting the minutes until you arrive. Now stop talking and get moving."

As he put the telephone down, Albert entered carrying a tray on which was a large whiskey, a jug of water and some ice. "How was your trip, Major?"

"Very eventful and quite revealing. At least the equipment all worked well but we had a few problems at the other end." Whilst enjoying his whiskey, he went on to explain briefly the problems they had with the Boers and the delay because of the bad weather.

When he mentioned they were a bit concerned coming back though Libya because of the British success, he realised Albert would probably not be aware of these changes of fortune. The propaganda news that was broadcast in Germany of these disasters would be portrayed in a completely different way to the public.

"What have you heard here about the fighting in Egypt and Libya, Albert?"

"Only that there has been some heavy fighting and attacks from the British but that they had been repulsed with heavy losses."

Von Lutzdorf then told him what they had heard on the BBC overseas service and how the Italians were bracing themselves for the worst.

It was forbidden for German citizens to listen to foreign broadcasts under threat of severe penalties if caught, so most law-abiding citizens knew only what they were told. Albert, however, being a soldier and a veteran, was more pragmatic and nodded as von Lutzdorf revealed the truth to him.

"The coming days and weeks should prove very interesting if what you say is true. Our Herr Goebbels will have his work cut out to explain his recent broadcasts. Not that it will cause him many sleepless nights as I'm sure he believes every word of his own propaganda."

Like von Lutzdorf, Albert was no Nazi but as a serving soldier and citizen, he had no alternative but to do his duty and make the best of things.

"Magda is on her way over and I expect we shall be here this evening so I will rely on you and Hannelore to look after us."

"We shall both be delighted to do so, Major. With you away, we've had little to do so it'll make a nice change for us."

"Thank you, Albert. Please bring me another whiskey."

He sat there enjoying the moment as he relaxed with his drink thinking over what he would put in his report for Goering and ruminating what these new matters were that he was anxious to discuss with him. He was still sitting there with his second drink when the sound of a car arriving and doors slamming broke him out of his ruminations. This was quickly followed by activity in the hallway then Magda burst into the room and threw her arms around him as she joined him on the settee.

"That was quick, darling."

"I told my driver it was an emergency so he broke all the speed limits getting here."

It was all he could do to stop Magda knocking the drink out of his hand in her enthusiasm but holding her off with one hand, he managed to dispose of the glass onto the side table and then turn his attention to the beautiful woman beside him. With both arms round each other, they kissed passionately for several minutes until their emotions calmed down enough for them to take a breath and relax.

"I must go away more often if this is how you're going to behave each time I come home."

"Don't be a beast, darling. Tell me how much you missed me too."

"Of course, I missed you, darling. I thought of you every day and went to sleep each night dreaming of you."

"Now you are teasing me but I like to hear you say that. How long have we got this time?"

"I'm not sure until I talk to your uncle, the big boss, tomorrow. But I'm sure we'll have enough time to get married as we planned. Perhaps you could have a word with him and get him to extend my leave," he added with a grin.

"What makes you think he'll listen to me?"

"I'm sure you can wheedle a few more days out of him to enable us to get married. After all, you did say in your letter that he would be there for you and had invited the Fuehrer himself."

"I'll try, darling. Now tell me about your trip."

Von Lutzdorf gave her a shortened version of what he had told Albert, leaving out the trouble with the Boers, saying it was just a proving flight and they had been held up by bad weather since the real purpose of the flight was secret, even from Magda. They spent the evening quietly with Albert and Hannelore fussing over them.

Chapter 26

❖

Steinberg and von Lutzdorf arrived early at the office as planned to prepare the report for Goering. They left out any mention about leaving the gold at the desert base or about the bag of diamonds they had concealed with it since it was the subject of a top secret order from Goering himself and limited the contents to the facts of the flight, the problems with the Boers and the delay caused by the weather. Suspecting that his secretary, who would type up the report, was a spy, willing or otherwise, for the Gestapo chief Heinrich Mueller, he knew a copy of the report would be on his desk probably even before Goering had a chance to read it.

They had agreed with Freiberg that they would give him a copy of the report for Goering as soon as it was ready so he had all the pertinent facts before their meeting.

***

Later that morning, after delivering the report to Freiberg, von Lutzdorf received a summons to the Reichsmarschall's office.

Not knowing how Goering would react to the abortive mission, he was a little apprehensive as he entered his office. He need not have worried however as the Reichsmarschall smiled as he waved him to the visitor's seat before him. "Come in and take a seat, my dear von Lutzdorf."

Relieved at this friendly greeting, he sat down as Goering continued, "Quite a trip," he said, waving the report. "You made no reference to the gold."

"No, Herr Reichsmarschall, I felt that the less said in writing, the better. There are as many eyes looking as ears listening where they shouldn't be."

"Quite so, Major. Very prudent of you."

"Your order concerning the gold was confidential so I felt it better that it should remain so."

"Your caution does you credit, Major, or I should say Oberst? I have decided that what I need to discuss with you about your next mission warrants a higher rank to go with it."

"This is an honour, Herr Reichsmarschall. I hope I shall be able to live up to it."

"Of that, I have no doubt. But before we get into that, I must give you some news and ask you what you learnt when passing through Libya."

"Well, to be frank, the news was not good. The Italian commandant in Tripoli was very pessimistic about the situation and I must confess we picked up a BBC broadcast whilst in the desert that supported what he told us. According to both reports, Rommel has lost the battle and our forces are in full retreat back towards Tripoli."

"I am afraid that is the case. It appears the British have unlimited supplies of tanks, ammunition and fuel from the Americans and their combined air forces have complete control of the skies. In addition to this bad news, I'm afraid that we've just received reports of a combined invasion of both Morocco and Algeria so we will have a real fight on our hands to retain a hold in North Africa."

"May I ask what my new mission will be and whether these setbacks in North Africa will affect it in any way?"

"Since any further South African missions seem to be in doubt for the moment and in light of the change of fortunes in North Africa, I have decided to bring forward the South American mission I had planned as a matter of priority. Tell me, how far had you got in planning possible routes to as far as Argentina?"

"Our preliminary planning called for refuelling points in the Vichy-controlled Ivory Coast and somewhere in Brazil but Brazil, as you know, declared war on Germany last August and are now cooperating with the allies. Paraguay and Uruguay are neutral, whereas in Argentina we have plenty of support. It all depends on whether or not we can establish a clandestine refuelling airstrip somewhere in the interior of Brazil."

"We have our agents in Brazil working on that and the Ivory Coast should not be a problem for now. If we can set up a refuelling stop in Brazil, are you confident of making the trip to Buenos Aires and back?"

"I don't see why not, Herr Reichsmarschall. If we fly over the Brazilian coastline at high altitude, I'm sure we'll be safe as the Brazilian air force is not equipped with interceptors of sufficient performance to reach us and I'm sure they wouldn't even have the radar coverage to detect us."

"Very well, Oberst. Please start planning the flight. I will instruct our agents to give priority to the Brazilian refuelling facility."

"I expect that will take a little time to establish. Can I therefore ask the Reichsmarschall if I will have enough time to marry his niece before the flight?"

"I think that can be arranged, my dear von Lutzdorf. Let me be the first to congratulate you," he said as he stretched his hand forwards to shake von Lutzdorf's.

Goering said he would give him a further full briefing on the purpose of the flight once they had satisfied the question of the landing site in Brazil and then dismissed him saying he would look forward to hearing about the preparations for the wedding in due course.

Von Lutzdorf returned to his office and related to Steinberg all that had been discussed at his meeting.

"There's quite a large community of German immigrants in Brazil and I read somewhere the Nazi Party was active there before the war so perhaps it won't be too difficult to get a landing site somewhere away from the coast and the main areas of population. It is, after all, a very large country with many sparsely populated and unexplored areas," said Steinberg.

"Let's hope so, Johann, because without a secure refuelling stop in Brazil, we won't be able to make the flight to Argentina."

"We must get Freiberg working with contacts in the Vichy government on the stop in the Ivory Coast. Looking at the map of that area, it should be close to the border with Liberia to shorten the transatlantic crossing as much as possible."

"We know our equipment is in order and we cannot do anything to plan the flight without the information and location of the refuelling sites so I suggest we take the opportunity to catch up with a little leisure time. What do you say, Johann?"

"It'll give me an opportunity to make some progress with my sister's friend. We had to cut short our dinner date last time if you remember."

"I do indeed, as did I. I don't think there's much more to do here today so I'll inform Freiberg we're leaving and ask him to start in the Ivory Coast site."

Chapter 27

❖

On the morning of the third day into their long-awaited leisure break, von Lutzdorf received a call from Hauptmann Freiberg requesting that he and Steinberg come to the office for an urgent meeting with Goering.

"That didn't last long, but I suppose two days is better that none," observed Steinberg as they sat in the staff car that had been sent to bring them to the Air Ministry.

They did not wait long in their office before Freiberg appeared and escorted them to his master's office.

Having observed the usual formalities, von Lutzdorf and Steinberg were left standing in front of Goering's desk as Freiberg took up a discreet position to one side.

We're obviously not going to have a friendly chat, thought von Lutzdorf.

Although friendly enough, Goering had a worried expression on his face as he addressed them. "I'm afraid I have some rather bad news to tell you this morning. Following the British and American landings in Morocco and Algeria, our gallant allies there, the Vichy French, have capitulated after only token resistance and gone over to the allied side. We must now re-evaluate the position with regard to future flights. Hauptmann Steinberg, please go with Freiberg who will brief you on the progress with landing sites in the Ivory Coast and Brazil. Oberst, please remain. We have much to discuss."

As ordered, Steinberg left the room with Goering's aide leaving von Lutzdorf standing in front of Goering's desk. When the door closed behind them, Goering indicated the chair and said, "Please, sit down."

"The Italian commandant estimated that the British forces would be in Tripoli by Christmas and we must expect that the Anglo-American forces will push east following their landings in Algeria," said von Lutzdorf.

"We are pushing supplies and troops into Tunis to support Rommel so we should be able to keep our hold in the west of Libya and Tunisia intact, at least for the foreseeable future," said Goering. "What I am about to tell you now, Oberst, is top secret and must remain so. You must not even reveal the details to Hauptmann Steinberg. I know he is a close and valued comrade of yours but until you are into your mission, please keep the details to yourself."

"You can rely on my discretion, Herr Reichsmarschall, and even though I will vouch for Hauptmann Steinberg in all matters, I will observe your order to say nothing to him until we leave Germany."

"Very good. This mission to Argentina is essential to the survival of the Nazi Party and the future of Germany in any post-war government in the event that Germany loses the war. Not that I am a pessimist or doubt the Fuehrer's ability to bring about a victory but we must make contingency plans to cover all eventualities."

"I agree, Herr Reichsmarschall. I am ready to do my utmost to help in any way I can." Privately, as a pragmatist, von Lutzdorf had his doubts about Hitler's ability as a military strategist or of Germany's ability to win the war now America had entered the conflict but he had his duty to do.

"If, with the new weapons the Fuehrer is promising, the war can be prolonged then the allies will tire of it and agree to a negotiated settlement with those of us presently in command having a position in the new government."

There was much talk and rumour about new wonder weapons that Germany was producing but so far nothing had emerged.

"I, as deputy Fuehrer, and with his agreement and authority, am assembling a portfolio of state documents which will constitute the basis of a new government if the worst happens. You will take these to our embassy in Buenos Aires, Argentina, where we enjoy great support from the government there. You will wait there to receive confirmation details and other documentation to bring back to me.

"We will communicate through the embassy via cablegrams encoded using the enigma machine but we shall also have our own secret authentication code which will be added to ensure our communications remain confidential."

"A wise precaution, Herr Reichsmarschall. When do you expect to have these ready for me?"

"This will probably take another week or two."

"Then Magda and I will still have time to get married as planned?"

"Yes, Oberst. I shall be there for Magda. I cannot disappoint her."

"She will be delighted."

"Remember, von Lutzdorf, this is all absolutely confidential. Now you should go off with Hauptmann Steinberg and start planning the flight."

Von Lutzdorf stood up, saluted and left the office in search of Steinberg who he found in Freiberg's office.

"Any luck with the landing sites, Johann?"

"Yes, it seems so. I'll explain back in our office."

"The landing site we can use in the Ivory Coast is a small Vichy military airfield in the provincial town of Yamoussoukro. It's in the middle of the country and well away from the British base at Takoradi on the Gold Coast," said Steinberg.

"What about Brazil, Johann?"

"In Brazil, they've arranged for a staging post near the city of Petrolina. I have all the navigation details and will plot it on the chart. It's on a farm belonging to an immigrant German who can arrange for the fuel. At an extortionate price but then I am sure the German government can afford it. Loyalty costs a lot of money in these times."

"Until then, the good news is that we have a week or more before we depart so Magda and I can go ahead with the wedding."

"Congratulations, my friend. I'm happy for you but what did the big boss tell you about the landings in Algeria and the latest situation in Libya? We have to fly the gauntlet through these areas."

"Not good news, I'm afraid. Now that the Vichy French in Morocco and Algeria have capitulated and joined with the Anglo-American forces, we can expect them to drive east to join up with the British forces under Montgomery. They are not yet in Tunis and the British are still a long way from Tripoli but I think we can expect that to be only a matter of time. We and the Italians still control the air from Sicily across to Tunisia so we should have a safe corridor to fly through for the time being."

"What's our mission this time?"

"I can't tell you the details at the moment but we have to fly to Buenos Aires in Argentina."

"That's a long round trip."

"Yes, but we should not run into any enemy air activity if we plan carefully. Get a preliminary route and distance for each leg worked out. My biggest concern is the transatlantic winds. We should have a tail wind outbound but coming back across could be a problem if we have any strong headwinds."

"I'll start on it right away, Walter. I think with our maximum range of nearly three thousand five hundred miles we'll have enough margin of reserve to cope with anything other than a constant strong headwind. I'll check on the prevailing winds for the next month and see how it works out."

"I must have a word with Freiberg and get all the details of the Vichy airfield at Yamoussoukro in the Ivory Coast and we must also find out whether or not they have sided with the allies as they have in Algeria."

Von Lutzdorf decided he would leave Steinberg to draw up the flight plan and left the office to meet with Magda and tell her Goering had approved them getting married before he left on his next flight out of Germany.

Magda was already at his apartment when he arrived. She was sitting in the drawing room talking animatedly to Hannelore about planning the wedding as he walked in. Hannelore, who had just served coffee from the tray she had prepared, excused herself and left the room.

"What did my uncle say, darling? How long have we got?"

"At least a week, so we should apply to the registry at the town hall right away to get things moving."

"I'll go there when I leave here on my way home."

"This is now your home," said von Lutzdorf smiling.

"Sorry, darling, I haven't gotten used to the idea yet."

"We'll go together when we finish our coffee as we may both need to fill in some document or other."

"I think we should go out tonight to celebrate, don't you, darling?"

"What about the Adlon Hotel? It was very nice there the last time and I enjoyed the music and dancing."

"It was lovely, all except for meeting that odious Gruppenfuehrer Mueller."

"Let's hope he will not be there tonight."

"Even if he does happen to turn up, nothing will spoil it for me."

"I'm sure he has a spy in my office so I would not be surprised if he knows we are to get married soon. Perhaps we should invite him," he said with a grin.

"Don't you dare, Walter."

Chapter 28

❖

It was a Monday when they arrived at the town hall and, after explaining to the clerk in the registry office the urgency of the wedding due to the duty obligations of von Lutzdorf and particularly when he realised one of the guests was Reichsmarschall Goering himself, they were given a priority appointment for the Friday afternoon.

That being settled, Magda returned to her apartment in the town and von Lutzdorf had the driver take him back to his office in order to inform Goering of the arrangements and to speak to Steinberg.

Since his secondment to the Air Ministry on special service, von Lutzdorf was not encumbered with any regular military routine or duties and was therefore free to do as he pleased. He decided to take Magda to see his parents in the country before the wedding.

Using his military authority stating the call was from the Air Ministry, he managed to get a telephone call through to his parents' estate in the country to the west of Berlin near the town of Dannenberg on the river Elbe.

He spoke to his mother who was delighted to hear from him, worried as all mothers are for their sons in war. When he told her he was in Berlin on permanent duty at the Air Ministry and not in the war zone, she was overwhelmed with relief. The sound of joy in her voice was even more difficult to contain when he told her of his impending marriage and his wish to bring his fiancée to visit her and his father. It was arranged that they would drive there the following day and stop over for one night to give his mother and Magda some time together. It would also give him some time with his father who he had not seen for almost a year.

He called Magda and said he had something to tell her regarding his family and they decided to meet that evening at the Adlon Hotel for dinner.

He decided he would call in at Hauptmann Freiberg's office to ask him to inform his chief, the Reichsmarschall, of the arrangements for the wedding instead of over the telephone.

As he entered the office, Freiberg stood up from his desk, saluted and said, "Congratulations on your promotion, Herr Oberst, and also for your coming wedding."

"Thank you, Freiberg. Please advise the Reichsmarschall that the wedding will be on Friday at three o'clock in the afternoon. There will also be a reception in the evening at the Adlon Hotel for guests which I hope he will be able to attend and I would like to take this opportunity to invite you also."

"Thank you, Herr Oberst. That is most kind of you. I shall be delighted to accept."

"Tomorrow, I wish to visit my parents so I will be out of Berlin until the following morning. I can be reached at this number in case of emergency," he continued as he gave a slip of paper to Freiberg on which he had written his parents' telephone number.

"In view of the circumstances, I think we will try to avoid any emergencies," said Freiberg, with a smile.

"Most understanding of you, Hauptmann," said von Lutzdorf returning the smile.

Before he left the office, von Lutzdorf spent some time with Steinberg going over the planning for the flight to South America.

"It all looks very feasible, Johann, and, from what I can see, we should not be troubled by enemy aircraft once past North Africa as long as we keep well away from the British base at Takoradi."

"I think you're right, but Takoradi is only used as a staging post by the British for ferrying aircraft to the Middle East via Nigeria and the Sudan. As they do not expect any enemy air activity, I don't think they mount any sort of combat patrols."

"Let's hope so."

Chapter 29

❖

Von Lutzdorf left early for the Adlon Hotel to ensure he would be there before Magda arrived. He did not want Magda to meet his parents without first explaining to her something about his family which he did not want to do over the telephone.

He was sitting at their secluded corner table when Magda arrived escorted by the maître d'. Standing up, he took both of her hands in his as they exchanged cheek to cheek kisses.

"You look more beautiful each time I see you, darling."

Magda, who was dressed in an elegant white cocktail dress with a diamond pendant at her neck and matching diamond stud earrings sparkling brightly in the reflected lights, squeezed their still held hands and said, "Thank you, my darling. I hope you will always think so and only have eyes for me."

"I think you can always count on that."

The maître d' smiled as he poured them both a glass of champagne and said, "May I offer you both the compliments of the hotel management on your forthcoming marriage?"

"Thank you, Enrico. Please thank your staff for their good wishes."

Enrico, like many of the staff at the hotel, was of Italian descent and part of the Italian community in Berlin.

Taking a sip of his champagne, von Lutzdorf replaced the glass on the table and took Magda's hand. "Darling, I have a little surprise for you and some things to tell you."

"More surprises? Something nice, I hope."

"I hope so too. I'm going to take you to see my parents tomorrow in the country."

"It's a bit late to seek their approval now, darling," she said with an impish grin.

"It's nothing like that, darling. In any case, I'm sure they will love you just like me. I just want you to know a bit more about my family and understand what our marriage will mean to them."

"It all sounds a bit mysterious. Do tell."

"The thing is, darling, my uncle is Baron Otto von Lutzdorf."

"That sounds impressive. So, I'm going to be related to the aristocracy?"

"In a way, yes, and it might be a bit more than that. You see, when my uncle dies, my father will inherit the title. My uncle had two sons, my cousins Hans and Frederic. Unfortunately, as a result of this dreadful war, they are both dead. Hans was an officer in the navy and was killed serving on the battleship Bismarck and Frederic was killed aboard his destroyer in the Norwegian campaign."

"How dreadful. I'm so sorry."

"That part of the family was all navy. My uncle was a naval captain in the first war and his father before him was an admiral. The family comes from a long line of military forbears going back several hundred years. My father served in the air force in the first war and was a highly decorated fighter pilot. That is why my brother and I chose the Luftwaffe."

"You have a brother?"

"No longer, unfortunately. Gerhard was killed over England in 1940 flying a Messerschmitt 109."

"My God, how dreadful for you all."

"So, you see, when my father dies and providing I survive the war, I shall become the next Baron von Lutzdorf. Do you think you could live with that?"

"Oh my darling, I don't know what to say. It's so much to take in," said Magda with tears welling up in her eyes. Taking a handkerchief from her purse, she dabbed at her eyes.

"I'm sorry, darling. I didn't mean to upset you."

"No, darling, don't worry. You didn't upset me. It's just that it's so sad what has happened to your family. I'm all right now," she said as she continued to sniff and dab her eyes.

"Have a sip of your champagne and let's talk of happier things."

A few glasses of champagne later, Magda's spirits were restored and later, after they had finished dinner and were enjoying the music, a familiar figure approached their table.

"Oh no," whispered Magda, "It's that odious Heinrich Mueller again."

"Good evening, Magda, and to you, Oberst. May I offer you my congratulations on your promotion? Well-deserved, I'm sure, and may I also offer you both my congratulations on your upcoming marriage?"

"Thank you, Herr Mueller," said Magda.

"Thank you, Herr Gruppenfuehrer, for both of your good wishes," replied von Lutzdorf.

"It seems as if I'm always intruding on your privacy. Please excuse me if that appears to be the case but I could not pass up the opportunity as before to speak to you, Oberst."

"Think nothing of it, Herr Gruppenfuehrer. I am always available if you wish to speak to me. Please, sit down."

Pulling up a chair, Mueller sat down and continued, "I understand you just returned from a very long flight. Successful, I trust?"

Knowing the Gestapo chief had access to all the information on his recent activities, it was pointless to deny his comment. However, he also did not want to give him any more information than necessary. "Yes, a very long flight indeed but whether it was successful or not depends on one's point of view."

"I know that you are a dutiful officer and that you are concerned, as I am, with the security of the state."

"Not exactly in the same way, Herr Gruppenfuehrer."

"Perhaps not, but we may have more things in common than you suppose. I know you have some more flights planned and there may well be something you could do for me on one of them."

"As you well know, I am under the direct orders of Reichsmarschall Goering, so anything I do for you must be with his knowledge and agreement."

"It might well be that the Reichsmarschall and I may have something in common to talk about shortly too."

"If the Reichsmarschall so orders then I would be happy to assist in any way that I can."

"Thank you, Oberst. You would not find me ungrateful for that assistance. Now I will bid you good night and leave you to your celebration and, once again, excuse me for intruding."

"Good night, Herr Gruppenfuehrer," replied von Lutzdorf whilst Magda just inclined her head and said nothing.

When he had gone, Magda looked at von Lutzdorf and said, "What's he up to? I really don't trust that man."

"You're not alone there. No one in the whole of Germany trusts that man. But there's nothing we can do about that, so let's forget him and have another dance."

Chapter 30

❖

Estimating the journey to his parents' estate would take approximately four hours allowing for troop convoys, road blocks and security checks, von Lutzdorf and Magda left Berlin early enough to arrive by lunchtime.

They settled into the rear seats of his staff car and closed the partition separating them from the driver to give them some privacy for conversation.

"What's it like being part of the German aristocracy, Walter?"

"Well, it's nothing like you may imagine, I'm sure."

"Does your uncle, the baron, have responsibilities?"

"Not like the old days when the aristocracy had a role in governing the country and had certain legal privileges to go with it. After the first war and the deposing of the Kaiser, all that changed. The hereditary titles remain as do their rights of ownership but their responsibilities now are largely confined to the welfare of their estate employees. My uncle is a good employer and is held in great respect by everyone."

"I'm really looking forward to meeting your family, especially your mother."

"Don't get too offended if she presses you about the importance of having children quickly. She's very concerned about the future."

"Don't worry. I'm sure your mother and I will get on marvellously."

"If I wasn't sure of that, I wouldn't have arranged our visit."

The von Lutzdorf estate was on the banks of the Elbe River and von Lutzdorf's father, as the younger son, and his wife occupied a grand manor house and land as part of the main estate. The baron, his elder brother, enjoyed the privilege of the residency of the castle which had been the seat of the barony for three hundred years.

At the gates of the impressive entrance, the gatekeeper, who had no doubt been warned of their impending arrival, saluted as they drove through. They continued on along an avenue of trees until turning off at a junction to the manor house from where the castle with its turrets and spires could be seen in the distance.

"Very impressive, Walter. So, this is your home?"

"I have very happy memories of growing up here with my brother and cousins. Now that they're gone, I hope that someday you and I will have children who will enjoy it as much as I did."

Squeezing his hand and kissing him on the cheek, Magda said, "Oh Walter, I do wish this war would end and we could bring up a family here just as you hope."

As the car pulled up at the main door of the manor, both parents were waiting out in front obviously alerted by the gatekeeper of their arrival. The driver opened the rear door on von Lutzdorf's side and saluted as he stepped out followed by Magda. Taking Magda by the hand, he led her to his parents and, first embracing his mother, he introduced her.

"Magda, this is my mother Christina. Mother, this is Magda."

His mother, tall with blonde hair and a slim aquiline nose set in clear skin with two remarkably blue eyes still retaining the beauty of her youth, stepped forwards and smiled displaying a set of pearl white perfect teeth as she embraced Magda and exchanged kisses on the cheek.

"Walter," said his mother in a mock scolding voice, "You didn't tell me to expect such a beautiful bride-to-be."

His father, tall and distinguished like an older version of von Lutzdorf, shook hands and embraced his son as he said enthusiastically, "Well done, my boy." Then turning to Magda, he clasped her hand in both of his and said, "Welcome to the family."

Standing quietly in the background was the butler Eduard Deerman, who now that the family greetings had been completed, came forwards to greet von Lutzdorf. "Welcome home, Master Walter, or should I say Oberst Master Walter?"

Grasping his outstretched hand, he replied, "How are you, Eduard? It's good to see you and good to be home. Have you any news of Wolfgang?"

"Yes, thank God. We heard through the Swiss Red Cross that he is a prisoner in England."

Wolfgang was Eduard's son and a boyhood friend of von Lutzdorf and his brother. Growing up on the estate together, the difference in status had no effect on the three of them. He had fond memories of their adventures and the pranks and scrapes they got into together. Eduard was always there in the background covering for them and protecting them from the more severe discipline likely to be handed out by his father. He and his brother spent more time eating in the kitchen with Wolfgang and his parents than they did with their own.

Wolfgang's mother was the housekeeper and, although he loved his mother deeply, it was Wolfgang's mother who was always there to tend the numerous cuts and bruises they sustained from their adventures. Because of this, there was a deep bond of affection between him and Wolfgang's parents.

His mother had written to him in the summer that year telling him Wolfgang had been reported missing in action but he had not heard anything since.

Von Lutzdorf's father was also fond of Wolfgang and had ensured he went to a good school and received a good education. At the outbreak of the war, he had sponsored and supported his cadetship at the military academy. Wolfgang had graduated as a second lieutenant and had been posted to Libya under Rommel. He had been reported missing during a battle near the town of Tobruk.

"That's good news, Eduard. When you write to him, please give him my best wishes and please ensure that before I leave here, you give me the address to which I can write myself."

"Of course, Master Walter, I shall not forget. I shall just direct your driver and car around to the service entrance and take your bags up to your rooms."

As an unmarried couple, convention decreed that Magda and he stay in separate rooms until they were married.

"I've put you both in the west wing. It's quieter there and you won't be disturbed," he added.

Acknowledging the message, von Lutzdorf replied, "Thank you, Eduard. Please take care of my driver and please tell Frau Deerman I shall come and see her as soon as we are settled in."

"She will be looking forward to that, Master Walter."

"I hope you're not too hungry," said his mother, as they walked in through the hallway. "We've only prepared a light lunch as Uncle Otto has invited us all to the castle this evening for dinner. He and Arabella are also looking forward to meeting Magda."

"Don't worry, darling," said von Lutzdorf, noticing the anxious look on his fiancée's face. "They won't bite. We're a very close family and they worry about me. They will love you."

"Let's go in for lunch now," said von Lutzdorf's mother and taking Magda affectionately by her arm, she led the way into the dining room.

Von Lutzdorf's father, who had been following at a discreet distance, quietly asked his son, "How is my fat friend Hermann these days?"

Frederick von Lutzdorf and Goering had served as fighter pilots in the first war and had both been awarded the Pour le Mérite, the highest award for gallantry during that conflict for airmen for which all fighter pilots strove to earn. Although not in the same squadron, they knew each other. Their squadrons had both been part of a larger wing, a formation led by the famous Baron von Richthofen, popularly known as the Red Baron because of the bright red colour of the fighter aircraft he flew, particularly the Fokker Triplane. He won many of the eighty air victories with which he was credited at the time of his death in that plane. The wing was known by the allies as "Von Richthofen's Flying Circus" because of the bright colours of all the aircraft.

Due to wounds received in combat, Frederick von Lutzdorf retired from active service before the war's end. Goering, however, went on to succeed von Richthofen commanding the wing until the war's end and becoming something of a national hero in the process. A status that was very much exploited by the Nazis to lend respectability to their party in the early days.

"How well do you remember him, Father?"

"I've not seen him now for many years but during the war, he was quite a jovial person and brave as a tiger. From what I see of him in the newsreels these days, he has been corrupted by those around him and by too much power and good living. How do you get on with him?"

"On the surface, he's still quite jovial and I cannot complain about his treatment of me. We are, after all, fellow aviators and he still puts great value in that. No doubt when you meet him at the wedding, he will treat you with the respect you deserve as a long-lost comrade and you will probably think him not a bad fellow."

"Can you tell me anything about your appointment to his staff at the Air Ministry or is it all top secret?"

"I don't even know all the details, but I'm making some long-distance proving flights, rather like I did before the war."

"That must be more hazardous now you have to contend with enemy fighters everywhere."

"We plan our routes to avoid any areas of intense enemy activity. Our biggest dangers are the long distances and the reliability of the equipment."

"Let's join the ladies. We can talk more later."

After lunch, Christina took Magda on a tour of the house and gardens whilst von Lutzdorf retired with his father to the study to catch up on the war and family matters.

Like most upper-class educated Germans, Frederick von Lutzdorf spoke fluent English like his son and listened into the BBC world service from time to time on his clandestine wireless.

"How do you think the war is going, Walter? You're very close to the centre of operations and have more knowledge and experience than most people. I only know what I hear on the wireless these days, on the one hand from that self-seeking propagandist Goebbels and the other from the BBC, who I am more inclined to believe. I do understand, however, that they must also gauge the morale of their people when giving out the news."

"I think we are about to lose our hold in North Africa. Rommel is in full retreat being pursued by overwhelming British forces and the British and Americans have launched a new invasion in Morocco and Algeria where the Vichy French have capitulated and gone over to the enemy. It's only a matter of time before the allies join up and clear North Africa of all German and Italian forces. And what then? The invasion of Italy and southern Europe is bound to follow."

"But we still hold most of Europe and a good portion of Russia, and the U-boats are wreaking havoc in the Atlantic."

"True, but because of Hitler's meddling, we are bleeding to death in Russia which has unlimited resources and manpower and now that the Americans are escorting Atlantic convoys, the U-boat losses will become untenable."

"This was never a good or just war. How did we let it come to this to let these bunch of criminals lead us into this catastrophe?"

"I don't know, Father, but it has cost our family dearly."

"There is a saying, from where I am not sure, but it is certainly true. For evil to triumph all that is required is for good men to do nothing. I fear that history will judge many of us Germans by that axiom."

"How does Uncle Otto feel about the situation?"

"As you can imagine, like myself, having lost sons, he is concerned for the future. You know we and most of our circle of friends were all anti-Nazi but were greatly outnumbered and out-manoeuvred and are now paying the price. No doubt he will have something to say on the subject this evening. I think you will see a great difference in both him and your aunt. They are still grieving from the loss of your cousins, although they will try to put on brave faces for you."

***

Knowing how much his mother liked to dress for dinner, von Lutzdorf had warned Magda to be sure to bring an evening dress. In the interests of security and to give him authority at the checkpoints en route to his parents, he had worn his uniform which he did not want to wear to dinner. Being much the same size as his father, he had an extensive wardrobe to choose from. When they assembled in the drawing room ready to go to the castle, he and his father were both dressed in formal dinner jackets and black bow ties. Magda had brought with her the stunning silver-coloured long evening dress she had first worn with him at the Adlon Hotel. His mother looked as beautiful and elegant as ever in an equally stunning black evening dress with family diamonds at her neck.

"A glass of champagne before we go, I think," said his father as Eduard came in bearing a tray and glasses which he put on the table next to the champagne bottle sitting in the bucket of ice. Expertly uncorking the bottle, Eduard filled four glasses and passed amongst them with the tray.

"A toast to the bride-to-be and to welcome her to the family," proposed Walter's father raising his glass to Magda.

They all raised their glasses as Walter and his parents said, "To Magda."

To which she replied, "Thank you. I am so looking forward to being a part of your family."

It had been arranged that von Lutzdorf's driver would drive them to the castle in the family Mercedes so the ladies donned their fur wraps against the evening chill and they all made their way to the waiting limousine.

The drive to the castle took only a few minutes and as they drew up under the archway of the imposing covered entrance to the massive double doors of the castle, a waiting butler dressed in a black topcoat came forwards and opened one door of the limousine while the driver, who had alighted quickly, opened the other. Christina and Magda followed by Walter and his father followed the butler through the open door into a grand foyer where the baron and his wife Arabella were waiting.

Christina and Arabella embraced and Christina introduced Magda to her sister-in-law who, taking her hand, she kissed on both cheeks. "You are very welcome, my dear."

Standing to one side, the baron shook hands with his brother and embraced his nephew. "How are you, Walter? Have you fully recovered from your wounds?"

"Yes, thank you, Uncle. I am quite recovered."

Turning his attention to Magda and taking her hands in his, his uncle said, "If there is one thing I can say about the von Lutzdorf men is that they have an unrivalled ability in choosing the most beautiful women. Welcome to our home. Please call me Otto." He raised her hand to his lips and gently kissed the back.

Meanwhile, Walter had embraced his aunt who clung to him with great affection no doubt thinking of her lost sons. Although still a beautiful woman, he noticed how the grief had aged her much more than the two years since last he had seen her.

The butler led them through the hallway to a reception room beautifully furnished with antiques and paintings where a large fire was burning and served them all with a before dinner aperitif.

Apart from the baronial banqueting room, the castle had several other smaller, though no less grand, dining rooms for less formal occasions and it was in one of these that they all sat down around a table which had been especially chosen to suit the size of the party of six.

The baron and his brother sat at each end of the dining table with Walter and his mother on each side of the baron while Magda sat next to his mother diagonally across from him with the baroness opposite her next to her brother-in-law.

"Well," said the baron, "This is quite an occasion. Since my brother Frederick told me you were both coming, Arabella and I have been very excited and anxious to meet Magda and to see our nephew. These are very difficult times but I would like to wish you both all the happiness for the future and we are looking forward to being at your wedding on Friday."

"Thank you, Uncle. Would you like to stay with me at the apartment? We have plenty of room."

"No, thank you, my boy. I have made reservations at the Adlon, so if we tire during your reception, we can sneak off to bed," he said with a smile.

With the constraints of wartime, the baron had been obliged to greatly reduce the number of staff he employed to maintain the castle but he still had an elderly footman, too old for military service, and two maids available as well as the butler to serve dinner so the meal proceeded in some style.

His father, obviously enchanted with Magda, kept the conversation flowing between her and his sister-in-law who was also greatly taken with her charm and easy manner.

The baron wanted to know everything his nephew was involved with and they discussed his recent flight and the recent turn of events in North Africa. Like his brother, the tone of his conversation was distinctly critical of the regime which he criticised openly secure in the knowledge that their isolation in the country and the loyalty of his staff was a secure safeguard against any reprisal from the state security services.

As a serving officer, von Lutzdorf refrained from open criticism of his commander-in-chief but he was inclined to politely agree with everything his uncle said.

When dinner was finished, the ladies, like all of their station, withdrew to the drawing room to allow the men to retire to the baron's study to their brandy and cigars and to talk of manly things.

Comfortably seated in winged club chairs, brandies at their elbow, the baron and his brother prepared and lit up Cuban cigars.

"Pre-war stock, and my reserves are getting perilously low," said the baron puffing contentedly, "You won't try one, Walter?"

"No, thank you, Uncle. I don't smoke at all."

"Walter, I know you and your father have already had some discussion on the subject but I would like to ask you some things which are very important to me and I think to the family and Germany."

"Uncle Otto, you know how much I respect both yours and my father's opinions. Please ask me anything you wish. I have no secrets from either of you."

"Both of us as ex-serving officers know how important an officer's oath is and what it means so I will try not to embarrass you."

"Uncle Otto, let me make this easier for you. Inside this room, the bond between us is far more important than any oath I may have taken. You will never embarrass me, so please speak freely."

"You don't know how much that means to me to hear you say that. How much can you tell us about your orders and the planned mission to South America?"

"Not much more than what I have already told Father. I am to fly to Argentina and deliver some documents to the embassy there and await for some in return and bring them back to the Reichsmarschall."

"Did he tell you what was in the documents?"

"No, Uncle."

"Did he say anything else at all?"

"He said that they were important for the future of Germany in the event that we lost the war."

"So, he admitted to the possibility of losing?"

"Not in so many words, but he is intelligent and he is not such a fool as Himmler, Goebbels, Borman and the other sycophants around the Fuehrer who do not admit to the overwhelming industrial might and resources of America, Russia and the British Empire, which will surely affect the final outcome as it did before."

"Did he say any more on how he saw the future for Germany?"

"He seems to think that the allies will eventually tire of the war and agree to a negotiated peace especially if Germany comes up with these new wonder weapons Hitler is promising and that he will have a role in any future government."

The baron looked at his brother and they exchanged knowing nods of understanding.

"So, that's his plan," said the baron, "Preparing his survival route and ready to stab the others in the back."

"In order to do that, he would have to be in a position to take over the leadership of the Nazi Party and to do that he would need to have control of its finances," said his brother.

"Hitler would never negotiate and would die rather than admit defeat, and the allies would never negotiate with madmen like Himmler and Goebbels. Goering, for all his faults, has a certain charisma and presence and may just be able to pull it off if he was able to take control."

"Then we must try to ensure he does not have the ability to take control. Walter, my son, it seems you have a greater role to play in this saga than we first thought."

Von Lutzdorf who had been following the conversation between his father and uncle said, "Is there something you would like to tell me, Uncle? It appears that you and Father have more than a casual interest in the affairs of state than normal for a pair of retired military officers."

"Your father told me that during a conversation with you earlier, the question of blame and responsibility came up regarding how Germany allowed a gang of criminals to take over the country and drag us into this war. Well, rather belatedly, some of us are trying to find ways to make amends for this failure of our duty."

"You must be very careful, Uncle. The Gestapo has eyes and ears everywhere and are quite ruthless in their methods. A person's station in society is no protection."

"We are both aware of this and, of course, we are careful. Nothing is ever written down and meetings are kept to a minimum and under the guise of a perfectly legitimate reason."

"Gruppenfuehrer Mueller has already been sniffing around the edges and lately has twice innocently accosted me in public and brought up the subject of my special duties for Goering. The second time he went so far as to request me to do something for him on my next flight. He seems to know more about the situation than I do."

"Very interesting. Not one of them in the upper echelon of the party trusts each other but the one to be most wary of is Mueller. His spies and informers keep him up-to-date with everything. He knows everyone's secrets, which makes him almost untouchable."

"Father, you say I may have a greater role to play. How exactly do you mean?"

"I think that we are all agreed that should it come to a negotiated settlement, the last thing Germany needs is for the Nazis to have any role in a post-war government. From what you have told us, Goering's plan to have a role in negotiations and government depends on the documents you have to take to Argentina and what you are supposed to bring back. We must find a way, therefore, to either ensure those documents never get to Argentina or the ones from Argentina never reach Goering. Since you are the courier for both, the solution is in your hands."

The baron broke in. "We must devise a plan that, however we do it, no blame attaches to Walter."

"Don't worry about me, Uncle. Outside of Germany, I have complete autonomy and can justify almost any action as there is only myself and Johann, my co-pilot and very close friend. He is more like a brother and very loyal and has no love for the Nazis either."

"Nevertheless, we will take no chances."

"Tell me more, Uncle, about your group and how did you start thinking in this way?"

"It started when some of us of the old aristocracy and families met at service reunions and discussed the war and the rumour of atrocities and it grew from there. We regularly exchange coded letters, nothing in detail but just to reaffirm our desire to do something. We call ourselves the Valkyrie. A little dramatic perhaps but it fits in with our open professed calling of helping old soldiers and families of those who died in battle."

"I think it's a very appropriate name and you can both rely on me to do whatever I can to avert Goering's plans. In that respect, we may have an unexpected ally, as I have already told you Gruppenfuehrer Mueller is taking an unusual interest in these activities. With his sources of information, I am sure he would have every detail of Goering's plans but is biding his time for the right moment to ensure he is well covered and involved in whatever the outcome. I shall cooperate with him and find out what I can. There is no point in having him as an enemy."

"Very wise, Walter, but be on your guard at all times."

They continued to discuss the war in general and speculate how long it would be before the allies launched an invasion of Europe and what these supposed wonder weapons were that were being hinted at.

"I've heard some rumours about jet powered aircraft that will outperform anything the allies have and some talk of long-range rockets," said von Lutzdorf, "But I don't see how even these can overcome the huge industrial might of America and we're not the only country capable of producing war-winning weapons."

They continued in this manner until Eduard knocked discreetly and advised them that the ladies were ready to retire.

The baron took his nephew's hand and shook it warmly. "It's been wonderful to see you, Walter. I will see you and your beautiful bride on Friday."

"It's been great to be home."

Kissing his aunt on both cheeks, they all said their good nights and entered the waiting limousine.

Back at the manor house, von Lutzdorf said good night to his parents and he and Magda made their way upstairs to the west wing of the house. Stopping outside the room prepared for Magda, he took her in his arms and said, "Good night, darling. I hope you sleep well. I know I will. I'm exhausted after such a day."

Magda looked at him with a quizzical smile on her face and said, "Are you serious, darling, or just teasing me?"

"I'm afraid, darling, that when you become part of the aristocracy, you must obey all of the conventions and you would not want to offend my parents, would you?"

"Tell me you're teasing me, darling. Or why would Eduard go to all the trouble of putting us here away in the west wing? I saw you wink at him when he brought us up here."

"Nothing escapes you, I see. But for the sake of propriety, we must use both bedrooms. I'll come back after I've changed and ruffled my bedclothes," he said with a laugh.

***

Von Lutzdorf and Magda came down separately for breakfast the following morning to join his parents who were already seated. Helping themselves from the range of silver salvers, they took their seats as Eduard served them with coffee.

"How did you sleep, Magda?" asked Christina.

"Very well. I was utterly exhausted after such a long and tiring day."

"And what about you, my son?"

"The same. It must be the country air and perhaps too much champagne. As soon as my head hit the pillow, I went out like a light."

Unseen by either of them, she exchanged knowing smiles with her husband. It amused her how naive the younger generation were sometimes to think that their parents had never experienced or had forgotten about love and sexual desires. In spite of convention, she was determined that Magda produce a grandchild for them without delay and she determined to assist in this to the best of her ability. Recognising how short the time was and how difficult it was in wartime for them to spend time together, she had specifically ordered Eduard to put them in the west guest wing where they would have privacy and not be disturbed. No doubt her son had thought his friend and ally Eduard had arranged this himself.

Directly after breakfast, they said their goodbyes in the foyer as Eduard carried their suitcases out to the awaiting car.

"Take care, darlings. See you on Friday," said his mother as she waved them off.

Chapter 31

❖

"Take me to my apartment in town, Walter darling. I have some shopping I need to do and I will see you at yours, or should I say *our*, new apartment this evening."

From Magda's apartment, he ordered his driver to take him to the Air Ministry where he joined Steinberg already adding final touches to his route planning.

"Has anything happened since I've been away?"

"Freiberg confirmed the landing arrangements in the Ivory Coast and Brazil and I have completed all the navigation and waypoint checks so when we get the word, we can leave within twenty-four hours if necessary."

"I'm hoping to have a little more time here before that. I know Magda would like to have at least the resemblance of a honeymoon."

"Of course. I must think up some reasons to delay our departure."

"I think the allied activity in North Africa will cause us a few problems and delay our departure. What's the latest intelligence report we have on that?"

"Depends on who you believe: Goebbels or the BBC."

"We must have absolutely accurate information on the dispersal and activity of all British and American fighter squadrons in the area before we try to run the gauntlet through Tunisia. Get on to Freiberg and see what he has to report."

"Let's give Gratziani a call. He'll be able to get up-to-date information from the Italian headquarters in Tripoli. The Italians are always closer to the truth. They've lost so many times that they're not ashamed to admit it. Nobody expects them to do well against the British. For them, confession is good for the soul. To be fair to them, however, they have lousy equipment, bad generals and poor discipline and their heart was never in this war or alliance with Germany."

There was a knock on the office door and Gratziani entered. "Good morning, Oberst von Lutzdorf, may I congratulate you on your promotion?"

"Thank you, Major. I'm glad you're here. I was about to call you. I want to ask you what information you have on the advancing British forces in Libya."

"Nothing good, I'm afraid. My latest information is that they've taken Misrata one hundred kilometres to the east of Tripoli and are poised to take the capital in the coming weeks."

"What about air activity? Are the German and Italian air forces holding their own?"

"I'm afraid not. The British have complete air superiority."

"Then we must prepare for the worst."

"With the Anglo-Americans advancing from the west, it can only be a matter of time."

"Thank you, Major. On a lighter note, I'm getting married on Friday and I wanted to invite you to the wedding and reception at the Adlon in the evening. I believe you know my bride-to-be, Magda, the niece of our illustrious Reichsmarschall Goering."

"Thank you, I shall be delighted. Congratulations and, if you don't mind me saying so, you are a very lucky man. I know Magda from meeting her at various embassy gatherings and I can say without fear of contradiction, she is always the most beautiful woman in the room on those occasions."

"That's very gracious of you to say so, Major. I shall pass on your congratulations."

Later that day, when they were both back in his apartment, von Lutzdorf told Magda about inviting Gratziani to the reception and of his comments.

"I'm glad to hear you invited him. He's such a convivial man and will make a nice contrast to the more formal guests."

"You said in your letter to me that you thought Hitler himself would come to the wedding."

"Yes. When I spoke to my uncle, he said he would ask the Fuehrer just to the wedding but I have since heard from him that it will not be possible because he is in his headquarters, the Wolfsschanze *(Wolf's Lair)*, at Rastenburg on the Eastern Front."

"Thank goodness for that. I wasn't really looking forward to him being at our wedding. It would have made it a very public affair and overshadowed what is, after all, our very personal day."

"I agree, darling. I too am very much relieved."

Chapter 32

❖

SIS HEADQUARTERS, LONDON

At the same time as they were having this conversation, in England, in a small room on the top floor of a building in St James in London, an officer in the service of MI6, the Secret Intelligence Service, was examining some photographs of an unusual enemy Heinkel 111 with a German civil aviation registration number. These were being examined in relation to a file being compiled on a Luftwaffe officer by the name of Major Walter von Lutzdorf.

He had come to the attention of MI6 because of a photograph that had been sent to them through their extensive network of agents working in Germany and the occupied territories. The photograph in question was of a group of three people seated around a table in the dining room of a hotel which they knew to be the Adlon, a favourite with Berlin society. MI6 had infiltrated a number of agents working as or with professional photographers who specialised in working in hotels in Berlin to photograph celebrities and other important people at social events.

In this way, they could keep track of associations and compile background information of many prominent Nazis. Of the many seemingly innocent associations, every once in a while, an important intelligence kernel of information emerged which, when fitted together with other pieces, formed an important picture of a clandestine operation.

The key figure in the photograph was Heinrich Mueller, the secretive head of the Gestapo. Gruppenfuehrer Heinrich Mueller, as head of the Gestapo Secret State Police, was their principal adversary in their battle to protect their network of agents. Photographs of him in public were very few and far between so any that came into their possession were closely examined and links to others in the photographs thoroughly investigated. The agent had supplied the names of those with Heinrich Mueller and as they were well-known figures, it was relatively easy to obtain their background information. Other than the fact that the woman was the niece of Hermann Goering, she was of little interest but the Luftwaffe officer was a different matter. His pre-war flying exploits and the fact he had recently been appointed to Goering's staff at the Air Ministry for special duties was of great interest especially since he had connections to two of the top Nazis.

Through their network, they soon discovered all about his visit to the Heinkel works and the special model 111. The chance photograph taken by the photo reconnaissance Mosquito was one of many such photographs that came their way but its significance was recognised by an alert analyst who, aware of the interest in Heinkel and von Lutzdorf's visit, noted the time and place that the photograph was taken and included in the growing file.

Chapter 33

❖

BERLIN

Shortly after arriving at his office the next morning, Hauptmann Freiberg called von Lutzdorf to inform him that Goering would like to see him immediately.

Replacing the handset, he looked at Steinberg and said, "The big boss wants to see me right away. I take it that we have everything in order and can go at short notice if necessary?"

"Yes, we're all prepared and only waiting on him for the order."

"Good."

Goering's support staff in his outer office ushered him directly into his office on his arrival.

Goering, as usual, waved a casual salute and invited him to take a seat.

"Good morning, Herr Reichsmarschall."

"Oberst, I have something I want you to do for me which may seem unusual after my previous comments."

"I am at your orders. What is it you need from me, sir?"

"Gruppenfuehrer Mueller and I have had some discussions and it appears we have some interests in common with regard to your flight to South America. These operations are strictly Air Ministry business and under my jurisdiction but I have been persuaded to assist the Gruppenfuehrer on this occasion."

"Am I to take orders from him, sir?"

"No, you will just do as he asks. He will contact you and you may discuss his requests and then report back to me."

"Very well, sir. I will do as you order."

***

Back in his office, Steinberg was eager to hear what Goering had wanted from them.

"Believe it or not, he has ordered me to assist Gruppenfuehrer Mueller."

"I wonder what dirt Mueller has on our big boss that he does not want to be spread around?"

"Whatever it is, I am to do what he asks, so I expect I shall get a summons to Prinz Albrecht Strasse shortly. Not my most favourite place to visit."

"From what I hear, not many of those that go in there, come out again in the same condition," said Steinberg. "Do you want me to go with you as your bodyguard?" he added with a smile.

"I don't think that'll be necessary. Our friend, Heinrich, wants a favour of us so let's see what he has to say."

They were still discussing the possibilities when the telephone rang and, to von Lutzdorf's surprise, it was Mueller himself.

"Good morning, Oberst. I am sorry to disturb you but could you do me a great favour and spare the time to come to my office? I have something to discuss with you. I believe that the Reichsmarschall has given you permission to help me in some small matter."

"That is so, Herr Gruppenfuehrer. I am free now, if that is convenient?"

"Excellent. I shall send an aide to collect you."

Turning to Steinberg, he said, "He didn't waste much time. At least he was very polite."

***

Ten minutes later, he had a call from security to say that a car was waiting for him outside.

The Gestapo was a part of the Reich security main office, an amalgamation of all the security services of the Reich under Reinhard Heydrich and housed in the one building on Prinz Albrecht Strasse.

Escorted through the building, he was shown into Mueller's office who greeted him effusively.

"My dear Oberst, how good of you to come so quickly. I know you are a busy man."

"Not at all, Herr Gruppenfuehrer. My commander-in-chief indicated to me that he was happy for me to help you in any way that I can but naturally my primary mission has priority."

"Of course, and I am sure our little matter will not impede or affect that in any way. In fact, it may be of considerable help. As I am sure you realise, my department of state security has agents and personnel throughout Germany and other countries both friendly and neutral most of which are easily reached. However, South America poses some difficulties due to the distance and isolation. These offices and services require funding and, from time-to-time, considerable funds are required. It would be of great help, therefore, if you could not only deliver and receive some documentation for me, but also to deliver some much-needed funding."

"I see no difficulty in that providing the weight is not excessive. Gold can be rather heavy."

"There will be no gold, just paper and nothing excessive."

"In that case, when we are ready to leave, I shall let you know and you can make your arrangements."

"Very good. That was all except to wish you congratulations for your wedding tomorrow."

"Thank you, Herr Gruppenfuehrer."

***

"I see you've come back all in one piece and have all your fingernails so I assume the interview went reasonably well, Walter," said Steinberg as soon as von Lutzdorf entered the office.

"Surprisingly short and sweet. He just wants us to be his postmen and deliver and collect some documentation from his agents."

"Seems simple enough, but Mueller is anything but simple so we should keep our eyes open."

"Indeed, we should. In the meantime, we need to know what enemy fighter aircraft we are likely to encounter in Tunisia and Algeria when we pass through that air space. We must therefore get as much intelligence on that as possible."

"I will ask Gratziani to get what he can from the Italian Air Force and Hauptmann Freiberg can get us the latest combat reports from Luftwaffe Intelligence. What do you need this for?"

"I'm concerned at the possibility of being intercepted at high altitude and need to know the altitude performance of their current fighters. We must conduct some high altitude trials to determine the absolute altitude we can attain in our 111. Altitude and speed are our only means of defence, so we must ensure we have sufficient margin of both to evade enemy attacks. Make arrangements to go to the Heinkel factory in the next week. We can discuss with them the possible extra modifications to improve performance."

"What other modifications do you think can be made to improve the performance?"

"The last time I spoke with the chief engineer at Heinkel, he said they could fit larger propellers with a broader chord which would be more efficient in the thin air at high altitude. This would result in more thrust and enable the aircraft to climb higher and go a little faster. Every extra foot in altitude and every extra mile per hour in speed could mean the difference between being intercepted and evading enemy fighters."

"I will get on to Hauptmann Freiberg to arrange the visit to Heinkel and also get the latest intelligence on enemy fighters operating in the area. Let's give Gratziani a call now and see what he knows."

Gratziani, who was in his office, came to their office immediately on receiving the call armed with a file containing the latest information from the Italian Air Force in Tripoli.

"What do you have for us, Major?"

"The British are still one hundred miles from Tripoli and are using the Spitfire mark Vc, the Hurricane and the P-40 Tomahawk. The Spitfire can reach approximately thirty-six thousand feet whilst the Hurricanes and Tomahawks can barely reach thirty-two thousand. and from where they are at present, they would not have the range to reach Tunis."

"What did you find out from Freiberg, Johann?"

"It appears that both the Americans and the British are using the P-40, which the Americans call the Warhawk. Neither have a good performance above thirty thousand feet."

"Very well. At least we know what to aim for when we do our trials."

****

Von Lutzdorf called the Heinkel works and spoke to the chief engineer who confirmed they would work on the aircraft as a matter of priority. He then called Hauptmann Freiberg to ensure the Junker 52 was available to collect them from the Heinkel works and bring them back to Berlin.

"Let's take the 111 to Warnemuende today and leave it with Heinkel to play with," said von Lutzdorf. "The Junker 52 will follow us and bring us back today. The sooner we get on with these modifications, the better. Call the Luftwaffe commandant and tell him to have the aircraft ready to depart within the hour."

It was midday when they arrived at the Heinkel works and, after spending an hour with the chief engineer, they decided on the new modifications. At his suggestion, they also would have fitted, in addition to the nitrous oxide injection system, the water methanol system since although this was effective at lower altitudes it would still give them some extra boost at extreme altitude. He warned them, however, not to run them at full boost for too long a period, as this could possibly over-stress the engines.

They also decided on fitting an observation blister in the underside cargo area to give them an all-round view below and behind to keep track of any pursuing fighter aircraft. Satisfied they had done all they could, von Lutzdorf and Steinberg returned to the waiting Ju 52 and flew back to Berlin.

***

The morning of their wedding day found von Lutzdorf in his apartment in the suburbs of Berlin and Magda in her own apartment in the centre. They had decided on this as Magda had agreed with her uncle, Hermann Goering, that he would collect her and bring her to the registry with his entourage. Both Magda and von Lutzdorf would have preferred a more low-key event but the showman in Goering would not hear of it.

"Don't worry, darling," said von Lutzdorf as he spoke to her on the telephone, "It'll soon be over and he has told you that he will only make a token appearance at the reception and then we can relax and just be with our friends and family."

"Yes, darling, I know. I just hope the British don't decide on an air raid this evening just to annoy him."

"I think they have better things to do than annoy him at the moment. There is some good news, however, as I think we'll have about a week to spend as a sort of honeymoon."

"That's wonderful. How did you arrange that?"

"Johann and I took the aircraft back to Heinkel yesterday for some further modifications and I had a quiet word with the chief engineer about us getting married and not to be in a hurry to finish them. He understood."

"There aren't many places we can go, so would you mind if we spent the time at your parents' and your uncle's estate? I would so much like to get to know your mother and your aunt."

"That's a splendid idea. We'll have a word with them this evening. I'm sure they'll be delighted too." Secretly he had hoped to spend the time there but coming from Magda, it made it all the easier.

Von Lutzdorf, with his family and friends, was already at the Registry Office at the town hall when Goering, together with his Luftwaffe bodyguard, arrived with the usual pomp and flurry of attendant reporters and photographers to record the moment. Security, however, was tight and no reporters were allowed inside the building and to von Lutzdorf and Magda's relief, the wedding passed off quietly. Afterwards, when they had all arrived at the Adlon Hotel, the bodyguards were ordered to remain outside and, as good as his word, Goering stayed just long enough to drink the newlyweds' good health and have a few words with von Lutzdorf's father.

"How are you, my old comrade?" he said as he gripped the outstretched hand of von Lutzdorf's father.

"I'm very well, thank you, Herr Reichsmarschall. Thank you for taking an interest in my boy."

"His qualifications and ability would have singled him out for special duties in any case. But I'm glad that we have this occasion to cement an old relationship and to meet again. You're still relatively young. Would you not consider re-joining the service? With your experience, we could find a place for you."

"I'm afraid not. That old wound of mine still gives me trouble from time to time and I'm fully occupied growing food for the war effort. Not so glamorous but still essential, I think. With Walter in the service and having lost my other son over England in 1940, there's no one else to run the estate."

"Quite so. I'm sorry, I didn't know about your other son."

After a few words with the baron and the wives, Goering took Magda and von Lutzdorf aside and wished them both good health and at the insistence of his niece, he confirmed that they would have time for a honeymoon on the family estate. Making his excuses on the grounds of pressing duties, Goering left the reception.

"There you are," said Magda, "Now, it's official. Goering himself has ordered you to have a honeymoon."

"Well done, darling. Now let's speak to Mother and Father about that."

***

The week away from the realities of war in the rural countryside on the banks of the river Elbe passed idyllically and all too soon. After eight days of bliss, von Lutzdorf received a call from Steinberg to say the chief engineer from Heinkel had telephoned to say the aircraft was ready for them.

Magda and his mother had become firm friends and confidants which pleased von Lutzdorf. They decided, therefore, to have a farewell dinner together at the castle with the baron and his wife and leave for Berlin in the morning.

Chapter 34

❖

During von Lutzdorf's absence, Steinberg had been busy working on the details for the flight to South America and he now had the navigational coordinates for the intermediate refuelling stops and the distances and tracks for each leg plotted on his set of charts. He had also been liaising with the Heinkel factory to ensure the new modifications were carried out as requested.

"Did you have any luck organising those fighters for some simulated interception trials, Johann?"

"Yes, the local Luftwaffe base commander was very cooperative and interested in trying out high altitude interceptions. He said it would be good experience for his pilots."

"We must be prepared to spend several days there as the weather at this time of year can be very unpredictable."

"I think we'll be fine as far as the weather is concerned. I called the airfield at Warnemuende this morning and they informed me that the prediction for the next few days is for high pressure so the weather should be stable for our trials."

"That's very good, Johann, so the sooner we get off, the better. Tell Freiberg to organise the Ju 52."

"Already done, Walter. Ready when you are," said Steinberg with a smile.

"Very efficient," said von Lutzdorf returning Steinberg's smile. "I must go away more often."

The Ju 52 was waiting for them at Berlin Templehof Airport and as they boarded the aircraft, Steinberg remarked, "Our pilot must have the best job in the Air Force. All he has to do is sit around in nice safe locations waiting for the boss and his staff and only flying when the weather is good. I think I'll apply for a transfer when we finish with these special flights. What about you, Walter? Now that you're married to the boss' niece surely she could arrange that for us."

"I think you would soon get bored doing this job, Johann."

"I can put up with boredom, especially safe comfortable boredom."

Von Lutzdorf laughed and said, "I think you may have a good idea. The way the war is going, if we lose our hold on North Africa, we'll never have an aircraft with the range to reach South America from Europe."

"It's important that we get on with this flight as soon as possible before the Americans and the British meet up in Tunisia and close this air space to us permanently," said Steinberg.

"Yes, with luck, we'll have time to complete one flight, possibly two."

The chief engineer was waiting for them as usual and greeted them as special visitors. He was greatly interested in their project. It incorporated several additions and other equipment which he had wanted to try out himself but had been restricted by the need to concentrate on producing ever-increasing numbers of the standard aircraft to keep up with demand from the Luftwaffe.

"Good morning, Oberst. Welcome back. I think you'll be pleased with the changes we have made."

"Thank you, I'm looking forward to testing them shortly. Fortunately, the weather seems suitable for some high-altitude flights today, so please show us over the aircraft and we'll get as much done today as we can."

They approached the aircraft which was parked in front of the hangar.

"The first thing you'll notice are the new broad chord propellers. These will certainly give them a better grip in the thinner air at high altitude and help to absorb the greater engine power when you use the boost system."

"They certainly look much bigger. What about their length?" asked von Lutzdorf.

"A small increase in length to improve the efficiency but not enough to cause a ground clearance problem."

They continued walking around the fuselage and inspected the new observation blisters under and to each side of the rear cargo area.

"These should give you an all-around view below and behind, Oberst."

"Good. Let's get on board and you can show me the new boost controls."

Once inside the cockpit area, the chief engineer pointed out the two control levers for each engine.

"You'll notice that they differ from the original system. Previously with the one system, you had only one on/off control knob. Working with the engine manufacturer, we have developed a continuously variable injection system which means you can apply the boost from low power right through to full power for both the nitrous oxide and the water methanol system. As you can see, they are labelled so you cannot mistake one for the other."

"That's a great improvement. So, we can run at low boost for a much longer period and, if necessary, full boost in an emergency?"

"That's correct, Oberst. Just apply enough boost to suit the situation. That will greatly reduce the stress on the engines."

"Excellent. Johann, what arrangement did you make with the local Luftwaffe commandant?"

"He has two Bf 109G fighters on standby. As soon as we advise him that we've activated our flight plan, he'll keep in contact with us by radio and coordinate trial interceptions tracking us by radar throughout."

"He already has a copy of the flight plan we agreed upon? Flying out over the Baltic Sea to gain altitude then flying in from the north crossing the coast to simulate us crossing into enemy air space at Tunis from the Mediterranean."

"Precisely so, Walter. We just need to alert him when we take off."

"Good. Let's take advantage of this clear weather. What's the local forecast?"

"High pressure dominating so should remain the same for the next two days at least."

Descending the crew boarding ladder, they collected their gear from the Ju 52, donned their bulky heated flying suits and completed a walk around check of the 111 whilst, as requested, the chief engineer telephoned the Luftwaffe base to inform them of the imminent departure.

Completing their engine start-up checks, they let the engines warm up to the operating temperatures and then taxied to the take-off position.

The extra bite of the larger propellers was immediately noticeable during their take-off run by the improved acceleration and they were airborne more quickly than usual.

"That seems better already, Johann."

"Let's hope they do their job at altitude. Those 109s can reach thirty-nine thousand feet. If they can't catch up to us, I don't think we'll have any trouble with those P-40s."

The plan was for the 111 to approach the coast at a high altitude and, when fifty miles out from the coast, the Bf 109Gs would take off and climb up to intercept. As soon as they were airborne, they called the Warnemuende Luftwaffe base on the prearranged special frequency and exchanged call signs for this special flight. The Heinkel 111 had been allocated the code name "Segler 1" *(Swift 1)* and the Bf 109Gs "Falke 1" and "Falke 2" *(Falcon 1 and Falcon 2).*

Keeping well away from Swedish air space, they climbed steadily on a northerly heading towards Copenhagen. With the new propellers and the two stage superchargers, they easily passed through the contrail level at twenty-six thousand feet and continued on up to thirty-three thousand feet without the need to apply boost. At that height, they were still climbing but at a very reduced rate.

"That's very impressive, Johann. Let's try a little nitrous oxide boost," von Lutzdorf said as he gradually eased the boost lever forwards. The climb rate increased significantly and they passed through thirty-six thousand feet with only a quarter of the available boost. Easing the lever back to zero, the climb rate stopped but did drop back as it held the altitude.

"Let's leave it at this altitude and see how those 109s get on. Let's turn back on our run-in to the coast and get our ground speed worked out and give the base a call and check it with radar."

Von Lutzdorf used the autopilot to enter a gradual one-hundred-and-eighty-degree turn back towards Warnemuende. They were one hundred miles from the coast as they made their turn and, settling on to a steady track and height, they called radar who confirmed their ground speed at three hundred and thirty miles per hour. At fifty miles, they would start the interception.

At fifty miles, they received confirmation that the 109Gs had taken off and were climbing to intercept. At that speed they would cross the coast in eight minutes. The 109s had to judge their climb rate and speed for a successful interception. If they climbed straight up from the coast, they would not reach that height in time. They would have to climb inland to intercept. Climbing would greatly reduce their ground speed which would mean that when they reached the height of the target aircraft, it would be well ahead resulting in a long tail chase and they would need sufficient fuel and range for that. All these factors had been considered so the result would be carefully considered after the trial. They could then change their approach altitude if necessary to ensure a safe penetration of the enemy air space.

Looking down from their height of thirty-six thousand feet, the recent snow provided a perfect background to spot any fighter aircraft climbing up to intercept them. As they crossed over the coast at Warnemuende, Steinberg moved into the bomb aimer's position in the nose where he could get an unobstructed view forwards and downwards as any interceptors at this stage would be ahead of them. Using a pair of binoculars, he scanned the area ahead looking for any sign of other aircraft.

"Anything in sight yet, Johann?"

"From the time they took off, it'll be about twenty minutes for those 109s to reach our height. I estimate from their performance, we should fly right over them and have about a ten-mile lead on them by the time they're at our altitude. With their greater speed, once they're level with us, they should overtake us in about ten minutes."

"Luckily, this is just a friendly trial run so we'll stick to our speed and height and see how they get on. Even if they do catch us, I doubt that one of the American P-40s could even get to this height so it'll be a useful comparison."

Just then the radar controller came on the radio. "Segler One, this is Warnemuende radar. Be advised that Falke 1 and Falke 2 are ten miles ahead of you at twenty thousand feet."

"Segler One, thank you, Warnemuende. Do you see them, Johann?"

"We should pass over them soon." A minute later, Steinberg came on the intercom. "I have them now straight ahead about ten thousand feet below. We'll pass over them in about one minute. They'll have quite a tail chase."

Shortly thereafter, he came back on. "Passing overhead now. I'll go back to the cargo hold blister to keep an eye on them."

"What ground speed do you estimate we're making?"

"Crossing the coast, we were making three hundred and thirty miles per hour. I estimate, judging on their present height, every minute it takes them to climb to our height, we will gain four miles on them." As he said this, he clicked his stopwatch to record the time until the fighters began their stern chase.

Changing frequency, von Lutzdorf called the Bf 109Gs. "Falke One, this is Segler One. What is your height and position?"

"Segler One, we are at twenty-three thousand feet and have you in sight approximately five miles ahead."

"Thank you, Falke One. Call me when you are at my level."

"Will do, Segler One. Falke One out."

"You have the performance figures on the 109, Johann. How long will it take them to reach our height?"

"About nine minutes at their best climb speed and angle."

"And what is their range and endurance without external fuel?"

"About two and a half hours but they're mostly at full throttle so not much more than two hours I would estimate."

"Good. Let's make it a little bit harder for them," said von Lutzdorf as he gradually eased the boost levers forwards on both systems on each engine to a quarter.

The effect was immediate but gradual as the indicated air speed increased by ten miles per hour and the altimeter showed a steady but positive climb rate as he gently pulled back on the control column.

Levelling off at thirty-seven thousand feet, he asked, "What is the lapsed time since we crossed the coast, Johann?"

"Coming up to ten minutes."

"Can you see Falke One or Falke Two?"

"No, they're too far back, at least forty miles or more."

"Falke One, this is Segler One. What is your height and do you have me in sight?"

"Segler One, we are in your contrail coming up to thirty-seven thousand feet but do not have you in sight."

Changing frequency, he called radar for a position check who confirmed that Falke One was forty-five miles behind them closing slowly.

"How long before they catch up to us, Johann?"

"I estimate about fifty minutes. They've been airborne now for twenty-five minutes. If they want to have enough fuel to return to base, they have no chance to catch us."

"Let's see how long it takes them to give up."

Thirty minutes into the stern chase, Falke One called. "Segler One, this is Falke One. I still do not have you in sight but radar tells me I am twenty miles behind you. I'm afraid I must break off the chase otherwise I won't have enough fuel to return to base. I hope this has been a useful exercise for you."

"Falke One, thank you for your cooperation. This has been a very useful test flight for us. Segler One out."

As he eased the boost levers back to the closed position, he said to Steinberg, "I don't think we have anything to worry about flying through the North African air space. The only enemy aircraft that could possibly worry us is a Spitfire IX and that would have to be already airborne on patrol in the area and we have no intelligence to suggest that the British have deployed any to the Mediterranean."

"I agree, but I think we should climb to our maximum altitude at least fifty miles out from Tunis just in case they have new aircraft by the time we plan to transit the area. We must also be aware, when we return, of any new deployments. That'll be Freiberg's responsibility to keep us informed."

"We'll set that up with him when we get back to Berlin. Now, let's get back to Heinkel and have the engines checked over before we go home."

Von Lutzdorf entered a slow one-hundred-and-eighty-degree turn back to Warnemuende and throttled back into a gradual descent to the airfield.

After a debriefing with the chief engineer, he promised to have both engines thoroughly checked over after the use of the boost systems. As this would take several days, von Lutzdorf and Steinberg decided to return to Berlin and boarded the waiting Ju 52.

Chapter 35

❖

Although the Vichy French forces in Tunisia had capitulated to the Anglo-Americans, the German Wehrmacht was still very much in control and holding up any advance by the allied forces whilst building up its own strength with an increasing influx of new troops and equipment from Sicily. To the east, Rommel's forces, together with the Italians, were fighting a strong rear-guard action against Montgomery's eighth army holding up its entry into the capital Tripoli.

Discussing the situation with Hauptmann Freiberg the following morning, von Lutzdorf was informed that so far intelligence had determined that the only Spitfires deployed in the area were the mark Vc versions and they did not have the performance to intercept the special Heinkel 111 at its proposed altitude. It was also determined that the only enemy fixed radar in the area was in Malta and its range did not extend to cover their proposed route through Tunisia. The only other radar available to the allies was their mobile GCI equipment which only had a range of ninety miles and therefore would not be a threat.

"How long before the Reichsmarschall will have all his documentation ready for us to leave for Argentina?" asked von Lutzdorf.

"My last information from him was that it would be several more weeks before he has everything in place, so you can stand down and make the most of the time."

"Thank you, Freiberg. However, please ensure we are always up-to-date with any intelligence information on the situation in North Africa and other Vichy-controlled territories we may need to transit."

"Of course, Oberst. It will be one of my priorities in the planning and execution of these missions."

Satisfied they had covered all the essential points, von Lutzdorf decided to take advantage of Hauptmann Freiberg's suggestion to make some time for himself and family.

"What are you planning to do with this welcome break, Johann?"

"I'll spend the time with my mother and sister and hopefully make some progress with my sister's friend. What about you?"

"I'm sure Magda will have some ideas about that. She was reluctant to leave my parents after our honeymoon so I expect she'll want to spend some of this time back there again. Not that I shall object as I would like it too. Although I haven't been married long, I think I'm becoming wise in the ways of women and will let her suggest it first."

"If I ever get married, Walter, I'll know who to come to for advice," said Steinberg with a grin.

Before they left the office, von Lutzdorf called Magda, who was still at the apartment, and told her of this piece of good news and said he was on his way home and for her to think about how she would like to spend this unexpected free time.

**

Magda threw her arms around him as he entered the sitting room where she had been waiting for him to return.

"Darling, how marvellous. You said perhaps several weeks. How many does that really mean?"

"Your guess is as good as mine. All I was told is that there will be several weeks' delay before my next flight due to the fact that not all the documentation is expected before then."

"If that's the case, then let's make the most of it. I would very much like to go back to your parents' estate to carry on where we left off. Would you mind?"

"I'm happy with anything that pleases you and I'm sure my mother would welcome you with open arms. But then I expect you and she have already made all the arrangements, have you not?"

"You are as wise as you are kind, Walter. It's true, your mother was overjoyed at this unexpected opportunity for her to have you back at home again."

"I feel that I have very little to do with arrangements where you two conspirators are concerned but seriously, darling, there's no place I would rather spend the next few weeks."

"That's settled then. I've already packed and Albert has packed everything you will need, so can we leave today?"

"I'll have a word with Albert to see if I can tear him away from the housekeeper for a couple of weeks in the country."

Magda raised her eyebrows and said with a half smile, "Do you think that he and Hannelore have developed a relationship?"

"You can hardly not have noticed how bright and joyful Hannelore has become since Albert joined the staff, can you?"

"Well, since you put it like that. There is a light-hearted atmosphere and laughter every time I go down to the kitchen area."

"I prefer to have Albert with me as my driver. The staff driver allocated to me here has other duties which I cannot take him away from for such a long period and I need a driver I can trust. I would not be surprised if Mueller himself had a hand in the choice of my driver. It's surprising what snatches of information can be picked up by innocent but indiscreet conversation and I do not want someone like that free to eavesdrop on my family and staff."

"Yes, of course. I understand your point. If you tell him now, we can get to your parents in time for dinner."

Von Lutzdorf sent Albert back to the Air Ministry with the driver and was ready when he returned with the official car. To ensure the journey did not suffer any delays, von Lutzdorf wore his uniform and carried a letter supplied by Hauptmann Freiberg bearing Goering's signature and seal. It stated he was on the personal staff of the Reichsmarschall and that all military personnel should offer any assistance requested at all times.

As before, the journey did encounter troop transports and several security road blocks but sight of the letter resulted in the officer in charge snapping to attention with a click of the heels and a Nazi salute as they were waved through.

***

It was dark by the time they arrived at the von Lutzdorf estate and the journey had taken longer than in daytime because of the need to use shielded dipped headlights.

When they pulled up in front of the manor house, Eduard appeared with a shielded lantern observing the blackout regulations.

"Welcome back again, Master Walter. Please go straight in. I'll go round to the back with your driver and see to the baggage."

"Thank you, Eduard."

Taking Magda by the hand, von Lutzdorf entered the hallway, careful to close the door behind them, and walked through to the drawing room where his parents were waiting. His mother immediately clasped Magda to her like a long-lost daughter. During their previous visits, his mother had developed a love for Magda more akin to the love a mother yearns to have for a daughter she never had. Smiling at this outward show of affection, von Lutzdorf took his father's outstretched hand in a strong affectionate grasp while putting his other hand on his father's shoulder.

"Good to see you again, my boy. Your mother has been beside herself with happiness at the thought of you both being back here so soon after your honeymoon."

"Thank you, Father. I know Magda feels exactly the same. She just couldn't wait to get here as soon as I told her about this extra leave. All she talks about is Mother and Aunt Arabella and how much she likes them. And you and Uncle Otto, of course."

"It's good to see them together. It's given your mother and your aunt both a new lease on life to know you are married with the prospect of grandchildren and nieces and nephews."

"You'll have to give me a little time for that, Father. We've only been married a couple of weeks but I'll do my best."

His father laughed. "I know you will, my boy. Now, let's go in for dinner. Frau Deerman and Eduard have been busy all afternoon preparing some of your favourite dishes."

Chapter 36

❖

SIS HEADQUARTERS, LONDON

General Stewart Menzies, director of Britain's Secret Intelligence Service SIS, a distinguished slightly balding man of medium height with a greying military style moustache, stood at the window of his office overlooking St James' Park. With him stood one of his agents from department six of military intelligence known as MI6: one of the subdivisions of SIS.

The agent, Commander William Downdale, was in charge of the collection of all enemy intelligence information and responsible for liaising with their extensive network of clandestine operatives throughout Germany. This network had been set up at the outbreak of war in collaboration with the Polish security service who had been responsible for providing information to the British government of the German secret military codes using their mechanical enciphering machine known as "enigma". As the war progressed, it enabled their code-breaking services to read much of the enemy wireless transmissions.

In Germany itself, there were large pockets of Polish emigres within the population and many of these technicians and others were pressed into forced labour in the vital military industries where they were able to collect and pass on secret and technical information essential to the allies.

"What do you make of this relationship that has developed between the Gestapo Mueller and this Luftwaffe officer Colonel Walter von Lutzdorf, Commander?" asked General Menzies, known as "C" within the service.

"Difficult to say at the moment, C. It appears that they only met recently. We were alerted to the meeting by one of our agents in Berlin who controls an organisation of professional photographers, one of whom snapped them together at a function at the Adlon Hotel."

"Ah, the Adlon. My favourite hotel in Berlin and the scene of some memorable moments in better times," mused the director. "What do we know about this officer von Lutzdorf?"

"Well, he was quite a celebrity pioneer aviator before the war. We've kept a file on him for some time. He was wounded recently on the Eastern Front and spent the last four months or so recovering in Berlin. He comes from a prominent German aristocratic family. His uncle is Baron Otto von Lutzdorf and his father, the younger brother, was a fighter ace in the first war, a contemporary of both Baron von Richthofen and Goering."

Menzies, who had returned to his desk going through the file, picked up a copy of the photograph. "Who is the woman sitting with them?"

The agent, who was sitting opposite him, took the offered photograph and said, "Now this is where it gets more interesting. She is the niece by marriage of the esteemed Reichsmarschall Goering."

"How so, by marriage?"

"She is the daughter of Goering's first wife Carin's younger sister."

"So, she's Swedish?"

"By birth, yes, but we think she has German nationality also."

"How is it she has become so close to Goering?"

"When she was just a child, her mother who suffered poor health was taken ill and her daughter Magda went to live in Germany with the aunt, Carin. Since she and Goering had no children, she was treated more like a daughter by Goering and became close and even more so after Carin's death and they have remained close ever since."

"What is her relationship with von Lutzdorf?"

"We understand that she and von Lutzdorf are engaged to be married."

"What else do we know about the von Lutzdorf family and their political allegiances?"

"By all accounts, the baron and his brother are vehemently anti-Nazi and we believe they have some connection to the German underground resistance although they are very careful and discreet of their feelings. The Gestapo have an extensive network of informers either willing or coerced by fear and they deal brutally with anyone even suspected at having any connection whatsoever with anti-government movements."

"This set of relationships makes for a very explosive situation if they all fell out in some way. On the other hand, it could be very useful to us if we could establish a discreet link with this officer."

"There's definitely something afoot here, C. Recently, von Lutzdorf was transferred to the personal staff of Reichsmarschall Goering based at the Air Ministry in Berlin. We have reports of him twice visiting the Heinkel works at Warnemuende on the Baltic coast and flight testing a specially modified Heinkel 111. By chance, thanks to the work of an alert analyst, we think we have a photograph of this particular 111. You have it there in the file somewhere."

Leafing through the file, Menzies produced the air-to-air photograph taken by the photo reconnaissance Mosquito. "Is this it?"

"Yes, C. It was taken, as you can see, at high altitude crossing the Mediterranean from Sicily to Tunisia. The markings and description correspond with the report we received out of the Heinkel works. It has a civil registration and no enemy markings other than the swastika on the tail."

"What happened to it after that encounter?"

"We had no reports of it for a few weeks until last week when it appeared back at Heinkel for some further modifications."

"What's your overall reading of the intelligence regarding this aircraft and von Lutzdorf?"

"Considering the fact that von Lutzdorf pioneered some pre-war long-distance flights to Africa and the Americas, I would say the Nazis are planning some clandestine long-distance flights, most likely to South America."

"I agree that seems the most likely outcome and whatever they are for, it must have something to do with Gestapo Mueller, either for state security or personal reasons, which means we must monitor these movements closely. Do you have enough resources to put a team on it?"

"Yes, C. I have some good people and we have excellent sources in Germany."

"Write me up a brief with everything you have up to now, together with your conclusions and I will get it to the Prime

Minister. He likes to keep right up-to-date with everything the Nazis are up to."

"I'll get onto it right away. I wonder if perhaps we could make an approach through the Swedish ambassador to von Lutzdorf's wife initially to sound out her opinion, bearing in mind she might have divided loyalties due to the closeness to Goering."

"It's worth a try but be extremely careful. We do not want to place either her or the von Lutzdorf family in any jeopardy."

"Perhaps we could try first to get some information from one of her Swedish aunts through our ambassador in Stockholm."

"Good idea. I'll leave the details to you."

"We do have an alternative line of communication which I will give some thought to however."

The director smiled and said, "Commander, you have my full support whichever route you take. I know your network is extensive and dedicated. What alternative are you thinking about?"

"Baron von Lutzdorf served as a naval officer in the first war and his father before him was an admiral. It is the naval link which I have in mind."

"I think I can guess what that link may be. Admiral Canaris, head of the Abwehr, the German Military Intelligence Service?"

"Quite so, C. Canaris, as you know, is anti-Nazi but plays his cards close to his chest. We have received information through this channel from time to time which we know could only have come to us with Canaris' approval. This information enabled us to thwart several enemy actions before they got off the drawing board."

"You're right. He's a clever, careful and principled man who has helped us in the past, although anonymously."

"He hated and fought against Reinhard Heydrich, the head of the State Security Service, the SD, who now fortunately is no longer with us thanks to those Czech officers who assassinated him this summer. He hates the SS and all they stand for so he will have no love for Gestapo Mueller."

"The whole situation is in your hands so get that brief to me and I will leave the rest to you. Keep me informed of progress or any other news on the principals in this mystery."

"Will do, C." Gathering up the file and its contents, the commander left the director's office to brief his team.

Chapter 37

❖

A couple of days after their arrival at the estate, von Lutzdorf found himself comfortably seated in the same wing chair he had occupied before in his uncle's study. His father and uncle were also comfortably seated enjoying the warmth from the log fire burning in the open hearth of the fireplace.

Magda, with his mother and Aunt Arabella, had gone off together to visit the small estate hospital which the baron had established for the health and wellbeing of his tenants and families.

"I must say, Walter, it's extremely pleasant and quite wonderful for your aunt and mother to have both you and Magda back here again for what we hope will be several more weeks."

"It's very fortunate that everything is not yet ready for me to make the trip. I know Magda is really enjoying being here. I think it won't be long before she suggests she moves out here permanently when I'm away on duty. Whenever that may be. She has grown very close to Mother and Aunt Arabella."

"We're both very pleased to hear that and hope what you say will come to be," said his father.

"Do you have any more information, from either Mueller or Goering, about what the purpose of these flights are for?" asked his uncle.

"Nothing in detail, of course, Uncle Otto. Just that they are to do with the security and future of the state."

"Whatever the purpose may be, I think that it will only be for the benefit of the Nazi Party and the criminals in charge, so we must do whatever we can to ensure they do not succeed. I know that you, like your father and I, are patriotic but that does not mean we have to be loyal to a despotic tyrannical leadership which, if left unopposed, will totally destroy the country we love. We both know this situation puts you in a very delicate situation as a serving officer."

"Uncle Otto, have no fear about where my loyalties lie. Father and I have already talked of such things and loyalty to my family and country are paramount in everything I do and think. Fate, if that's what it is, has put me in a unique position to be pivotal in helping to thwart what might be the intentions of a gang of criminals who somehow have come to hold all our fates in their hands."

"Well said, my boy, but you must promise us you will be extremely careful who you confide in and what you say."

"Of course, Uncle. Nothing we discuss here will ever go outside these walls. The only other person involved is my great friend and co-pilot Johann Steinberg and we only discuss the aspects of the mission and never anything political or subversive. However, I know without a doubt that, when the time comes to act, he will be one hundred percent with me."

"It's a good thing to have such loyal friends at times like these, Walter. When we met him at the wedding, he seemed a very decent person and comrade."

"None better, Uncle."

***

Baron von Lutzdorf's wife, Arabella, and her sister-in-law, Christina, sat in Arabella's cosier private drawing room having tea after returning from their visit to the hospital.

Magda had excused herself as she wanted to go riding for an hour before it got dark. Magda, an accomplished rider, had discovered a particularly spirited but gentle horse in the stables kept by the baron during her honeymoon and was keen make the most of this opportunity to ride as much as possible.

"It's been a lovely day and so good to have someone like Magda with us. I do miss not having younger people here and I hate this war for what it has done to us," said Arabella.

"Yes, it's been marvellous to have Walter and Magda here again so soon and unexpectedly."

"I do hope that this new duty of Walter's keeps him out of the more dangerous front line flying that he's been exposed to. It's a miracle he survived this last incident."

Both women had married before the last war and knew well the anxieties of having their husbands away from home fighting and in danger every day so they could well imagine what thoughts went through Magda's mind when Walter was away flying.

"I do hope so too. We have both paid enough already. You more than me, my dear," said Christina.

"Yes, it's been hard to bear losing both sons but worse still with having no known grave to visit and put flowers on, both having gone down with their ships."

Christina grasped Arabella's hand and said, "It's so unfair for you losing both Hans and Frederic like that. I do have some little comfort knowing Gerhard was buried with full military honours by the British and has a grave that I can visit when this dreadful war is over."

"Under the circumstance, I hope you don't mind me sharing Magda with you and, God willing, if they have children, I can share them also."

"We're all one close family and need to look after each other and share whatever good fortune comes along," said Christina. With tears welling in both their eyes, they hugged each other.

"Everyone wants to have sons but when war comes, they are the first to be lost. It's a great pity we didn't have any daughters to see the family through but it seems that fate has given us a daughter who we must hope will keep our family together."

***

It was almost three weeks and just before Christmas when von Lutzdorf received a call from Hauptmann Freiberg to inform him the documentation that was being prepared for him to take to Argentina would be ready in the coming days and he should prepare to return to Berlin soon. Thanking Freiberg for giving him some advanced notice, he broke the news to his wife who had been expecting the summons every day for the last week, thankful for each day that passed without a call.

"It had to happen someday, darling," she said, "We've had a most wonderful time here these last few weeks for which I am most grateful."

"Mother and Aunt Arabella will be most upset, but there's no need for you to return to Berlin with me. I'm sure I can wrangle a few more days and spend Christmas here. Johann has everything in hand ready to depart without any need for me to be there."

"That would be wonderful, darling. I would love to stay here whilst you're away. Your mother and aunt have been so kind to me. It's like having two mothers fussing over me all the time. Something I have missed all these years."

"That's settled then. Let's tell Mother and then we can plan for Christmas."

Before the war, Christmas for the von Lutzdorf family at the castle was quite a festive affair. After service in the church on the estate, all the tenants, families and estate workers were invited to the huge baronial hall in the castle for dinner where all the family members waited on their guests and all the children received presents handed out by the baron. Since the beginning of the war, however, that had been suspended since not only were all the sons away but many of the tenants were also serving. The practice of giving presents to the children, however, was still part of the Christmas festivities. This was always organised by the baron's wife and her sister-in-law and now Magda was happily engaged in helping to choose and wrap them.

During the weeks leading up to Christmas, she had visited all the estate families either at home or at the school and had been introduced as the future baroness. This year instead of all the tenants coming to the castle, it had been arranged that Magda, her mother-in-law and Aunt Arabella would be driven around the estate to the families and deliver the children's presents on Christmas Eve. This freed up Christmas Day for the family to enjoy a private dinner together at the castle.

Although von Lutzdorf's mother was disappointed her son had to return to duty, she was pleased they would be together for Christmas and that Magda would stay on at the estate while he was away.

On Christmas morning, the family, tenants, children and those not away serving in the armed forces attended a Christmas service at the church, where the baron gave a reading and read out a list of those who had sadly been killed, remembering all those who had gone before, including his sons and nephew.

After the priest had concluded the service and given his blessing to all those there, the baron, together with his family, stood at the entrance to the church shaking hands and exchanging a few words of greeting or condolence with everyone as they left. Walter shook hands with everyone and in particular spoke to some of the younger men who he had known growing up who had either been wounded and discharged from the service or who had been unfit for military duty. All congratulated him on his marriage and looked forward to the day when things on the estate returned to normal.

The following day, von Lutzdorf announced he would be returning to Berlin in the morning as everything was now ready and the weather was right for their departure.

That evening, as he and Magda retired to their bedroom, she asked him, "How long do you think you'll be away on this trip, darling?"

"Allowing for the weather and providing there are no holdups at each refuelling stop, I estimate it will take four to five days to reach our destination and allowing for a stay of perhaps one week, I should be back within three weeks."

"It will seem like three months."

"I'm sure Mother and Aunt Arabella will keep you so busy and occupied on the estate helping them with their good works it will pass in no time."

"I do hope so. I must say, I am enjoying helping out. I didn't realise how much there is to do on an estate of this size, especially looking after the welfare of the tenant families."

"It's always been a tradition of the family to take care of everyone. That's why my uncle and grandfather before him are held in such respect. It will always be a part of our lives."

"That is something I'm really looking forward to when this war is over."

"Keep thinking that way and things will work out."

***

Next morning, Albert, dressed in his uniform, brought the car to the front of the manor house where von Lutzdorf, also in his uniform, was waiting with Magda and his parents. Shaking hands with his father and kissing his mother on the cheek, he took Magda in his arms and kissed her passionately completely against convention whilst winking at his father over her shoulder and then smiling at his mother.

Chapter 38

❖

Reporting back to the office, von Lutzdorf was immediately informed by Hauptmann Freiberg that he had a meeting scheduled with Goering as soon as he arrived for a last briefing before departure early the following morning.

The Reichsmarschall greeted him with his usual familiarity and asked after his niece and his father.

"They are both well and they thank you for allowing us to spend Christmas together."

"Christmas is a family occasion and, whenever possible in these difficult times, we must do our best keep families together."

Even though he knew that sentiment was completely disingenuous and cynical, von Lutzdorf said, "We all did appreciate the time together even though many were missing from better times."

"To get down to business, Hauptmann Freiberg has all the documentation ready and prepared for you along with a detailed set of instructions on who to see and deal with in Argentina. Also, he has details of your intermediate stops and contacts at each."

"What about Gruppenfuehrer Mueller? Will I see him before I leave?"

"I believe he has a meeting with you arranged for this afternoon and has all the documentation he has asked to be delivered. No doubt he will give you instructions concerning these at the same time."

Anxious to get back to discussing arrangements with Steinberg, von Lutzdorf stood and said, "If that will be all, Herr Reichsmarschall, I would like to get back to my office and see to the details for the mission and then meet Gruppenfuehrer Mueller."

"Yes, Oberst, that is all for now. I know I can rely on you. Good luck and keep regular contact with us here at the ministry in case the situation changes and we have to initiate new orders. Whilst in Argentina, of course, you will have the facilities of the embassy communications department to assist you but, as you know, we will use our own private encoding ciphers for all communications."

"Yes, Herr Reichsmarschall. Freiberg and I have established a very secure system of communicating with each other."

"Excellent. I shall detain you no longer." And without rising from his chair, Goering dismissed von Lutzdorf with a casual salute that he had become accustomed to which he returned with the pre-war Luftwaffe salute and left the room.

Waiting outside, he found Hauptmann Freiberg who accompanied him to his office. When they were together with Steinberg and settled around von Lutzdorf's desk, Freiberg placed the file he had with him on the desk and said, "In this, you will find all the details for the entire flight plus contact names and instructions of how to deal with those officials at the embassy in Buenos Aires, as well as what you must receive from them in return for the documents you will hand over. Remember, you are acting with the full authority of the Reichsmarschall himself and if you have any difficulties or are not satisfied with results, you can send a coded telegram here for instructions and support. Sometimes these embassy officials think because they are so far away, they are in charge of their little empires and can be uncooperative."

"And the documentation?" von Lutzdorf asked.

"I will bring it to the aircraft when you are ready to depart. I prefer that you supervise the loading. The documents will be in a sealed container and you will have a separate container with funds to cover fuel costs and other expenses."

"What currency will it be this time? Last time, you gave me some British sterling."

"It will be the same as before. Unfortunately, Reichsmarks are not universally acceptable like sterling or US dollars."

A great oversight by the Nazis was the fact that even though they might start a war with overwhelming military superiority, especially against England, what they didn't take into account was the fact England was the head of a great empire and international banking system. England's currency was stable and supported by its many holdings, industries and assets held not only in its colonies but also in many neutral countries including the United States of America. The huge internal natural resources of the US and its immense industrial potential far outweighed that of Germany even when including those forcibly taken over in the occupied territories.

"I imagine the same will apply to the documentation I will be carrying for Gruppenfuehrer Mueller," said von Lutzdorf. "Do you have any idea what it is he's sending to Argentina?"

Freiberg smiled and said, "Herr Oberst, you know as well as I that the Gruppenfuehrer is a law unto himself and the SS have their own agenda. The fact that Mueller has managed to persuade the Reichsmarschall to allow him access to these flights must mean he has some leverage which cannot be ignored. What that might be, I will leave to your imagination."

"As long as all it entails is being a postman, I can accept that. I have never been comfortable in the company of the Gestapo or SS. They're like a pack of vipers who will strike you when you least expect it."

"All I can advise is to just do as asked and watch your back."

"I shall certainly do that, Freiberg."

***

The visit to Gestapo headquarters at Prinz Albrecht Strasse went as expected with Heinrich Mueller putting on his best charming approach to von Lutzdorf.

"Thank you, Oberst, for coming to see me. I hope you have had a pleasant leave and Christmas with your family," he said, making von Lutzdorf aware that he was always well-informed as to his movements.

"Yes, thank you, Herr Gruppenfuehrer. I understand you have everything ready for me. I take it you will arrange delivery to the aircraft in the morning before we depart?"

"Yes, indeed. In the meantime, here is a confidential file for you which sets out what I would like you to do for me and whom to speak to. Once again, I am most grateful for your assistance in this matter."

"It seems like very little bother to me. After all, I'm just a glorified postman."

"Much more than that, my dear Oberst. I don't think a mere postman would have your skills and accomplishments."

Playing the game in the same manner, von Lutzdorf responded with, "Thank you, Herr Gruppenfuehrer, for the compliment. If there is nothing more, I must get back to my office as I still have some last-minute things to attend to."

"Of course. My aide will see you out of the building."

***

"Still have all your fingernails, I see, Walter," said Steinberg as von Lutzdorf entered the office. "How was the beast of Prinz Albrecht Strasse?"

"At his most obsequious best. All compliments and good humour, like a slithery serpent."

Von Lutzdorf and Steinberg had recently come to using derogatory humour when describing Mueller and others as it amused them to think of these pompous and evil Nazis in this way.

"Here's the file he gave me with instructions to go through it and make sure they're straightforward. He will also arrange delivery of his documentation to the aircraft at the same time as Freiberg. He's also giving us a bunch of money for costs and distribution."

"I hope that includes some high living in Argentina. I hear the night life in Buenos Aires is quite exciting and after all, long-distance postmen deserve a little relaxation."

"I daresay that we will be well looked after by the embassy. Remember to pack civilian clothes. It would not do to be seen in uniform in public in a neutral country. We're supposed to be a civil flight. Meantime, what news do we have regarding the allies in North Africa?"

"The latest intelligence indicates that, following the Vichy collapse, the Americans have made no move to advance from Algiers to Tunisia due to political wrangling with the Free French. General de Gaulle, it appears, is as much an asset to us at the moment as he is a thorn in the side of the allies. The British are still held up to the east of Tripoli so we have a pretty wide corridor between advancing allied forces to exploit."

"What about allied fighters?"

"Still the same. The only ones encountered so far are the P-40 Tomahawks."

"Let's not waste the opportunity. I take it that apart from loading the cargo, we're all ready to leave?"

"Yes, the aircraft is ready and we will top up the refuelling just prior to departure."

***

Von Lutzdorf and Steinberg were on hand early the next morning when the containers from Goering and Mueller arrived. Both consignments consisted of a sealed metal-bound box and a similar container with a lock holding the British sterling. Von Lutzdorf signed for both consignments and received the keys for both boxes of currency. Ensuring all boxes were securely tied down, he secured the cargo hatch door and shook hands with Hauptmann Freiberg while ignoring the SS courier.

"Good luck and remember what I said. I am at your disposal for any aid you might require."

"Thank you, Freiberg. I shall not forget."

With that, von Lutzdorf joined Steinberg who was supervising the fuel topping up.

"Ready when you are, Johann. I will get on board."

He had no sooner settled in his seat when Steinberg appeared from behind him and took up his place in the co-pilot's seat.

Through the glazed cockpit canopy, they observed the fuel bowser pull away and the ground crew take up positions for engine start up. Switching on the electrics, they allowed the radio to warm up before calling the tower for permission to start engines following which they went through the normal checklists and started both engines. When all the gauges were registering normally, they called for clearance to taxi and proceeded to the hold position.

Receiving permission to take off, von Lutzdorf looked across at Steinberg and said, "Well, Johann, here we go again."

With Steinberg's hand covering his, he advanced the throttles to take-off power and held the aircraft straight as it accelerated down the runway.

The climb to altitude on autopilot was steady and uneventful as they levelled off at twenty-five thousand feet.

Chapter 39

❖

The recent low pressure which passed through Germany had resulted in a heavy layer of snow throughout central Europe. The cold front which followed together with high pressure cleared away the remnants of low cloud and left the atmosphere sparkling bright and clear. As they climbed, the countryside of Germany glistened in the rising sun and the snow-capped peaks of the Alps were visible ahead in the distance. Passing over the eastern part of neutral Switzerland, they looked down on the Swiss Alps where unseen twenty thousand feet below, the citizens were enjoying the pleasures of skiing unaffected by the rigours of war.

In preparation for their flight, they had notified all the military air spaces in their flight path to expect them to avoid unnecessary interceptions by friendly aircraft. As they passed through each area, they called using their allocated call sign of Segler One.

Leaving the French Alps, they crossed the coastline near the Franco-Italian border and headed out over the silvery Mediterranean Sea. Below them, ahead and to starboard, they could make out Cap Corse, the northern tip of Corsica. about ninety miles from the French coast. Their track would take them down the east coasts of Corsica and Sardinia and then past the western tip of Sicily to Tunis, their reporting point for entry into North Africa.

"Do you want to climb any higher, Walter?"

"I don't think it'll be necessary. Intelligence reports that there is much air activity between Sicily and Tunisia by both the Italians and our own air force transporting new troops and supplies to bolster our position against the expected pincer movement from the allies. This is all taking place at a much lower level and the allied air forces will be fully occupied trying to stop them so I don't think they'll be very interested in a lone aircraft at our height. We have a long way to go and I don't want to use the boost systems and stress the engines unnecessarily. Except, of course, in an emergency."

"A sensible idea. And from this height and clear visibility, we will have ample warning of any approaching aircraft."

With southern Sardinia on their starboard beam, they were beginning their approach to the tip of Sicily when Johann exclaimed, "Look up there, Walter."

Straight ahead, about five thousand feet above and perhaps ten miles distance, there appeared a vapour trail crossing their path.

"I think that might be our old friend the photo reconnaissance Mosquito."

"I do believe you're right, Johann. He must be keeping an eye on the ship movements from Sicily to Tunis and reporting back to Malta for the torpedo squadrons there."

"I think most of the supplies being sent to North Africa will end up at the bottom of the Mediterranean. Between the allied air forces and the submarines based at Malta, I don't think they'll stand much of a chance."

"I think it's an absolute folly to try to bolster our forces in Tunisia diverting desperately needed supplies and men from the Russian front. A complete waste of scarce resources."

As they watched, the reconnaissance Mosquito, now to the west of them, made a gradual turn southward and returned on a reciprocal course to the east, keeping a watch on the straights between Tunis and Sicily.

As predicted, their flight through this area was uneventful and setting their course from Tunis directly to Sebha, they flew on into the Sahara Desert towards their clandestine airfield known to them as TBS1.

It had now become a routine matter locating and recognising the three rock formation which gave them their approach heading for the landing strip, as was the landing and taxiing into position to be pulled back into the hangar. Relieved to be able to exercise their limbs and relax their aching muscles, von Lutzdorf opened the hangar doors and Steinberg hitched up the tractor unit to the tail wheel and pulled the aircraft inside.

"You know, Walter, this is becoming quite pleasant having our own private airfield with plenty of supplies including some decent Italian wines. We should think about sitting out the war here and retiring on the proceeds we have buried. I don't think anyone will be disputing ownership of all that gold and sterling after the war."

"If it wasn't for the fact that I recently married, I would be inclined to consider your suggestion seriously but I think Magda would have something to say about it," replied von Lutzdorf with a laugh.

"Perhaps you're right," said Steinberg with a sigh.

"Let's encode and send a signal that we've completed the first leg of our flight safely to keep them all happy back at the Air Ministry. Then we can refuel and check over the engines ready for early departure tomorrow."

Chapter 40

❖

Steinberg had calculated the distance from their base at TBS1 to the staging airfield at Yamoussoukro in the Vichy French controlled Ivory Coast to be approximately two thousand miles. At the most economical cruising speed at twenty thousand feet at two hundred and fifty miles per hour, they would be in for an eight-hour flight. They decided therefore to be ready for take-off at first light to ensure it was still daylight when they arrived.

The German Embassy in Lisbon had relayed messages via the undersea telegraph cable network from Europe to Africa to their embassy in the Ivory Coast confirming the arrangements and the expected time of arrival. In addition, they had the radio frequencies to use when they neared their destination.

"This first part over much of Niger is pretty well uninhabited with no navigational aids so it will be map reading all the way with some sun sights to check our position, Johann."

"The sun sights are easy with the bubble sextant so I don't expect any problems and it will relieve the monotony."

The tip of the sun was just appearing above the horizon as they took off and began the steady climb to their cruising altitude. As they crossed the unmarked borders between Libya, Chad and on into Niger, the terrain below revealed the vastness of the inhospitable Sahara Desert. Without water, life was untenable except for the indigenous reptiles and creatures that lived there who managed to exist on the moisture in the atmosphere and occasional rainfall. They would congregate around the rare oases that formed where deep subterranean wells seeped to the surface. Such a place was Séguedine, an isolated oasis on the old trans-Saharan trade route inhabited by a mixture of local ethnic African tribes and wandering Tuareg, semi-nomadic people. Steinberg had marked it on his chart as one of the few places of interest on their intended track which would serve as a navigational checkpoint.

Their southwesterly course took them over the length of Niger which was still mostly a part of the Sahara Desert and from their height, the inhospitable vastness of the country stretched out in every direction.

"I wouldn't like to be forced down anywhere in this country, Johann. I don't think we would last long down there."

"I agree with that, Walter. It must be a pretty hard life trying to exist in those conditions."

It was four hours into the flight before the mostly barren desert landscape started to change and then, as they crossed into the tropical African landscape, it was transformed into the lush green covering of fields and trees of the British protectorate of the Gold Coast and the Vichy French colony of the Ivory Coast. Numerous sun sights had kept them accurately on track and, as they flew on, more areas of habitation and development replaced the barren desert spaces.

When they were in radio range of the airfield at Yamoussoukro, they called for permission to land and were surprised when they received instructions to transmit for a QDM: an aeronautical Q code for a magnetic bearing, so that they could be given a magnetic heading to steer for the airfield.

"It seems they are better equipped than we thought," said von Lutzdorf.

Adjusting their track to the given heading, the airfield soon came into sight and, after receiving clearance, they landed safely and taxied to the reception area near the control tower.

They were dressed, as instructed, in flying overalls without military insignia or badges of rank. A civilian who turned out to be the consul and a Vichy French Air Force officer with the rank of captain were on hand to meet them as they disembarked the aircraft.

Accompanying them to the reception offices, the captain asked the purpose of their flight. In response, von Lutzdorf presented the aircraft's registration documents showing it to belong to the German Air Ministry and said, "We are, as you see, a civil aircraft on a courier flight for the government. I trust this was cleared by our embassy with your authorities." As he said this, he turned to the consul who had previously introduced himself as Hans Schmalbach. "Herr Schmalbach, if you please." Acknowledging the introduction, he stepped forwards and produced a file containing a number of documents and telegrams confirming authorisation of the flight and the request for fuel.

"What cargo are you carrying?" asked the Vichy French officer.

"Everything on board is listed in the manifest which has a diplomatic status, as you can see," replied the consul.

The Vichy French officer leafed through the file and finally agreed that everything was in order. Although officially the Vichy French were allies of the Germans, a large number of the Vichy military had reluctantly accepted this situation. Many regretted it strongly and felt it was a matter of national shame that those forces outside of mainland France had not all joined the Free French, especially now since the Vichy forces in Morocco and Algeria had now sided with the allies.

The air force officer, obviously one of those who would rather be with the Free French, smiled as he said, "My commandant has ordered me to give you every assistance in this matter and specific orders regarding payment. We have a fuel bowser ready to refuel the aircraft. How will you pay for it? We do not accept Reichsmarks, I'm afraid."

The irony of the moment of offering to pay using the enemy's currency did not escape von Lutzdorf as he said, "I trust British sterling will be acceptable in this case?"

"Quite acceptable," said the Vichy officer continuing to smile, also acknowledging the irony of the situation, he added, "It's very acceptable in most of Africa."

Rather than being irritated by the officer's provocative attitude, von Lutzdorf's anti-Nazi sentiments sympathised with him as he reflected how he would have felt had their roles been reversed. In keeping with these feelings, he kept his composure and continued, "The matter of the payment will be dealt with by our embassy, which I trust has been agreed to by your commandant. We intend to leave early tomorrow morning, so could this be done right away?"

"It is, as you say, Captain, the currency, and the method of payment has been agreed by my commandant," responded the officer, addressing von Lutzdorf as the commander of the aircraft and not alluding to a military rank.

He waved to the driver of the fuel bowser who drove forwards and positioned the vehicle in front of the parked aircraft. His assistant came forwards with a ladder and, under Steinberg's supervision, proceeded with the refuelling.

Taking this opportunity, von Lutzdorf addressed the consul. "Herr Schmalbach, due to the sensitivity of the cargo items, I will need to have twenty-four-hour security posted around the aircraft. It cannot be left to the Vichy authorities to be arranged. Can you provide some security personnel from the consulate?"

"I have already arranged for that and I have two of my best men with me who will stay with the aircraft at all times."

"Please stress on them not to refer to or address either myself or my co-pilot by our military ranks. As far as they are concerned, this is a civil flight."

"It shall be as you wish."

"In that case, as soon as the refuelling is completed, my co-pilot and I would like to be taken to a hotel."

"Tonight, you will be guests at the consulate where the ambassador shall also be staying. As you know, the embassy is in Abidjan on the coast and too long a journey by road to go there tonight. We understand why you did not wish to fly via the capital and draw too much attention to yourself but the ambassador is anxious to meet with you and catch up with some real news from Berlin, as am I."

"Thank you, Herr Schmalbach, for your help so far. It has been invaluable and, of course, I shall endeavour to bring the ambassador up to date with the latest news from Berlin." Privately, von Lutzdorf was not at all looking forward to spending an evening with German officials, pretending to be a loyal Nazi expounding on the genius of the Fuehrer and the glories of the third Reich. From his experiences on the Russian front and now the news from the Anglo-American victories in North Africa, he knew it was only a matter of time before the Reich began to crumble on all fronts.

***

The German Consulate in the town centre turned out to be a rather impressive French colonial mansion, no doubt previously the property of a wealthy French merchant, set in a garden of tropical plants and blooms all surrounded by a walled enclosure. They entered through an iron gate manned by a local police sentry and were led into a marble floored entrance foyer and through to the sitting room furnished in the French Regency style which seemed out of place here in the remoter parts of Africa.

Von Lutzdorf and Steinberg were firstly taken to their rooms where they freshened up and then returned to the sitting room where they joined the consul and his wife, a thin middle-aged waspish blonde woman overdressed with too much jewellery and makeup.

"This is my wife, Annalise," said the consul introducing his wife. "Darling, this is Oberst Walter von Lutzdorf."

"Good evening, Frau Schmalbach," said von Lutzdorf. As he took her hand and inclined his head, she smiled demurely trying to look younger than her years.

"Good evening. Welcome to Yamoussoukro. How I envy you coming straight from Berlin. I hope you have some interesting stories of the social life of the capital to entertain us with. Nothing of interest ever happens here in this godforsaken outpost of the Reich."

"Thank you, Frau Schmalbach. I will do my best, although I have only spent little time there recently myself and not had much time for socialising."

"What a pity. I suppose I shall have to listen to you men discussing boring war news all evening."

Wishing to avoid any further embarrassment, the consul broke in to change the subject. "We have received a message confirming the ambassador will be with us within the hour. In the meantime, can I offer you both a drink? You would be surprised to learn that the French here have managed to produce some very decent wines here since they first arrived in Africa."

"Good idea, Hans. Open up some of the local champagne and let's celebrate our visitors' arrival. At least it will make a break from the usual monotony."

"Thank you, Frau Schmalbach. It is most kind of you," said von Lutzdorf feeling a sudden sympathy for the woman regretting his flippant remark and realising how lonely and boring it must be for her with little or no social life to occupy her. "This is my very good friend and co-pilot, Johann Steinberg. I am sure he would also like a glass of champagne to celebrate and thank you for your hospitality."

Attuned as Johann was to his friend's feelings and personality, he followed his lead and, intent to set her at her ease, responded and took her hand in his, raised it to his lips and gently placed a kiss on it as he said, "Good evening, Frau Schmalbach. My colleague and I have had a long journey and I can think of nothing better than a glass of champagne or two to relax us and to drink to your health and kindness for your hospitality, which we did not expect to find at this remote spot in Africa."

Von Lutzdorf observed her face as his friend spoke and noticed how it changed as the lines and pursing around the lips brought on by years of bitterness of being exiled to this remote posting disappeared and were replaced with a softer gentler smile. It revealed a woman although not beautiful but who was certainly much more attractive than had first appeared.

The consul, grateful at von Lutzdorf's and Steinberg's mollifying remarks, was busy pouring champagne, a glass of which he handed to von Lutzdorf who in turn smoothly handed it on to the consul's wife while deftly picking up another for himself. When all four of them had a glass, he raised his to his hostess and said, "To your kindness and hospitality, madam," echoing his friend's earlier remark.

Responding to the toast, Frau Schmalbach said, "There you are, Hans. We are in the company of gentlemen." To von Lutzdorf, she continued. "Thank you, Oberst von Lutzdorf. Please forgive me for my earlier demeanour. It's so seldom we have the chance to entertain."

"Think nothing of it. I can well understand the privations and lack of opportunities of a place like this, especially in wartime."

"I suppose in some respects we are lucky not to be facing enemy activity and bombing, so can you tell us if this is having much effect in Berlin?"

"In Berlin, so far, the bombing has been sporadic but in the industrial cities and ports, it has been quite heavy and disruptive. I do fear, however, now with America allied with Britain, it will get much worse."

At this point, they were interrupted by the arrival of the ambassador who was shown into the room by the maid.

Unlike the consul, who was a career civil servant, the ambassador was a Nazi Party member, given the position as a reward for services to the party. The man who entered the room was of medium height with dark hair cut in a similar style to Adolf Hitler but without the moustache. He was wearing a suit with the jacket cut in a military style as affected by the Fuehrer with a gold party badge in the lapel. To the assembled party, he raised his right hand in the Nazi salute and said, "Heil Hitler!"

The consul replied in a half-hearted manner and stepped back. Neither von Lutzdorf nor Steinberg responded to the ambassador's greeting other than to say, "Good evening, Herr Ambassador."

Unperturbed by the response of von Lutzdorf, the ambassador stepped forwards and proffered his hand to him and said, "Welcome to the Ivory Coast, Oberst," using his military rank.

Von Lutzdorf shook the outstretched hand and, introducing Steinberg, he said, "Thank you. This is my colleague Hauptmann Steinberg," prefixing Johann's name with his military rank since obviously the ambassador had been informed who they were.

Belatedly remembering there was a woman present, the ambassador acknowledged her and said, "Good evening, Frau Schmalbach. I trust you are well?"

"Good evening, Ambassador. Yes, thank you," she replied in a curt manner, which was wasted on her inquirer but admired by von Lutzdorf.

The consul, a conservative man whose only ambition was to do his job and rise by gradual steps in his chosen profession without any black marks on the way to his retirement, caught his wife's tone of voice and quickly intervened by handing a glass of champagne to the ambassador, who raised his glass and said, "A toast to a safe flight and the success of your mission, von Lutzdorf."

"Thank you, Herr Schmalbach."

"I have received a message from SS Gruppenfuehrer Heinrich Mueller to give you every assistance," said the ambassador. "Now, what more can we do to assist you and what can you tell us of this mission of yours?"

"Your people have been very helpful and have done all that was needed." Deciding he needed to prick the ambassador's pompous bubble, von Lutzdorf continued. "As for the mission, I'm afraid I can tell you nothing. We are on a confidential mission for the Fuehrer, which has been organised by Goering himself and, as Luftwaffe officers, we come under his command and are sworn to secrecy."

Clearing his throat, the ambassador attempted to put on a good face at this put down to his assumption that he should be informed of the details of the mission. "Quite so, I understand. State security must be observed at all times."

Out of the corner of his eye, von Lutzdorf caught the smile of satisfaction on the face of the consul's wife and, as the ambassador turned to speak to the consul, he caught her attention and winked at her which made her smile even wider.

Having successfully pricked his bubble, von Lutzdorf decided that a little compliment for the ambassador would lighten the atmosphere as he said, "You are correct, Herr Ambassador, state security is paramount. However, we understand that there is a degree of cooperation between the Air Ministry and the SS in making certain of the arrangements for this flight and Gruppenfuehrer Mueller has given me a package for delivery to you personally, Ambassador."

At this acknowledgement of his importance and connection to the SS, the ambassador puffed himself up and preened as he said, "The Gruppenfuehrer has many contacts throughout the axis and neutral countries which depend on the close cooperation and help from those of us who serve the Reich outside the Fatherland."

"I shall be sure to mention your help to the Gruppenfuehrer when I next see him in Berlin."

Taking the initiative as the hostess, Frau Schmalbach said, "Gentlemen, I think we can all go in to dinner." She took von Lutzdorf's arm indicating that she considered him to be the most important guest and led him into the dining room.

As the hostess, she placed herself at the head of the table with von Lutzdorf on her right and the ambassador on her left with the consul next to von Lutzdorf opposite Steinberg. The Ivory Coast, a French colony, did not suffer from the shortages currently being experienced in wartime Europe. There was no lack of fresh food available or lack of wines from the local vineyards established by the settlers to ensure the same level of comforts they enjoyed at home.

For this evening, the consul's wife had obtained the services of a French-trained chef and, following the humorous exchanges between herself and von Lutzdorf, she was determined to enjoy herself and make the most of this rare social occasion.

Von Lutzdorf, aware of her change of demeanour and underlying humour, was ready to play his part.

Following their initial conversation regarding the purpose of their flight, the ambassador kept his conversation and inquiries limited to news from the home front and the personalities of the Nazi hierarchy. Proud of his gold party badge, he sought von Lutzdorf's opinion on those he boasted of knowing and of being on intimate terms with, such as von Ribbentrop, the Foreign Minister. Von Lutzdorf confessed he had not had been as fortunate as the ambassador in being invited to his house for dinner.

Frau Schmalbach, making the best of this opportunity to deflate the ambassador's boasting, raised her glass of champagne and said with the hint of a smile, "I wonder what the Foreign Minister would make of this locally produced champagne?" referring to his previous occupation as a champagne salesman.

Von Lutzdorf, picking up the baton, commented, "Unless we could take a case back with us for him, I don't think he will have much opportunity to visit the Ivory Coast to sample it. Now that most of the Vichy French territories have capitulated to the allies."

The ambassador, attempting to overcome this deflation of his position, said, "A temporary setback, surely. Once the Fuehrer has dealt with those Russians, he will turn his attention back to France and Britain which is on its knees at the moment due to our successful U-boat campaign."

Not wishing to completely destroy the ambassador's uninformed and blind acceptance of Goebbels' propaganda, von Lutzdorf, who sought to play the patriotic and loyal officer and not reveal his true anti-Nazi feelings, tempered his reply and said, "It is true we are making heroic efforts on the Eastern Front and there is news of new weapons being produced which may turn the tide."

"There, you see, the genius of the Fuehrer will see us through to ultimate victory," responded the ambassador.

This gave the consul's wife another opportunity to prick his bubble but with caution as she did not want to cause her husband a problem. "That is very reassuring, Ambassador. But at what final cost to Germany? How long will this war go on for? Now that the Americans have joined the allies, it will be an enormous task."

"The Americans are fully occupied in the Pacific fighting the Japanese and will not have enough resources or men to fight on both fronts."

"That is something that has always puzzled me, Ambassador, and I do not mean to question the tactics or strategy of our glorious Fuehrer but perhaps you can explain it to me."

"What is it that puzzles you exactly, Frau Schmalbach?"

"America was neutral when Japan attacked it, so why did the Fuehrer declare war against America and ally himself with Japan, an alien nation on the far side of the world?"

Listening to this discourse, von Lutzdorf was impressed with her knowledge and argument and how cleverly she had put the ambassador on the spot and found himself warming to her and reassessing his original opinion of her.

The ambassador was momentarily wrong-footed by this approach from a woman who had not openly criticised the Fuehrer but had asked him to explain and justify his actions with a perfectly reasonable question.

In an attempt to gain the advantage and divert the awkward question away from himself, he said, "Not being a military man myself, perhaps Oberst von Lutzdorf here can best explain the strategy of the situation."

Von Lutzdorf, now beginning to enjoy himself, responded with, "Well, Ambassador, I must say that the decision to declare war on America and ally Germany with Japan also puzzled me. But then, as a mere major, I was not privy to the thinking and intelligence available to the high command of the Wehrmacht at that time."

This response elicited a smile from the consul's wife who pushed the knife in a little further. "There you are, Ambassador, if the Oberst admits he also has no rational explanation for those decisions, it is hardly surprising that someone as uninformed as a mere woman could understand them either."

Desperate to extricate himself from this line of questioning, the ambassador said, "As you say, Oberst, none of us are privy to the reasoning behind decisions of such import but surely the Fuehrer will have taken everything into consideration and acted in the best interests of Germany."

"One can only assume that was the reason," concurred von Lutzdorf.

"Changing the subject, I understand you come from a military family of some repute, von Lutzdorf."

"Some may consider that to be so but in times of war, it is not always such an advantage and can be quite costly."

"Costly? In which way?"

"Not in money, Ambassador, but in lives."

The consul's wife, much more aware and sympathetic, understood immediately the significance of his remark and said, "I'm sorry to hear that, Oberst. There's no need to elaborate. These things can be quite painful."

Grateful for her intervention, he said, "What's done is done and I'm sure my family has suffered no more than many others due to this conflict. My grandfather, the baron, was an admiral before the first war and his son, my uncle Otto, was a destroyer captain in the Imperial Navy. He served with distinction and survived the war.

"His two sons, my cousins, both joined the navy. One was lost in the Bismarck and the other went down in command of his ship in the Norwegian campaign. My father, his second son, served in the Imperial Air Force as a fighter pilot and was a contemporary of Baron von Richthofen and Reichsmarschall Goering. He was wounded but survived and was awarded the Pour le Mérite. My brother and I naturally joined the Luftwaffe. My brother Gerhard was killed in what is now known as the Battle of Britain. I am the only surviving son, so you see what I mean when I say costly in lives."

There was silence for a moment when von Lutzdorf finished speaking and then the consul's wife said, "I am so terribly sorry you had to relive that. How dreadful for your family."

"Thank you for your sympathy, but as I said, it's over and done with and no more than many others have suffered."

The ambassador was quietly thinking, recognising that as the last surviving son, one day the von Lutzdorf before him would become Baron von Lutzdorf and that he and his family were connected with the highest in the land. This made his earlier attempts at trying to impress him with his connections to the Nazi hierarchy rather puerile.

Quickly recovering his composure and anxious to ingratiate himself to someone who may one day be an important and influential contact, he said, "My dear Oberst, please forgive me for my earlier remarks. I had no idea your family had been through so much."

"Think nothing of it, Ambassador. It's really of no importance."

"On the contrary. We cannot afford to lose men like your brother and cousins. When Germany has won the war, it will need as many men of their calibre as possible to permanently establish Germany's position as the leader of the New Order with strong military traditions at the centre of the Greater Third Reich."

Not wanting to become embroiled in a discussion with a devoted follower of the Fuehrer on his fantasies of a thousand-year Reich, von Lutzdorf commented only on his brother and cousins in his response. "You are quite right, Ambassador. The deaths of my brother and cousins were a great blow to me and my family and Germany can ill afford the loss of men like these."

The consul's wife broke in and said, "Please forgive me for asking but did either you or your cousins have any sisters?"

"I'm afraid not." Then with a smile, he added, "But I did get married recently."

"Congratulations."

"Thank you, Frau Schmalbach, but I'm not sure that getting married is the right thing to do in wartime."

"Don't worry. If she is the right person, and I'm sure she must be, that will not worry her."

"That's a great comfort to hear that from a woman's point of view."

"Hauptmann Steinberg, what about you? Are you married or engaged?"

"No, madam. So far, I've not had the desire to marry or the good fortune to meet someone as beautiful as Oberst von Lutzdorf's lady."

Not wishing to pursue this line of conversation, von Lutzdorf changed the subject by announcing the time was getting late and that they had an early departure in the morning. "It has been a most delightful evening, Frau Schmalbach. I am most grateful for your hospitality and have enjoyed our conversation very much. I look forward to continuing it when we return, if you would be so good as to invite us again."

"My dear, it is my husband and I who are grateful to you and your colleague, Hauptmann Steinberg, for making this evening a memorable one. We seldom have the opportunity to have such informed and interesting guests to dinner. You are both most welcome to stay with us again on your return. I know you cannot reveal details of your flight but I hope that it will be soon."

"Rest assured, as soon as we are able, we will inform you via the embassy of our expected date of arrival." To the ambassador, von Lutzdorf said, "Herr Ambassador, we shall keep in touch with you during our time away and will rely on you to ensure our same smooth clearance into Yamoussoukro on our return and the refuelling facilities that your staff have provided for us so far."

"Rest assured, Oberst, all our facilities and personnel are at your service."

"Thank you, Ambassador. I shall make a point in my report of commending your cooperation to my commander, Reichsmarschall Goering and to the Foreign Ministry."

"Now, perhaps, Oberst, we could have a few minutes together for a private conversation? And for me to collect the package you have for me. I am sure the consul will not mind if we use his private study."

Excusing themselves from the dinner party, they retired to the study.

"Here is the package and a separate envelope containing twenty thousand pounds in British sterling notes which I was instructed to give to you, Ambassador."

"Thank you. I am sure it will not always be necessary to use the enemy's currency in the future but, for the time being, I am told it has its uses and helps to cause an imbalance in their foreign exchange mechanism."

"So I am led to believe, Ambassador. I assume it is to you that I should give my thanks for arranging things with the Vichy commandant at the airfield?"

"Indeed so, Oberst. Even so-called collaborators have their price."

This confirmed von Lutzdorf's suspicions that the commandant had been paid off. At the same time, he wondered how much of the twenty thousand pounds would stick to the ambassador's hands.

**

The consul himself was ready the next morning before first light to take them to the airfield. They found the two security men from the consulate who reported that no one had approached the aircraft or attempted to enter it.

At that time of the morning, there were no personnel on duty at the office or tower. It had been agreed the day before that, as they were a diplomatic flight, they would depart at their own convenience and authority without the need to file a flight plan.

After a routine walk around and ground check, they thanked the consul for all his help and confirmed they would advise him via the embassy of their next ETA on their return trip.

Chapter 41

❖ `

The weather forecast for the next twenty-four hours predicted high pressure and clear skies across the part of the Atlantic near the equator.

"Looks like we'll have about a ten-hour journey, perhaps a bit less, with the prevailing easterly wind behind us, Johann."

"Should be a calm flight but perhaps a bit boring."

They had decided on the same height of twenty-five thousand feet cruising their most economical speed.

The take-off and climb to altitude was uneventful and as soon as they had levelled off on track, they could see the coastline before them and, beyond, the vast expanse of the northern part of the South Atlantic stretching for some two thousand miles to the coast of Brazil.

"Keep a good record of the strength of our tail wind, Johann. We'll have it on our nose on the return trip."

"Yes, Walter. I've made a point of studying the prevailing winds here at various altitudes throughout the year and am sure we'll be able to adjust our height on the return leg to give us the most favourable headwind. We have about one thousand miles of reserve fuel for the west to east crossing so we should be well within our safety margin."

***

At their latitude of departure this time of the year, the sun rose quickly behind them as they climbed. Their track of two hundred and forty-five degrees would cross the equator approximately halfway across the South Atlantic from the African continent to Brazil in South America when they would pass into the southern hemisphere.

By mid-morning, the sun was climbing well behind their shoulders to reach almost directly above them by midday. Steinberg assiduously took sun sights every hour keeping them on track by measuring the sun's altitude and calculating their latitude as it gradually decreased down towards zero. From the meridian sight, when the sun was directly overhead, he was able to calculate their longitude position and confirm they were exactly on track for their predicted point of landfall at the Brazilian coast.

"We've had a tail wind of thirty miles per hour for almost all of our crossing, Walter. This will reduce our total flight time to landing to just over nine hours."

"Excellent. How long to landfall?"

"Two hours should see us cross the coastline just north of Recife well south of Natal in Rio Grande do Norte province where the Americans have established an air base. Intelligence tells us the base is used only for maritime patrols and as a ferry depot for aircraft being sent to North Africa. Neither the Americans or Brazilians have coastal air defence radar so at our height, we should be unobserved. From landfall, it will take us one hour and forty minutes to landing."

"Let's hope Hauptmann Freiberg's information regarding this German immigrant's ability and willingness to help is accurate."

"The farmer in South Africa he produced for us was first class. If he's as good as him, we should have no trouble."

The coastline of Brazil came into view on the horizon and, right on time, they crossed at their predicted entry point without any indication of being detected. When they were two hundred miles inland over largely uninhabited territory, von Lutzdorf eased back the throttles and began a long slow descent towards their destination.

Steinberg had sketched a drawing of the landing site close to a bend in the Sao Francisco River, the longest and most prominent in the area, leading to the nearest city, Petrolina. On the sketch, he had marked various aids for identification from the information supplied.

At ten thousand feet and fifty miles from Petrolina, they easily identified the river and, continuing their descent, they followed the river towards the city. They soon recognised the bend in the river some thirty miles northeast of the city and further reduced their height to one thousand feet. They made one pass over the landing site before completing a wide turn and then performing another pass at five hundred feet easily identifying the approach arrow set out in white and the landing strip beyond. Off to one side of the landing strip, they could make out some buildings and signs of life.

Satisfied they had correctly identified their destination, von Lutzdorf configured the aircraft for landing and began his approach procedure and landed on an area of grass that had been cut and rolled to make a hard smooth runway. As they rolled to a stop, a small truck drove out in front of them and indicated for them to follow. It led them towards the area of farm buildings where they were able to park on a prepared hard strip.

Von Lutzdorf turned to Steinberg and said, "Well done on the navigation, Johann. How did we do on time?"

"Nine hours and ten minutes. Let's hope our host is as good as the landing strip."

Von Lutzdorf shut down the engines and turned off all the electrics. Steinberg then unlatched the entry hatch and lowered the boarding ladder.

When they had both exited the aircraft, they stood in front of the nose. A tall, slim broad-shouldered man with short hair and a neatly trimmed beard who had driven the truck approached them and, giving a pre-war air force salute, said, "Former Oberleutnant *(Lieutenant)* Eric Bachmann at your service, Oberst."

Returning the salute, von Lutzdorf said, "Thank you. My first officer and I thank you for your assistance and compliment you on the airstrip."

"It's a pleasure to be able to help. I served in the first war as an engineering officer and worked on all types of aircraft but they were nothing like this rather sleek and beautiful aircraft you have here today."

"Design and technology have developed at quite a pace since that time. My father, who flew during that war, always said every time he took off, he gave a prayer hoping it would stay together long enough to get him home safely."

"I always felt the same, whenever I was required to fly in them," said Bachmann with a laugh.

"What about the local inhabitants and authorities? Are we secure here from prying eyes?"

"No neighbours for twenty miles and haven't seen a police or militia man for months."

"Very good. When we leave, we'll climb out to the north over what looks like a mostly uninhabited area."

"Yes, there are no inhabited areas of importance for one hundred miles to the north."

"Did you manage to get the fuel we requested?"

"Yes, Oberst. Fortunately, that was all organised by the agent who first recruited me to provide this airstrip. A fuel bowser was delivered here a few days ago with fifteen thousand litres."

"Can we refuel right away so we can get an early start in the morning?"

"I will get my men to bring out the bowser from the barn and get started."

The refuelling was carried out smoothly and efficiently by two of Bachmann's workers who, he assured von Lutzdorf, were reliable and loyal German immigrants like himself. They would keep the area secure and be available for refuelling them again on their return.

When they had finished refuelling, the two men returned with what turned out to be a rolled-up camouflage net. They proceeded to drape it over the aircraft and secure it with tie downs through rings fixed in the parking area.

"Is that necessary?" asked von Lutzdorf.

"Probably not, sir, but old habits die hard. If I learnt anything from my service in the first war, it was always expect the unexpected."

"A good habit indeed," said von Lutzdorf with a laugh. "Do you ever have any military patrol flights or other air activity this far inland?"

"I've never seen one before, Oberst, and the only other aircraft I've seen is an occasional civil flight way off in the distance."

"However, as you say, beware the unexpected."

"We're finished here now, sir. Please come with me. We have quarters for you both and some good German cooking."

***

The farmhouse, set in a secluded grove surrounded by trees, had the distinct style of Bavarian architecture, which von Lutzdorf remarked on as soon as they had settled down and were seated in a spacious living room enjoying a refreshment.

"Designed and built by my grandfather. He emigrated here before the first war with his second wife who was Brazilian. My father stayed on in Germany and was killed in that war. Following the defeat and the great depression which hit Germany in the twenties, I came out here to join him."

"It seems you have made a nice life for yourself here, Bachmann."

"I like to think so, sir." Bachmann paused for a moment. "I have something to ask you and something to explain, if you will excuse me for bringing it up."

"I'm intrigued. Please go ahead."

"I do not know your politics, Oberst, but I have to confess my reason for agreeing to assist you in this matter was not for the reason of supporting the present government of Germany.

But rather because I once knew your father and served in his squadron during the first war."

"You have my full attention. Please go on."

"I soon discovered that the agent who contacted me was an ardent Nazi and I was not disposed to have any involvement in what he proposed until he happened to mention your family name. When I found out that you would be at the forefront of the mission, I agreed."

"What about my involvement made you change your mind?"

"If you will pardon me, sir, your father was a very fine man who I respected very much. He was always very decent to me and in fact tried to help me during the hard times in Germany before I left. I thought that you, his son, would be of much the same character and therefore I would do my best to help you."

Von Lutzdorf smiled. "So, what you are saying is that you are no Nazi and you want to know if I have become one. Is that correct?"

"I wouldn't have put it so bluntly, sir, but yes, that is what I'm asking."

"Put your mind at rest, Bachmann. I and all my family are no lovers of Nazism."

"That's good to know, Oberst. The agent who you will meet this evening is normally based across the border in Paraguay where the government is very pro-Nazi. I understand the Nazis have a very extensive network in South America, particularly in Paraguay and Argentina which is no doubt the reason for your flight. Not that I want to know the details. I am, like you, a patriotic German and will always do my duty but I despair sometimes when I see and hear what they have done to my country."

"I am undertaking this flight under orders as a serving Luftwaffe officer which, as you understand, I have no option but to obey. However, by being at the forefront, as you put it, gives me an insight as to the reason which will perhaps prove to be of some benefit to those of a more patriotic leaning at some future date."

"You could not have explained it to me more clearly or given me a better reason to help you in every way possible, Oberst."

"It is fortunate that our Nazi agent friend, who is no doubt under the orders of SS Gruppenfuehrer Heinrich Mueller, came to you to provide our refuelling stop. For the moment, we must continue to rely on him and his network to give us the support we need so we must treat him with courtesy and cooperation."

"Agreed. We don't have to like the man and I don't expect to see much of him after you have gone."

"What arrangement do you have with him to advise you of my next date and time of arrival?"

"He is presently in Petrolina where he has a local Nazi group who will send someone out to let me know. I'm afraid I do not have the luxury of a telephone out here in this remote part of the country. He must communicate with them from time to time by coded telegram."

"I will check that with him before we leave."

***

The agent duly arrived accompanied by a driver also of German descent who was from the local clandestine group in the city.

As Bachmann showed him into the room, he raised his arm in the Nazi salute. "Heil Hitler! Good evening, Oberst.

I am Reinhard Schneider and have the honour to represent Gruppenfuehrer Mueller here in South America. I hope everything has been organised to your satisfaction."

"Everything went strictly according to plan. Herr Bachmann has been extremely helpful," responded von Lutzdorf ignoring the Nazi greeting.

"That's good, that's very good. I hope you will inform the Gruppenfuehrer that we operate an efficient group here."

"Rest assured, my report will be very complimentary, Herr Schneider."

"I prefer the use of my honorary SS title of Hauptsturmfuehrer *(Captain)* that Gruppenfuehrer Mueller has been kind enough to bestow on me for services to the Reich. If it pleases you, Oberst."

"Of course, Hauptsturmfuehrer. It is good that those who represent the Reich in the way that you do should be so rewarded for future recognition."

"Thank you, sir. It is very good of you to say so."

Von Lutzdorf suppressed the urge to smile in response to the grin on Steinberg's face who was standing unnoticed behind Schneider.

"Oberst, I believe you have some documents for me. If you don't mind, I would like to get our business concluded as soon as possible. I have to get back to another meeting in the city this evening and then I must start back to Paraguay first thing in the morning."

"Of course, Hauptsturmfuehrer. Johann, please let me have those packages we brought in from the aircraft."

Taking the packages, von Lutzdorf and Schneider retired to a separate room arranged beforehand by Bachmann.

"Here is the package of confidential documents I was requested to hand to you and in this package, there are British sterling notes in the amount of fifty thousand pounds."

Taking the two packages, Schneider said, "Thank you, Oberst. I shall see that it is put to good use in the service of the Reich."

"In my discussions with Gruppenfuehrer Mueller, I was assured his agents would arrange for clearance through Paraguayan air space and on into Argentina. What arrangements have you made for this, Hauptsturmfuehrer?"

"That is correct, sir. You may fly through Paraguayan air space unmolested although I am sure intelligence has informed you that Paraguay has no radar facilities and certainly no aircraft capable of intercepting you. However, as a matter of political protocol, I have indeed applied for and obtained the necessary clearance for you as we need to maintain our good relations with all friendly governments. Your entry into Argentina will be as for any other international flight. You have the approach and control tower radio frequencies for Buenos Aires airport and they have your call sign and civil registration code. They have been advised to expect your arrival some time tomorrow."

"That's very efficient. Thank you."

"The party and my department under Gruppenfuehrer Mueller have worked very hard at establishing good relationships with both Paraguay and Argentina whose governments are well disposed towards Germany."

"It seems all your hard work is having the right result for us. You said you will be travelling back to Paraguay tomorrow, Hauptsturmfuehrer. How is it that you can travel so freely in

Brazil now that they have sided with the allies and declared war on Germany?"

"I emigrated to Paraguay with my parents after the first war and now have Paraguayan citizenship and can travel freely anywhere in South America, Oberst."

"I see. Well, I wish you a safe journey and thank you for your assistance."

"It was my pleasure to be of service to the Reich. Now, if we have nothing more to discuss, I will leave you. Please get the embassy in Buenos Aires to advise me of your departure date and ETA at Bachmann's farm so I can ensure you are well received again."

The information gained from Schneider made von Lutzdorf realise how deeply entrenched the Nazi Party were in South America and how powerful the Gestapo was in all its institutions in carrying out its policy.

Von Lutzdorf and Schneider returned to join the others and, after Schneider and his driver had made their farewells and left, von Lutzdorf expressed his relief at not having to spend the evening with them.

"It seems that Schneider, with Paraguayan citizenship, can come and go freely here in Brazil without fear of being harassed or charged with being an agent of Germany. But what about yourself, Bachmann? We would not want you to be in trouble on our account."

"Don't worry, sir. I have Brazilian citizenship through my grandfather and the moment you leave on your return flight to Germany, I shall plough up the airstrip ready for planting. All my workers are entirely loyal to me so it will be as though you were never here."

"I hope that you never have to face that sort of issue."

"In any case, my conscience is clear since neither of us would do anything to support the Nazi cause nor would I betray my new homeland Brazil."

Chapter 42

❖

The flight from the Bachmann farm to Buenos Aires would take them approximately eight hours so they decided on a departure time of 0600 hours to arrive in the daylight with ample time in reserve in case of any emergency.

After take-off, they proceeded in a northerly direction away from Petrolina in a steady climb for twenty miles. They then began a gradual turn to port climbing all the time until they came on to their track for Asunción, the capital of Paraguay, which they would use as a navigation check. From there, they would fly on directly to Buenos Aires airport as a normal civil flight. Their flight path after take-off took them well clear at a distance and height out of sight and sound of any observer on the ground in the vicinity of Petrolina. This was in order to reduce to the minimum any possible sighting that could be reported to the authorities.

With the autopilot switched on keeping them on track for their initial destination, von Lutzdorf and Steinberg prepared for their long flight. Ahead of them were signs of cloud forming at a lower level which gradually began to thicken obscuring their view of the ground below. From their height, as far as they could see to the horizon, the cloud layer extended at the level of about ten thousand feet like a white blanket.

"So much for map reading, Johann."

"No problem, Walter. I'm rather enjoying practising my sun sights and brushing up on my basis navigation skills. Besides, as long as we are in Brazilian air space, no one can see us and we can see any other aircraft against the white background."

"I think the chances of seeing another aircraft are quite remote but you're right. This cloud is helpful to us as long as it does not cause us a problem later."

The cloud layer continued before them as Steinberg continued taking sun sights at regular intervals and more frequently as they approached their estimated position overhead the Paraguayan capital where they were required to change track.

"You may come on to our new heading, Walter. We're just passing Asunción below now."

From Asunción, their new track was almost due south six hundred and fifty miles to Buenos Aires just skirting the frontier of Uruguay and Argentina. As soon as they crossed the border into Argentina, they were flying over the Pampas, an area of low-lying agricultural and cattle-rearing land that extended all the way to Buenos Aires.

One hour after changing track, the cloud layer started to disperse and areas of the landscape below began to appear through the broken cloud. Von Lutzdorf decided to put the aircraft into a gentle descent to a lower altitude to pick up landmarks to aid his approach to Buenos Aires airport.

Descending at five hundred feet per minute, it took forty minutes to descend to five thousand feet at which height he levelled off with two hundred miles still to go to his destination. When they were within one hundred miles, they could recognise the outline of the estuary of the river Plate.

At fifty miles, von Lutzdorf made his initial call on the airport approach frequency giving his call sign Segler One and his civil registration code D-RLM. Buenos Aires approach replied immediately directing him to proceed to a designated visual reporting point ten miles from the airport and to change to the control tower frequency.

Following procedure, von Lutzdorf called at the reporting point, requested landing instructions and was given directions to join the landing circuit and proceed to land.

After touching down, they rolled to the end of the runway where they were met by an airport vehicle which they were directed by the tower to follow to the parking area.

***

True to the assurance of Schneider, von Lutzdorf and Steinberg were efficiently dealt with when they presented their identification and aircraft registration documents. Their manifest declaration confirming the diplomatic status of the cargo also ensured a swift clearance through customs. The cargo was collected by waiting embassy staff, one of whom approached von Lutzdorf and said, "Welcome to Argentina, Oberst. I am the commercial attaché, Manfreid Stroheim, at your service."

"Thank you, Herr Stroheim. This is my colleague, Hauptmann Johann Steinberg."

"You are most welcome, Hauptmann. Now, if you are both ready, I shall take you to your hotel."

"I would, first of all, like to hand over the sealed diplomatic box of documents to the ambassador and also have the two other boxes to which I have the keys placed in a secure location in the embassy."

"We can do that on the way to the hotel if that is what you prefer, sir."

***

The drive into the centre of Buenos Aires was more impressive than von Lutzdorf expected with its wide avenues and beautiful buildings in the neoclassical style favoured by the Spanish and Italians who made up a large portion of the historic immigrant population.

At the embassy, they were ushered into the ambassador's office who greeted them briefly and excused himself to attend another meeting assuring them he would be available for a more extended meeting in the morning. Their unexpected departure from the schedule to go straight to the hotel had obviously disrupted his planned routine. Before he left, however, he confirmed that they could safely leave the documents and other cases in the safe hands of the commercial attaché.

Satisfied that he had delivered the documents as requested directly to the ambassador, von Lutzdorf acceded to Stroheim's suggestion to proceed to the hotel.

"At least we cannot complain about the accommodation," said Steinberg as they were shown into a luxurious suite with two adjoining bedrooms in one of the best hotels in the city.

"It's nothing less than we deserve, Johann, after a journey of more than eight thousand miles. I think it's time we relaxed and enjoyed ourselves for a few days," said von Lutzdorf with a smile and a sigh of satisfaction as he sat down in one of the comfortable arm chairs.

"We should drink to that, Walter," said Steinberg as he handed von Lutzdorf a glass of champagne and joined him in the other chair. "I still cannot believe how things have changed. Each time I go to bed, I think that, in the morning, I will wake up on the Russian front and it has all been a dream. Yet here we are in one of the best hotels in Buenos Aires, a place I had hardly heard of a couple of months ago, sipping champagne."

"We might as well make the most of it because if things don't improve in North Africa, I don't think we'll be able to do this again."

"In that case, we should take advantage of the most amazing menu that is available in the hotel restaurant this evening for dinner. There are some things in it that I have never heard of and that are certainly not obtainable in Germany today."

Before he left them, the commercial attaché had told them that an embassy car would collect them in the morning and until then, they were on their own. He did, however, add a note of caution saying Buenos Aires was a hot bed of espionage and to be careful of what they said and to whom they spoke especially in the hotel's public areas like the restaurant and bar.

Steinberg emptied the last of the champagne into their glasses and said, "Let's go down to dinner, Walter, and see how many Mata Haris we can spot. I wouldn't mind being seduced by a beautiful woman spy. I know you, as a newly married man, must resist that sort of temptation but I am a free man and must take advantage of every opportunity."

"I think Mata Hari was on our side in the last war, Johann, and she was shot by the French."

"In this conflict, especially here in South America with all these different loyalties, for, against or neutral, it's becoming difficult to know whose side to be on."

"We've been friends for a long time, Johann, but never expressed opinions about the Nazis except to make fun of their ardent and often comical attitudes. But a time is coming when we will need to treat the subject more seriously."

"Put your mind at rest, Walter. I know that you and your family are anti-Nazi but also intensely patriotic. I would not have remained friends with you all this time if I was not of the same mind and conviction."

"I never doubted that, Johann. It's just that what we are involved in now is a world apart from our previous service together where we just did our job and left the politics to others. We are caught up in the world of political intrigue now, whether we like it or not, and what we do can have considerable effect on the future for Germany after this war is over."

"Whatever you decide, Walter, you can count on my full support."

"I think only a fool could believe Germany could win this misconceived war, now America, with her full industrial might and her armed forces, has joined the allies. Whilst we, as serving officers, must do our duty, we must do all we can to ensure the Nazis do not completely destroy our country or have any part in its future."

Chapter 43

❖

SIS HEADQUARTERS, LONDON

Stewart Menzies, head of SIS, had summoned his most senior agent William Downdale, who headed up MI6, to a meeting in his office where they were now seated having coffee.

"Have you made any progress through the Polish connection to Canaris, William?"

"Not yet, C. But then I did not expect immediate results. Canaris is the most cautious man in the business. He only moves on his own terms which is natural enough considering what he has at stake."

"I understand. In the meantime, we've had a report in from one of our agents in Buenos Aires. Our friends von Lutzdorf and Steinberg arrived there yesterday afternoon. It's the same unmarked aircraft with the civil registration D-RLM.

"We had an earlier report from a Free French source in the Vichy-held Ivory Coast that it had landed at a place called Yamoussoukro and then left after an overnight stop. It follows that it must have stopped somewhere in Brazil to refuel which must have been clandestine. Now that Brazil has declared for the allies, they would not have sanctioned an official stop over. I think this may be an opportunity to make contact with von Lutzdorf. We have many operatives there working with British companies who continue to do business with Argentina."

"I never knew we were so involved over there, C."

"We're one of the biggest foreign investors in Argentina and own a number of Argentinian companies and land as well as much of the railroad network."

"We know that von Lutzdorf and his family are anti-Nazi, but do you think that will induce him to collaborate with us? He is still a loyal serving officer and that counts for much in his class."

"We can only make contact and leave the rest to his conscience. It's worth a try at least."

"Do we have anyone suitable in our embassy there who speaks German and is trained in this work?"

"According to his file, von Lutzdorf speaks fluent English and spent three years in England at a top public school. His class always ensured their children spoke English."

"Let's get the foreign office on to it and check through their personnel files to see who we have either in the embassy or on our list of informed employees who feed us with intelligence from time to time."

"Can I leave this to you, William? I know Europe is your particular brief but this is too important to leave to anyone unfamiliar with the whole matter."

"I'll get on to it right away, C."

Chapter 44

❖

The commercial attaché was waiting for them in the elegant columned foyer of the Savoy Hotel after they had breakfasted.

"Good morning, Oberst. I hope you are both fully refreshed after your long journey. I have a car waiting to take us to see the ambassador."

"Yes, thank you, Herr Stroheim. The hotel is very comfortable. Just as elegant as its namesake in London."

"You have experience of the famous London hotel?"

"Indeed I have. I was fortunate to stay there several times in happier days with my parents. I spent part of my education in England and also stayed there on other visits involving my pre-war flying career."

"You were indeed fortunate. Perhaps when we have won the war, you may visit it again."

"I fear that may be a long way off, but who can foretell the fortunes of war?"

"As you say, Oberst, who can tell? We must maintain our faith in the ability of the Fuehrer to lead us to victory."

Not wishing to prolong the inane dialogue with the attaché, von Lutzdorf turned to Steinberg and said, "Johann, if you are ready, let's get our business with the ambassador moving so we can return to Germany as soon as possible."

***

In contrast to their previous brief meeting, the ambassador was effusive and full of apologies for their abortive meeting of the day before.

Showing them to an area of his grand office containing chairs placed around a low coffee table, he bade them to make themselves comfortable whilst he poured them coffee himself. "One of the perquisites of the job is being able to enjoy real South American coffee as opposed to that awful ersatz coffee made from acorns one has to endure back in Germany."

"It is, as you say, one of the many shortages one has to endure."

"Oberst, I feel I must explain to you why I was tied up when you came yesterday. Germany, as you know, enjoys good relations with Argentina and it is important that we keep them in good standing. We do a lot of business with Argentina through two most important German banks and I had a long-awaited meeting booked with the heads of both banks which could not be rescheduled."

"Think nothing of it, Herr Ambassador. Our arrival could not be precisely predicted due to its unorthodox nature. The main thing is we are here now. We have delivered certain documents to you to deal with and have been instructed to await for certain measures to be taken and commercial investments to be concluded. Following which, we are to carry back with us certain confirmation documents to be held in safe keeping in Germany and presumably Switzerland.

"We are not, and will not, be privy to the contents but are charged with their safe conduct and transportation. How long, may I ask, do you expect it to take for the completion of these measures and investments?"

"As it happens, the meeting I had yesterday was important for the very same reason. I am happy to say that I think we can conclude the business within one week, or two at the most. So, please take advantage of this time to see and enjoy something of the country here. I am sure a short holiday for you both is well-deserved."

"Thank you, Herr Ambassador. A break from flying duties and planning will be most welcome."

"All the facilities of the embassy will be available to you. Just ask Herr Stroheim for what you need."

"I have left one box containing some funds and a package for the representative of Gruppenfuehrer Mueller in your keeping."

"You may safely leave that to me. I have the box here. I understand you have the key."

Von Lutzdorf, relieved to be rid of this responsibility, opened the box and gave the package of confidential documents and a separate package containing fifty thousand pound sterling to the ambassador. The box containing the balance of the money was re-locked and left at the embassy pending their departure.

"Now, gentlemen, I believe that concludes our business for the time being so the driver will take you back to your hotel or wherever else you may wish. We shall see each other again as we have several diplomatic functions during the coming week to which you will be invited."

The commercial attaché conducted them out of the embassy to the waiting car and confirmed that the driver, who spoke English, was at their disposal for whatever they wished to do during their stay. He confirmed that the embassy was responsible for all costs at the hotel and if they needed any local currency, they could sign for it at the hotel cashier's office.

As they settled themselves in the back seat, the driver turned round and introduced himself speaking in English. "Good morning, señors, I have been told that you both speak English. I am Juan Gomez and I will be your driver during your stay in Buenos Aires. I am at your service at all times, day or night."

"Thank you, Juan. Since my colleague and I do not speak Spanish we will always speak English together and you will have to translate for us from time to time."

"That will be my pleasure, señor, but you will find many people here speak English as there are many English settlers here and a large number of English companies."

"So I understand and there is also quite a large German community."

"Yes, señor, and also Italian. We are really quite international and cosmopolitan in Argentina."

Chapter 45

❖

"**D**o you realise what day it is, Johann? It's New Year's Eve. At home, it's midwinter but here we are in the southern hemisphere where it's midsummer."

"Yes, for any Europeans visiting or living in the southern hemisphere, it must be difficult to get used to Christmas and New Year without snow."

"I think we should take the opportunity to have a tour of the town."

Fortunately, the embassy driver was a former taxi driver and knew all the places of interest to visit. They passed a very pleasant afternoon sight-seeing including a stop at a popular riverside cafe where they watched the river traffic on the Plate estuary including the ferries which operated from Buenos Aires to Montevideo, the capital of Uruguay, Argentina's neighbour.

Both von Lutzdorf and Steinberg were mindful of the fact that the first naval battle of the war was fought off the mouth of the Plate estuary between a cruiser squadron of the Royal Navy and the German Kriegsmarine Heavy Cruiser, Admiral Graf Spee, which after being damaged was scuttled by her commander, Langsdorff, in the mouth of the estuary. Three days later, on a matter of honour, he committed suicide.

"That was quite a battle at the beginning of the war," said Steinberg, "I believe that the upper works and superstructure of the Admiral Graf Spee are visible at low tide."

"So I believe, Johann," said von Lutzdorf. "My uncle, Otto, knew Langsdorff from the first war. They were both in the Kiel Naval Academy at the same time. He often mentioned him and when he died, he wrote to his widow."

"I believe he's buried here in Buenos Aires."

"I think perhaps we should visit the grave and lay a wreath so we can tell my uncle and his widow when we get back home. I'm sure she would appreciate the gesture."

When they were ready to leave, they signalled to their driver who was seated at another table with some of his taxi driver friends. As they entered the car, von Lutzdorf asked the driver, "Juan, do you know where the commander of the Admiral Graf Spee is buried?"

"Oh yes, certainly, señor. Kapitän Langsdorff's funeral here in Buenos Aires was a very big event. Many people attended it. We all listened to the news following the battle every day right up until the end. You know that he and all of his crew came here from the ship after it was blown up and scuttled."

"We would like to visit the grave site. Can you drive us there tomorrow morning?"

"Of course, señor. As I said, I am at your disposal at any time. What time would you like to go to the cemetery?"

"Directly after breakfast but we would like to arrange a wreath or some flowers. Do you know a good florist where we could order something today and pick up on the way in the morning?"

"Yes, señor. The embassy has an account at one of the best florists in the city. We can go there on the way back to your hotel."

"Excellent. Let's do that now, Johann, and then we're free for the rest of the evening."

"The thing is, Walter, we're free all of the time while we wait for the ambassador and Mueller's man to give us the documents we are to take back with us to Germany. We can only spend so much time sight-seeing and I'm not used to just sitting around not doing anything. Perhaps we could meet up with some of the crew of the Graf Spee or other German organisations here in the city to help pass the time."

"Good idea, Johann. We must speak to the commercial attaché, Stroheim, and see what he can suggest."

"Here we are, señor," said the driver as he stopped outside a large double-fronted shop on one of the fashionable avenues in the town centre. Outside of the shop, on the wide pavement, was a display of flowers of many colours and other exotic plants.

"This looks promising, Johann. We should find something suitable here."

"I assure you, señor," broke in the driver, "They will make anything that you wish. They specialise in all sorts of floral displays and products."

"Sounds like you have done business with them before, Juan."

"As a former taxi driver, señor, it was my job to know where to take clients, especially foreign visitors."

They entered the shop with Juan in the lead who introduced them to the manager, who was obviously well-acquainted with him. As they shook hands, Juan spoke to him in Spanish while the manager smiled and nodded his head.

"I have explained to the manager who you are and what you need and that everything should be charged to the embassy's account. He assures me your order will be ready tomorrow morning whenever you wish to collect."

"Thank you, Juan. Please take us to our hotel and we will see you in the morning."

***

When they had returned to their suite, von Lutzdorf called the embassy and asked to be put through to the commercial attaché.

"Good afternoon, Oberst. I trust everything is all right. What can I do for you?"

"Yes, thank you, Herr Stroheim. We have passed a perfectly pleasant afternoon. We would like to go to visit the grave of Kapitän Langsdorff tomorrow and we took the liberty today of ordering a wreath on your account with the help of your driver Juan."

"That's perfectly in order, Oberst. Juan is a very enterprising and competent employee. I am sure he can find you anything you may need in Buenos Aires," he added with a chuckle.

"We have arranged for him to pick us up tomorrow and take us to the cemetery."

"He is assigned to you for the duration of your stay so he will follow your orders. In the meantime, you are invited to a social function here at the embassy tomorrow at 6 p.m. It is just one of many such functions which the diplomatic fraternity put on and have to endure. They are useful, however, because it gives all of the legations here an opportunity to invite each other and local dignitaries to speak off the record about the war situation and occasionally gain a useful piece of intelligence. You will, no doubt, be a topic of interest so please be careful to whom you speak and what you say as there will be personnel from many of the various legations friendly to us as well as neutrals. Some of whom have contacts with the allies."

"Have no fear, Herr Stroheim. We have been well-briefed and, as serving officers, we know our duty."

"Quite so. I hope you're not offended at my mentioning it."

"Not at all. You have your duty just as we have ours. What is the dress code for such a function? Will it be in order to wear our uniforms? I'm afraid we do not have an extensive wardrobe for social occasions."

"An important consideration. Although I'm sure most of the legations and dignitaries will be aware of your aircraft arriving, we must not unnecessarily advertise your military standing as the aircraft has a civil registration identity. Tomorrow, you will be taken by Juan to a good firm of tailors to provide you both with suitable attire. I shall instruct him to take you directly after you have visited the cemetery."

Chapter 46

❖

As arranged, Juan was waiting for them at ten o'clock the next morning as they emerged from the hotel.

"Buenos dias, señors," said Juan as he opened the door for them.

"Good morning, Juan. First, the florist and then the cemetery. Is it far?"

"No, señors. La Chacarita Cemetery is in the centre of the city just a few minutes' drive from the hotel and the florist is on the way."

"Has Herr Stroheim instructed you to take us on a shopping trip after we are finished there?"

"Yes, señor. All is in hand."

***

They collected an impressive wreath to which was attached an equally impressive gold bordered card on which the names of von Lutzdorf and Steinberg had been written in a classic script expressing their condolences on this occasion and giving the date.

"This is rather impressive, Juan. I didn't expect something so grand."

"I took the liberty, señor, of telling the florist on your behalf not to worry about the cost. The embassy can afford it and it is not often that someone so distinguished as yourself comes all the way from Germany to lay a wreath on the Kapitän's grave. Is it, señor?" said Juan with a smile.

"If you put it like that, I suppose you are right, Juan."

As Juan took charge of the wreath and carried it out to the car, von Lutzdorf smiled and turned to Steinberg who was also smiling and said, "I don't suppose it hurts the size of his commission either."

"I imagine the tailor where he will take us will be told the same thing as the florist," said Steinberg with a laugh.

"No doubt at all, Johann."

As Juan had said, within a few minutes of leaving the florist, they found themselves entering the La Chacarita Cemetery and driving along between rows of impressive mausoleums decorated with angels and other religious icons.

"This is enormous, Juan. Are you sure you know how to find the grave?"

"Yes, señor. It is nearly one hundred hectares but do not worry, the Kapitän is buried in the German section and it is easy to find. I have taken other Germans there before, when I was a taxi driver."

They drove on through a bewildering display of mausoleums and grand buildings and occasionally open spaces of more modest gravestones until they entered a section amongst some trees and laid out to gardens.

"This is now the German and British section of the cemetery," said Juan, as he drove through a neat garden area and stopped in front of Kapitän zur See Hans Langsdorff's gravestone. The headstone was in the form of a cross set above a stone plinth in a small grassed area with a backdrop of shrubs and trees. Von Lutzdorf and Steinberg carried the wreath between them and placed it at the base of the stone plinth then, standing to attention, they both saluted in the pre-war military fashion.

After standing for a full minute to honour a fellow warrior who had taken the honourable way out for the sake of his crew, they stepped back, turned and walked back to the waiting car.

As Juan drove them from the cemetery, they were both quiet in keeping with the solemn occasion until Steinberg broke the silence and said, "Do you remember seeing the newsreels at the time? It was very well attended."

"Yes, I think perhaps he was one of the luckier ones. At that time, there was still some honour in this war. At least he did not live long enough to see the way this war has turned out with the needless slaughter of so many young men, women and children on both sides all to feed the twisted ambition of a madman."

Steinberg did not respond right away to his friend's obviously deeply felt feelings which he understood and totally agreed with. Due to their long intimate friendship, they had already expressed their anti-Nazi feelings and confirmed their loyalty to each other.

"Like it or not, Walter, we are involved in supporting this madman albeit in a different manner."

"Yes, Johann, you're right and we must think how we can do something about it but that is not for today. Let's go and spend some more of the embassy's money and at least enjoy our time here before we return to our homeland and loved ones."

"Here we are, señor," said Juan. "This is one of the best gentlemen's clothing stores in Buenos Aires."

"The manager is no doubt your uncle or cousin, Juan?"

"My wife's second cousin, señor, but I am sure he will still be very helpful to you. He has a good eye for fashion and will be able to advise you what will be suitable for the occasion. I took the liberty of speaking to him and explaining what you required."

"That was very thoughtful and helpful of you, Juan," said von Lutzdorf with a smile.

"I'm just following orders, señor, to be of service to you while you are here."

"We are most grateful, Juan."

Throughout the exchange, Steinberg contrived a deadpan look to avoid laughing whilst Juan maintained his look of total innocence.

The manager greeted them effusively as special customers with only a casual acknowledgement of Juan. He then, with the help of two assistants, proceeded to produce an extensive range of suits and accessories with the flare of a fashion expert designed to convince the customer they could not possibly leave the store without at least two suits apiece with all of the accessories, including matching shoes.

Von Lutzdorf noticed that all the time Juan sat in the background, he exchanged an occasional smile with the manager each time he concluded a sale, no doubt mentally adding up his commission.

Von Lutzdorf and Steinberg, who both liked Juan, saw no reason to deny him his commission, played the game and accepted the manager's choice of suits and extensive list of accessories.

"Gentlemen, as you see, we have taken your measurements and the suits require some little alterations here and there to fit perfectly. These will be done today and everything will be delivered to your hotel in time for your evening function."

"Thank you," said von Lutzdorf, "It has been a most interesting and almost unreal experience as it has been a long time since we have visited a tailor for civilian clothes having spent most of our time in uniform."

"Let us hope, gentlemen, that this war will soon end and that when peace time comes, you will still have these excellent quality clothes to enjoy and remember your time here in Argentina with pleasure."

"That is certainly something worth hoping for and thank you for your advice and courtesy. Juan, can you please now drive us back to the hotel?"

***

As promised, the clothes arrived on time and all neatly packed and labelled.

"Let's see, Johann. I bought a light grey and a dark blue suit and you bought a dark grey with a light stripe and pale blue suit. I suggest we wear opposite colours this evening. We don't want to look like a double act."

"Good idea, Walter."

Dressed in their new unaccustomed clothes and feeling somewhat self-conscious, they decided to have a drink in the hotel bar before leaving for the embassy.

Just as they prepared to leave their suite, the telephone rang which von Lutzdorf picked up and answered to find the commercial attaché Herr Stroheim on the other end.

"Good evening, Oberst. I'm glad I caught you before you left for the embassy. I hope I'm not disturbing you."

"Not at all, Herr Stroheim. Steinberg and I were just going to the bar before leaving."

"Do you mind if I join you there? I would like to have a word with you before you come to the reception."

"We shall look forward to seeing you."

Putting down the phone, he said to Steinberg, "That was Stroheim. He wants a word with us before we mingle with the other guests. A matter of protocol, no doubt. He'll meet us in the bar."

***

They had just given their order to the waiter when Stroheim appeared at the entrance and, having espied them, he made his way over to them speaking to the waiter on the way.

"Have a seat, Herr Stroheim. Can I order you a drink?"

"Thank you, but I ordered something from the waiter as I came in. Oberst, I just wanted to give you a brief on what to expect at the reception and who will be there. I also just wanted to reiterate my previous warning about what you should say when asked about being in Buenos Aires. The ambassador and I were discussing your presence here and felt you should have some sort of innocent explanation for it."

"Never fear, Stroheim. We will not be giving away any state secrets and already have our story straight."

"Forgive me, but you know how we diplomats worry about saying the right thing to the right people. There will be a number of representatives from the other legations but only from those who are either neutral or friendly to us. Obviously, there will be nobody from either the British or American Embassies. There will be, however, a number of prominent members of the Argentinian government and also some of the more important businessmen and members of the financial institutions. Remember that Buenos Aires is a hot bed of political intrigue."

"Herr Stroheim, we will keep our conversation purely limited to flying and how we are seconded to the Air Ministry seeking out new possible civil routes for Lufthansa or the new range of long-distance civil airliners under development. What can be simpler and more innocent than that?"

"Excellent. However, be on guard for questions from some quarters which may appear innocent. Some diplomats are noted for their devious ways of asking seemingly innocent questions."

"Your advice is well taken and understood. Please relax and enjoy your drink."

Herr Stroheim did as he was bid and relaxed with his drink and smiled as he said, "Let me compliment you both on your choice of tailor."

"Thank you, Herr Stroheim. We had a great deal of help and advice."

"Obviously good advice. Most suitable for the occasion."

"I hope the ambassador thinks so when he gets the bill," said von Lutzdorf with a laugh which was echoed by Steinberg.

As they finished their drinks, Stroheim looked at his watch and said, "Time to leave, I think. We can go together. I have a car waiting outside."

***

Guests were already arriving as they approached the embassy and they had to take their turn in a queue of limousines flying the different flags of their various nations.

The embassy was an imposing building built in the classical style as a residence for an obviously wealthy owner during the previous century. After passing through the entrance foyer, they entered a large hall with a curving staircase leading up to an imposing balcony which ran completely around the hall from which corridors ran off to the different parts of the second floor. Leading off from the hall at the ground floor were two large reception rooms each with large double doors which had been opened and folded back to provide an unobstructed access throughout the area allowing guests to mingle freely with one another.

The ambassador was standing to one side of the entrance to the hall with several staff greeting guests as they arrived. He quickly passed them on to his staff to lead them into the wider reception area, ensuring they were served immediately by a number of waiters balancing trays covered with glasses of champagne.

Completing the greeting formalities, Stroheim escorted them through to the centre of the hall nodding and exchanging greetings with others as he passed. He said to von Lutzdorf, "I will leave you here to mingle for a while but I will be back and introduce you to some of the more interesting guests shortly."

"Please don't worry about us. Go and attend to your duties," said von Lutzdorf. As Stroheim left, von Lutzdorf whispered to Steinberg, "What he means, Johann, is he will find some bores to keep us occupied so that we don't get into trouble."

"I don't know about you, Walter, but I have already noticed one or two attractive ladies I would rather talk to."

As more guests kept arriving, the background noise increased with a mixture of different languages. Since they did not speak Spanish, they concentrated on picking out snatches of English as being more likely to be interesting.

Von Lutzdorf suddenly felt the presence of someone close to his side and, turning in that direction, he came face to face with a very attractive tall blonde woman in her late twenties, bare-shouldered and wearing an elegant black cocktail dress who addressed him in English. "It is Herr von Lutzdorf or Captain, is it not? Or how else should one address you?"

"Von Lutzdorf is fine. To whom do I have the pleasure of speaking?"

"My name is Maria Olavsonn and I am secretary to the Swedish ambassador."

"I am very pleased to make your acquaintance, Maria. Forgive me for asking but how did you know my name and that I spoke English?"

"The secrets and intrigues of the diplomatic scene are full of mysteries," she replied with a laugh and a dazzling smile.

"I take it that I am now to rack my brain to try to remember when and where we met before?"

"Nothing quite so difficult or mysterious. I am with the air attaché from my embassy. It was he who recognised you and it was I who volunteered to come over and speak to you as he was tied up with someone else for the moment." As she explained, she looked over across the room to where a group of three men were talking and caught the eye of one of them who smiled and nodded in their direction. Von Lutzdorf had a vague feeling he recognised him from somewhere in the past.

"Lars said he met you some years ago before the war in England."

"That must be it. He is vaguely familiar but I cannot recall the occasion for the moment."

"Don't worry. I'm sure it will come to you but, in any case, Lars will join us shortly when he can make his excuses and come over."

Von Lutzdorf turned to introduce Johann only to find he had drifted off in the direction of another attractive woman who appeared to be on her own.

"If you're looking for your colleague, I see he has an eye for the ladies. He is quite safe. He is talking to Anna, a friend of mine. She is a secretary at the embassy with me."

Just then, they saw the air attaché had left the group and was making his way towards them. As he approached, von Lutzdorf could see he was about the same height and build as himself with dark blonde hair and blue eyes with strong Nordic features.

"Von Lutzdorf, this is my colleague, Lars Erikson."

"Good evening," said von Lutzdorf, "Both of you, please call me Walter."

"Good evening, Walter. Please call me Lars."

"Now, Lars, please remind me, where did we meet before? Maria told me we met once in London and although you are extremely familiar, I cannot place where it was."

"It was five years ago at the Royal Aero Club of Great Britain on Piccadilly on the occasion of you being presented with a certificate for one of your pre-war pioneering flights. I was one of many guests so I am not surprised you cannot remember. We only spoke for a few minutes but I recognised you when you came in."

"Yes, of course. Please forgive me for not recalling you right away. As you say, there were many guests there that day."

"Is it indiscreet of me to ask what you are doing here in Argentina so far away from Europe?"

"Not at all. I'm still flying and, as you know, I am a serving officer but it is no secret that I am on secondment to the Air Ministry looking at potential civil routes for commercial flights on behalf of Lufthansa. These should become possible with the new long-range civil airliners being developed in Germany."

"Very interesting. When do you think these will be in operation?"

"Forgive me, Lars, I'm only the pilot. I do not know the politics or reasons behind the plan. For me and my colleague, it was a welcome turn of events to get away from combat flying and back into a semblance of normality away from the wartime exigencies, especially since my recent marriage."

Lars was pleased that it was von Lutzdorf who had brought up the subject of his recent marriage, providing him with an opening. "Yes, congratulations. I do believe I read something about that in some news release we occasionally get through the international press. If I recall, your wife is Swedish, is she not?"

"Yes. In fact, she is the daughter of one of the sisters of Goering's first wife, Carin, who, as you know, was Swedish."

"Was she indeed? How very interesting. So, we have a Swedish connection?"

In fact, Erikson knew all about Magda and her connection to Goering having been fully briefed by Swedish intelligence who cooperated covertly with British intelligence and MI6 on many matters.

"Yes, it would appear so."

"How long do you think you will be staying in Buenos Aires, Walter? It would be nice if we could all get together over lunch one day to talk about better things and hopefully better days to come," said Maria breaking into the conversation on cue from Lars.

"That would be very nice and a welcome break from sight-seeing. Johann and I have little to do until we are ready to leave. Since we're already here, we've been requested by our foreign ministry to courier some diplomatic papers back with us so we must wait until ordered which we have been told will be a week or two."

"That's fine. That will give us time to arrange something. There are many fine restaurants and venues here in Buenos Aires and no wartime shortages as in Europe."

Suddenly, Stroheim appeared with an anxious look on his face. "Sorry I had to leave you, von Lutzdorf. How are you all getting on with our Swedish friends?"

"We're getting on very well, Stroheim. We're discussing our Swedish connection," said von Lutzdorf knowing it would make him more anxious.

"What connection is that?" said Stroheim with a worried look on his face.

"Why, my Swedish wife and her relationship to Goering who also had a Swedish wife, of course. What other connection could there be?"

"Quite, quite, as you say, a very interesting connection and parallel."

"Oh, I wouldn't say parallel. I don't put myself on the same plane as our illustrious deputy Fuehrer. Other than a Swedish wife, I don't think we have much in common," said von Lutzdorf with the hint of loathing in his voice and a smirk on his face unnoticed by Stroheim but noted by Lars and Maria.

"Perhaps not. So, if you will excuse me again, I must make my rounds and chat to other guests."

"Please, carry on. We are having an interesting time catching up."

As Stroheim left, Maria remarked, "He looks a worried man but then, was I mistaken or were you teasing him a little?"

Von Lutzdorf laughed. "Some people are easy to tease, especially those who have little or no minds of their own and have closed their eyes and minds to reality."

Erikson picked up the conversation and taking a chance he said, "Do I take it from your remarks that you have some misgivings concerning the possible outcome of the war and the conduct of your government?"

Von Lutzdorf looked straight at Erikson for a few moments without speaking and then with steady eye contact he said, "Lars, make no mistake. I am a patriotic German as are all my family but that does not mean that I or them agree with the policies and conduct of the current government. I don't think I can put it clearer than that."

Returning his steady gaze, Erikson replied, "That is very clear and understood. Now, I see that our glasses are empty. Shall we join your friend and Anna, refill our glasses and talk of more pleasant things?"

"I think that would be an excellent idea. I don't want my friend Johann thinking he has been abandoned and left out in the cold."

"He seems very happy and not in the least bit abandoned chatting with Anna," said Maria as they moved through the throng to the corner where Steinberg and Anna were having a very animated conversation.

Maria made the introductions as they collected fresh glasses of champagne from a passing waiter.

"How long do these functions usually go on for?" asked von Lutzdorf.

"Two to three hours. Mostly everyone is gone by nine o'clock on to dinner somewhere," said Maria.

"What a good idea. Why don't you all join Johann and me for dinner at our hotel? The menu at the Savoy is quite exceptional."

Quick to take the opportunity of continuing the conversation with von Lutzdorf, Erikson agreed and Anna prodded by Maria also quickly accepted.

"That's splendid," said von Lutzdorf, "This is turning out to be a most enjoyable evening."

By eight thirty, the throng was beginning to thin out as people began to leave and as was usual for ladies, they tended to gravitate to the women's restrooms to refresh their makeup and hair so Maria and Anna excused themselves and left the group.

Once inside, Anna said, "You didn't need to prod me, although I don't usually have much time for Germans, Johann is very nice and I would have accepted the invitation to dinner."

"I just wanted to make sure, that's all. You're right, Johann is very nice and I can reassure you that he and Walter are no Nazis."

"So, what are you and Lars up to cultivating these two German glamour boys?"

"Never you mind. We're just doing a favour for someone in London."

"Be careful. You know what happened to Mata Hari."

"It's nothing like that. Just making a connection, that's all."

When Maria and Anna returned and they moved towards the exit, von Lutzdorf said, "We don't have our designated driver with us tonight. If you have cars, can we join you?"

Erikson spoke up right away and said, "Maria, why don't you take Johann and go with Anna in her car? I will take Walter."

Taking the hint, Maria took Johann's arm and guided him towards where Anna's car and driver were waiting. "We will see you at the Savoy," she said as von Lutzdorf followed Erikson to his awaiting car.

Von Lutzdorf got in first as Erikson gave instructions to his driver to take them to the Savoy Hotel and, as he got in, he closed the partition between the driver and the passenger seats.

"Why do I get the feeling that you want to speak to me privately about something, Lars?"

"Am I that obvious, Walter? My diplomatic skills must be failing."

"Not in the least, Lars. I think you are very adept at getting your meaning across."

"I do want to speak to you about something confidential but I do not want to offend you at the same time."

"We are in a neutral country, so please say what you want to say and let me be the judge of whether or not to take offence."

"Sweden, as you know, is also neutral but we are stuck in the middle of the warring nations and although we owe no allegiance to either the allies or the axis, we have our opinions and preferences. As a peace-loving nation, I am sure it would hardly be a surprise to you to realise with whom our sympathies lie."

"Very diplomatically put, Lars. Please get to the point."

"Very well. I have a friend in London who has taken a very great interest in your activities and he has asked me, diplomatically of course, to make contact with you. He says if at any time you felt that, for the greater good of Germany, you had some information you would like to pass on then you have the means to do so through me. I must stress that I know nothing and am merely acting as a conduit."

"What makes you think that I would even contemplate passing confidential information to the enemy?"

"At the risk once more of offending you, it is known by those in London that your family, meaning your father and his brother, the baron, are not members of the Nazi Party and have been critical of their policies before the war broke out, especially their anti-Jewish laws. You yourself spent part of your education in England and have some affection for it and its people."

"It is true what you say, Lars, so don't worry, I am not offended. At times like these, it is important that unofficial connections are established. I think you are aware that as a patriot, I could never do anything that could cause hurt or danger to the German people but the Nazis are a different matter."

"Thank you, Walter. You cannot imagine how tense I have been ever since being asked to speak to you. I'm very glad that it is over and we can hopefully help each other. Before we get to the hotel, is there anything you have that you can tell me now?"

"I'm afraid not. I know nothing of what I am being asked to courier other than it is important to the Nazi Party. All documents that I brought with me were securely sealed and I understand that those I am to take back to Germany will be the same. However, there is something that I would like to be clear and understood by your friend in London and why I am prepared to help if I can."

"I understand that what I am asking is not easy for you as you must have conflicting loyalties."

"My only loyalty is to Germany itself and, of course, to my family. The last time I was at home with my father and uncle, we discussed this very subject and something that my father said to me has become the deciding factor in any action I may take to assist your friend. He quoted me a saying which he was not sure of its origin but it is more relevant today than when it was originally stated. He said, 'For evil to succeed all that is required is for good men to do nothing.' This is exactly the reason Germany is in the dreadful state it is in today.

"There are a great number of good men in Germany, many of them responsible for doing nothing and allowing a great evil force take control of their country. I am not exactly sure of what it is that the Nazis are planning in South America. But, from what I have learnt from my talks with Goering and Gestapo Mueller, I believe they are planning to build up a strong Nazi base with large financial resources here. If they have a certain amount of support, they would be able to launch a bid to build a Fourth Reich if they lose the current war."

"That is indeed a frightening prospect, Walter."

"The Nazis started this war in the belief that they could win by force of arms on the battlefield as they had built up a formidable army and air force and were building a navy to oppose the might of the Royal Navy. However, they overlooked one thing, a lesson they should have learnt from the first war. They underestimated the economic strength of the British Empire and its influence around the world.

"Wars cost money and need a constant supply of raw materials. They thought they could starve England into submission by using U-boats to cut off supplies of food and fuel but two can play at that game. The Royal Navy's huge surface fleet has effectively cut off the supply of desperately needed raw materials and, more importantly, rare minerals and industrial diamonds. On top of that, England, through its department of economic warfare, has denied Germany access to international credit and funds to purchase these desperately needed materials.

"True, Germany has plundered the occupied countries but the tide is turning. It is only a matter of months before we are thrown out of North Africa and with the Russian Bear getting stronger every day, we will soon be on the defensive all along the Eastern Front. Now that America is in the war, those of any intelligence can see the writing on the wall that it is only a matter of time before Germany's total collapse and defeat."

"I will pass on your thoughts and opinions. Is there anything else you would like to say?"

"You must tell your friend that he will have to trust me for the time being. I will find a way to discover what is in the documents and at least I will keep them secure until then. There is no point just destroying the documents as there will be copies of everything at the embassy here and your friend needs to know what they contain so they can destroy whatever it is that the Nazis hope to achieve.

"What is needed is that your friend gets them, unknown to the Nazis. There will be no chance of breaking the seals and photocopying them as they will be delivered to the aircraft under guard just before we leave. Even if we could, it might be detected and lead to the Nazis changing their plans. I will have to contrive an accident of some sort to cause them to be lost or destroyed in such a way that it will not cause suspicion."

"Very well. Now, let's leave it at that and enjoy the rest of the evening."

"One more thing you can do for me before I leave. Speak to your friend and get me a radio frequency on which we can communicate with a call sign. We can use the book cypher method to encode messages so you will have to provide a suitable book for this. Make sure you get two books, one for each of us from the same edition. I may need to get in touch with him if something happens on my flight back to Germany."

"I will speak to my contact in the British Embassy here tomorrow and get that organised for you."

"One last thing. Any contact will be strictly through me and one designated contact at their end. This arrangement will be known to only us and the head man who I take it is your friend in London. I will not risk any of this getting out and putting my family in any danger."

"Of course, Walter. I will make that condition absolutely clear."

"Good. Here we are at the hotel, so let's enjoy dinner on the embassy."

Chapter 47

❖

SIS HEADQUARTERS, LONDON

"Good news, William," said Stewart Menzies, speaking on the telephone to his agent William Downdale. "Our man in Argentina has made contact. Come to my office right away and we will go through the arrangements we must put in place."

"I'll be with you straight away, C," said Downdale using the internal code for the chief.

Within a few minutes, there was a tap on the door and Downdale came in with a beaming smile on his face. "Good news indeed and good work by our man there. How did he achieve it?"

"I fortunately had a good contact at the Swedish Embassy who I had met in London before the war. He's done little favours for us in the past which we have been able to reciprocate. I gave his name to our man at the embassy and told him to remember me to him and to ask him to do us another little favour. I left the rest to him. Our man learnt that von Lutzdorf would be at a cocktail party at the German Embassy to which the diplomatic fraternity are always invited, apart from us and the Americans, of course. The little favour was for my Swedish friend to make an approach. As it turned out, von Lutzdorf was very receptive and agreed to help us, with certain conditions, of course."

"Naturally. He is in a very sensitive position."

"He will only deal with one designated contact and the arrangement will be known only to me and that contact which I would like to be you."

"That's fine. I will be pleased to handle it personally."

"One more thing. He has requested a radio frequency and call sign on which to communicate in case of emergency and a book for encoding any messages. Make sure that our man at the embassy provides him with one from the same edition we will use. We do not want any errors caused by differences in the narrative."

"I shall make sure that nothing is overlooked and I think we should provide him with several different frequencies to ensure he can always make contact under differing atmospheric conditions and times."

"Yes, of course. I will leave that all to you. It appears von Lutzdorf had already been giving this matter a great deal of thought even before the approach was made which probably accounts for his receptive attitude.

"He made the point that it was of no use just preventing the documents getting back to Germany and there was no benefit in us getting copies if the Germans knew about it as they would just change their plans. We need somehow to get these documents without them knowing we have them. The last thing he said was that we must trust him to get them to us with the Germans believing them to have been irretrievably lost or destroyed en route."

"I think von Lutzdorf has already shown us that he is a very capable person and an ardent anti-Nazi. I believe we can safely leave it to him to come up with a plan to secure the documents for us. After all, there's no great hurry at the moment. The main object is to ensure they remain intact and available to us when the time comes."

"Agreed. And with that in mind, we must make sure he is not intercepted and shot down on his return flight. Perhaps we should speak to our cousins at OSS and also have a word with the FBI. They have a big presence in South America especially in Argentina who are sympathetic to the Nazis. Can we get an idea of his planned route back? That way we can alert the Americans, who have a base at Natal in Brazil, not to try to intercept him."

"I've had an aviation expert looking into the technical aspects of the Heinkel 111 and the possible modifications they could have applied to it to increase its performance and range. He's quite sure that the maximum range they could obtain would be perhaps three thousand two hundred miles and a speed up to three hundred and fifty miles per hour. That means they would have had to have staged from somewhere in the Vichy-controlled Ivory Coast to some clandestine airfield in Brazil crossing the coast near Recife."

"On second thoughts," said the director, "I don't know if we should inform the OSS and FBI as we do not want any leaks concerning our interest in this flight to get back to Germany, especially since we have given our assurance to von Lutzdorf about secrecy."

"Perhaps you're right, C," said Downdale. "Von Lutzdorf seems very capable and managed the flight to Buenos Aires without being detected or intercepted."

"His only chance of being intercepted would be from an aircraft from the American ferry airfield at Natal. Check with the RAF and see what aircraft the Americans have which would be capable of intercepting the Heinkel at thirty thousand feet doing three hundred plus miles per hour and whether or not they have any GCI radar there."

"I'll get on to it right away. If their information is that they would have no chance of a successful interception, I think we should leave von Lutzdorf to his own resources and abilities. He would know about the American base at Natal and keep well clear of it."

"Whatever the situation, we must get our Swedish contact to speak to him again when we get the information back from the RAF and let him make his own decision."

Chapter 48

❖

Von Lutzdorf and Steinberg were sitting in the hotel dining room having breakfast the day following the embassy reception.

"That turned out to be a very interesting evening, Walter, especially the way Maria cornered you and then how she and Lars manipulated our transport back to the hotel. Are you going to tell me what Lars said to you during your car journey?"

"Of course, Johann, we have no secrets. When it comes to espionage, you and I are just naive babes in the woods. Stroheim was right. Buenos Aires is a hot bed of political intrigue."

"So, what have we got ourselves into and what did he say?"

"You have to hand it to the British. Their intelligence network is extremely subtle and efficient and, of course, very extensive throughout the world, far more so than ours. The result of several hundred years of the Empire and its influence."

"I appreciate the history lesson and the comparison of our respective intelligence organisations, Walter, but what did you learn from Erikson?"

"He's working for British Intelligence albeit in a clandestine manner but with them nevertheless."

"Makes you wonder who you can trust these days, doesn't it?" said Steinberg with a wry smile.

"He's offered his services as a conduit to the British if we feel so inclined. Apparently, the British have been taking a great interest in us and seem to know very much about us but not what we're actually up to. They know we have a connection to Goering and the Nazi Party and also Gestapo Mueller and would dearly like to know the details."

"Is that all? What did you say to him?"

"I said we would think about it."

"We?"

"We have both declared to each other that we are not Nazis nor do we support their policies so we must decide together on any future actions we may take."

"You're my superior officer and I owe my position to you. You have my one hundred percent support on whatever you decide to do."

"Rank doesn't come into it, Johann. Whatever we decide, we do it as friends and comrades."

"Then as your friend and comrade, you have my full support and agreement on what you decide. This is not open for debate."

"Very well, my friend. I've decided that we must make sure all the documentation we are tasked with getting back to Germany somehow gets into the hands of the British without the Nazis knowing about it."

"That shouldn't be difficult. We can make copies and pass them on through Erikson."

"I already thought of that, but it's a question of opportunity and being able to make undetected copies. You forget that the documents will be delivered to the plane just before take-off in sealed packages inside locked steel-bound boxes. Even if we could find a way to copy them en route, it may be difficult to disguise tampering with the seals. In which case, if this was detected, the Nazis may change their plans and whatever we are able to pass on will become useless. To say nothing of the consequences to us and our families."

"I take your point, Walter. We'll have to find another way."

"I've given this whole matter a considerable amount of thought and whilst I have no compunction against ensuring the documents end up in the hands of the British, it has occurred to me from the information I had from Goering that they would become important for the survival of the Nazis in the event that Germany was defeated. Therefore, I see no great urgency in getting them to the British until that time.

"We are both anti-Nazi but we are both still serving officers and patriots. Because of this, it goes against the grain somewhat to hand over material to the enemy whilst we are still in conflict as, whatever the circumstances, it is still an act of treason. It would ease my conscience if we can avoid that especially since I have persuaded you to follow my lead."

"Have no fear about that, Walter. I'm completely of the same opinion and agree with your reasoning and, I'm sure, with your eventual solution."

"We must somehow contrive a situation that makes it impossible to complete our return flight all the way back to Germany and make it necessary to conceal the material somewhere safe so that it can be recovered by either party when convenient at the war's end, whoever wins. That way both sides will be satisfied and our position will be secure. We will be blameless."

"That would work. We could fake engine trouble and report that back to base. I would still like to get back home though. How do you propose we manage that?"

"We could leave the aircraft at TBS1 and take one of the trucks and make for Tunisia to join up with the Afrika Korps. From there, we could fly to Italy and back to Berlin."

"Why would we not be expected to take the documents with us in the truck?"

"I'm sure Goering and Mueller will agree that, under the present circumstances in Libya, which may be worse by the time we get there, we could be in danger of being captured by British or American forces and the documents falling into their hands."

"Yes, there is that risk. Better to conceal them with the other material."

"I'll arrange to meet with Erikson to discuss the plan and for him to liaise with London."

***

Von Lutzdorf telephoned Erikson later that morning and arranged a meeting in their suite in the afternoon. This gave time for him to speak to his contact in the British Embassy who informed London of the proposed meeting.

Promptly at three o'clock, Erikson knocked on the door which was opened by Steinberg who welcomed him warmly.

"Good afternoon, Lars. How's that delightful colleague of yours Maria?"

"As always, she is, as you say, a most delightful person. We are lucky to have her at the embassy."

Erikson and von Lutzdorf shook hands and made themselves comfortable in the sitting area of the suite reception room.

"Thank you for coming, Lars. We've decided on a plan to deal with the request of your friend in London which we would like you to pass on for comment and any suggestion they might have to facilitate what we have in mind."

"My embassy contact is on standby to forward any messages to London as a matter of priority at any time, day or night."

Von Lutzdorf proceeded to explain in detail what he and Steinberg thought would be the best way to deal with the problem.

"Of course, your presence here is well-known, thanks to the press both here in Argentina and other countries," said Lars. "No doubt there's much speculation on the route you took by both the allies and neutral countries. Brazil will be somewhat annoyed that you overflew her territory without permission and will probably be considering ways with the Americans of intercepting you on your return."

"Yes, of course, that's a possible danger, so you must ensure the British persuade them not to interfere."

"Even the Germans would expect an attempt at interception to be made on your return flight. If not, they could be suspicious. Perhaps a failed attempt could be arranged which could be reported and get back to the Germans to allay any suspicion."

"Good idea. Propose that to London and let them come up with a plan."

They spent the rest of the afternoon going over various options but finally agreed to put von Lutzdorf's proposal to London and to allow them to organise things with the Americans and arrange a realistic interception attempt.

Chapter 49

❖

SIS HEADQUARTERS, LONDON

The coded signal from their embassy in Buenos Aires came in overnight and the decoded text setting out von Lutzdorf's plan and suggestions were on Stewart Menzies' desk waiting for him when he arrived at his office in the morning.

The agent designated to handle the operation dealing with von Lutzdorf, William Downdale, had also been notified of the incoming signal which had been copied to him.

Within a few minutes of having read the decoded signal, William Downdale's telephone rang.

"William, have you read the signal from our man in Argentina?" asked Menzies.

"Yes, I'm just looking at it right now."

"I don't know about you, William, but I think von Lutzdorf's reasoning is quite sound and his suggestion of us organising a failed interception adds a nice touch to keep his bosses quiet. The thing is, where do we plan for this to take place?"

"There are only two possible areas where we could organise an interception attempt and those are crossing the coast near the American air base at Natal in Brazil or somewhere within range of our base in Takoradi on the Gold Coast.

"I think we should try both places especially in Brazil because they will very happily advertise the attempt as they'll want to put on a display of annoyance at the unauthorised intrusion of their air space. Then we could put on a show by advertising our attempt as they fly through the Ivory Coast from Yamoussoukro into our air space on the Gold Coast in support of Brazil."

"It'll take some planning and coordination and require precise timing. What information did you get from the RAF about what fighter aircraft they have at Natal and if they have ground control interception radar?"

"The Americans have some Curtiss P-40 Tomahawks which can reach just over thirty thousand feet and have a speed of three hundred and fifty miles per hour. They could make an attempt but if what my aeronautical experts say is true, they would be lucky to catch this modified Heinkel 111."

"That doesn't matter, as long as they can make a credible attempt. After all, we don't want them to actually shoot down von Lutzdorf, do we?" said Menzies with a laugh.

"Quite so, C," said Downdale with a smile.

"What about our fighter capability on the Gold Coast?"

"We have plenty of Hurricane fighters as they're assembled there and flown on via the southern Sahara route via Nigeria, Libya, the Sudan and Egypt to our forces in the Middle East. They have a similar performance to the P-40 but have a higher ceiling because of their superior Rolls Royce Merlin engine with supercharger."

"Very well. Get on to our friends at OSS and advise them that this is an important operation and we need their cooperation from their air force in Brazil. Make sure they understand that this interception is only for show. We don't want some trigger-happy pilot losing the plot and getting in a lucky shot."

"I will personally brief my opposite number at the American Embassy."

"Very good. Now I will prepare a reply to this signal and tell von Lutzdorf we agree with his idea and will send him a detailed plan as soon as we can. How long do you think it'll take you to organise things with the Americans?"

"Allowing for permissions and coordinating between the various departments and command structures, I would say at least four or five days for the signals to go back and forth."

"Very well. Let's hope that von Lutzdorf has at least another week to spend in Buenos Aires."

Chapter 50

❖

Von Lutzdorf and Steinberg were sitting in their suite considering what to do for the day when the telephone rang. Steinberg picked up the handset and responded to the caller at the other end. "Yes, thank you. Tell him to come up." He put the phone down and turned to von Lutzdorf. "That was reception. Lars is downstairs. I expect he has something back from London for us."

"Hopefully, yes. It's all very pleasant here but I'm anxious to get back home to Magda."

"Me too. I was just making some headway with my sister's friend. She's extremely pretty."

Just then, there was a knock on the door which von Lutzdorf, already on his feet, opened to admit their new Swedish friend.

"Good morning, gentlemen. I have some news for you from London."

Erikson produced a decoded copy of the signal from London which his contact at the British Embassy had given him.

"You can read it for yourself but I can tell you it's all good news. They agree completely with your idea and will respond shortly with a more detailed plan of their own. But first of all, they need from you a detailed flight plan of your intended return trip."

"No problem there. We have all the information to hand and can soon put that together."

"You'll see they expect it to take four or five days to organise the intercept with the Americans so I hope you don't suddenly get the order to leave before that's in place."

"Last time we spoke with Stroheim, it'll be at least one week from now before they have all the documents ready for us, so it shouldn't be a problem."

"Excellent. Well, I'll leave you to get your flight plan details set out. I suggest that when you're ready, give me a call and I will come over and collect it. The sooner we get it off to London, the better."

As Erikson left them, von Lutzdorf said to Steinberg, "That's your job for the day, Johann. Make sure you put in all the navigation coordinates for each staging post and journey times for each leg. They can then work out all the estimated times of arrival from our departure time from here. I see they've suggested we cross the Brazilian coast near to Natal rather than further south as we did coming in, so you'll have to rework that part of the flight plan. They must want to make it easier for the Americans to intercept us. Frankly, I think I shall enjoy that part. It'll give us the opportunity to see what our bird can really do to make it hard for them. When we tested it against our own fighters at Warnemuende, we only played with them a little and never used the full power boost."

"It should be an interesting little game. I must say that I'm also interested in seeing what she will do when pushed to the limit."

"One thing I would like to change to the return flight plan is to not reveal the location of our secret base in Libya TBS1 for the moment. Change our destination in Libya to the town of Sebha. The difference in track is only minor and should not cause a problem for their proposed plan."

"I'll get on with it right away and should have it ready by midday for Lars to pick up."

Good as his word, Steinberg had the flight plan ready by midday and, after Erikson had collected it and left for the embassy, he and von Lutzdorf were left to their own devices.

"You know, Walter, this has been a very interesting mission so far and infinitely better than being on the Russian front and I never thought I would say it but I'm bored. What would you say if I gave Anna a call and asked her out to lunch?"

"She's a lovely woman. Go ahead, don't worry about me."

"There's something about Swedish girls that I find very attractive. They're very liberal-minded and independent, not like our German women."

"I know what you mean, Johann," said von Lutzdorf with a smile, "I'm married to one."

"Oh, I'm sorry, Walter, I forgot. I didn't mean anything personal."

"Think nothing of it. I would recommend it to anyone. That's why I'm anxious to get back to Magda."

Steinberg picked up the telephone and placed a call to the Swedish Embassy. When the operator answered, he asked for Anna and was put through.

"Hello?" said Anna.

"Hello Anna. It's Johann."

"Johann, how nice to hear from you. What can I do for you?"

"Would it be an imposition if I asked you to lunch?"

"How delightful. I would love it."

"I'll pick you up with my driver in twenty minutes, if that's convenient for you? You can choose the restaurant."

"That's fine and I know a very lovely place for lunch."

"Wonderful. See you soon."

As he put the handset back on the rest, von Lutzdorf grinned and said, "There you are, Johann. That was easy, wasn't it?"

"Better than expected, but I feel guilty leaving you here alone."

"Don't worry about me. Go and enjoy yourself."

***

As soon as Steinberg had left for his lunch appointment with Anna, von Lutzdorf placed a call to the German Embassy and asked to speak with Stroheim, the commercial attaché.

"Good morning, Oberst. What can I do for you?"

"Can you tell me if there have been any complaints from the Brazilians concerning our overflight of their air space and how much longer it will be before we can leave?"

"Yes, they have lodged a complaint through the Portuguese government with whom we have contact through our consulate in Lisbon."

"Can you tell me what was the nature of their complaint? I would like to start planning our return flight as soon as you have all the documentation ready for us. Depending on what they've said, I may need to change the route of our return flight."

"Yes, I can see that it may be a factor to take into consideration. They said they reserve the right to take any steps they feel necessary to preserve the integrity of their air space against unauthorised intrusions notwithstanding whether the aircraft is civil or military."

"That's unequivocal. At least we know what to expect if they locate us."

"What will you do? Do you think it's safe to fly into Brazilian air space?"

"We don't have any other option, I'm afraid. We don't have the range to fly around Brazil. We have to fly over part of it but I'm not so concerned about that. They have to detect us first and then intercept us. Unless they have new aircraft, they don't have anything that can reach us easily."

"They will, of course, know of your exact time of departure from here as there are many members of the world press here observing your every move. As soon as you take off, the information will be transmitted to the press and news services around the world."

"Unfortunately, what you say is true but it can't be helped. However, we have a few tricks that we can play to put them off as to our exact route which will make things difficult for them." He smiled to himself as he said that. It amused him to wonder what Stroheim would think if he knew he was working in collaboration with the British to ensure an interception, albeit a contrived failed one.

"As soon as we know our departure date, you must inform Reinhard Schneider so he can advise of our ETA at Bachmann's farm," said von Lutzdorf.

"Of course, Oberst, that is all in hand. We have plenty of time as we expect it to be one more week before we have everything ready for you."

Thanking Stroheim for the information, von Lutzdorf replaced the handset and sat for a moment thinking over the plan, trying to think of anything he may have overlooked.

He had much to think about and, although he knew his close friend Johann was absolutely one hundred percent loyal to him and would follow his lead, he was still bothered to some extent at the level of his collaboration with the British.

As Hitler had stated several times in the past, England was not Germany's natural enemy. As much as he hated and loathed everything he and the Nazis stood for, on this point he absolutely agreed with him.

Three years in an English public school had instilled in him a strong sense of freedom of thought and the rights of the individual as espoused in English Common Law based on the principles set out in the Magna Carta. Something he was sure Hitler was totally unfamiliar with or even if he was, it certainly did not fit in with the Nazi ideology of total control of the individual whose life, thoughts and ambitions were to be subjugated to the state. During those three years, he had made many friends in England and he also knew his parents had a wide social circle amongst the English upper classes, including the parents of some of his fellow students who were in politics or government.

It was at times like this of reflection that he remembered his conversations with his father and uncle, which strengthened his resolve to do whatever he could to thwart the plans of the Nazi Party. To von Lutzdorf's way of thinking, it was not Germany who was England's enemy but Hitler and the Nazi Party.

Having reassured himself that his thinking and chosen path were right and correct for the greater benefit of the German people and that he was a patriot and not a traitor, he resolved to carry out his plan and continue to collaborate with the British.

***

The next day, Erikson delivered their plan of the proposed interceptions to coordinate with Steinberg's flight plan which gave details of the aircraft that would be involved which were, as von Lutzdorf had expected from his original information, Curtiss P-40 Warhawks, the latest version with a slightly more powerful Allison engine. It was proposed that a flight of three Warhawks would make an attempt as they approached the Brazilian coastline between Recife and Natal. It was left to von Lutzdorf how he would deal with the interception. The pilots had been briefed not to shoot at them but to try to get close enough to take photos for the press to make it appear that a real attempt had been made to try to force them down to land at the Natal air base.

"I think what we'll do, Johann, is to climb above the contrail level to help the P-40s locate us as we approach the coast at twenty-eight thousand feet. This version of the P-40 can climb to about thirty-one thousand feet so we'll let them get close enough to photograph us and them apply maximum boost on both systems and see if they can keep up with us as we climb."

"It'll be interesting to see how long before they stall out as we climb out of their reach," replied Steinberg.

"We might have a bit of trouble out-climbing the Hurricanes as they have a higher operational ceiling so we'll use this test to see how high we can get with both boost systems in operation."

***

Von Lutzdorf and Steinberg managed to keep themselves occupied with some more sight-seeing and the occasional social lunch or dinner with Maria, Anna and Erikson until the day came when they received a call from Stroheim that everything was ready for them and proposed they plan to leave the following morning.

Relieved their waiting was finally over, von Lutzdorf informed Erikson of their proposed departure time in the morning so he could inform London.

Later that afternoon, they arrived at the airport to supervise the loading of three boxes. Two of them, one each with diplomatic seals, were for Hermann Goering and Heinrich Mueller respectively and the third locked one contained fifty thousand pounds sterling for which von Lutzdorf had the key.

Stroheim very efficiently produced their official cargo manifest stamped by the embassy and asked von Lutzdorf to sign a document confirming he had received everything intact.

"I trust you will have a guard in place during the night, Herr Stroheim, and that you will inform Schneider that our planned time of departure is 0700 hours tomorrow morning."

"Everything is as you request, Oberst. Bachmann will have your ETA later today so he will be ready for your arrival."

"Excellent. Now we would like to refuel the aircraft ready for tomorrow."

The bowser crew waiting nearby responded to his hand signal and proceeded to refuel the Heinkel under Steinberg's supervision.

***

Precisely at 6 a.m. the following morning, von Lutzdorf and Steinberg exited the hotel to find their driver Juan waiting for them.

"Buenos dias, señors," said Juan with a cheerful smile.

"Good morning, Juan. Thank you for being on time."

"My pleasure, señors, I'm sorry you're leaving us but I wish you a safe and pleasant journey back home."

Both von Lutzdorf and Steinberg were dressed in plain flying overalls without any insignia. They would don the heavy heated flying suits and boots which were stored on the aircraft before they took off. In spite of this and trying not to attract attention, there were several journalists tipped off by their contacts in the hotel that they were checking out that morning waiting to catch sight of them and take photos. Several of them shouted questions asking if they were leaving Argentina.

Von Lutzdorf smiled and, wanting to be polite, he said, "Thank you, gentlemen. Yes, we are leaving today and we have enjoyed very much our visit to your country. We hope there will be a time in the future when we will be able to return."

With that, they both got in the car and ordered Juan to get moving to the airport, where no doubt they would be followed and have to run the gauntlet to the aircraft. Hopefully airport security would keep them at a distance.

Forewarned by the German Embassy of the intended departure that morning of their aircraft, the airport authorities, anticipating more than a usual interest by the press and radio, had arranged a cordoned-off area for them, secure from the active areas of the airport but with ample view of the aircraft and runway.

Von Lutzdorf and Steinberg were passed through a security barrier manned by armed airport police who directed all other cars containing the reporters to the designated area. Juan drove then straight to the parked Heinkel and assisted them with their suitcases.

Retrieving their equipment from the aircraft, von Lutzdorf and Steinberg made their way to the control office to formerly present their departure documents and change into the flight suits. By prior arrangement, their flight plan did not list their route or way points but just stated Berlin as their destination. Formalities completed, they returned to their aircraft where a ground crew and firemen were waiting to ensure engine start-up proceeded without any problems.

"Well, Johann," said von Lutzdorf as they settled into their seats and fastened their safety harnesses, "Let's get our checks done and get on our way."

"Right, my friend. It's been very pleasant here but I'm glad to be on our way home."

They worked their way methodically through the checklists quickly but efficiently; the result of many years of working together as a team who trusted each other implicitly. With both engines ticking over smoothly, they called the tower for clearance to taxi to the take-off runway. When granted, von Lutzdorf eased the two throttles open and slowly taxied the aircraft via the taxiway to the threshold of the runway where he stopped and turned into the wind.

With his final engine checks complete, he called for permission to enter the runway and depart. As he lined up the aircraft, he noted the time which was just five minutes after their intended departure time of 7 a.m.

"Pretty good timing, Johann."

"Yes, and the weather forecast is clear pretty much the whole route so we should have good visibility for landing."

Chapter 51

❖

The take-off was routine born of long practice and, as they climbed away and turned on to their northerly heading towards Asunción, their first navigational way point, the tower wished them bon voyage to which von Lutzdorf responded with thanks.

Climbing on track, the expanse of the Plate estuary opened up to starboard with the shores of Uruguay in the distance. Since it was unlikely they would encounter any other aircraft on this leg nor expect any interference as their track took them over only Argentina and Paraguay, both friendly towards Germany, they decided on a cruising altitude of fourteen thousand feet. This was a practical choice as it was economical on fuel and required only an occasional whiff of oxygen so they could dispense with the discomfort of continuously wearing a mask.

Boring as these long-distance flights could be, von Lutzdorf and Steinberg had their routines which helped the time to pass quickly. Von Lutzdorf continuously checked the engine instruments and weather whilst keeping a lookout for the unexpected; a practice instilled in him by many hours of combat flying and hard to break. Steinberg kept a continuous record of their track, calculating drift and ground speed and taking an occasional sun sight to check their latitude which, because their track was largely along a longitudinal line, gave him a very accurate figure for distance over the ground.

As they passed Asunción over to their port side, Steinberg pressed his microphone button and said over the intercom, "We have a little headwind but nothing to affect our ETA at Petrolina."

"I hope Bachmann has not had any nosy officials sniffing around since our last visit. It would be a problem if he had to prematurely plough up the runway," said von Lutzdorf with a laugh.

"I'm sure our friend Schneider would have got a message to us if that was the case."

"Let's hope so."

At their way point of Asunción, they turned on to a north-easterly course towards Petrolina in Brazil and started a gradual climb to cross the border into Brazil at twenty-five thousand feet to be out of sight and sound from any ground observer. Even though they expected the British had cleared their flight with the Brazilian authorities, they did not want to advertise their presence unduly, especially where they intended to land in case some over-enthusiastic local official not in the know decided to intervene.

One hundred miles from Petrolina, von Lutzdorf eased the throttles back and put the Heinkel into a gradual descent. From that height, the city was visible so he altered course slightly to pass twenty miles to the east of it and with the Sao Francisco River in sight, he overflew the landing site and flew on for another twenty miles to a lightly populated area of wilderness suggested by the farmer. He continued descending in wide circles until one thousand feet when he levelled off and set course for the makeshift airstrip.

As he approached the bend in the river where the farm was located, he observed a column of white smoke rising almost vertically which Bachmann had lit by prior arrangement to aid location and give the wind direction to ensure they landed as best they could into wind.

Bachmann and a couple of his workers were waiting at the end of the runway close to the farm buildings as von Lutzdorf taxied up to them and parked the aircraft in the same spot as previously and shut down the engines.

"Pretty much spot on our ETA, just over eight hours," said Steinberg.

"Yes, we've been fortunate with the weather. Time to stretch our legs, Johann."

Once on the ground, they were greeted enthusiastically by Bachmann while his men went about draping the camouflage netting over the aircraft as before.

"Have you had anyone looking around and asking questions since we left?" asked von Lutzdorf.

"No, Oberst, and I have seen no strangers in the area on my visits to town so I think we're quite safe from any unwanted snoopers."

"We will refuel while it's still light as we want to be off early tomorrow morning."

"Very good, sir," said Bachmann as he turned to his men and ordered them to keep the netting clear of the refuelling caps on the wings for the moment and instructed one of them to bring the fuel bowser from the barn.

"How was your visit to Buenos Aires? I hear it's a very interesting place."

"Everything went according to plan, albeit a bit longer stay than I had anticipated. And yes, it is a very beautiful city."

***

Later that evening, after a plain but substantial evening meal produced by the farmer's wife, the three men were sitting enjoying a glass of the farmer's locally produced schnapps.

"I apologise for the plainness of the food, Oberst, but we live quite simply here in the country."

"Think nothing of it, Eric," said von Lutzdorf using Bachmann's Christian name much to his delight. "Good wholesome food is always welcome and I'm really a country boy myself."

"Tell me, since you are close to those in government in Germany, how is the war going and how will it turn out? We're so very remote from things here in Brazil especially here in the interior. Please speak freely as you did before. We are all anti-Nazi here."

"To be honest, as long as the Nazis remain in power, nothing can be good but I have every hope that now America has entered the war. I think there can only be one outcome and that cannot come too soon."

"My fear is that there are a great number of Nazi groups all over South America being organised by the Nazis, like that odious Schneider."

"Unfortunately, you're right and I've only just recently, because of my visit here, come to realise how extensive that network is. The only comfort I can give you is that I know the British are aware of this and will, I'm sure, take the appropriate steps to deal with them when the time comes."

"That is indeed a comfort. One feels so helpless here so far away. Even though I and my immediate family are safe, I still have many relatives back in Germany for whom I fear."

The conversation continued on the same subject for a while until von Lutzdorf suggested it was time to retire as they had an early start in the morning and a long flight of more than ten hours.

***

Von Lutzdorf had a restless night with much on his mind. He was well-accustomed to the hazards of flying but he always felt a little apprehensive when preparing for a long flight over water. Any mechanical failure could result in having to land on the water in the vast expanse of the Atlantic with little chance of rescue.

However, once daylight came and he awoke, he put such thoughts behind him and his professional instincts took over and his faith in German engineering banished any doubts he had about the flight ahead.

They had decided on a departure of six o'clock local time as they would be flying west to east against the sun which would shorten their actual daylight period as well as the possibility of a headwind to extend their flying time. Fortunately, they would be landing at the airfield at Yamoussoukro which had been very efficient before, equipped as it was with radio direction finding to give them a heading to steer and landing lights.

Bachmann was up and about long before von Lutzdorf and Steinberg rose and sat down for breakfast half an hour before their intended departure. They were just finishing when he came into the kitchen.

"Good morning, gentlemen. I trust you both slept well. Your aircraft is all ready for you. My men and I have removed the netting and I've done my best with a walk around external check to see if everything is in order but no doubt you will have your own routine."

"Good morning, Eric. Thank you. I'm sure that, as a former Luftwaffe engineering officer, you know what to look for."

"She looks good to me. I'm only sad I never got the chance to experience a flight in it with you, Oberst."

"Who knows, Eric? Perhaps after the war we might have a chance to fly together."

"Something to look forward to, sir."

Their pleasantries completed, von Lutzdorf and Steinberg, already dressed in their heavier heated flying suits, thanked and bade farewell to Bachmann's wife and, accompanied by Bachmann, walked out to the aircraft.

After a quick walk around to check the controls and tyres, von Lutzdorf turned to Bachmann and said with a grin, "Just making sure, Eric."

Steinberg was already on board when von Lutzdorf entered the cabin and took up his position in the left-hand seat.

Both engines started after turning over a couple of times, coughing into life with a puff of white smoke as the oil, which had drained onto the cylinder heads over night, burnt off and settled into a steady subdued rhythm at their normal warm-up revolutions of one thousand per minute. They ran through the rest of their checklist and von Lutzdorf put his hand out of the cabin window with a thumbs up sign and a wave to signal everything was in order and they were ready to taxi.

Bachmann and his men moved away from the aircraft as they taxied into position and did their final magneto and pitch control tests, opened up the throttles, sped down the makeshift airstrip, took off and climbed away to the northeast.

Chapter 52

❖

Their plan called for a climb to twenty-five thousand feet and to approach the coast between Natal and Recife at that height where the P-40s would attempt an interception. When they were within fifty miles from the coast, von Lutzdorf began a steady climb to enter the contrail level.

"Let's give them a little help, Johann. Go back and see what our contrail looks like."

"Look up ahead, Walter. You can see their contrails at about thirty thousand feet. That's about their limit as they don't have supercharged engines."

Looking up, von Lutzdorf could make out three contrails curving across their flight path about twenty miles ahead as the three interceptors patrolled in a wide circle waiting for the Heinkel to appear.

"We'll level off at thirty thousand and see how they get on. Let's hope they've been properly briefed."

"Too late now to worry about that."

As they got nearer to the patrolling P-40s, they changed their direction as they spotted the approaching Heinkel and manoeuvred to intercept.

"We'll let them get on our tail to take some photographs and then see what they can do as we speed up and climb."

The flight of three fighters came around, closing up on the tail in a classic interception manoeuvre as von Lutzdorf flew straight and level.

While one stayed on the Heinkel's tail astern, the other two split up and pulled up alongside obviously curious to see an enemy bomber up close for the first time.

"I think that's enough to satisfy everyone. Let's give them something to think about. We're doing close on three hundred miles per hour at the moment. Time to see what we can really do, Johann."

Von Lutzdorf opened both throttles, gradually pushing them up to their fully open position and, at the same time, he pulled back on the control column into a climb. The effect was immediately apparent as the P-40s fell back until they too opened their throttles in an attempt to keep up. As they gradually closed in again, von Lutzdorf pushed both boost system levers slowly forwards, injecting both water methanol and nitrous oxide into the cylinders. This time, the effect was more dramatic as the Heinkel not only pulled away but climbed steadily ever higher away from the fighters. At that moment, Steinberg, who was watching them from the observation windows in the cargo area, suddenly exclaimed, "They're shooting at us, Walter."

Von Lutzdorf continued to hold the Heinkel in the climb without attempting to take avoiding action.

"Don't worry, Johann. I can see the tracers falling away below us in front. They're deliberately aiming under us for the benefit of their wing gun cameras. They'll make for good publicity shots."

"There they go, Walter. They can't maintain the climb at this altitude. They've each stalled out below us and are diving away."

Von Lutzdorf kept going in the climb and, as they approached thirty-eight thousand feet, he levelled off and reduced both boost systems to zero and throttled back.

"No point in wasting fuel. We're way above any chance of interception and probably will do three hundred and fifty miles per hour if we tried. We must keep a track of our speed and any possible headwind from now on. We have a long way to go."

"That little show will give the British and the Americans something to think about, Walter. We're just crossing the coast. I think we can descend to a lower altitude now. It's quite cold up here in spite of our heated suits and, even with oxygen, it's hard on the breathing being unpressurised."

"What height would you suggest for comfort and best economy?"

"Try coming down in stages while I check for the best height for drift and headwind."

Deciding ultimately on fifteen thousand feet, they commenced their long Atlantic crossing to South West Africa to make landfall at Liberia, south of the capital Monrovia.

Steinberg calculated that their headwind would only add an effective additional two hundred and fifty miles to their distance, well within their fuel reserves.

**

By the time they crossed into Africa, the sun was still some distance above the horizon and there was still enough daylight as they called Yamoussoukro tower for permission to land.

Dusk was rapidly approaching as they called, airfield in sight, which had the runway lights on ready for their approach.

The German consul was on hand to meet them as they taxied up to the apron in front of the tower.

"Good evening, Herr Schmalbach," said von Lutzdorf after he and Steinberg had descended from the aircraft.

"Welcome back, Oberst. It's good to see you back again safe and sound."

The same Vichy Air Force officer they had dealt with before was waiting for them in the administration office below the tower.

"Good evening, Captain," he said, using the normal form of address for an aircraft commander, "I trust you have had an interesting flight."

"Yes, thank you, Captain," replied von Lutzdorf referring to his military rank.

While the consul hovered in the background ready to be of assistance if needed, von Lutzdorf dealt with the normal formalities of an arriving aircraft and arranged for the refuelling to be done first thing in the morning before their departure. Formalities completed and the aircraft secured with two armed security guards from the consulate to keep an overnight watch, he and Steinberg accompanied the consul to his waiting car.

"The ambassador sends his apologies that he will not be able to meet with you on this occasion, Oberst."

Much to his relief at this good news, von Lutzdorf expressed his regret as required by protocol and inquired of the consul's wife who he genuinely wanted to meet again.

"She is well and looking forward to hearing of your trip to South America. A place she has heard much of and always wanted to visit."

"We only spent time in Buenos Aires, but we have a few stories which I hope will entertain her."

***

It was obvious to von Lutzdorf that the consul's wife had made an extra effort with her appearance for the occasion, not only with her fashionable new hairstyle and dress but also in her demeanour. While he knew it was not because she wanted to appear desirable to him, as he thought better of her than that, but rather it was in response to the effect his last visit had had on her in making her feel more feminine and bringing a little style and gallantry into her bored existence buried, as she was, in this remote part of Africa.

Her smile and greeting made her appear ten years younger than she was and von Lutzdorf responded to her in his most gallant manner taking her hand and gently raising it to his lips as he said, "Frau Schmalbach, how well you look. This is indeed a pleasure to see you again."

"Oberst, you cannot imagine how much I have been looking forward to your safe return. Please, call me Annalise."

"My friends call me Walter, so please dispense with rank for this evening. It makes me feel like I'm on parade."

"Thank you, Walter, for including me in your list of friends."

"I'm sure my comrade would like you to call him Johann as he is also my best friend."

Steinberg stepped forwards, taking her hand. He smiled broadly and said, "It's also my pleasure to be back here again, Annalise."

"Thank you, Johann." Linking her arms into both those of von Lutzdorf and Steinberg, she guided them into the drawing room where a bottle of champagne was sitting in ice with a tray of glasses. "Would either of you two gallant gentlemen please do the honours and open the champagne?"

The consul entered the room behind them and, picking up the bottle, said, "Please, gentlemen, let me as your host welcome you to our home again and drink a toast to your safe return to Germany."

Without the ambassador, the evening passed in friendly and open conversation with no mention of any member of the government or Nazi hierarchy to spoil the occasion. Von Lutzdorf entertained the consul and his wife with stories of the social life in Buenos Aires, about which the consul's wife asked many questions obviously wishing she too could experience the city. He told them about their visit to the grave of the commander of the Admiral Graf Spee and the antics of their driver Juan which had them all laughing.

Finally, he told them of the attempted interception by the American aircraft as they flew out of Brazil not disclosing the organisational part played by the British.

Von Lutzdorf felt a tinge of guilt at the look of shock on the face of the consul's wife as she gasped and put her hand to her mouth as he related dramatically how close they came to being shot down.

"Oh, how dreadful for you, Walter," she said with a tone of genuine distress in her voice.

In an effort to downplay the moment, von Lutzdorf replied, "Oh, it wasn't so bad. We managed to outpace them and get away quite easily."

"You still have a long way to go. Is there any chance the British or the Free French may try to catch you?"

"There's always a chance and there is always a risk when flying through enemy air space but I think we're well-equipped to evade any attempt. Please, put your mind at rest on that point. Now, let's talk of more cheerful matters."

The evening progressed until, by mutual consent, they agreed they had an early start in the morning and a long flight before they reached their next destination and retired.

***

The consul and his driver were on standby the next morning and drove them out to the airport as dawn was breaking.

As arranged the previous day, employees of the fuel company were ready for them and commenced the refuelling under Steinberg's supervision while von Lutzdorf dealt with the departure details. He was surprised to find the same Vichy French Air Force officer on duty this early and although they were, for the moment, still reluctant allies, there was an undisguised feeling of animosity in the air.

"I see your flight plan is to Sebha in Libya and then via Tripoli to Berlin."

"That is my intention, Captain. Why do you ask?"

"From the news, we hear the British are poised on the outskirts of Tripoli ready to take the city which will make your stopover there somewhat precarious," said the officer with a smirk on his face.

Not wanting to rise to the obvious provocation, von Lutzdorf smiled and said, "Possibly, but we have other options and we still retain control over most of the western part of Tripolitania and all of Tunisia."

"Maybe so for the moment, but for how long?" replied the officer, relishing baiting the German officer.

Not wishing to indulge the Vichy officer with further debate, von Lutzdorf picked up his documents and, bidding the officer good day, he left the office.

***

The Vichy officer was frustratingly disappointed that the Ivory Coast government still remained loyal to the Vichy French government and that the Vichy French forces had not capitulated to the allies as they had in Morocco and Algeria and joined the Free French. In spite of this, he was in touch with former colleagues and officers in Algeria and passed on any information and intelligence that was useful to them. He had alerted them as to the intended flight of von Lutzdorf and would now send them the exact details and the ETA at Sebha. He was aware the Vichy French Air Force in Algeria was equipped with the Dewoitine D-520, one of the latest French fighters that had come into production at the outbreak of war. This sleek-looking fighter, a contemporary of the Spitfire with a similar performance to the early models, could well pose a problem for von Lutzdorf if he was unlucky enough to encounter one of them. It would be a great propaganda coup for the Free French if they could intercept and shoot down von Lutzdorf's Heinkel.

His Free French contact quickly passed on the information to the air force in Algeria who alerted the commander of a flight of D-520s based in Djanet close to the Libya border and almost directly on the intended track of the Heinkel's flight from Yamoussoukro to Sebha.

From the flight details and the time of departure, the commander was able to calculate, to a reasonable degree of accuracy, the time when the aircraft would cross the border between Algeria and Libya. He therefore ordered the flight to standby and be ready to take up a patrol of the area and effect an interception.

***

Steinberg had completed the refuelling and all the pre-flight checks when von Lutzdorf returned, thanked the consul for his assistance and bade him farewell. They ran through the engine start-up procedures and, when ready, taxied out to the runway.

Chapter 53

❖

They had already planned to climb to twenty-five thousand feet; the agreed height for the RAF interception. Their take-off was precisely at seven o'clock and they estimated that the interception would be approximately one hour from take-off.

Almost on the estimated time, von Lutzdorf and Steinberg spotted a pair of Hurricanes, about five miles ahead and slightly above, fly across their track from right to left. Keeping them in sight, they observed the Hurricanes split up and each make a long curving turn to come in from astern and forwards, one on each wing with the Heinkel.

After his three years in England, von Lutzdorf was very familiar with the English sense of humour and panache the RAF pilots could indulge in when they were inclined. As with their previous encounter with the Mosquito over the Mediterranean, the pilots smiled and waved at them and then, gently dropping astern of them, they took it in turns to fire a stream of tracers which shot out under the nose alarmingly close to the underside of the Heinkel. Confident in the skill of the RAF pilots, von Lutzdorf held a steady course until they had finished and was then surprised as they both appeared once more on each wing and flew in formation with him for another few minutes. Finally giving the thumbs up sign, to which von Lutzdorf responded in like fashion, they each peeled away and descended out of view.

"If the British release some of those photos to the press, we'll be able to report that, although we managed to out fly them at that altitude, we did sustain a couple of hits in one engine."

"Luckily, they weren't serious, Walter."

Immediately after the Hurricanes departed, von Lutzdorf changed the setting of the automatic pilot gyroscope controller five degrees to starboard to bring their heading back on track for their real destination TBS1 and not that of Sebha which he had declared to the Vichy officer at Yamoussoukro.

The weather continued clear throughout their long flight across Niger towards the Libyan border with still plenty of daylight as they neared their destination. The change of heading would put the Heinkel nearly two hundred miles southeast of the position calculated by the commander of the Free French flight based at Djanet for his intended interception.

By the time the commander realised they had missed the Heinkel and widened the search area, von Lutzdorf and Steinberg were preparing their approach to their secret airstrip. The familiar sight of the three rock formation came into view giving them the heading for the airstrip as they configured the aircraft for landing. With the precision born of great experience and practice, von Lutzdorf flew a perfect approach and the Heinkel touched lightly down at the threshold and, as he throttled back both engines, they rolled gently to a stop.

Following their, by now, usual routine, von Lutzdorf positioned the aircraft with the tail pointing at the hangar doors and they both exited the aircraft. As he opened the doors, Steinberg entered and emerged shortly after driving the towing tractor which he attached to the tail. He then towed the Heinkel inside the cavernous interior.

Meanwhile, von Lutzdorf had started the generator and, as the doors closed, he switched on the interior lighting. Having made themselves more comfortable by discarding their heavy flying suits, they retired to the living quarters at the rear of the hangar.

"Do you realise that this is probably the last time we'll be using this place, Walter? It's not too late to change your mind and sit out the rest of the war here in safety and comfort," he added in a mock wistful tone.

"If I didn't know you were joking, I might take you up on that suggestion, Johann. Unfortunately, we have a job to do and a mission to complete albeit for our own reasons. Why don't you see what there is in the store while I write out and encode some signals? One for our masters in Berlin and one for our friend in London."

"I'll get on to it right away. But first, a glass of schnapps to celebrate our safe arrival."

As Steinberg busied himself in the store, von Lutzdorf set to work using the enigma machine for the signal to Berlin and the book cypher for the signal to London.

Chapter 54

❖

SIS HEADQUARTERS, LONDON

Stewart Menzies and his agent, William Downdale, were discussing the signal that had come in from von Lutzdorf that evening.

"This fellow von Lutzdorf is without doubt a very astute and redoubtable operator. After the war, I must ask him if he would like a permanent job with us," said Menzies with a wry grin.

"He certainly knows how to play this game and keep his cards close to his chest," replied Downdale.

"By keeping the location of all these documents secret from us until either the end of the war or unless he happens to be captured by us attempting to continue his journey by land across Libya, he retains control and can demand almost anything he wants from us.

"If in the event he manages to join up with the axis forces in Tunisia and get back to Berlin, he has the perfect excuse and reason for leaving the documents concealed somewhere in southern Libya. In either case, he achieves what we both want. That is, they would be available to us without the enemy knowing. If in the million to one chance Germany is victorious, the whole situation is moot."

"We must alert Montgomery's intelligence to the possibility of von Lutzdorf falling into their hands. We should inform them of his great importance, instructing them to treat him with utmost care and get him back to England to us by the quickest and safest method."

"Yes, William. Please give the matter utmost secrecy and priority."

Chapter 55

❖

After laboriously encoding both signals, von Lutzdorf used the base's communications equipment with its efficient external aerial concealed in the cliff above the hangar and then signed off not wanting to receive or acknowledge any replies as they might interfere with his plan.

In order to substantiate any newsreel footage of the RAF interception released by the British, von Lutzdorf had reported they had sustained some damage to the starboard engine and, even though they had managed get back to their base in Libya, he was concerned about flying back to Germany.

He and Steinberg then enjoyed a convivial evening with a dinner consisting of a number of Italian delicacies accompanied by a bottle or two of the best wine to be found in the store. During the meal, von Lutzdorf explained what he had said in both signals so his friend was fully in the picture especially the explanation why they had to continue by land due to damage sustained in the unsuccessful attack.

What they both were not to know, however, as they discussed the matter, was that the contents of the signals were of little importance to their future as they would not be called upon by either recipient for an explanation of their actions or decisions.

***

They awoke the following morning both feeling the effects of their overindulgence the previous evening but soon felt better after inhaling pure oxygen for a few minutes which cleared their headaches better that any amount of aspirin.

They chose the former Afrika Korps medium truck for their journey to the coast due to its better mechanical condition and reliability and proceeded to load it with extra cans of fuel and water as well as a selection of canned food. They decided to also take with them the box containing the British currency in case of the need to purchase any further supplies or pay for assistance from the locals en route. The boxes containing the documents, they buried with the gold, diamonds and other cash, replaced the rocks covering the site and brushed away all signs of any disturbance.

"They should be safe there until needed," observed Steinberg. "Perhaps one day we will return and have another meal. The wine should be very nice and mature by then."

They shut down the generator, switched off the electricity and securely closed the hangar doors before one last look around and then climbed into the cab. Von Lutzdorf elected to drive the first part while Steinberg, with his map of the Libyan Sahara and his hand compass, sat in the front passenger seat.

Their initial direction was to the northwest towards the southern tip of Tunisia. The terrain was a mixture of hard packed sand and rocks with occasional sand dunes.

***

In Djanet, across the border in southern Algeria, the commander of the Free French D-520 flight was cursing himself for missing the Heinkel the previous day. But now, rather than dwell on the missed opportunity and free now from the restraints imposed on him by the Vichy government, he decided to mount a series of patrols out from his base into Libya to see if he could make contact with any axis forces fleeing the British Juggernaut from the east attempting to escape to the south of Libya and avoid the Americans coming from the west.

The commander had decided to make the best use of his limited resources by sending out the aircraft on single patrols one to the northeast, one due east and the third to the southeast to cover as great an area as possible.

The pilot on patrol to the southeast was reaching the limit of his range and was about to turn about and head back to base when he spotted a cloud of dust straight ahead obviously made by some sort of moving vehicle. Checking his fuel gauge, he decided he had sufficient to investigate and commenced a gradual dive towards the vehicle.

**

Von Lutzdorf and Steinberg had been travelling for barely two hours when they were startled by the roar of an aircraft as it flashed low overhead. As the pilot neared what he could now see was a military truck, he was also shocked into the realisation it was German by the sight of the Afrika Korps insignia on the cabin door. Elated at this unexpected and lucky encounter, he pulled up and made a sweeping turn to port and came round for a head on approach.

Von Lutzdorf and Steinberg, unaccustomed to encountering the enemy on the ground, were momentarily rendered unable to react until the aircraft dove down directly at them head on and unleashed a stream of cannon shells and machine gun bullets kicking up plumes of sand in a line heading directly towards them. By the time von Lutzdorf reacted and started to turn the wheel to avoid the onslaught, it was too late. The cannon shells smashed into the radiator and engine which erupted in a cloud of steam and smoke while the machine gun bullets stitched a row of holes up and across the bonnet and windscreen tearing into von Lutzdorf and Steinberg killing them both instantly.

Elated at his success, the pilot flew over the truck again executing a victory roll then, conscious of his fuel state, turned on a heading back to base leaving the truck enveloped in a cloud of steam.

The young pilot, jubilant at his first taste of action during a war which had until now confined his activities to boring local patrols and exercises, reported the incident to his commanding officer on his return to base. The commander recorded it in his daily report but put it down as an isolated event of stragglers attempting to evade capture and decided it did not merit any further investigation.

Chapter 56

❖

SIS HEADQUARTERS, LONDON

"William, it has been two weeks now since we received that signal from von Lutzdorf. What arrangement did you have for contact with him once he returned to Germany?" said the director of SIS as he spoke to his agent William Downdale on the telephone.

"We had no formal arrangement, C, as we deemed it too dangerous to continue contact with him once he returned to Berlin. We rather left it to him to make contact if he had anything he wanted to pass on to us."

"He should, by now, have been either back in Berlin or in our custody which obviously he is not. How can we check whether or not he's in Berlin?"

"I'll get one of our people in contact with our Polish network to make inquiries and get back to you."

"Check with Montgomery's intelligence people to see if they've come into possession of any identification documents recovered off enemy casualties that would identify him."

"They had been alerted to look out for him as a matter of utmost priority so I assume they would also check that possibility."

"Nevertheless, send a high priority urgent signal to them to check all enemy casualties and, if necessary, also check with the Americans. We must find him, dead or alive."

***

The following day, William Downdale responded to a summons from Menzies to come to his office.

"What have you found out about von Lutzdorf, William?"

"Our people in Berlin say he hasn't returned to his office in the Air Ministry and other inquiries say he hasn't been seen either at his parents' home in the country or his usual haunts in Berlin. Neither has anyone seen his wife."

"Well, I have something for you, William. We've been contacted through the Red Cross in Geneva whether or not we have him in custody as a prisoner of war."

"We must assume the authorities in Germany have posted him as missing."

"It looks like it. What about that signal you sent to Montgomery's intelligence?"

"They're adamant they have no information on him whatsoever and say if he was alive, they would know but also say that there's so much chaos there checking casualties that he could easily be amongst the missing."

"What about the Americans?"

"Intelligence reports that, at the moment, they are nowhere near that theatre of operations."

"For the time being then, we must be patient and hope for the best."

Chapter 57

❖

Magda von Lutzdorf received the news of her husband being posted as missing directly from Reichsmarschall Goering.

"I'm sorry, my dear, to be the bearer of bad news but we haven't heard anything from Walter for two weeks and it's way past the time when we would have expected a scheduled communication. We're continuing our inquiries and have asked the Red Cross to inquire if he is a prisoner of war which is our fervent hope."

"Thank you, Uncle, for letting me know. I will also pray he is a prisoner."

Magda, who was staying at von Lutzdorf's family estate with his parents, put down the telephone and, with tears in her eyes, looked at her mother-in-law and said, "Walter is missing."

The two women embraced each other in mutual despair as Magda in a voice strangled with emotion whispered hoarsely, "He may be a prisoner."

"Let us both pray so."

***

Following the attack, the truck containing the bodies of von Lutzdorf and Steinberg came to rest in the lee of a sand dune. The whole area through which they were travelling was categorised as being of shifting sand dunes.

From above looking down, they would appear like stationary ocean swells with troughs and peaks albeit moving at a much slower indiscernible speed. The dune with a peak of one hundred feet or more loomed over the stranded vehicle and, in the few weeks since the incident, the sand was already encroaching up the wheels and its side as the fine sand blew off the crest of the dune with the prevailing wind and even more so with the frequent sandstorms.

As time passed, the sand would completely engulf the truck and hide it, and its human remains, from view until the dune moved on and chose to reveal its secret to the awaiting world once more.

Chapter 59

❖

TRIPOLI, 1963

Jaime arrived at the British Embassy as arranged at ten o'clock the following morning for his meeting with the man from MI6. Mary met him in the reception and conducted him through security to her office on the second floor where she introduced him to the waiting MI6 agent.

"Jaime, this is Alan Sherbourne."

Jaime shook hands with the agent and said, "James St Clair, please call me Jaime."

"Good to meet you, Jaime. I suppose you're wondering what this is all about."

"Well, it seems that my discovery has aroused a lot of interest."

"Of that, you can be sure, Jaime. We have a file on your von Lutzdorf going back twenty years and your discovery may be the answer to a twenty-year-old mystery."

"Sounds very exciting and interesting. What can you tell me? I take it that after all this time, there are no secrets."

"That's yet to be decided. For the moment, I'll tell you what I can. But first of all, I would like to ask you a few questions, if you don't mind."

"Go ahead. I'm here to help all I can."

"First of all, do you think you'll be able to find the truck again? I understand from Mary here that it was in a rather remote part of the desert."

"I've been back over my flight plan and log book where I made some notes and I'm pretty certain I can narrow down the location sufficiently to find it again."

"That's excellent, Jaime. Now, did you find anything in the truck?"

"No, I'm afraid not. Only the front as far back as the cab was clear of the sand dune. It'll take several men with shovels and a great deal of work to clear the whole truck to see what's in the rear."

"Did you find anything in the cab itself?"

"Such as what?"

"Anything. Like a briefcase or notebook."

"No, nothing like that. But there was still a considerable amount of sand in the cab, as far up as the waistline of the bodies. There may have been something under or behind the seats but I was not inclined or had any reason to be looking for something specific. And I didn't want to unduly disturb the remains too much."

"That's understandable, but as far as you could tell, the rest of the truck was intact?"

"As far as I could tell, yes. It had suffered a frontal strafing attack. The motor and the cab bore the brunt of the damage and it hadn't appeared to have caught fire. So, I would say there's a good chance the back, and whatever was in it, remains intact."

"Excellent. Let's hope that's so."

"Your turn. What can you tell me about this twenty-year-old mystery?"

"What I'm about to tell you is totally confidential even after all this time as it's possible that what we discover may have far reaching effects on events that have happened since the Second World War."

"It gets more mysterious by the second. Please go on."

"You know who von Lutzdorf was, don't you, Jaime?"

"Yes, but only up to a point. I know that, pre-war, he was quite a celebrity pioneering long-distance flying but that's all."

"Well, amongst other things, he was strongly anti-Nazi and, up until the time he disappeared, he was collaborating with my department."

"This has all the makings of a spy story. By the way, have you seen that new film just out featuring an MI6 agent called James Bond?"

Sherbourne laughed and said, "Yes, it's a bit fanciful. Nothing like reality. To be serious, Jaime, have you ever heard of the name ODESSA?"

"As far as I remember from my geography, Odessa is a port in the Black Sea."

"Quite right, but it also has another more sinister meaning. It is the acronym for the organisation of former SS members. In German, it stands for Organisation Der ehemaligen SS-Angehoerigen."

"Is that so? What is its significance in this matter?"

"We have reason to believe von Lutzdorf was transporting documentation relating to the initial formation of this organization during the war and we would desperately like to get our hands on it."

"For what purpose?"

"The Nuremburg trials did not end the hunt for Nazi war criminals. Very many of them still remain at large and we suspect that some, who have managed to conceal their crimes, are active in politics and business in Germany today. We have reason to believe ODESSA was also set up to ensure that the Nazis' ambitions would not die if they lost the war and that it would be the basis for establishing a Fourth Reich. We think this documentation would help us catch up with them."

"I see. That's definitely a worthwhile quest. When do you want to start?"

"First of all, Jaime, I must warn you that we won't be the only interested party in trying to recover this information. Your discovery was widely circulated in the press in both England and Germany and most definitely will have come to the notice of ODESSA. Even though it is clandestine, ODESSA is a powerful and influential organization and will stop at nothing to prevent this information falling into our hands. So, we must take precautions on how we proceed. As far as we know, the Germans had no idea of our relationship with von Lutzdorf nor that we were aware of what he was transporting. For the moment, we have the advantage since you are the only person who knows of von Lutzdorf's location. We also have a bigger involvement and resources in Libya than the opposition and good relations with its government. We do not, however, want to advertise our interest as a government in this matter as it may arouse suspicions that there is more to this than just the discovery of a long-lost wartime casualty."

"How is it then that you would like to proceed?"

"I understand you've had some discussions with an attaché at the German Embassy on the matter?"

"Yes, the air attaché, Hugo von Oppersdorf. A solid sort who, in my opinion, is most definitely anti-Nazi."

"What did you discuss with him?"

"Only cooperating to assist them in recovering the bodies to be brought back to their families for a Christian burial. I observed your request via the ambassador to be vague about the location and stressed it would require an extensive search over a fairly large area."

"Good, well done. We'll make an agent of you yet."

"Mary has already started on that. I'm thinking of calling her Mata after Mata Hari instead of Mary."

"She was supposedly on the other side," said Sherbourne with a laugh.

"Same flower, different colour," retorted Jaime.

"That's very nice of you, Jaime, to refer to me as a flower," Mary said. "What kind?"

"Without a doubt, a rose, most certainly."

To bring the conversation back to the subject in hand, Sherbourne broke in. "What did you suggest to them as the best way to recover the bodies, Jaime?"

"I said we would need to mount an air search supported by a land expedition. We'll need the air search to relocate the truck and then we could guide the land party the final stage by radio or some other type of visual signal."

"That sounds a very practical way of doing things. Why do you need a land party?"

"The landing area is very restricted and will only accommodate a small aircraft such as the Twin Beech that I was flying. We could not carry all the personnel and equipment needed. It's a long way from Tripoli and, if we use the Twin Beech, it doesn't have the range to get there and back without some extra fuel which the land party could bring with them."

"That settles it then. You must be the team leader for this project because of your knowledge and experience. I suggest you speak again to von Oppersdorf and organize a joint expedition with our two embassies working together. The German Embassy can charter the aircraft from your company Air Libya, and Mary and I will accompany you in the aircraft. Von Oppersdorf can organize the land party which I suggest should consist of two vehicles suitable for travelling in the desert and capable of carrying your aviation fuel, water and other supplies."

"What if von Oppersdorf wants to come in the aircraft with us? After all, they'll be paying for it," asked Jaime.

"I would prefer that he didn't as I would like to search the cab before they arrive."

"In that case, why doesn't our embassy charter the aircraft and leave the land expedition to the Germans?"

"I didn't want us to appear to be too interested. After all, it's German nationals we're talking about. But you're quite right, of course. You can say that, in the interests of goodwill, we will organize the flight. I'll then authorize the embassy to charter the aircraft on behalf of my department."

"As a matter of interest, why is it that you don't want von Oppersdorf with us when we get to the truck? Is there something you haven't told me?"

"Well, yes. I suppose I had better tell you the whole story as I know it from the files."

"I think that's the least you can do if you expect me to lead this team."

"Von Lutzdorf was operating from a secret base in the south of Libya near to the border with Chad. It had been set up by the Italians years earlier. We've tried to discover its whereabouts but before the Italians quit Libya fleeing from Montgomery's forces, they destroyed all of their records and archives so we've had no luck there."

"What's the significance of that?"

"According to the file, von Lutzdorf concealed all of the documentation he brought back from South America somewhere near this secret base but the Germans don't know exactly where. I believe they think the documents are in the truck. I'm hoping he had with him some form of evidence showing not only the location of the base but also the concealed documentation."

"Why do you think that?"

"Because he was a very clever and resourceful man. He would have anticipated the possibility of something going wrong and would have made provisions to cover every eventuality of either getting back to Germany, being captured by us or being killed. He was determined, no matter what, that these documents should get to the allies as he had no desire to see a resurgent Nazi Party post-war. That much is clear from the file."

"Now I understand the importance of this matter. I'll do my best to persuade von Oppersdorf to travel out with the trucks but I won't insist if he prefers to fly with us."

"I agree. If that's the case, we'll deal with it at the time but whatever else happens, we must not let them know I'm from MI6. I will pose as a representative of the British War Graves Commission here to assist in the recovery. There's a very large British and Commonwealth grave site here in Tripoli. The main German war grave is in Benghazi."

"It'll take a week or so to organize the expedition so we have time to get things right."

"What arrangement do you have for meeting with von Oppersdorf?"

"No problem, just a simple phone call. I'll call him from here when we've finished."

"I think we're done for the moment, so please make your call."

***

Von Oppersdorf was pleased to hear from Jaime after he explained he was at the British Embassy discussing the ways and means of recovering the bodies. Von Oppersdorf invited Jaime to come straight to the German Embassy as soon as he was finished there.

"Good to see you again so soon, Wing Commander," said von Oppersdorf as Jaime was shown into his office.

"Please call me Jaime. Wing Commander is a bit formal after all these years."

"Of course, Jaime. Please forgive me, force of habit. I stayed on in the post-war Luftwaffe until I joined the diplomatic service where even now rank is important."

"If I may, I'll call you Hugo."

"Please do, Jaime. I would like that we become friends and perhaps, as we get to know each other, we may spend some time discussing some of our more pleasant memories of our wartime experiences,"

"I would like that, Hugo. Now the reason for this visit is to organize jointly the recovery of two of the more unfortunate members of our former fraternity."

"Indeed so, and I like the way you have described them."

"In death, everyone is equal, Hugo. We must count ourselves as amongst the more fortunate ones."

"I do believe, Jaime, that you are a philosopher at heart just like myself."

"Perhaps so, but to get down to the immediate issue. I have discussed it with some of my embassy people and they have proposed that I organize the flight to locate the truck again and that you organize a land party to bring up some equipment and stores to enable us to excavate the truck and recover the bodies. What do you think of that proposal?"

"It sounds a good and practical solution. Could you explain your plan in a little more detail?"

Jaime proceeded to set out his reasoning for the need for an air search and a supporting land expedition which von Oppersdorf enthusiastically agreed with and said he would discuss the logistics of it with his government and get back to him as soon as he had the confirmation to proceed along those lines.

Chapter 60

❖

When he got back to his apartment after leaving the German Embassy, Jaime telephoned Mary to confirm von Oppersdorf had agreed with the plan and would get back to him after he had cleared it with his government department.

They agreed to meet, together with the MI6 agent, for dinner that evening to continue their discussion on the matter as Jaime still had a number of questions he wanted ask about the ODESSA connection.

Much against the objection of Jaime and Sherbourne, Mary insisted they all meet for dinner at her apartment; her argument concerning security winning out in the end.

"We really didn't want you to have to produce a meal for us," said Sherbourne.

"Don't worry. It's only a salad and cold cuts. Nothing too laborious."

"Mary is a Cordon Bleu chef, Alan. What a pity you won't have the pleasure of her cooking."

"Another time perhaps," added Mary. "What would you all like to drink?"

"A glass of cold white wine for me," said Jaime.

"Me too please," said Sherbourne. Seated on the terrace enjoying the warm evening breeze, Sherbourne spoke up. "Mary mentioned you might have some further questions of me concerning the ODESSA connection, Jaime."

"Yes, as it's all so new to me, never having heard the name before, I wondered what you really know about it since you intimated it was a shadowy secret kind of organization."

"That's true, Jaime, and there are many in government, both at home and in other countries, who do not believe in its existence but I can assure you it's true."

"What can you tell me about von Lutzdorf and his involvement in the movement?"

"He was never involved in ODESSA, quite the contrary. In fact, at the time, the movement was in its embryo state and the name ODESSA had not been coined. Before I came out here, I had a meeting with Stewart Menzies. He's retired now but he was formerly the head of SIS during wartime from 1939 right up until 1952. It was he who recruited von Lutzdorf into working with us sometime in early 1943. He was astonished at the news of his discovery and, when I went to see him at his home, he told me all about that period and how von Lutzdorf was involved. A fascinating story."

"That's why I'm here. For you to tell me all about it."

"It's clear now that the two major architects of ODESSA in the beginning were Goering and Heinrich Mueller. Goering, you know, was head of the Luftwaffe but Mueller was an altogether different character. Where Goering was an extrovert and reveled in public exposure in the press and films, Mueller was very secretive and liked to keep his exposure down to a minimum. Everyone in Germany and the outside world knew of Goering but very few people, even in Germany, knew

Mueller was head of the Gestapo, the secret state police, and then even less what he looked like. Only a few photographs of him ever appeared in public and that was by design.

"Of course, Himmler was involved as Mueller's boss but he had no direct involvement in the setting up of ODESSA. As you know, both Goering and Himmler committed suicide at the end of the war whereas Heinrich Mueller just disappeared like Bormann and many others. To date, Mueller is still sought after as one of the biggest and most important of the Nazi war criminals who escaped justice."

"That's a very interesting history lesson, but where does von Lutzdorf fit in?"

Sherbourne smiled as he continued. "Be patient, Jaime. It's a long story."

"Sorry, please go on," replied Jaime as he topped up everyone's glass from the bottle cooling in an ice bucket.

"Menzies told me about how von Lutzdorf had been seconded to Goering's private staff at the Air Ministry and commissioned to plan a series of flights to Africa and then South America. It was the flight to South America that first interested Heinrich Mueller.

"Whereas Goering, it's now clear, was preparing to transfer huge state assets out of Germany to ensure that, if Germany lost the war, a new Reich could be well-funded as could any of the leaders who managed to escape.

"Mueller, on the other hand, was busy setting up a network of Nazi cells throughout the countries of South America to support the eventual establishment of a Fourth Reich. At some point, Goering's and Mueller's plans coincided and they agreed to cooperate. Von Lutzdorf was instructed by Goering to accommodate Mueller's needs.

"Menzies also told me von Lutzdorf did not know exactly what the diplomatic boxes contained but from what he had managed to understand from his discussions with Goering was they contained original, signed and notarized copies of banking documents relating to the huge gold deposits resting in banks in Switzerland. These were being pledged as security for the issuance of letters of credit and certificates of deposit to banks all over South America to fund nominee companies. They were also used to acquire shares in established companies and industries in both North and South America and even probably Great Britain.

"We know Germany, throughout the war, did business through nominee companies in Switzerland with many countries and had established banks in Argentina, Paraguay, Chile and Brazil. They also did business directly with Sweden who was officially neutral but then Sweden was a great help to us in the more clandestine aspects of war. So, we don't hold that against them.

"America, on the other hand, had companies with subsidiaries in Germany and was making profits from their wartime industries. Switzerland's secret banking laws make it impossible to trace any assets or money deposited by Germany even to this day. Switzerland jealously guards her secrets and this is unlikely to change at any time in the future unless we can find some documentary evidence to allow us to penetrate that veil of secrecy."

"This all sounds terribly complicated and I'm still not sure where all this is leading."

"It cannot have escaped your notice, Jaime, that the most successful economy in Europe since the war is Germany. Albeit Germany received funds under the Marshall Plan, those alone do not account for the thriving economy of today. There must have been, and still is, another source of funding underwriting the rebuilding and development of her industries.

"Britain also received funds under the Marshall Plan but we also had incurred a massive debt under the lend lease programme which largely negated these funds. We're still burdened with the repayments which are continuing to this day. Germany had to repay nothing."

"As interesting as this all is, Alan, I'm still not sure how it's connected to the recovery of these documents. Surely they won't change the events of the last twenty years."

"No, of course not, but that's not the intention. I told you Nuremberg wasn't the end of the quest for justice and retribution. As the war was coming to a close, the only person who saw a new conflict was looming was Churchill. President Roosevelt was a sick man and no match for the wiles of Stalin.

"In an act of unprecedented ingratitude, the British people voted Churchill out of office and installed a socialist government. Granted, there were reasons for the people wanting a change after all the social upheaval of the war but then was the wrong time. The socialist government did some good things but they were politically naive and the communists took over control of all of eastern Europe.

"The Americans then became politically obsessed with communism and invested their time and politics into courting the Germans as a bulwark against the Russians. So much so that they were prepared to ignore many of the wartime atrocities and the pursuit of those who perpetrated them. They felt secure in their fortress, being the possessor of the atomic bomb technology, and were concentrating on the boom in their post-war economy made possible by the vast increase in industrial capacity due to the wartime research and development and the captured German technology and scientists.

"It was left to us, therefore, being closer to Europe not only geographically but mentally, to try to right many of the wrongs that had happened. Apart from enabling us to break into the very core of ODESSA, what these documents will enable us to do is to seek out some of those criminals still at large and force the Swiss banks to return many of the stolen funds and other items of value to their rightful owners and to force the German government to make reparations where suitable."

"Now I understand. A noble quest indeed and, from what you have explained, I can see that ODESSA could not only be exposed as real but could stand to lose much of their wealth."

"I'm glad I've managed to get that across to you, Jaime, and you now understand the need for absolute secrecy. There could be much danger in this for us all. ODESSA will have operatives that will think nothing of eliminating any one of us if they think it'll keep themselves safe and secure."

"A sobering thought. What do you suggest we do about it?"

"I don't think they'll try anything here in Tripoli. Especially not when we're working together with a team from the German Embassy which will be highlighted by the press."

"But if they think the documents are in the truck, they cannot afford to stand back and let us find them."

"True enough, Jaime, but they also have a problem with that as they cannot do anything before we leave and they won't know where we're going."

"What if they try to follow us?"

"Well, they certainly wouldn't be able to follow you flying."

"True enough but they could keep a trail on the land party."

"That may be a problem. How would you explain that to von Oppersdorf without disclosing to him the possible danger from ODESSA? As far as he's concerned, this is just a straightforward recovery of two war victims. How about von Oppersdorf? Do you trust him?"

"From the things he's told me and the sentiments he has expressed, I would be inclined to trust him with my life."

"It might very well come to that."

"I think we should give it some further thought when I hear back from him and we know who else will be in his party."

"Good idea but as an MI6 operative, I'm licensed to carry a gun which I shall take the precaution of doing."

"This is becoming quite dramatic. Let's hope it doesn't come to the need to use it."

"I think that's quite enough drama for the evening. Now, come and sit at the table," said Mary. "We have some of that soup you liked so much, Jaime, before the cold cuts and salad."

"I thought I could smell that delicious aroma coming from the kitchen. Now's your chance, Alan, to try one of Mary's specialities."

The rest of the evening passed in a more light-hearted atmosphere and when Alan said he was ready to leave, Jaime joined him saying that, as he was flying the next day, he needed an early night.

***

Two days after their last meeting, Jaime, who was unexpectedly not flying that day due to a faulty aircraft, received a call from von Oppersdorf saying he had someone he would like him to meet and asked him to come to the embassy.

Assuming it was someone who would be joining their expedition, Jaime arrived at the embassy at the appointed time and was shown directly to von Oppersdorf's office.

As he was shown in to the office, he was surprised to see two women sitting together on the settee around the coffee table. Von Oppersdorf rose immediately from one of the easy chairs and clasped Jaime by the hand.

"Jaime, I would like you to meet Frau von Lutzdorf and her daughter."

Somewhat taken aback by both the unexpected nature of the event but also by the sight of two extremely beautiful women, Jaime was momentarily lost for words but saved by von Oppersdorf's interjection. "Frau von Lutzdorf, this is James St Clair who I've told you so much about."

Jaime, having recovered his composure, stepped forwards and, leaning slightly, he took her outstretched hand and said, "How do you do, Frau von Lutzdorf?"

"I am very pleased to meet you, James. Please call me Magda and this is my daughter, Alexis," said Frau von Lutzdorf in perfect unaccented English.

Releasing her hand, Jaime exchanged it for Alexis' and said, "This is indeed a pleasure. I'm very pleased to meet you both."

The introductions over, von Oppersdorf invited Jaime to join them around the coffee table.

Frau von Lutzdorf was a woman in her mid-forties at the peak of her beauty; her blonde hair coiffed on top showing her elegant neck and ears which were adorned by two sparkling stud diamond earrings. Her makeup was lightly applied but to perfection showing off her azure blue eyes, flawless complexion and full lips. Her daughter could have passed for her younger sister so alike were they facially. In contrast, Alexis wore her hair down in a fashionable style which revealed her ears displaying a pair of younger, coloured drop earrings. They were both dressed in similar summer dresses suitable for the climate in Libya.

It was obvious from the way von Oppersdorf looked at Frau von Lutzdorf he was considerably smitten with his guest.

"Hugo has told me you are the person who found my late husband and for that I shall be eternally grateful to you."

"No need for that. It was a lucky chance that led me to find him."

"Nevertheless, it will enable me to afford him a proper burial and give closure to twenty years of sadness not knowing what happened to him. His parents also will be greatly comforted to have him back."

"His parents are still living then?"

"Yes, as are his aunt and uncle, Baron von Lutzdorf. We, as a family, remember him with great love and affection. Only our daughter Alexis never knew that pleasure."

"The fact that we will be able to bring him back home will give me something to be happy about knowing he was real and has a resting place back with his family. So, I am very grateful to you also for giving me that," said Alexis also in perfect English sounding like a younger version of her mother.

To bring the subject back to the more practical, Jaime asked, "Hugo, have you heard anything back from Berlin regarding who they will be sending out to help with the recovery?"

"Not yet but I'm expecting a signal tomorrow. How have you got on?"

"I've put my company on notice that we'll need to charter one of our Beech 18 aircraft and that I'll need some time off to fly it. There will be no problem with that when we're ready."

"I have at least been able to hire two suitable trucks from a local company who transport stores and equipment out to the oil survey companies."

"Would it be possible for me and my daughter to come with you?" asked Magda.

"I wouldn't recommend it," said Jaime, "It's a long and tiring journey by land and the desert is no place for the unaccustomed at this time of year and in this heat. I venture to say you may find the circumstances and sight of your husband and his friend in their present state somewhat distressing. I assure you, your husband will be treated with all the respect and dignity that should be afforded to a fallen soldier.

"We will have with us a representative of the British War Graves Commission who has just arrived who is very experienced in this sort of work so he will be in good hands. We have a large British war graves cemetery here in Tripoli and he regularly comes and has dealings with the local authorities so he has offered to assist with all the usual paperwork. You will be better staying in Tripoli and enjoying the comforts of air conditioning. If all goes well, we should only be gone for four days, five at the most."

"I will defer to your recommendation and good sense, Jaime."

"Where are you staying whilst you're here?"

"We are in the Uaddan Hotel. It's very pleasant and we have a nice sea view."

"It's the best place in Tripoli."

"Perhaps we could all have dinner there this evening," said von Oppersdorf.

"That would be very nice. Thank you, Hugo, for suggesting it," said Frau von Lutzdorf.

"Why don't you ask Mary if she would like to join us?" added von Oppersdorf.

"I'll do that and perhaps, if you don't mind, I would also like to ask the War Graves representative, who I just mentioned, to join us."

"By all means, please do ask him. I would like to thank him for his kind offer," said Frau von Lutzdorf.

"That's settled. Until this evening then," said Jaime as he rose. "Excuse me for now, Hugo. I have some things I must get done today."

"I'll see you out, Jaime," said von Oppersdorf also rising. "Please stay here, Magda. I will be right back."

As Jaime and von Oppersdorf reached the exit of the embassy, Jaime turned and smiled at him and said, "My goodness, Hugo, what a beauty!"

"Which one?" said von Oppersdorf returning his smile.

"Which one indeed. Both, of course, but the daughter's a bit young for you, Hugo," Jaime replied, laughing this time.

"Nothing like that has crossed my mind, Jaime, but I agree she is a remarkable beauty."

Chapter 61

❖

Jaime returned to his apartment and immediately called Mary and told her of the arrival of Frau von Lutzdorf and her daughter and the invitation to join them and von Oppersdorf for dinner at the Uaddan Hotel.

"Put on your best frock this evening, Mary. I think you'll have a little competition."

"What do you mean by that, Jaime?"

"Well, knowing how women are, you would never forgive me if I didn't forewarn you that Frau von Lutzdorf and her daughter are considerable beauties. But don't worry, darling, you're in the same class and I'll only have eyes for you."

"That remains to be seen. What about Alan?"

"He's been invited also and I've explained that he is our War Graves representative who has offered his services to help so be sure to give him a proper briefing. I suggest we meet at your apartment as it's closest to the Uaddan."

***

Jaime, Mary and Alan arrived at the appointed time to find von Oppersdorf and his two companions already seated at a round table in a quiet corner of the terrace. After the formal introductions, they quickly arranged the seating so Sherbourne was between Frau von Lutzdorf and her daughter with von Oppersdorf on the other side of Frau von Lutzdorf next to Mary with Jaime between the daughter and Mary.

In spite of the serious nature of the underlying reason that had contrived to bring them all together at this place, they all managed to contribute to a convivial and pleasant evening keeping the conversation light and about their work and experiences and occasionally current world affairs as well as local situations and what it was like living in Tripoli.

"I must say," said Frau von Lutzdorf, "I envy you these nice warm evenings. Dining outside is so pleasant."

"It isn't always so nice, especially when we have the hot winds from the desert covering everything with fine sand. But on the whole, it's a very nice climate," said Jaime.

Throughout the evening, Jaime noticed how attentive von Oppersdorf was to Frau von Lutzdorf, obviously entranced with her beauty and character, occasionally causing her to break into a smile and laugh at some remark.

Occasionally, Mary squeezed his hand under the table and whispered in his ear, "Remember what you said about eyes only."

Sherbourne managed to portray himself as an urbane civil servant acting the part well and keeping up a conversation with the whole table.

Von Oppersdorf, conscious he was the host acting for his embassy, recognized Frau von Lutzdorf was beginning to tire and that it was getting to that time to bring the evening to a close. He looked at Jaime and nodded. "Gentlemen, I think it is time to call an end to a most delightful evening. Magda and Alexis have had a long day travelling and I'm sure they're feeling the effects."

Frau von Lutzdorf smiled at von Oppersdorf and said, "Thank you, Hugo. You're right. It has been a long day and we girls need our beauty sleep."

Both Jaime and Sherbourne rose and, with von Oppersdorf, stood behind each lady's chair and removed them as they also rose from the table.

In the lobby of the hotel, they bade each other goodnight, leaving von Oppersdorf with his guests. Jaime, Mary and Sherbourne left and walked together down to the avenue along the harbour facing the hotel. Jaime and Mary turned to the left towards both his and her apartments as Sherbourne said goodnight and turned right towards the ambassador's residence where he was staying in one of the VIP guest apartments.

Mary put her arm through Jaime's as they strolled slowly along, enjoying the still warm evening and the scent and smells of the tropical night.

"What did you think of von Lutzdorf's widow and daughter?" asked Jaime.

"Delightful, the both of them. Though I must say the daughter was a surprise. They were only married for a couple of months before he disappeared."

"I think that was a very fortunate thing for the family as now there's an heir to carry on the family title. Alexis will ultimately inherit the barony when the baron and his brother die."

"Yes, she will make a very glamorous baroness."

When they reached Mary's apartment, she said, "Would you like a coffee or something?"

"I think I would prefer a something."

Mary took him by the hand and said goodnight to Anna as they entered the lift.

Chapter 62

❖

Jaime had an early flight the next day but it was only of short duration and he was back in his apartment by early afternoon when he received a call from von Oppersdorf.

"I've had a signal from Berlin. They're sending out someone from a military benevolent organization that specializes in looking after disabled veterans and recovering war victims. There will also be two volunteers from the same organization who served in North Africa and have desert experience. They'll be very useful to drive the trucks."

"That sounds an admirable arrangement. When do you expect them?"

"In a day or two. They'll let me know. I was thinking, Jaime, if you don't mind now we'll have some competent help to deal with the land party, I could fly out with you. I would really like to get back in the cockpit if possible."

"Of course, Hugo. That would be fine. I look forward to you flying with me."

Jaime had discussed this possibility with Sherbourne and was confident he could keep von Oppersdorf busy in the aircraft while

Sherbourne conducted a thorough search of the truck's cabin for any likely evidence concerning the location of the documents.

"Perhaps we can get together to draw up a plan to enable the land party to rendezvous with us at the site. How would you suggest we organize that?" asked von Oppersdorf.

"I can give them an approximate location to head for and then, when we're on the ground, we can give them directions by radio for the last few miles or so. At night, we could aim a searchlight in the sky which would be visible for miles or fire a rocket flare for them to home in on."

"That sounds simple enough and should do the trick."

Jaime and Sherbourne had discussed the possibility of having a talk with Magda von Lutzdorf to see if she had any information on her husband's last mission which might be useful to them. Perhaps he had mentioned something that might help to locate what he was transporting or even where their secret base was located. Sherbourne was sure from the file they would not find anything in the truck and, if there was no clue as to where von Lutzdorf had secreted the documents, they must make every effort to locate the base.

"Thank you for organizing last evening, Hugo. It was very nice to meet Magda and Alexis. Mary and I would like to see them again if possible."

"I'm sure they would like that too. When would you be available?"

"I have the next couple of days off flying so any time during then."

"I will organize a lunch and get back to you."

After they finished the call, Jaime called Mary at the embassy and told her what he planned. "She might have some useful information but I don't want to appear too inquisitive or appear insensitive."

"Don't worry. Between us, we'll see what she knows."

"It's a pity we couldn't involve von Oppersdorf in our inquiries. I'm sure he would be cooperative as I'm sure he's completely anti-Nazi. But after what Alan has told me about the extent of the ODESSA infiltration and its reach, we cannot take the chance."

"I agree. In this business, we can trust no one until proved otherwise."

"Spoken like a true professional, Mata."

"Now you're beginning to get the hang of it, Jaime."

An hour after he finished speaking with Mary, von Oppersdorf called and told Jaime he had organized a lunch for the following day and gave him directions to a well-known and popular Italian restaurant on the main square near to the old city and gold souk.

***

Jaime arranged to meet Mary at her apartment and then walk together the short distance to the restaurant with which they were both familiar.

"I'll say one thing for living in Tripoli, everything is nicely within walking distance," remarked Jaime as they left Mary's apartment.

"I know that Libya is now an independent kingdom, but the Italians have left it with some nice buildings and amenities especially their cuisine to complement the local dishes which I find delicious," said Mary.

"It certainly has a nice cosmopolitan atmosphere. The Libyan people are extremely friendly and the Libyans and the

Italians seem to have no animosity of the past under Italian occupation. It was a wise move on the part of the Libyan government to allow the Italians who live here and were born here to remain and keep their property and businesses. They contribute a great amount to the economy and the functioning of local government."

"Let's hope it stays like that."

Von Oppersdorf and his guests had just arrived as they entered the restaurant and, when they were all seated, Magda von Lutzdorf smiled at Jaime and Mary and said, "I'm so pleased to see you both again. I really enjoyed the evening yesterday."

"It's always very pleasant dining outside at the Uaddan."

"Yes, it's a very nice spot but it's the company that counts and my daughter and I enjoyed yours and Mary's very much. We talked a lot in general but it would be really nice if we could talk a bit about each other. I would love to know more about you both."

This gave Jaime the opening he was hoping for as he said, "That would be very nice, Magda. Ever since I found your husband, I've been consumed with curiosity to know more of his life and background and, now that you're here, perhaps you could satisfy that curiosity. That is, if you don't mind talking about him."

"Not at all, Jaime. It's been twenty years and, although I still miss him, time is a great healer and it'll give me great pleasure to share some of my memories with you. It helps to bring back some of those happy times."

Relieved at her attitude and willingness to talk about the past, Jaime pondered how best to start.

"I understand you were married in Berlin not long before his last mission and that Goering attended the ceremony," said Mary, coming to his rescue, "It must have been quite an affair."

"Of course, you would know that from my letter which you found with him. Thank you, by the way, for returning it to me. It was a very poignant moment for me to see it and read it after all those years. To answer your question, yes, but it was not so big, what with security and all those considerations in those days.

"Goering, who you may or may not know was my uncle by marriage, was there. His first wife Karin, who was Swedish, was my aunt, my mother's sister. When my mother became ill with a very debilitating illness, I went to live with them in Germany as a young girl. I know the world looks on him today as a monster but my memories of him are much fonder. He was almost like a father to me and very kind."

"There are many facets to a person's character and I don't suppose Goering was any different," said von Oppersdorf, "I met him once when he visited my squadron and he was very jovial and full of good humour. But that was, of course, before all the Nazi secrets came out."

"Of course, he had a lot to answer for and I make no excuses for him but, from what I know of him in his own mind, he was never an ardent Nazi. He most definitely supported them and used them for his own ambitions because they were his route to power and riches. His real loves were the Luftwaffe, art and the good things of life."

"You said in the letter that you thought Hitler might also attend. Did he?" asked Jaime.

"No, thank goodness. Much to our relief, he was busy away at his bunker in Rastenburg on the Eastern Front."

"How did your husband get on with Goering?"

"I must tell you my husband and his whole family were intensely anti-Nazi but, as a serving officer, he was patriotic and would always do his duty. Goering admired him and, as you know, there is always a special bond between aviators. Whatever else he was, Goering was courageous and who knows, if he had not been seduced by the Nazis and they had not come to power, he could have had perhaps a constructive career in politics. He certainly had the energy for it."

"Did your husband ever talk to you about his missions?" asked Jaime.

"Not about the missions as such. He was always security conscious but he did talk about the flying and the people he had to deal with sometimes. He was very upset at having to deal with Heinrich Mueller when Goering ordered him to cooperate with him."

"How did Mueller fit in to the picture? Wasn't he the head of the Gestapo?" said Jaime, knowing very well the connection from what Sherbourne had told him but he did not want to reveal his hand.

"Yes, he was a most odious creature. Made my skin crawl every time I met him."

"You knew him also then?"

"Yes, I met him on numerous occasions when Goering invited me to party functions. It was because of knowing him that he introduced himself to Walter one evening when we were having dinner at the Adlon Hotel to celebrate our engagement. He came to our table and made the excuse that he would like to be introduced to Walter because, as a fellow aviator, he admired his pre-war exploits and would like to meet him."

"What was he like as a person?"

"I don't know the right word to describe him in English but he had a sinister sort of air about him, very chilling and the most striking feature about him was his piercing grey eyes. When he looked at you, it was the look of a snake about strike. I'm sure he would have been very frightening when interrogating prisoners."

"He disappeared after the war and has never been seen since. It seems he got clean away," said von Oppersdorf.

"May I ask you one more thing?" asked Jaime. "I know this must be tedious but one thing that has always puzzled me is why your husband was driving across the Libyan desert. There was still an opportunity to continue his flight back to Germany as the allies had not, at that time, taken over all of North Africa. Where did he leave the aircraft and where did he obtain the vehicle he was driving? It's a real puzzle."

"I think I can help you there," said Magda, "I know he made a test flight before his missions to establish a staging post to refuel the aircraft. It was somewhere in the vicinity of the Libyan border with Chad near the Tibesti Mountains. Apparently, it was a former secret Italian base because he was accompanied by the Italian air liaison officer attached to the Air Ministry. I knew him very well and he came to our wedding. He is, in fact, Count Mario Gratziani. He would know where it is."

"That's extremely interesting and solves that part of the mystery. Did he tell you anything more about it?"

"Only that it was close to the mountains and that the airstrip was just sand and not obvious from the air. He had to fly the approach from a line of three rocks to be able to land safely on the hard part of the sand and not get bogged down in the soft areas."

"A fascinating story, Magda. Sorry to have asked you so many questions."

"It has been a pleasure, Jaime. After all, it was you that found my husband and understandable you would have questions concerning the mystery of his disappearance as I have had all these years. I'm glad I was able to help clear up some of the circumstances for you."

The lunch continued in a convivial atmosphere with Jaime telling Magda of his family, home and background, touching on his wartime flying and subsequent post-war flying career and tragedy that caused him to leave his position in England and end up flying in Libya.

Magda and her daughter were visibly moved when he mentioned the loss of his wife having suffered a loss themselves. Jaime thanked them but brushed aside the incident as being a long time ago and moved on in a lighter note. He explained how he really enjoyed the freedom of the type of flying he was now engaged in as opposed to the more regimented routine and sometimes boring civil flying with BOAC. Mary squeezed his hand under the table to convey her feelings silently having already heard of the tragedy.

Magda and Alexis had decided they wanted to explore the gold souk after lunch and Mary had to get back to the embassy so she and Jaime excused themselves and left von Oppersdorf to escort them as their most willing guide, pleased to keep them to himself.

"That was a most useful discussion, especially the description of this secret refuelling post. We must tell Alan about what we've found out from Magda. If we don't find anything in the truck, at least we'll have a plan B to try to locate it," said Jaime.

"Let's go back to the embassy and we can call Alan to join us and he can send a signal to SIS to get in touch with this Count Mario Gratziani. It shouldn't be too difficult to locate him."

When they arrived at the embassy, they found Sherbourne was already there in a meeting with the ambassador. Mary spoke to the ambassador's secretary and asked her to inform Sherbourne that she and Jaime were in her office and would like to see him when he finished his meeting.

"The spot where I found von Lutzdorf is only about sixty miles from the border with Chad so I think, after we've recovered him and his colleague and they're safely on their way back with the land party, we could fly along the border to see if we can locate this three rock formation Magda mentioned," said Jaime.

They were still discussing the situation when there was a knock on the door and Sherbourne entered. He was aware of their lunch meeting with the widow and what information they would try to elicit from her.

"How did you get on with the beautiful widow?"

"We managed to get some very useful information regarding the location of the secret staging airstrip. We also got the name of an Italian Air Force officer who first disclosed its location to von Lutzdorf. His name is Mario Gratziani and he was attached to the German Air Ministry. Magda knew him well and apparently, nowadays, he is Count Mario Gratziani. Your people in London should easily be able to locate a member of the Italian aristocracy."

"I'll get on to it right away."

"Anything important with the ambassador?"

"No, just routine. It appears von Lutzdorf's father and uncle are very well connected with some of our members of the

House of Lords and the PM has taken an interest and wanted to know how we're progressing."

"It seems our hero has generated quite a lot of interest."

"Yes, particularly in the press. I had another signal from my boss this morning to be on our guard for any unusual interest from other persons who may be in Libya. He is concerned about ODESSA trying to interfere."

"If, as you say, you're convinced the documents are not in the truck, we don't have anything to worry about. We'll get there first and search the cab thoroughly for any evidence left by von Lutzdorf where he concealed them and then recover the bodies and let the land party return to Tripoli while we proceed on our own."

"If we don't find any evidence in the cab, where do you suggest we go? We may eventually find this secret base but we still need directions to where the documents are hidden."

"At least if we can't find them then neither can ODESSA and we're back to square one."

"I don't think it's just a question of ODESSA wanting to find the documents. From their point of view, it's rather stopping anyone else from finding them and that's where the danger lies."

"I see your point. Then we must just rely on your instinct and conviction that von Lutzdorf thought of this eventuality and made certain he left evidence somewhere in some form or other that would lead us to the place of concealment while keeping a wary eye open for any move from ODESSA."

"I 'm afraid that's the only path open to us for us at the moment."

***

Later that afternoon, Jaime received a call from von Oppersdorf who had returned to his office to find a signal waiting for him.

"Hello Jaime. I've just received details that the people from the veterans' organisation are coming out to Tripoli tomorrow. The leader is called Kurt Hartmann, apparently a decorated and injured veteran, with two assistants who have the desert experience I told you about. They'll arrive around midday and will be staying in their own apartment that was arranged for them through the organization. They do not need picking up from the airport. They seem to be well-organized and independent. They'll see us here at the embassy later in the afternoon when they've settled in. Can you make it or will you be flying tomorrow?"

"I should be back in Tripoli by four o'clock so make the meeting for… say, four thirty?"

"I'll speak to Hartmann and arrange it for that time. See you tomorrow."

Chapter 63

❖

As Jaime entered von Oppersdorf's office the following afternoon, he was confronted with the sight of four men, including von Oppersdorf, seated around the coffee table. As one, they all rose and turned towards him.

"Wing Commander," said von Oppersdorf, "May I introduce Captain Hartmann?"

At the same time he said it, von Oppersdorf, who was standing behind Hartmann and facing out of the line of sight of the other two men, nodded at Jaime with a serious sort of expression on his face.

"Good afternoon, Wing Commander. I am Kurt Hartmann and these are my men," he said, indicating the two men as he put out his hand to Jaime.

Jaime was about to say they could dispense with the need to use their former wartime ranks when he realized why von Oppersdorf had nodded and made the face at him. From the way Hartmann had addressed him and referred to the others as "my men", it was obvious they were not former officers and that rank was still observed between them even now in peacetime. Von Oppersdorf was indicating that, between those present, rank was important to establish the hierarchy of who was in charge. Something important to the German mentality.

Jaime tried not to stare at the man facing him which was difficult since he still bore the scars and results of an obvious wartime injury. He was of medium height, perhaps three inches shorter than Jaime, with dark hair containing flecks of grey. His most striking feature was the black patch over his right eye. He also wore a pair of dark glasses so his eyes were not visible. From his temple and around part of the cheek below his glasses and nose, there was some healed scar tissue that was obviously from the wound that had cost him his eye.

"Good afternoon, Captain," replied Jaime, grasping his hand in a firm grip.

Hartmann indicated his men once more and said, "This is Bruno Neumann and Claus Schmitt."

The two men were both stocky with blond hair cut short in the military style and obviously former soldiers. They both nodded towards Jaime and said, "Good afternoon, Wing Commander," but both refrained from putting out their hands.

Jaime had the distinct feeling they had to severely restrain themselves from giving a Nazi salute and clicking their heels. Turning to Hartmann, he said, "It's good of you to come to Libya to organize the recovery of two of your fallen."

"It's what we do, Wing Commander, and we thank you for your help."

"I'm only too pleased to be able to help in this matter. It is the duty of those of us who survived to recover those of our more unfortunate comrades and return them to their loved ones whenever we can."

"Well said, Wing Commander. It is indeed an unusual chance of fate that brings us together here in the land of our former conflict on a mission of good will."

"Indeed so, Captain. I expect that Major von Oppersdorf here has explained the proposal of both a land party and me leading the way by air?" said Jaime using von Oppersdorf's wartime rank to keep up the charade.

"Yes, and it seems a very admirable and practical solution as I understand the location is far down in the Libyan desert and you do not have a precise position due to the random and lucky sighting in that remote area."

"That is so, but I'm sure I'll be able to find it again as I made meticulous notes of my track returning to Tripoli. I shall be able to give you an approximate position and guide you in for the final few miles."

"Excellent, Wing Commander."

"I understand your men, Neumann and Schmitt, have experience of the desert?"

"Yes. All three of us fought in the desert campaign together. That was where I suffered this unfortunate wound and was invalided out back to Germany before the collapse. Neumann and Schmitt were taken prisoner and spent three years in a camp in England. That is why they speak such good English."

"That's very useful and they'll be familiar with driving in the desert also."

"Yes, they will each drive one of the trucks the major has so kindly hired for us. Now I think that is all we need for now. If you will excuse us, me and my men will take possession of the trucks and fit them out with what we may need for the trip. I understand you would also like us to transport some extra aviation fuel for you. Where can we obtain that?"

"I will arrange for you to pick it up from the airport at my company's refuelling facility."

"One more thing, Wing Commander. Do you know if there was anything in the rear of the truck?"

"I couldn't see as the entire rear of the truck behind the cab was buried in sand. Why do you ask?"

"Only because it might contain items of a personal nature and of interest to the families. We would like to return as much as possible as it helps to heal the loss, especially if we find something of value."

Von Oppersdorf took over and saw Hartmann and his men out of his office indicating to Jaime to remain for him to return.

"Quite a trio, Jaime. What do you think of them?"

"Hartmann is quite a striking character. Doesn't seem the type to be running a benevolent society but then he does seem to be a man of action which is what you need for this business. As for the other two, I expected them to click their heels when he addressed them."

"Yes, they're a strange combination but obviously he commanded them during the war and those habits are hard to break. Hartmann came with impeccable references. Any organization that works for the government in Germany is thoroughly checked out. At least they will be efficient."

"Does he know von Lutzdorf's widow and daughter are here in Tripoli?"

"Yes, I told him before you arrived and asked him if he would like to meet with them. He declined saying there would be time for that when he returned with the bodies."

"I suppose that's a reasonable attitude to take. He doesn't appear to be much for socializing. Perhaps he's self-conscious of his appearance."

"Perhaps."

"As from today, I'm off flying duties on standby to prepare for the flight. It seems we can get going by the day after tomorrow. That'll give us time to find the truck again and await the arrival of Hartmann. I'll draw up a chart for you to give to him to find the search area and wait for my signal."

"Hartmann is confident he can have everything ready by the day after tomorrow, so we should plan on that."

***

Jaime's first call when he left von Oppersdorf was to Sherbourne to tell him about his meeting with Hartmann and that he thought it worth investigating his past.

"I'll get my people in London to check him out straight away. As a war veteran, they shouldn't have too much trouble tracing his history. I'm glad to see my disclosure to you on the potential dangers has made you security conscious."

"We'll be ready to leave in two days, Alan. Can you have the information back by then?"

"I'll mark it urgent and I'm sure we can get clearance by then."

His next call was to Mary telling her of the imminent departure and to make sure she had the appropriate clothing and necessities packed.

"Come round to my apartment this evening. You have my permission to make a personal inspection of my readiness for duty, sir."

"That's something I shall look forward to."

***

The two trucks von Oppersdorf had managed to acquire were later versions of the ubiquitous WC model four-wheel drive light truck built by the American Dodge company during and after World War Two. Many of them were still in use in Libya because of their performance in the desert. With a closed cab, they could carry a load of half a ton and were still very popular with the oil companies for transporting personnel and stores.

Hartmann had been very proficient throughout the day following his meeting with von Oppersdorf and Jaime, acquiring all the supplies and equipment needed for the expedition to the southern Libyan Sahara, including two wooden caskets he had made by a local Italian carpentry shop. He had informed them he would be ready to leave on schedule the following day.

***

The news back from SIS in London was they had managed to check out the background of Hartmann and he appeared to be all he claimed. Wounded during the North African campaign, he returned to Germany where he was invalided out of the army and went back to live with his parents, since deceased, on their farm in Bavaria. His only other relatives, two brothers, were killed on the Russian front. Although something of a lone wolf, he had busied himself in setting up an organisation to rehabilitate wounded veterans; many of whom he employed on the farm. He also specialised in looking for and recovering missing wartime personnel and played a very active part in taking care of the maintenance of established German military cemeteries in various locations which had included several previous visits to the German military cemetery in Libya.

"My people have given Hartmann a clean sheet, Jaime," said Sherbourne, as he explained what he had received back from London. "It seems he's well-respected and has been commended by several high-ranking ministers for his achievements and care of former veterans."

"That's good to know, Alan. Have you managed to buy the kit you need for the trip? I plan to get off early tomorrow morning."

"Packed and ready to go, Captain."

"I'm going off now to see von Oppersdorf and give Hartmann a final briefing. I shall go out to the airport with von Oppersdorf at least one hour before you and Mary need to arrive. He's so keen to be able to fly again, he insisted on picking me up. So, we'll see you out there at 8 a.m."

***

Jaime was ready outside of his apartment at sunrise shortly after the speakers on the mosques in the nearby souk and other parts of the city began calling the faithful to the first prayers of the day. Von Oppersdorf, with an embassy car and driver, pulled up and opened the rear door.

"Jump in, Jaime."

The driver picked up Jaime's flight bag and small overnight valise, put them in the boot and then closed the rear door behind him.

"Good morning, Hugo. You're bright and early this morning."

"I just can't wait to get in a cockpit again, so forgive me if I seem a little eager."

"It'll be good to have a co-pilot for a change. You can do the flying while I relax."

"I'm afraid I'll be a bit rusty after all these years."

"Don't worry. It's like riding a bike. Once a flyer, always a flyer."

On arrival at the airport, von Oppersdorf thanked and dismissed his driver and followed Jaime to the Air Libya office where Jaime went through the formalities of taking charge of the Beech 18 on charter for the British Embassy. He checked the aircraft was fully fueled and the refueling facility had the correct instructions and permission to supply a drum of high-octane aviation fuel to Hartmann for collection. He checked the weather for the area for the following seven days and professed himself satisfied and filed a VFR flight plan to be sent to the tower.

"Right, Hugo. We're all done here. We can go and do the pre-flight walk around ground check, if you're ready. I'm sure you'll be familiar with those. They'll be the same for any aircraft."

"Yes. I'm sure we've both done enough of those in our flying careers."

They were just completing the check when Mary and Alan Sherbourne arrived.

The Beech 18, in its normal passenger configuration, had eight seats but the Air Libya version had four of the seats removed to make more space for cargo since this was more of a priority for the oil company work.

Jaime took their small suitcases and stowed them together with the other equipment and essential stores in the cargo space. Von Oppersdorf had already entered and moved up to occupy the co-pilot's seat on the right side of the cockpit. Jaime had a word with the ground crew operator who would standby with a fire extinguisher during engine start and then entered and closed the passenger door from the inside. Making sure Mary and Sherbourne were securely seated, he entered the cockpit and sat in the left-hand captain's seat.

Turning to von Oppersdorf, he said, "I don't know if you're familiar with the cockpit layout in American and British aircraft but Beechcraft, for some peculiar reason, are different from almost all the other manufacturers in that the throttles are in the middle of the control pedestal instead of on the left-hand side. Propeller pitch controls are on the left and fuel mixtures on the right."

"Don't worry, Jaime. Whatever the layout, it won't confuse me because both of those layouts are entirely different to what I'm used to in the Luftwaffe aircraft I've flown. In any case, I'm just going to watch you and learn what I can by asking questions. All I would like is to just feel my hands on the controls when you've got everything settled down in trim in the cruise."

"Fair enough, Hugo. Just watch. I'll explain as I go through the checklist and engine start."

Making sure there were no ground personnel near the propellers, Jaime went, first of all, through the prescribed safety checklist. Then he went through the start-up procedure explaining every move as he went along until the engines had settled down to a satisfying throaty rumble letting the oil pressures and temperature climb to their normal operating levels.

Leaning his head around and back over his right shoulder, he called to his passengers loud enough above the engine noise to ensure they were comfortable and let them know he was ready to depart. Calling the tower for taxi clearance to the take-off position, he opened the throttles and they trundled gently away from the apron to the runway.

At that time of the morning, Tripoli airport was busy with departing aircraft taking personnel and stores to oil camps and survey parties in many parts of the Libyan desert. Jaime found himself taxiing in a queue with three DC-3 Dakotas ahead of him: one from his own company and two were from a rival company whose hangar was next to that of Air Libya. The pilots of the aircraft ahead were not above a bit of good-natured banter on the radio even though they were supposed to leave the airwaves clear for air traffic control.

One of them said, "Good morning, Jaime. I see you're off on a cushy charter this morning."

"Lucky devil," broke in another, "Did you see that glamorous blonde getting into the Beech?"

"It's strictly business, my friends," replied Jaime.

"Some business, if you can get it. Any chance of passing some our way?" came a taunt from a third.

The crisp professional tones of the English controller in the tower broke in. "Okay, gentlemen, you've had your fun. Now, can we get back to the serious business of traffic control?"

By this time, the lead DC-3 was about to enter the runway and, in contrast, the casual drawl of the American captain came over the radio giving his call sign and continued, "Sorry about that, sir. Permission to take off."

The controller responded in the affirmative and the aircraft proceeded with its take off followed in consecutive order by the awaiting aircraft as order was restored to the airwaves.

Von Oppersdorf, who had been listening in unaccustomed to this non-regulation use of the radio, was greatly amused and said, "You seem to have some good friends amongst the pilots here, Jaime."

"They're a good bunch. Mostly Americans and a few Brits."

By the time it was Jaime's turn to enter the runway, the three DC-3s were climbing away heading off in a southeasterly direction where most of the current oil exploration activity was taking place.

All checks complete, Jaime opened the throttles keeping the Beech straight by use of the twin rudders and, as the aircraft accelerated down the runway, the tail lifted and they passed VMC: the minimum control speed. At ninety miles per hour, Jaime eased back gently on the control column. As the aircraft lifted off the ground climbing steadily ahead with the speed increasing, Jaime raised the undercarriage and told von Oppersdorf to place his hands on the controls and follow his movements.

Chapter 64

❖

Instead of following the preceding aircraft, Jaime continued straight ahead on to a southerly heading towards the Libyan border with Chad and the Tibesti Mountains. From his pilot notes he had entered in his log book detailing the discovery of the Afrika Korps truck and his flight back to Tripoli, he had been able to calculate a fairly accurate position by noting the proximity of some ground features and centres of habitation in this sparsely populated area.

The area where he found the truck was in the Murzuk Sand Sea, an area of shifting sand dunes with the oasis of Murzuk its centre of population. The prominent feature of this ancient town was the old Turkish fortress which Jaime noted as he flew towards Tripoli. He now would use this a navigation reference point for the return flight.

Jaime had already given von Oppersdorf a copy of his proposed flight plan and, as they climbed ahead, he set the giro compass on the southerly heading and said, "If you're comfortable with the feel of the aircraft, you can climb to eight thousand feet and level off on this heading. Use the trim wheel to lessen the pressure on the column to suit yourself, Hugo."

"Thank you, Jaime. This is wonderful and you're right. It's all coming back and feels so natural."

"You have control. I'm going back to speak to Mary and Alan."

Jaime unfastened his seat belt and got up out of his seat and, stepping over the main spar, entered the cabin through the cockpit door which was hooked back in the open position.

The passenger seats in the cabin consisted of three single seats on each side of the aisle. Mary and Sherbourne were occupying the centre seat of each row opposite each other as Jaime slipped into the front seat on the port side and turned to face them both.

"Who's driving?" asked Sherbourne with a grin.

"I'm giving Hugo a refresher course. Don't worry, he's got the hang of it."

"How long will the flight be?" asked Mary.

"If all goes well and we locate the truck without too much difficulty, about three and a half hours."

"What's the terrain like in the search area?" asked Sherbourne.

"It's in the region known as the great Murzuk Sand Sea. An area of shifting sand dunes interspersed with flat basin areas. It was on one of these flat areas I managed to land the first time."

"What about Hartmann? When do you think he'll arrive?"

"I gave him a full briefing and advised him to drive first to Sebha. There's a reasonable road as far as that. Then stop overnight in Sebha and make his way to the Murzuk Oasis by what's not much more than a rough track. From Murzuk, it's all desert and he shouldn't attempt that at night. So, we'll have today and tomorrow to ourselves and probably expect to see him the morning of the day after tomorrow."

"Good. That will give us ample time to search for any evidence of the documents."

"Have either of you spent any time in the desert before?"

"I drove from Tripoli to Gharyan one day. That's about all," said Mary.

"My career has kept me mostly in capital cities, so I'm afraid not," said Sherbourne.

"Well, you'll have an experience to remember then. The days are extremely hot and the nights, surprisingly, get quite cold. You'll be sleeping under canvas so a few things to watch out for are scorpions, both black and green. Well, a sort of greeny brown. They'll give you a nasty sting so make sure you keep your shoes concealed. Otherwise, be sure to shake them out in the morning. And don't open your sleeping bag until you use it. Likewise, if you leave it open, shake it out before you get in.

"You may see some camel spiders. They grow to around six inches and look ferocious and nasty. They're not usually aggressive but they will bite you if you annoy them. Finally, there's the horned viper snake. Its bite is very poisonous. They burrow in the sand during the day and come out to hunt at night. They won't bother you, if you don't bother them."

"Sounds delightful," said Mary.

"We have plenty of water for this trip so drink when you feel like it and also take the salt tablets you've been given. I see you've both brought hats as advised, so keep your heads covered to prevent heatstroke. End of lesson."

"Are there any other creatures we may see that might be dangerous?" asked Sherbourne.

"I think I've covered those you're most likely to encounter. Be careful, however, when you're searching around in the truck.

Scorpions like the shade and will hide in the cabin, under seats or under the bonnet if there are any about."

"It's a wonder anyone survives out there."

"People have learned how to live with the desert. It's a fascinating and beautiful place once you learn its moods and character."

"You make it sound like a living creature, Jaime," said Mary.

"I think that's a good analogy. There's a surprising amount of life in the desert that, on first sight, appears to be quite desolate and barren."

"I do believe you're becoming poetical, Jaime."

"Wait until you see and experience it. Then tell me what you think."

"Fair enough," said Mary.

"Excuse me, I must get back to the cockpit to check our progress."

Slipping back into his seat, Jaime put on his earphones and looked across at von Oppersdorf as he pressed the microphone button and said, "How are you getting on?"

"This is absolutely wonderful, Jaime. It's bringing back so many good memories for me. I cannot thank you enough for this opportunity."

"I see you leveled off and trimmed the aircraft precisely at eight thousand feet and throttled back exactly to the right engine revs for the cruise. You're a very good student, Hugo," said Jaime smiling.

"As you said, once a flyer, always a flyer. You don't forget the technique after so much rigorous training. I think when I go back to Germany, I will brush up and get my licence back."

"As we used to say in the RAF: a piece of cake."

Von Oppersdorf, unfamiliar with this colloquial bit of air force slang, smiled and nodded his head in agreement but didn't understand what Jaime meant.

Realizing that, Jaime grinned back and didn't think it worth the trouble to explain .

***

Three hours into the cruise brought them in sight of Murzuk and its hilltop fortress where Jaime checked his flight plan and made a minor heading adjustment and clicked the start button on his panel mounted stopwatch.

Pressing his microphone button, he said, "I'll take it now, Hugo."

Von Oppersdorf took his hands off the control wheel and said, "You have control, Jaime."

Throttling back both engines, Jaime put the Beechcraft into a gradual descent towards the Murzuk Sand Sea visible in the distance. The descent to one thousand feet took fifteen minutes where they leveled off and began to scour the terrain ahead. Jaime concentrated from dead ahead out to port and von Oppersdorf, the opposite quarter.

Checking the time elapsed from leaving the fortress navigation reference point, Jaime pressed his microphone button and said, "We should see something in the next two minutes, if my timing is correct."

"Roger," replied von Oppersdorf, using the international acknowledgement.

It was von Oppersdorf who excitedly tapped Jaime on the arm and exclaimed, "There, straight ahead. I saw a flash of sunlight reflecting off something."

Jaime immediately concentrated his attention in that direction and lowered the nose a fraction. He was immediately rewarded with a flash and then another.

"Well done, Hugo. I can see it now." Jaime throttled back a little more, lowered five degrees of flap for more slow speed control and concentrated on the small dot of something standing out differently from the sand-coloured background about a half a mile away, growing larger and more distinct with every second.

They were now down to five hundred feet as they swept over the object which they had been able to clearly identify as their desired objective. Banking into a gentle turn to port, Jaime scanned the area around the truck and recognized the strip where he had managed to land before. Staying at five hundred feet, he quickly configured the aircraft for landing by lowering the undercarriage and keeping it at a safe manoeuvring speed. He lined up for an approach and landing using the truck as his reference point. In the final approach, he lowered full flap and closed the throttles as they gently touched down on the threshold and coasted finally to a stop.

Von Oppersdorf was full of praise for Jaime's quick response and slick landing.

"Well, I didn't want to lose sight of the truck by making too wide a circuit. We were lucky the sun was at the right angle to give us that flash off the windscreen. Without that, we might have missed it."

Turning the aircraft around, Jaime taxied back to the spot where he touched down, passing the truck on the way about two hundred yards off the harder landing strip still in the soft sand of the windward side of the dune. By this time, it was approaching midday with the sun at its highest, so Jaime

441

suggested they first pitch their larger communal tent where they would eat as this, with both front and rear flaps open, would provide a breeze and some cool shade.

"What's wrong with using the aircraft?"

"Just wait a while and see," said Jaime, "Now we're stopped in this sun, it'll heat up like an oven."

"So speaks the voice of the desert expert," said Sherbourne, "Give me a hand, Hugo, to haul this tent out and see if I can remember my Boy Scout training."

While Sherbourne and von Oppersdorf were engrossed in unfolding and erecting the main tent, Jaime and Mary unloaded four lightweight folding chairs and a similarly constructed table.

"All the comforts of home, I see, Jaime," said Mary.

"We'll be here for probably three or four days so we might as well be as comfortable as possible."

"I can go along with that," said Mary.

As well as the main tent, Jaime, who had made out the list of equipment, had also loaded two one-man tents, one of which he allocated to Mary. Another item consisted of a number of poles six feet long rolled up in a length of canvas secured by a couple of straps.

"What's that for?" asked Mary.

"Well, there's no delicate way of putting this, but, when erected, it'll serve as a portable toilet. I'm afraid no plumbing comes with it so you must use your imagination. We men can manage quite well under any conditions but as gentlemen, I thought we would make some allowance for your female status."

"That's very thoughtful of you, Jaime, and I'm touched. But don't worry too much about my modesty, I was in the Girl Guides and we did go camping."

They both laughed as Jaime said, "That's good to know."

They decided to leave the food stores and utensils in the aircraft until the tent was ready. Sherbourne and von Oppersdorf had successfully managed to lay out the tent in the correct position indicated by Jaime and were just fitting the supporting poles when Jaime and Mary gave them a hand to lift them into a vertical position.

With Jaime and Mary holding the poles upright, it was a relatively simple matter for the others to anchor the supporting guy ropes and stretch out the tent and peg it down. When erected, it measured twelve feet long by ten feet wide with a ridge of eight feet high between the poles. With the entry flaps at each end tied back, it provided good shade with a gentle breeze flowing through. The final touch was a canvas groundsheet, pegged down inside to provide a sand-free interior.

Jaime set up the table and chairs and, with a flourish of his hands, he said, "There you are. Home sweet home."

By the time the tent was ready, they were all feeling the effects of the midday heat and from their physical efforts. It was with welcome relief they sat down at the table and poured themselves some cold drinks which they had packed in an insulated cool tub filled with ice.

"That's all the ice we have," said Jaime, "So, if you want some with your gin and tonic this evening, be sure to keep the lid on."

"Wise words, as always, from the desert expert," said Sherbourne, "It's very fortunate the desert Arabs don't drink alcohol. Otherwise, how would they survive without their sundowner gin and tonic?"

This elicited a laugh from all round as they relaxed in the coolness of the shade.

They decided to have a light lunch and wait until the midday sun had descended a few hours towards the west before tackling the cabin search of the truck.

Whilst Mary and von Oppersdorf remained in the tent, Jaime and Sherbourne, each carrying a short-handled shovel which was standard equipment carried in the aircraft in case of getting bogged down in soft sand, made their way along the harder surface of the landing area until they came abreast of the truck. From here, the going was harder through the soft sand and they were grateful to be wearing the desert boots worn as standard by the oil field workers which prevented sand from filling normal footwear. The two hundred yards seemed longer by the time they reached the truck where they took a breather.

Jaime had already warned Sherbourne what to expect concerning the bodies in the cabin but, in spite of that, both men took a moment to look at the remains of von Lutzdorf and Steinberg in silent contemplation and respect.

"Remember what I said about scorpions and snakes," said Jaime, "Let's lift the bonnet first to see if there's anything lurking in the engine compartment."

The safety catch had already been released by the impact of the cannon shells. Taking a side each, they gingerly lifted the bonnet accompanied by a creaking sound from the long dried-out hinges. Nothing scuttled or slid away as they raised it high enough for Jamie to lift up and slot in the safety rod.

Jaime poked his shovel into the engine compartment and rattled it around to disturb anything that might be still lurking there. Satisfied, they proceeded, one each side, to open the cabin doors to let the sand begin to trickle out. They decided not to disturb the bodies and leave the removal to Hartmann's men when they arrived with the caskets.

They first poked the sand, which was still at waist height, with their shovels to disturb any horned vipers that might be sleeping under the surface. When nothing moved, they became a little bolder and began to scrape the sand out of the open doors, gradually working their way down to the floor level and foot controls.

Between the back of the seats and the rear of the cabin which formed the bulkhead between the cabin and the cargo area, they uncovered a hinged flap forming the lid of what was designed to hold tools and a lifting jack, essential for changing wheels. Over the years, the lid had kept out the majority of the sand and when lifted, revealed the tools and jack and also a canvas-wrapped package.

"This looks interesting, Jaime," said Sherbourne as he lifted out the package. "It feels quite heavy."

Undoing the two straps which secured the package, they found a bundle further wrapped in what was once an oil-soaked piece of cloth. Although mostly dried out, it was still supple to the feel.

"I know what this is," said Sherbourne as he unwrapped the bundle to reveal a Schmeisser MP 40 machine pistol and two magazines still in surprisingly clean condition. "I haven't seen one of these for a while. Last time was in Berlin when I was a young intelligence officer attached to HQ. What about you, Jaime?"

"I came across a few during the advance from the Western desert. But being in the air force, they all got snaffled by the army. Some of them preferred them to the Tommy gun."

"Quite a souvenir. What shall we do with it?"

"Wrap it back up and I'll stow it in the aircraft."

Having rewrapped the Schmeisser, Sherbourne set it to one side as he and Jaime continued the search. The tool box revealed nothing further than some more tools and what looked like some engine spare parts. Jaime, who was on the driver's side, remembered the Luger pistol he had taken off von Lutzdorf and stowed under the seat in its holster. As he tried to pull the holster out from where it was jammed between the bottom of the seat and the springs, he found it was caught and would not move. Bending right down so he could put his head below the bottom of the seat, he discovered the holster buckle had got caught between another object jammed between the seat and the springs.

On further inspection, he determined that the object appeared to be a leather-bound book approximately eight by ten inches and nearly an inch thick. Grabbing a tyre lever out of the tool box, he prized it between the springs and the seat bottom which gave him enough space to slide the book out from its place of concealment and also release the holster containing the Luger.

Looking across at Sherbourne, he said, "See what I've found. It looks like a pilot's log book." As he spoke, he opened the book and continued. "How's your German?"

"Not good. Mostly schoolboy stuff. How's yours?"

"The same. Fortunately, Mary's fluent so we'll let her have a look but not in front of Hugo for the moment. I'll conceal it for the time being in my flight bag with my own log book and charts. If von Lutzdorf left anything by way of evidence, the chances are we'll find it in his log book."

"Good. Let's make our way back to the aircraft so we can stow these things out of sight."

"I shall be happier when these poor devils are safely in their caskets. It's a bit unsettling chatting away about them with them sitting there looking on, don't you think?"

Stuffing the log book inside his shirt, Jaime picked up the holster and Luger while Sherbourne tucked the Schmeisser bundle under his arm. They trudged back through the soft sand to base camp.

As they entered the coolness of the tent, von Oppersdorf looked up and said, "How did you get on? Did you find anything of interest?"

"A couple of wartime souvenirs," said Sherbourne as he plonked the Schmeisser on the table next to the holster which Jaime had put down.

Jaime winked at Sherbourne and nodded towards the objects on the table as he said, "Alan, why don't you and Hugo see if these relics are in working order?"

Taking the hint, Sherbourne picked up the bundle and began to undo the straps. "Come on, Hugo. How long since you last handled one of these?"

With von Oppersdorf occupied with Sherbourne, Jaime said, "Mary, can you come and help me with something in the aircraft?"

"Of course. What is it that you want?"

Taking Mary by the hand, he led her towards the aircraft. "Wait and see."

Once inside the Beechcraft, he went to the two front passenger seats and indicated that she should sit down. Taking the log book from his shirt, he handed it to her and said, "What do you make of this? Your German is much better than mine."

Mary opened the book and began to read. "This is amazing. It's a complete record of the South African and South

447

American flights right up until the time he started on his final land journey to where you found him. This is an incredible historic account of his life and flying from the time he was seconded to the special duties under Goering. This is a gold mine of information."

"Does it say anything about where he concealed the documents he was transporting from Argentina?"

"Jaime, I've only had a quick scan through, but most of it seems to relate to the operational aspects such as the navigational details. It'll take me hours, if not days, to read all of this."

Mary kept turning the pages and flipping through the book until she came to the last page where she exclaimed, "Hold on a minute. Here's something which is different."

"What do you think it is, Mary?"

"Here, Jaime, have a look. I can't make much sense out of it. It's groups of numbers. Perhaps some sort of code."

Jaime took the log book and looked at what she had found. "It's a cypher-encoded message. We'll have to get Alan to look at it. Perhaps his people in London will know what it is."

Jaime took the log book and put it back in his flight bag. "Let's get back to the others. Don't say a word until I've spoken with Alan."

Back at the tent, Sherbourne and von Oppersdorf had cleaned both the MP 40 and the Luger pistol and had unloaded the magazines.

"They seem to be as good as new," said von Oppersdorf as he began loading the rounds back into the magazines and the Luger.

"It's like the recent discovery of the USAF B-24D Liberator bomber called Lady Be Good, which went missing in 1943. It was found in the great Calanscio Sand Sea by a survey team from British Petroleum. Most of its equipment was in working order including the radio. It's due to the dry heat and lack of humidity."

"Whatever the reason," said Sherbourne with a laugh, "We're well-armed to fight off an attack."

"Wrap them up again, Alan, and bring them over to the aircraft. I think it best if I find a safe place to stow them out of the way," said Jaime.

Mary busied herself checking through the stores to prepare something for dinner: a duty she had volunteered for and which was gratefully accepted by Jaime.

Together, he and Sherbourne picked up the guns and carried them to the Beechcraft. Jaime entered first and opened a door in the rear bulkhead at the back of the cabin where there was space for a limited number of items. Above the door, there was a shelf where he placed both the MP 40 and the Luger, still in its holster, and secured them in place with a couple of straps.

"Come on up to the cockpit, Alan. I want to show you what Mary found in the log book. Perhaps you can make something of it."

Retrieving his flight bag from behind his seat in the cockpit, he and Sherbourne sat opposite each other in the two front passenger seats. Opening the log book, Jaime turned to the back of the book showing the pages covered in text made up of groups of figures and passed it over to Sherbourne who studied the pages with a growing expression of excitement.

"This could be exactly what we're looking for. It's a message in cipher. When I met recently with Stewart Menzies, he told me that he and von Lutzdorf had communicated in code using a book cipher method."

"How does that work?"

"The sender and receiver both use the same book to refer to words in the text by using numbers to indicate the page, line and position in the line of certain words to construct a message. It's essential both ends have the same book and the same edition to enable them to encipher and decipher the messages."

"That was really useful information from Menzies."

"Better than that, Jaime. He even told me the name of the book. One they had both read. Remember von Lutzdorf went to school in England, so he was familiar with a number of favourite books read in school."

"What was the title? Don't keep me in suspense."

"One I expect you read in school also. *The Wind in the Willows* by Kenneth Grahame."

"A good choice. I did read it and enjoyed it immensely. Where do we get a copy of the same edition?"

"Well, we're in luck there because Menzies has the self same book in his library which he kept as a souvenir after the war. Problem is, it doesn't help us here unless I can transmit the enciphered message back to London and get them to decode it. But I don't have the radio equipment here to communicate with the embassy in Tripoli."

"I might be able to help there," said Jaime, "I can call Aeradio Libya in Tripoli on the Flight Information Service frequency and give them the cipher groups which they can send to the embassy who in turn can pass them on securely to MI6. They'll have to decipher the message and send it back via FIS to us here, but anyone can listen in on that frequency so it won't be secure."

"That won't be a problem because they can encode it in an MI6 code which I can decode when we get it back. When can you call Tripoli?"

"I think I might have to rig up an external aerial to get through from here as we normally communicate when we're in the air. The other problem is it'll be quite laborious having to spell out each figure group. Do you have an identifier code name and department code which I can include to ensure the embassy knows what to do?"

"Yes, and don't worry, I'll take over once you've established communications. I think we should try to do it as soon as possible before Hartmann and his men turn up."

"Agreed. Let me try to establish contact now using the aircraft aerial only. If I can get through, I'll tell them to standby for an important diplomatic message to be relayed to the British Embassy."

Jaime and Sherbourne settled themselves in the cockpit and Jaime switched on the aircraft electric power. Selecting the HF SSB frequency used by all aircraft to call Tripoli Flight Information Service, he pressed the transmit button and called Tripoli giving his aircraft registration call sign.

He was pleasantly surprised when he received an immediate response acknowledging his call. The signal was clear but a little weak so they agreed to switch to an alternate channel more suitable for the time of day. On changing to a lower frequency, the signal came through loud and clear. Jaime quickly explained he had an urgent message to be passed on to the embassy saying it was enciphered and would need to be taken down by hand. The operator at Tripoli, intrigued by the unusual request, was eager to assist.

Taking over from Jaime, Sherbourne identified himself and spoke confidently and slowly into the microphone to ensure the operator got everything down accurately. When he finished, he emphasized the extreme urgency of the situation saying they would be listening out every hour on the hour for a reply from 6 a.m. the following morning.

Thanking the operator for his cooperation, Alan signed off and said to Jaime, "I think that will get them all going in London overnight, so we should have what we want first thing in the morning."

"I think we've done a good day's work here today and it's time for our sundowner gin and tonic before all the ice melts."

"I'll certainly drink to that, Jaime."

As they left the aircraft and walked towards the tent, their nostrils were assailed by a delicious aroma coming from inside. Mary turned to them as they entered from where she was standing over a little two-burner paraffin stove.

"That smells delicious. What is it?" asked Jaime.

"My version of beef stroganoff. I hope you like it. It's not easy working on a tiny stove in these conditions."

"That's very ingenious of you. Where did you get the ingredients?"

"It's just as well I didn't leave everything to you. Otherwise, we would be living on tinned beans and corned beef," said Mary as she pointed to a wicker hamper underneath the table. "I took the precaution of bringing a few fresh items from my freezer and some herbs and spices."

Turning to Sherbourne, Jaime said, "Fancy finding a Cordon Bleu chef out here in the desert."

"Sit down," said Mary as she opened the hamper and took out a bottle of gin and some tonics as well as a large thermos flask which she opened to reveal it was full of ice cubes. With a final flourish, she produced a fresh lemon and put it on the table with the rest of the items.

"Will one of you fix the chef a drink? And then help yourselves."

Sherbourne looked at Jaime and with a huge grin and said, "I thought we had done well today, Jaime, but where would we be without an efficient woman like Mary to look after our essential needs?"

***

While Jaime and Sherbourne had been communicating with Tripoli, von Oppersdorf had set up the two single tents ensuring there were no scorpions or other unwelcome visitors likely to disturb the sleep of himself or Mary who would use them. Jaime and Sherbourne had elected to use the main tent where there was ample space to lay out their air beds and sleeping bags.

Jaime explained over dinner that he and Sherbourne had contacted Tripoli and had passed a message on to the embassy confirming their safe arrival. He really wanted to get Mary started on reading von Lutzdorf's log book and discussing the contents with her and Sherbourne but, with von Oppersdorf present, he did not want to reveal to him what they had found, or disclose that Sherbourne was in fact an MI6 agent and not the innocent employee of the British War Graves Commission. Whilst he felt instinctively Hugo was to be trusted, Jaime had taken seriously Sherbourne's warning that ODESSA had long tentacles which had reached out and infiltrated many aspects of society and government; seemingly normal and innocent-appearing members of both may well belong to this clandestine organization. He decided, therefore, that he would leave any further examination of the log book until the morning when von Oppersdorf could be distracted with some other employment.

During the discussions between von Oppersdorf at the embassy in Tripoli and the German government, it had been agreed that some form of radio communication would be necessary in the desert and Captain Hartmann and his team were supplied with two battery-powered HF transceivers, one of which had been given to Jaime. He proposed to von Oppersdorf that he set up the radio on a ridge near the camp to give the best reception and to monitor calls from midday onwards the following day. This would give Mary the opportunity to study the log book unobserved with Sherbourne and for him to decode any message he got back from the embassy in Tripoli.

They had all enjoyed Mary's surprise dinner together with a few bottles of wine which, on top of a somewhat busy and tiring day, made them all drowsy enough to turn in early.

***

Sherbourne and Jaime rose before 6 a.m. and were sitting in the cockpit monitoring the radio when FIS in Tripoli came on the air at the prescribed hour. The operator confirmed he had a long encoded message for them which Sherbourne proceeded to write down on a pad which he had prepared.

When he finished, he thanked the operator for his assistance and signed off.

"Just as I expected. Jaime. The boys in London must have got the book from Menzies and worked on it during the night."

"How long will it take you to decode their message?"

"Not too long," said Sherbourne, producing a small leather-bound notebook which he leafed through to access the appropriate key to unlock the code.

Jaime decided to leave him alone while he returned to the tent to help Mary with breakfast. He found both Mary and von Oppersdorf there with the Primus stove alight heating water for tea or coffee.

"You were both up early, Jaime," said von Oppersdorf.

"Yes, we had a prearranged call with Flight Information Service at 6 a.m. in case there were any messages for us from the embassy. Just routine," Jaime replied.

"I hope we have as good communications with Hartmann today. But you said you didn't expect him to be here until tomorrow morning, Jaime."

"Depends on how much progress he made yesterday. If he got to Murzuk late yesterday evening, we could hear something from him today. The tough bit is driving from Murzuk to here."

After breakfast, von Oppersdorf set about erecting a sunshade on the ridge then set up the transceiver on a crate top together with a folding seat to monitor any calls from Hartmann. While he was busy engaged doing this, Jaime handed the log book to Mary to study for any other useful information. She was leafing through the log book making notes when Sherbourne returned from the aircraft.

"I'm very pleased to inform you that faith in von Lutzdorf's integrity and ingenuity has been restored. The enciphered message he wrote in the back of his log book disclosed specific directions of where he concealed the documents. All we have to do now is find their base of operations."

"I can help there," interjected Mary, "I've just found the exact navigational coordinates and directions for it in his log book. So, it looks like we have game, set and match."

"Well done, the pair of you. Mary, let me have those coordinates and I'll mark them on my chart. Give me the log book and I'll put it back in my flight bag."

Producing an aeronautical chart from his flight bag, Jaime unfolded it and set it out on the table. With a pencil and ruler, he measured off the latitude and longitude and penciled in a cross, marking the exact location. With a set of dividers, he then measured the distance from their present position and declared, "We're not so far away from where they started out on their last journey. I make it just over sixty miles. A couple of hours by truck and less than twenty minutes by air."

A beaming Sherbourne said, "The sooner our friend Hartmann gets here and recovers the bodies, the better."

"Yes," said Jaime, "As soon as he's gone, we'll just make a short hop there, recover the documents and get back to Tripoli. Mission accomplished."

Now they had found what they needed, all three were impatient for the arrival of Hartmann.

"I think I'll see if we can raise Hartmann on the radio. If he's in range, we can get an estimate of his time of arrival," said Jaime.

As he approached von Oppersdorf on the ridge, he called out. "Any contact with Hartmann yet, Hugo?"

"Nothing yet. Shall I try giving him a call?"

"It's worth a try."

Von Oppersdorf keyed the transmit button and made the call using their agreed call signs. When he released the transmit button, all they could hear in the speaker was the mush of atmospheric noise.

"Maybe he's not listening out for us yet," said Jaime. "Keep trying."

Jaime left von Oppersdorf to try calling at regular intervals.

As Jaime entered the tent, Mary and Sherbourne were transfixed looking at what appeared to be a large spider that had emerged from beneath one of the beds in the corner. Jaime, who was no stranger to what they were looking at, smiled to himself and said, "Don't move. It's a camel spider. They won't attack you if you ignore them and leave them alone."

"How can you ignore something as horrible as that?"

"Just stand still. I'll deal with it," said Jaime.

Concealing the smile on his face, Jaime picked up the empty biscuit tin which Mary had used to pack some food in and half filled it with sand. Setting it on the table, he selected one of the larger pots and approached the camel spider very slowly in order not to alarm it. He then turned the pot upside down and deftly clamped it over the spider. Taking a small round flat tray larger in diameter than the pot, he slid it underneath and picked both of them up together. All the while he contrived to put on a severe face as Mary stared in horror at his actions.

"Oh Jaime, do be careful," she said as he held the pot over the biscuit tin. With a flourish like a conjurer performing a card trick, he whisked away the tray and gave the pot a shake. As the spider dropped onto the sand, it stood there quivering in an outraged stance with its feelers raised as if to attack. Mary instinctively reacted and jumped back with a gasp of horror.

"Oh Jaime, that was foolish. He could have bitten you."

Sherbourne, in the meantime, stood there motionlessly and said, "I see you've handled these before, Jaime. It's a good job I didn't know he was under the bed last night. I wouldn't have got a wink of sleep."

"He probably crept in this morning to find some shade. They're nocturnal and hunt at night like most desert creatures."

"Nevertheless, I shall look under it tonight and shake out my sleeping bag."

As they all stood there looking at the spider, Jaime picked up a fly swat and knocked down one of the many flies that buzzed around in the tent.

"Watch this," he said as he scooped up the stunned fly with the swatter and dropped it into the tin, still fluttering, in front of the spider.

In a movement so fast they almost missed it, the spider leaped forwards and grabbed the fly in its jaws and proceeded to devour it.

"It deserved a little treat after being knocked about like that," said Jaime.

"How horrible," said Mary staring at the spectacle, "I've never seen a spider eat its prey like that. I thought they sank their fangs in and dissolved their meal."

"You're quite right, Mary, they do. But these are not strictly spiders as you know them. They're called solifuges: a different species altogether. As a matter of fact, they're not poisonous in the normal sense. They don't inject a venom. But if they bite you, it can be quite painful and become infected and poisonous so it's best not to annoy them."

"You beast," said Mary, "You knew all the time it wasn't poisonous. You frightened me to death on purpose, didn't you?"

Jaime laughed and said, "Guilty, but the scorpions and snakes are, so I was just reminding you to be careful in the desert, that's all."

Being a good sport, Mary saw the joke and, smiling, said, "You're quite right. I wouldn't want one of those in bed with me."

As they stood there looking at the camel spider reduce its meal to a pulp, a shadow fell across the table as von Oppersdorf appeared in the open tent flap; his approach unheard in the soft sand.

"Hello, what do we have here?" he said, peering at the creature in the tin. "What a perfectly horrible thing to find. Where did it come from?"

"Out from under my bed," said Sherbourne.

"It's a camel spider," said Mary.

"I've heard of them but never seen one. I hope we've not erected the tent on a nest of them," said von Oppersdorf.

"Don't worry," said Jaime, "They're quite individual creatures and won't bother you if you leave them alone."

"I came down to let you know that I got through to Hartman finally. He's about halfway from Murzuk to the estimated position you gave him. Apparently, they drove all day yesterday and got to Murzuk last night and started out from there very early this morning. The going is hard but he thinks he could be here by late afternoon."

"I'll give him a more accurate position after I take a noon sight. I managed three star sights before dawn this morning so it'll be accurate to within a half mile."

Jaime had brought with him an aviation bubble sextant which was easier to use in the desert because it had an artificial horizon essential for measuring the altitude of the sun and stars. He was also very proud of his Breitling Navitimer pilot's watch which kept very accurate time as a certified chronometer.

As the sun approached its local noon meridian, Jaime started taking a series of sun sights which he noted down together with the time. Using these figures, he was able to plot a graph of altitude against time from which he was able to read off the zenith and time from which he could calculate the local hour angle giving him the distance in degrees of longitude from the Greenwich meridian.

Writing down the latitude and longitude of their revised position, he gave it to von Oppersdorf to relay it to Hartmann.

As it worked out, they were only four miles from Jaime's original estimated position. Not a long distance at sea where visibility is largely unobstructed but in the desert, where the topography and sand dunes can severely obstruct one's line of sight, it is far more important.

Armed with the new information, Hartman had given them an ETA of 5 p.m. and Jaime had agreed to fire off a white smoke flare every fifteen minutes from 4:30 p.m. until Hartmann reported back it had been spotted.

At 5:15 p.m., Hartmann reported in the affirmative that the flare had been seen and would arrive within the next half hour.

Chapter 65

❖

The sound of two truck engines labouring up the slope of a sand dune announced the arrival of Captain Hartmann and his men as they topped the dune and came into sight.

They pulled up to a stop alongside the aircraft and clambered out of the trucks relieved to have arrived after such an arduous journey.

Jaime greeted Hartmann by shaking hands as he said, "Welcome to our camp. You made good time. We didn't really expect you until tomorrow."

"Thank you, Wing Commander. I did not see much point in wasting time and my men are fit so we took advantage of all the daylight hours."

He shook hands with the others in turn and, when he came to Mary, he said, "It's nice to meet you, Miss Loveday. I am sorry we did not have the opportunity to meet in Tripoli but we were very occupied preparing for this trip. I trust you are not finding the desert too disagreeable?"

"Well, there are some rather nasty creatures to be aware of but, apart from that, it's so far been an experience to remember."

While Hartmann was engaged with the others, Jaime turned his attention to his two men who were standing back from Hartmann in their usual subservient manner which Jaime felt was unnecessary. In an attempt to put them at their ease, he said, "You two have had a hard drive getting here so soon. Well done."

Obviously unaccustomed to compliments or praise from Hartmann, they hesitated until Schmitt replied, "Thank you, Commander. We are on a mission and do as we are ordered."

Jaime couldn't think of a suitable reply to that as Captain Hartmann came back to him and asked, "Where do you want me to park the vehicles?"

Jaime had given this some thought prior to their arrival and said, "We're parked here at the beginning of the take-off area which is a little way from the truck where you'll need the caskets. I suggest you move the truck with the caskets further down the airstrip closest to the truck with the bodies. Then you can make camp there or wherever you prefer."

"I have your aviation fuel and cans of water loaded in the same truck with the caskets. We have our own supplies and water in the other truck. Do you want to refuel your aircraft first?"

"No, we can leave that until later when we're ready to return."

Hartmann issued a number of orders to his men who proceeded to drive the truck about two hundred yards further on. The second truck moved on a further hundred yards where the men erected their tent and unloaded stores. They no doubt preferred their own company, much to the relief of Jaime and the others.

"You didn't say anything to Hartmann and his men about the scorpions, snakes and camel spiders," said Sherbourne.

"No. Hartmann and his men have lots of desert experience so I expect they're used to them. Anyway, they'll be in good company," he added with a smile.

**

Early the next morning, Jaime and Sherbourne were awake as usual before the dawn and, after making themselves tea, they decided to walk over to join Hartmann and his men to help with the excavation only to find them already hard at work.

"You've got to admire their discipline and work ethic," said Jaime as they trudged up the slope towards the truck.

They were surprised to find that the bodies of von Lutzdorf and Steinberg had already been removed and placed in their caskets which had been sealed and stenciled with their respective names and rank: Oberst Walter von Lutzdorf and Hauptmann Johann Steinberg. The caskets had been set to one side, clear of the truck, so as not to obstruct the excavation.

"Good morning, Captain," said Jaime, "It's a good idea to have an early start before the sun gets too high."

"Indeed so, Wing Commander."

"Your men look exceedingly fit, Captain. But take care not to let them become dehydrated in the heat. Ensure they drink sufficient amounts of water and take their salt tablets."

"Thank you for your concern, Wing Commander, and advice which is noted. You are quite right. These conditions are outside the normal and can cause problems to the inexperienced."

Taking this as a mild rebuke to his experience and control, Jaime nodded and said, "If there's anything you need from us, please let me know. I've been thinking it might be a good idea if you placed the caskets in my aircraft for us to transport them back to Tripoli instead of taking them back in one of your trucks. It would be quicker and more reliable as we'll have more space without the stores and equipment. We'll also have diplomatic representatives on board from both embassies in case of any difficulties."

"A very good suggestion. I will get my men to bring them over when they take a break."

Sherbourne and Jaime watched for a while and admired the enthusiasm of Neumann and Schmitt as they moved copious amounts of sand.

As they walked back to camp, Sherbourne looked at Jaime and said, "Why did you say that to Hartmann?"

"I don't really know. just a hunch. Having found them, I have this feeling of personal responsibility of seeing them back safe and sound with their loved ones. Especially after having met von Lutzdorf's widow and daughter. There's something very cold and impersonal about Hartmann that doesn't sit well with me. He was very quick at absolving himself from his primary responsibility almost as if they were a burden."

"I can understand your feelings on that point."

"Anyway, we have what we came for and, as far as I'm concerned, the sooner we can leave, the better. Hartmann and his men can carry on digging while we fly on to von Lutzdorf's base and search for the documents he described. If all goes well, we'll be back in Tripoli before them and von Oppersdorf can take possession of the bodies officially on behalf of the widow and arrange for them to be transported back to Germany."

"When do you plan to leave?"

"We still have some things to do here and we'll need daylight to be sure of landing safely at the base. So, if we leave first thing in the morning, we'll have all day to recover the documents and fly to Tripoli. I'll talk to Hartmann later and tell him of our plans."

***

Later that afternoon, after Jaime had observed Hartmann was back at the truck, he decided to walk over and tell him he planned to leave the following morning.

When he arrived at the truck, Hartmann, who had been sitting in the cab, emerged and greeted him as he indicated the two caskets placed side by side next to the truck and said, "As you suggested, my men brought the caskets down a while ago and will bring them over to you later."

"Thank you, Captain. Now that our part of the expedition is complete, I plan to leave first thing in the morning. With your agreement, I will ensure the bodies of von Lutzdorf and Steinberg are properly handed over to the German Embassy in Tripoli for onward transportation back to their families in Germany. His widow and daughter are waiting in Tripoli, as you know. It's a pity you did not have the opportunity to meet with them when you passed through."

"Yes, that was unfortunate but I'm happy to leave them in yours and von Oppersdorf's good hands. Please give my respects to Frau von Lutzdorf and her daughter and tell them if we discover any personal items, I will ensure they are forwarded to her through the embassy."

"How's the excavation going?"

"We still have a way to go to ensure we do not miss anything but I'm sure we'll finish today. If so, then we will also leave for Tripoli in the morning and may still have the opportunity of meeting Frau von Lutzdorf."

"Let's hope so."

With that, Jaime walked back to the camp. As he reached the tent, Mary and von Oppersdorf came out carrying between them the cool box water container.

"We're going over to fill this up from Hartmann's truck. Is he there?"

"Yes, I just left him and told him we're leaving in the morning."

As they approached, Hartmann, who had observed them from a distance, waited for them at the rear of the truck.

"We would like to fill up. If you don't mind, Captain?" said Mary.

"Please, help yourself, Miss Loveday. There are plenty of cans in the back."

Von Oppersdorf had already clambered aboard and, taking Mary's hand, he easily pulled her up when she placed one foot on the fender and stepped inside.

Moving to the back, they manhandled one of the water cans and proceeded to fill their container.

Occupied as they were, they neither saw nor heard the approach of Hartmann's men carrying between them a heavy steel-bound box by the handles.

"*Herr Oberst-Gruppenfuehrer, wir haben etwas gefunden.*"

Hartmann, who was still standing at the rear, glanced towards Mary who had obviously heard what had been said turned to his men and, in an authoritative tone, said, "*Stille, sagen sie nicht mehr.*"

By this time, his men had come closer and, seeing Mary and von Oppersdorf, realised they had committed a grave error and stood still with looks of shock and surprise on their faces.

Hartmann looked at Mary and, smiling, he said, "My men forget themselves sometimes and use old expressions in German." He hoped she had not recognized the significance of the indiscretion.

Von Oppersdorf appeared not to have heard what had been said and did not comment. Mary, on the other hand, having read the file on von Lutzdorf and also his log book, knew there could be only one explanation for the unintended disclosure. However, aware of the potential danger, she smiled and said nothing, deciding not to reveal she spoke German.

Smiling, she said, "That looks interesting. What have you got there?"

Relieved that it appeared he had defused the incident, Hartmann offered his hand to Mary to help her down from the truck and said, "It's locked. We will have to wait and see. If it is anything personal of von Lutzdorf and Steinberg, we will ensure it gets to their families."

"Perhaps it's full of gold bars," said Mary with a laugh to further diffuse the incident.

"Perhaps so," said Hartmann, joining in the laughter.

Hartmann's men, who now felt relieved their indiscreet outburst had not resulted in anything more serious, stepped forwards and lifted the heavy water container down and insisted on carrying it back for Mary to the tent.

As Neumann and Schmitt left, von Oppersdorf took Mary to one side and said, "I know you speak German fluently, Mary. Did you catch what his men said to Hartmann back there?"

Not sure whether or not to discuss the incident without first talking to Jaime and Sherbourne, Mary looked at von Oppersdorf in a quizzical way and said, "What do you mean, Hugo?"

Von Oppersdorf hesitated a moment before he replied. "It's just that I was right at the back of the truck and only caught a bit about them having found something."

"Before I answer that, Hugo, I think we must discuss it with Jaime and Alan Sherbourne."

With a puzzled expression on his face, he said, "Is there something going on here that I don't know about, Mary?"

"Perhaps. Let me get Jaime and Alan in here and we can talk."

Jaime and Sherbourne responded to Mary's call to come over to the tent and all four sat around the table.

Mary proceeded to explain what had happened at the truck.

"You mean to say that one of his men addressed Hartmann as Herr Oberst-Gruppenfuehrer. That's an SS rank of a general."

"Yes, I know. Hartmann was noticeably shaken but I pretended as if I didn't understand German then we joked about what might be in the box they had found."

"What did you hear, Hugo?" asked Jaime.

"I just caught the bit about finding something but Mary handled the situation very well. But she also indicated there's something I should know that so far you have not disclosed to me."

"Under the circumstances, I think we should tell Hugo what we know about von Lutzdorf and his mission," said Mary.

"I think it's best if you explain the situation to him, Mary," said Jaime. "After all, it was your report from the embassy to the Foreign Office in London that resulted in you and Sherbourne becoming involved."

Addressing herself to von Oppersdorf, she began. "When Jaime came to the embassy and reported the discovery of von Lutzdorf's body, a routine signal was sent to London. The reply was unexpected and quite mysterious. Instead of just a formal acknowledgement, they asked if anything had been found in the truck with the bodies.

"We informed them that Jaime had found nothing as the truck was almost completely buried in the sand and only the bodies in the front cab were visible and that he had left them undisturbed. Jaime, as you know, is, for all intents and purposes, an innocent bystander who, so it appears, happened to have stumbled onto something of great interest to both our governments."

"I see," said von Oppersdorf, "Did they explain or describe what they thought von Lutzdorf might be carrying with him?"

"No, they just said that when an expedition was organized to recover the bodies, a representative from our embassy should accompany them and lay claim to anything found in the truck. They also, as a matter of protocol, informed the War Graves Commission of the discovery who sent out Alan here to assist. They have much experience here in Libya looking after a number of war grave cemeteries." In making this statement, Mary felt it would be prudent not to reveal who Sherbourne really was at this stage nor that they had found von Lutzdorf's log book with all the details of the base and the coded information where the documents he was carrying were concealed.

"Did they say anything about other organizations who might be interested in the discovery?"

"Not specifically but they did say to be on our guard against any unusual interest from any third persons."

"Have you had any unusual interest?"

"Not until today. The one person we did not suspect was our friend Hartmann since your people in Germany and my people in London gave him a clean sheet," said Mary. "We still don't know who he really is except it seems he was infiltrated into the expedition for their own ends."

"Perhaps I can answer that."

As one, they all looked in the direction of the sound of the voice to find Captain Hartmann standing in the front entrance of the tent with Neumann standing behind him holding an MP 40 Schmeisser. At the same time as he appeared, they also became aware of movement behind them at the rear entrance as Schmitt entered, also carrying an MP 40.

Von Oppersdorf was the first to react as he stood up and addressed Hartmann. "What is the meaning of this?"

"Please sit down, Major," said Hartmann, "All in good time."

"I demand an explanation," replied von Oppersdorf.

"You are in no position to demand anything, Major, but you might be interested to know it was on account of you that we had to take these steps."

"What on earth do you mean by that?"

"It was your reaction to the unfortunate outburst of one of my men that put me on my guard."

"What reaction was that?"

"Exactly. You showed no reaction at all. A former military man as yourself could not have missed the significance of the reference to my SS rank. You just ignored the whole incident. As for the delightful Miss Loveday, her reaction was very professional. She gave the impression she did not understand German. I now know she understood every word. From a lifetime of caution, when my men returned from helping carry the water here, I ordered them to come back under the pretext of bringing the caskets. Taking care to avoid being noticed, they listened to your discussion from outside the tent. I did tell you their English was good when we first met."

"What is it you hope to gain by this show of force?" asked Sherbourne.

"It would appear we are both after the same thing. Something far more important than the recovery of bodies."

"And what would that be?"

"Please don't take me for a fool. My men overheard enough for me to know that your government have been aware of what von Lutzdorf was transporting since the war."

"I thought you had just recovered what you were looking for," said Mary.

"I'm afraid not. The box only contained English currency."

"Your men excavated the whole truck. If there was anything there, they would have found it."

"Not the whole truck. You were here a whole day before us and could have found something."

"There was nothing else except the bodies in the cab which we left for you to remove. We left everything untouched until you arrived."

"Why would you do that?"

"For the simple reason that we had no reason to suspect you were anything other than what you professed to be. It was only your men's recent indiscretion that gave us reason to think otherwise."

"I suppose there's a certain logic in that. Nevertheless, we will search your camp and the aircraft. Please remain seated while my men carry on."

Taking one of the MP 40s to keep everyone covered, Hartmann issued orders to his men who left the tent and started a systematic search of the aircraft and camp looking for whatever appeared to be documents.

In the aircraft, Neumann entered the cockpit and found a number of charts tucked in pockets or under the seat. Opening Jaime's flight bag, he found it full of other charts and navigational accessories including reference books for radio and navigational aids. Amongst these were his own and von Lutzdorf's log books over which he gave a cursory glance. Satisfied there were no documents of interest, he closed the bag and returned it to its position behind the captain's seat and started on the passenger cabin. Finding nothing in the pockets at the back of the seats or in the overhead lockers, he turned his attention to the rear cargo compartment but found only a life raft and life belts, shovels and a fire extinguisher and some other emergency tools.

Meanwhile, Schmitt had been riffling through Mary's and von Oppersdorf's tents and personal baggage without success. They both returned to the tent and shook their heads and told Hartmann there was nothing to be found.

The main tent itself contained only the table, chairs and beds which they quickly stripped and searched.

"It appears you are telling the truth. Neither of us have found what we were looking for."

"We weren't instructed to look for anything in particular," said Mary.

"Maybe so, but you said your government told you to lay claim to anything that was found."

"True but we never found anything and there appears to be nothing to find."

"Perhaps, whatever it was, was destroyed when their plane crashed," said Jaime.

"We don't know if the plane crashed," said Hartmann.

"There has to be an explanation why nothing was found in the truck."

"Perhaps so, but whatever that might be is of little consequence now and will remain a mystery."

"What do you intend to do now?" asked von Oppersdorf.

"Why, leave you, of course," said Hartmann with a smile like a snake looking at its prey before the strike.

"Who are you really? Certainly not Captain Hartmann," said Mary.

"Under the circumstances, I see no reason not to introduce myself to you properly, my dear Miss Loveday, as it will go no further. Oberst-Gruppenfuehrer Heinrich Mueller at your service. Note the correct rank this time," he added with a smile as he removed his dark glasses and eyepatch to reveal two piercing grey eyes.

His announcement was greeted with a collective gasp as the significance of his statement sank in.

"Good lord, it's Gestapo Mueller," said Sherbourne.

"Quite so. The reports of my death were somewhat premature. Don't you agree, Herr Sherbourne?"

Stuck for some suitable comment to say in response, all four of them stared at Mueller dumbfounded as he issued more orders to his men who went outside to carry them out.

They were shocked back into reality at the sound of several bursts of gunfire.

"Please walk outside," said Mueller, gesturing with his pistol.

As they stood together, still covered by Mueller, his men came back and, while Neumann raised his weapons allowing Mueller to return his pistol to his pocket, Schmitt went into the tent. The first thing Jaime noticed was that both tyres of the aircraft were flat having been shredded with bullets. From inside the tent came the sound of things being broken and overturned. When he came out, Schmitt took out a knife and slashed the guy ropes causing the tent to collapse.

Looking around at the destruction, Mueller looked at them as they stood together still in a group and said, "We will take our leave of you now. Please do not attempt to follow or do anything foolish."

With that, he and his men backed off and headed back to the truck and, as a parting act, one of the men threw a petrol-soaked flaming rag onto the tent which quickly caught fire.

"What do we do now?" said Sherbourne, looking for a lead from Jaime.

"Not much we can do for the moment. Let me look inside the aircraft and see what other damage they may have done."

They all walked over to the Beechcraft and waited as Jaime entered, re-emerging shortly shaking his head. "As I feared, they have wrecked the radio so we have no means of communication."

"What about the transceiver on the ridge?" said Sherbourne.

"Have a look but I'm sure they destroyed that too."

Von Oppersdorf offered to go and look at the transceiver and when he returned from the ridge, he had a puzzled look on his face. "That's a funny thing. The transceiver is intact but they removed the battery."

"Perhaps they needed it as a spare. But, in any case, without a battery, it's useless to us," said Jaime. "Our first and most important need is water. I'm sure they overturned our water container but see if they left any liquids, including wine, tonics and soups, intact."

While the others searched the camp, Jaime entered the aircraft again and opened the cargo door. In the corner behind the bulkhead, he uncovered an emergency one-gallon water container which had been missed underneath a pile of life jackets. Setting that to one side, he recovered the MP 40 and the Luger pistol.

As expected, Mueller's men had made a thorough job of destroying all water and liquids.

"For the moment, we have just this one-gallon emergency container of water. But we also have some arms and we may well need to fight to get some from Mueller and his men before they leave. What do you say?"

"We can't let them get away with this," said Sherbourne, "I'm up for it. How do you want to play it?"

"I think the first thing is to immobilise the truck so they cannot drive it away. A burst of fire into the tyres should do the trick. It'll also put them on notice that we're armed so they won't try to rush us. Have you used one of these before, Alan?" asked Jaime, as he offered him the MP 40. "No, but I'm familiar with automatic weapons, having used the Sten gun in the army."

"You take this then and I'll hang on to the Luger."

With the MP 40, he handed over the two full magazines of thirty-two rounds each.

From where they were standing behind the aircraft fuselage at the threshold of the landing area, it was two hundred yards to the truck containing the water and aviation fuel. Mueller and his men had moved the other truck a further one hundred yards down the airstrip and set up their tent. The whole landing area was approximately eight hundred yards long and one hundred yards wide. The far end of the flat hardened surface ended with a gradual slope leading up to a sand dune which rose to a peak of nearly one hundred feet. The two trucks and the aircraft were all parked on the same side of the hardened landing area. On the opposite side of this area, a defile of approximately five feet in depth ran the whole length.

"Mary, you stay here by the aircraft. We'll use the defile as cover to get closer to the truck without being seen by Mueller and his men."

Using his binoculars, Jaime studied the Mueller encampment to ensure they were not looking in their direction and, satisfied they would not be observed, he said, "Come on. Keep low and make for the defile as quickly as you can."

Once the three of them were safely hidden in the defile, Jaime scanned the camp again to ensure there was no movement and gave the word to proceed. At two hundred yards, they were almost exactly opposite their intended target. Raising his head for a final look, he saw one of Mueller's men walking towards the truck.

"Quickly, Alan, see if you can put a burst into the rear tyres."

Sherbourne raised the MP 40 above the lip of the defile and sighted it as ordered.

The ripping sound of the short burst caused Mueller's man, who they recognized as Neumann, to stop and look towards where the sound had come from. At the same time, he raised his own MP 40 and loosed off a short burst in their direction, which kicked up a few bursts of sand but well wide of the mark, to distract them as he ran towards the truck.

Sherbourne did not return his fire as it was not their intention to engage in a fire fight at this stage and Neumann made it to the cover of the truck.

All automatic weapons have a tendency for the barrel to raise when fired and the MP 40 was no exception. Of the burst of seven rounds fired by Sherbourne, four had hit their intended target of the rear tyre but the trajectory of the remaining three, being higher, had hit the drum of aviation fuel causing it to start leaking out onto the floor. The fuel sealed in its liquid form would be difficult to ignite unless the bullets were of the incendiary type. The MP 40 rounds were solid and sank to the bottom of the drum. As the fuel slowly drained from the drum down to the level of the bullet holes, the space inside above the fuel level filled with air forming an extremely volatile explosive mixture.

"What do we do now, Jaime?" asked von Oppersdorf.

"Leave it and see if he tries to start the engine. If he does, give the front tyre a burst."

As they watched, they saw Neumann enter the cab and then heard the starter motor whine as he attempted to start the engine. It did not start on the first attempt, neither on the second. As Neumann continued to press the starter, finally on the third attempt, there was a cough as the engine fired. What happened next took them all unawares and too quickly to fully comprehend. Petrol, which had flooded the exhaust from the failed attempts, ignited and a flame shot out the rear which in turn ignited the aviation fuel dripping off the floor at the back. The whole interior behind the cab was instantly engulfed in flames which flashed back through the holes in the drum causing the volatile mixture to explode. Fed by the remainder of the fuel in the drum, it created an enormous deafening blast and a giant fireball rising hundreds of feet into the sky.

Protected by the defile, the blast of hot air and sand passed over their heads as they cringed in shock.

"My God!" said Sherbourne.

As the dust settled, they ventured a look above the lip of the defile and were greeted with the spectacle of the broken and twisted chassis burning furiously within which was the remains of the unfortunate Neumann. The huge fireball had now transformed itself into a black, brown and red mushroom-shaped cloud boiling and climbing up above the wreck.

The sound of Mueller's truck starting up drew their attention in that direction and they watched it move off down towards the end of the take-off area.

"What shall we do about him?" asked von Oppersdorf.

"Let him go," said Jaime, "We have nothing left to fight over now and he obviously doesn't like the odds. There's no point provoking another confrontation. We have other things to worry about."

Climbing out of the defile, they cautiously approached the burning wreck which was now smouldering. All the combustible material had been consumed or blown apart in the explosion save for the charred remains of Neumann which had been protected from the worst of the blast by the cab.

"I'll get a shovel from the plane," said Jaime, "We should bury the poor devil. Would one of you follow where Mueller has gone? Go up to the top of that dune and see what direction they've taken. We don't want to be surprised if they try to get back around behind us."

"I'll go," said von Oppersdorf, taking the MP 40 from Sherbourne. He slung it over his shoulder by the strap and, with the binoculars hanging from his neck, strode off in the path of the departing Mueller.

"I'll help you with the body," said Sherbourne as they walked back to the aircraft.

Mary was waiting for them at the doorway to the Beechcraft, a look of relief on her face.

"Thank goodness. You're all okay. What happened?"

"Somehow the aviation fuel exploded. We don't know how. It was nothing we did. It must have been caused by a spark or something when he started the engine."

"You mean there was someone in there when it exploded?" gasped Mary.

"It was Mueller's man, Neumann. We're just going to bury him."

Jaime and Sherbourne collected two shovels from the plane and a blanket from the debris of the camp.

Back at the truck, they went through the gruesome task of prizing the corpse's hands from the steering wheel where the heat had bonded flesh and plastic together. Then by draping it with the blanket, they were able to keep the rest of the flesh of the charred skeleton together whilst they removed it from the cab. Laying it down on the sand, they wrapped the blanket tightly around and secured both ends with rope.

Although it was hard packed sand, the pointed shovels made easy work of digging the grave and they soon had a hole four feet deep sufficient to lay Neumann to rest.

They had just finished filling the grave when von Oppersdorf returned.

"What did you see, Hugo?"

"They were still in sight when I reached the top of the dune on the other side of which is another area similar to this. It stretches on for another half mile or more to another row of dunes. With the binoculars, I watched as they topped the first dune and carried on watching as they topped the second dune, all the while going in the same direction which I estimated to be southwest. I don't think they have any intention of trying to get around behind us."

"So it appears. In any case, we shall be long gone before they could manage that," said Jaime.

"What do you have in mind?" asked Sherbourne.

"Let's get back to the plane and I'll explain the options open to us."

Chapter 66

❖

It was now late afternoon and, with the cockpit windows and the rear door open, a cool breeze flowed through the aircraft.

Jaime and Sherbourne were seated in the two front passenger seats facing back towards Mary and von Oppersdorf in the other two.

"Here's where we stand," began Jaime, "The nearest centre of known population where we could find water is Murzuk, approximately a hundred and twenty miles over hard-going desert terrain. Achievable on foot if we had sufficient water. As far as that's concerned, we have exactly one gallon. Two pints for each person. With the best efforts, we could make perhaps twenty miles per day over that terrain, but we don't have enough water for six days.

"On the other hand, we know from von Lutzdorf's log book that his secret base of operations had a water reservoir fed by a spring from the mountains. I've been able to calculate with a high degree of accuracy that it's sixty miles from here. Therefore, do we make for Murzuk severely rationing the water and hope to make contact on the way with a Taureg encampment? Or do we go for von Lutzdorf's base hoping the spring is still active? If we get there and it's not, we've shot our bolt."

"From what I've read in his log book, this base was very well-established with stores and equipment including a radio and had been in operation for some time. I'm sure they wouldn't have put so much into it if the water supply had been erratic or irregular which would point to a well-established and reliable water source," said Mary.

"What's this about von Lutzdorf's log book? You didn't mention this before," said von Oppersdorf.

Realising Mary's comments had let the cat out of the bag, Jaime quickly broke in and said, "It's just a navigation log book that all pilots keep, as you know. We found it in the cab. It just happens to give the navigational coordinates of their base and a brief description of the facilities. It was with a chart of the desert here which he was obviously using to navigate his way back to the coast in Tunisia."

"Oh, I see," said von Oppersdorf, "That's very useful. I agree that would be the best place to head for as it would appear there should be a water supply, as Mary has said."

"I happen to agree with both of you," said Jaime. "What about you, Alan?"

"Since I'm just the spare wheel here," said Sherbourne with a smile, "And don't read German. I'm with the majority."

"That's it then. A good decision, I'm sure. Now, this is what I propose. We'll travel by night. It's now 4 p.m. Dusk is in about two hours. We'll have some moonlight for much of the night so visibility won't be a problem and, apart from my hand compass, we'll have a clear night with stars visible to help guide us. Navigation is not a problem. Food and water are. Let's gather up what food there is that Mueller's men did not destroy and take stock."

They all searched through the dishevelled camp in overturned crates and cartons and the remains of the tents. The sum total of their search was four tins of corned beef, two tins of baked beans and two tins of soup: one vegetable and one beef.

They also found an empty unbroken gin bottle and whisky bottle as well as two empty wine bottles.

The Primus stove was still in working order so Jaime said to Mary, "Do you think you can make an edible stew out of what we have here?"

"I think it'll test my Cordon Bleu skills," said Mary with a laugh, "But I'll do my best."

Jaime proceeded to fill the empty bottles each with a pint of water using the measuring cup that came with the emergency water container and gave one to each of them.

Von Oppersdorf helped Mary re-set up the table and the folding chairs. With the Primus stove alight, Mary found a discarded saucepan and, using two tins of corned beef, a tin of beans and one of the soups, she made a thick stew.

Sharing it out in equal portions on four surviving tin plates, she said, "Whatever it tastes like, it's full of protein and very nutritious. Just what you need for energy."

"I think it's rather good," said von Oppersdorf, "This, what you call corned beef, is rather tasty."

Jaime laughed and said, "The trouble is, Hugo, you didn't have to eat it all through the war as we did."

"I'm sorry there's no wine to go with it," said Mary.

"You can all wash it down with a swig of water from your bottles," added Jaime. "We'll travel as lightly as we can carrying only the essentials. Each will carry his own water bottle. That leaves the four tins of food, one each again. We must take the latrine canvas and the four poles for the sunshade, and the remaining water.

"I'll carry my flight bag with the log books, charts and sextant. Hugo, can you carry the canvas screen? And Alan, if you please, the water container? We can each also take one of the poles. They'll be helpful when walking up some of the dunes."

"What about me?" asked Mary.

"I don't think the age of chivalry has completely gone yet," he said with a grin as he handed her the Luger pistol. "Just bring that and yourself to keep us cheerful."

Jaime attached some loops of rope to his flight bag through which he could place his arms and carry it like a rucksack and slung the MP 40 by the strap on his shoulder. Von Oppersdorf rolled up the canvas and, with some rope, strapped it across his back and carried one of the two Schmeisser magazines, while Sherbourne carried the other and made a sling out of a piece of blanket to take the weight of the water container.

Wanting to do her bit, Mary slung the binoculars around her neck and pronounced herself ready.

They had each selected a jacket from their clothing to keep out the nightly chill and, more importantly, had taken note of Jaime's advice before they came to acquire sensible desert boots which zipped up above the ankle and, when worn with suitable socks, prevented loose sand from getting in their footwear causing blisters and abrasions.

"It's now 6 p.m.," said Jaime. "We'll stop every three hours for a five-minute break and drink a half cup of water. There are four cups to a pint, so that's eight drinks from now until the same time tomorrow. If we stick to this routine, we should manage twenty-five miles overnight depending on the terrain.

"From first light, it'll still be cool enough for us to carry on for two more hours perhaps until 8 a.m. when we could have covered nearer thirty miles. We'll rest and get as much sleep as we can between 8 a.m. and 4 p.m. We'll then eat the remaining food. Cold this time, I'm afraid, but just as nutritious. If we do as well tomorrow night, we'll be in sight of our destination by the following morning."

Von Oppersdorf said, "That sounds like a good plan. Since you are the navigator, you had better lead off, Jaime."

As they all murmured their agreement, Jaime checked his hand compass and strode off at an angle climbing the first dune heading southeast. As the twilight faded, their first glimpse of the moon appeared above the horizon off to the left of their direction of travel.

As it rose, the three-quarter moon cast a silvery luminescent light over the terrain ahead of them revealing a landscape of dunes interspersed with areas of open flat sand. The dunes in their line of march were of a modest height with a gentle windward slope making the going relatively easy, Between the dunes, the surface was hard packed and they made good time. After the first three hours, they rested at the top of one of the dunes and Jaime scanned the area ahead through the binoculars. "It looks as if we'll be coming to the end of the dunes shortly. The area ahead of them appears, from here, to be gently sloping hills. How do you all feel?"

They all confirmed themselves fit to continue with no problems. Passing the measuring cup around, Jaime said, "Each take your half cup ration and we'll get off."

As Jaime had observed, the dunes came to an end and they found themselves on an area of gently sloping low hills and valleys, the surface of which, although not hard packed, was much easier going than the soft powdery sand of the dunes. By now, the moon had risen higher and they could see the way ahead for several miles.

Jaime, in the lead, kept to a steady pace as planned, to preserve their energy but also to achieve their goal of between twenty-five and thirty miles for their first night's march.

At their second stop at midnight local time by his watch, Jaime took three star sights with his bubble sextant and, from the three intersecting position lines, he marked an accurate fix of their position on the chart he had.

"I'm pleased to tell you, my friends, for the past six hours, we have averaged two miles per hour. Right on target." As they rested and drank their second ration of water, Jaime asked, "Are you all still feeling fit to carry on?"

"It's past my bedtime," said Mary, "But I've had later nights than this. I'll soon get my second wind and will be able to party until the sun comes up."

They all laughed at this remark and the humour bonded them together in the spirit of determination not to succumb to the elements.

The terrain remained largely the same for the rest of the night and, as the sky began to lighten in the east with the approaching dawn, Jaime called a halt at 6 a.m. for their water break.

"The sun is just about to come up, Mary. Do you think you can party for another two hours?"

With the lines of fatigue beginning to show around her eyes, Mary smiled and said, "I can, but I don't know if you men can keep up with me."

With that remark, Jaime knew this was one very exceptional woman whose spirit would be the last to break.

"You both heard her, chaps," said Jaime, addressing von Oppersdorf and Sherbourne, "Are you going to let her put us to shame?"

Tired as they were, they all laughed and got to their feet. "Lead on, MacDuff," said Sherbourne, "We're right behind you."

At eight o'clock, with the sun well above the horizon and beginning to feel its heat, they stopped and erected the canvas sheet as a sunshade. Exhausted from the fourteen-hour trek, they all soon fell into a deep sleep.

***

Jaime awoke and, for a few seconds, although conscious, was unaware of his surroundings or what it was that had woken him. As awareness filtered through his consciousness, he remembered where he was but not what had awakened him. That morning, as a precaution against the flies which proliferated in the desert, he had draped a piece of fly net across all of their faces in order to prevent them from irritating and disturbing their sleep.

He was lying on his back with his head propped up resting on his flight bag. Looking down to his chest, he came eye to eye with a small lizard which had obviously woken him as it scuttled across his face and neck. Raising his left arm to look at his watch, the lizard, startled by the movement in a move almost too quick to follow, scurried off from under the netting and disappeared. From his watch, which had shown nearly three o'clock in the afternoon, Jaime realised he had slept for almost seven hours. He lay there for a few moments listening for sounds from the others who all appeared still to be sleeping.

Mary, who had her head on his chest, was breathing gently. His right arm was across her back and her hair was almost in his face. Raising his arm, he gently stroked her hair as his nostrils inhaled the still sweet smell of shampoo. With a deep sigh, Mary's eyes fluttered as she awoke.

"Good morning," she murmured, "What time is it?"

"Good afternoon," corrected Jaime, "It's three o'clock."

"Did you sleep all right?"

"Yes, I managed seven hours until a lizard on my chest woke me up."

"How awful."

"Rather that than a camel spider."

"Don't mention those dreadful creatures. All I've dreamed of lately is creepy crawlies."

"Time to get everyone up," he said as he nudged Sherbourne who was next to him in the back. "Give Hugo a shake, Alan. It's time we were up."

One by one, they all sat up and rubbed the sleep from their eyes.

The sun was still hot as they sat under the makeshift sunshade preparing themselves for the night's march. Jaime opened the two tins of corned beef and sliced them into four portions each on the tin plate he had carried with him in his flight bag while the others opened the beans and soup. With the plate between them, they each used a spoon they had brought with them to eat their share of the soup and beans while helping themselves to the corned beef in equal measures.

"We can afford to drink one cup each before we set off," said Jaime, passing round the cup.

"After a meal like that," said Sherbourne, "What I need now is a bit of vigorous exercise. What about a thirty-mile route march?"

They all joined in the humour while Jaime marveled at the strength of the human spirit that can come to the surface in moments of crisis.

"As near as I can measure it," he said, "We covered twenty-nine miles yesterday, so thirty miles tonight should put us on the doorstep at first light."

As planned, it was close to 4 p.m. when they resumed their journey having refilled their empty bottles from the water remaining in the container. The sun was still relatively high in the western sky but its heat was rapidly diminishing as it sank towards the horizon behind them.

Two hours into the march, its lower limb touched the horizon and, as it sank lower, the short period of twilight began. As the sun disappeared completely, there was still enough light in the western sky to illuminate their way ahead.

With the light in the west fading, it was replaced by an ever-brightening eastern sky as the moon emerged and, as was usual in these tropical latitudes, began to climb almost vertically towards the heavens overhead adding its light to the ever-increasing number of stars now visible.

As it continued its climb, the intensity of the moon's light increased, casting a silvery luminescence over the terrain ahead clearly illustrating the landscape of low hills and hollows stretching out before them.

When their first water break came, Jaime asked, "How's everyone making out?"

He was greeted with a chorus of spirited replies from, "Just like a stroll in the park," to "What are we stopping for?"

Jaime, heartened by this show of positive morale, responded with, "If we keep this rate up, we shall arrive there in the dark so we don't have to overdo it."

"If we're pushing you too hard, we'll slow down a bit," retorted Sherbourne.

What a fine bunch of people I'm with, thought Jamie, conscious of his responsibility towards them. He knew it was the way he set out the options leaning in favour of their present course that had persuaded them to head to their present destination.

Throughout their march, he had continually questioned his judgement and reason for opting for von Lutzdorf's secret base instead of taking the chance of finding water on the way to a certain source of water at Murzuk. One hundred and twenty miles was, after all, no great distance compared to their present trek and people had survived that and greater distances during the war on the same amounts of water.

He was persuaded largely by the argument that the base, as described in von Lutzdorf's log book, was clearly chosen after considerable surveys had been carried out by the Italians. The main condition for a permanent base of any sort was a regular and reliable source of water, which appeared to be the case here.

At midnight, during their second stop of the night, Jaime took three more star sights quickly reducing the readings to position lines and marking them on the chart with the use of his torch. Although sure of their progress, it was reassuring to see they were exactly on track and slightly ahead of expectations.

In the desert, just as at sea, the night sky, away from the industrial haze and the backdrop of artificial lighting of the cities and inhabited areas of the world, was of a darker more intense blackness which had the effect of increasing the density of the heavenly bodies to an almost overwhelming degree.

"How can you find what you're looking for amongst all those millions of stars up there?" asked Mary who had been watching Jaime as he peered into the scope of the bubble sextant and, after looking at his watch, scribbled figures on his notepad.

"It's not as difficult as you might think," said Jaime.

"How so?"

"Well, if you can imagine that we're standing on a certain unknown spot on the surface of the Earth which we're trying to identify. This is known as our geographical position or GP. Every heavenly body is at one point in time exactly directly overhead a particular spot on the surface of the Earth. This is known as their geographical position.

"Since the Earth is rotating, this geographical position is constantly changing with time so it's essential that, when I measure the altitude of certain identifiable stars, I also make a note of the time. The GP of these stars has been tabulated against the time for each day of the year so we have that as a reference point. Then, by a relatively simple matter of trigonometry, I can calculate our distance and bearing from the GPs of the selected stars and find our position. Do you understand?"

"Maths and trigonometry were not my strongest subjects so I'll take your word for it," said Mary with a smile.

With the moon high overhead, the landscape was almost as clearly lit as in sunlight such that they were able to make out several areas of rock formations indicating they were moving into the area of the foothills of the Tibesti Mountains. Now certain they would reach their goal soon, they were impatient for the dawn to arrive.

⁕

The moon was still high in the western sky when the first signs of the approaching dawn were heralded by a lightening of the sky to the east. Tropical sunrises, like the sunsets, happened at a greater pace than in the more northern latitudes and it was not long before the tip of the sun appeared at the horizon. The moon and its light were soon overwhelmed by the power of the rising sun and its image faded and disappeared. In contrast, the sunlight increased in intensity and etched out the horizon in sharp relief.

Raising his binoculars, Jaime was able to make out the irregular shape of the Tibesti Mountains' foothills a few miles ahead. Passing the binoculars around, he invited them all to take a look.

It was Mary who first spoke. "Jaime, I think I can see those three rocks mentioned in the log book. Here, take a look."

Accepting the binoculars, Jaime scanned in the direction indicated by Mary and exclaimed, "I do believe you're right. And not more than a couple of miles."

"Well done, navigator," said Sherbourne with a smile.

"Well done, all of you," said Jaime, "That was quite a trek."

Encouraged by what they had achieved, they felt infused with new energy as they all increased their pace towards the now clearer foothills.

Chapter 67

❖

They were all familiar with the description and directions written in the log book to locate the hidden hangar and airstrip. Their first point of reference and task was to correctly identify the three rock formation which gave the approach heading to the landing and take-off area of the base. They quickly covered the remaining two miles and it soon became apparent there was only the three rock formation which they had seen from a distance that could possibly fit the description von Lutzdorf had written in his log book. It was then a simple matter of standing in front of the last one and lining it up with the other two to give them the heading which Jaime checked with his hand compass.

"From here, we walk five hundred yards to the threshold. We should find the surface is hard enough to support the weight of an aircraft without its wheels sinking into the sand. From there, we turn at right angles to the right of the heading and walk a hundred yards towards the cliff face which should bring us to the hidden entrance of the hangar."

"We've come this far. This last bit shouldn't be too difficult," said Sherbourne, "And I'm thirsty as well as curious, so let's go."

With Jaime in the lead pacing out the distance, they eventually found themselves walking on a hard packed surface as described. In unison, they all looked towards the cliff face.

"Are you sure we're in the right place? All I see is something that looks exactly like a cliff face," said Sherbourne, keeping up the humour.

"There's only one way to find out," said Mary as she strode forwards.

"It's amazing," said von Oppersdorf as, even from the distance of ten yards, the camouflage was impressive. Instead of just paint, the Italians had covered the surface with a mixture of plaster or cement embedded with pieces of rock and rubble to closely resemble the surrounding rock surface.

"According to the next instruction, we must find a cleft in the cliff face off to the right where we should find some sort of lever to operate the opening mechanism," said Mary who had already started walking in that direction. After fifty yards, Mary gave a shout of glee and said, "Here it is."

Just as she was about to reach into the cleft, Jaime grabbed her hand and said, "Wait a moment, Mary. Just stand back a bit." He poked the pole he had been carrying into the cleft and rattled it around.

Mary gasped as two large black scorpions scuttled out and crawled away. Giving the cleft another poke or two, he then peered in as far as he could see and, satisfied there were no other lurking predators, he reached in and found what felt like a metal lever.

Mary, in the meantime, recovered from the shock and said, "You're quite right, Jaime. The desert is no place for a lady without a Sir Galahad."

"At your service, milady," said Jaime with a grin. "Now all stand back. This is the moment of truth."

With that, he reached in and grasped the lever. First applying pressure in one direction, he found it would not budge. Using the other hand, he applied pressure in the other direction and was rewarded with a slight movement. Using the pole as a crowbar, he applied more pressure and moved it a little more.

"Trouble, Jaime?" asked von Oppersdorf.

"It's a bit stiff, but that's not surprising after all these years."

Removing the pole, he changed hands again and applied backwards pressure as he moved it back to the closed position. Alternatively changing the direction of movement eased the shaft of the valve in its sleeve and, on the third attempt, he managed to move the lever through ninety degrees to its open position. As he did so, there was a hissing sound of escaping air accompanied by a rumbling sound as the cliff face began to move.

They all stood back in amazement as two large sections of the cliff face started to move apart. They all walked towards the opening and stood there gaping in awe and surprise as the hangar doors opened. No matter what they had read in the log book, they were not prepared for the scene unfolding before their eyes. The gap between the now fully open hangar doors was over one hundred and fifty feet but the width of the hangar behind them was nearly twice that figure and the depth nearer two hundred and fifty feet.

The centrepiece and star of the show was a gleaming wartime Heinkel 111 bomber which looked as if it had just come from the factory.

Overcoming their initial surprise, they all entered the hangar to be greeted with a slightly musty smell with a hint of oil and, apart from a very fine film of dust, everything was surprisingly clean.

"This is amazing," said Sherbourne, "No doubt due to being practically hermetically sealed for all these years."

"First things first," added Jaime. "Alan, Mary, see if you can find the water reservoir. Hugo, give me a hand looking at the electrical panel to see if we can get some lighting going."

The electrical panel next to the plumbing and compressed air piping was clearly and logically laid out on one wall. To one side of the electrical panel was a room containing two generators which had been insulated to reduce the noise of them in operation. After some study, Jaime was able to work out the compressed air starting procedure for the generators. Firstly, however, he checked the fuel supply for them and found the feed line from the tank mounted on a pedestal between the two generators. The sight glass attached to the tank indicated it was three quarters full. Each generator had its own feed line and shut-off valve, both of which were closed.

Choosing one of the generators, he opened the appropriate fuel valve and then traced out the compressed air piping.

"It looks like this one should start it, Hugo," said Jaime, with his hand on a lever.

Von Oppersdorf, standing next to him, said, "Open the valve and let's see what happens."

Depressing the lever resulted in a hissing sound as the generator motor turned over and, after a few revolutions, it burst into life. At the electrical panel, Jaime closed one of two main breaker switches and the hangar was suddenly illuminated by a number of wall and hanging lamps. Closing a row of secondary breaker switches caused more lights to come on all around the hangar.

Mary and Alan suddenly appeared from the back of the hangar each carrying a glass of water which they offered to Jaime and von Oppersdorf.

"Believe it or not," said Mary, "There's a tap in the kitchen at the back which we let run for a few minutes. The water tastes as fresh as if it just came from a spring which must constantly trickle into the reservoir keeping it topped up and fresh."

"Thank goodness for that," said Jaime. "At least that takes care of our immediate needs. I must confess, however, that I'm totally overwhelmed by this amazing installation. Now I know what it must be like when one first opens an ancient Egyptian tomb."

"I don't think you'll find any Heinkel 111s in an old tomb," said Sherbourne, with a laugh.

"Now you have all the lights on, we'll have a more thorough search," said Mary.

"Yes, we must find the food store and see what there is."

All the store rooms were at the rear of the hangar and, as Mary and Sherbourne searched for foodstuffs, Jaime found the large workshop area and associated electrical and mechanical stores full of all the tools and spares to maintain the installation for long periods.

Mary came into the workshop and said, "There are enough provisions, all tinned or in sealed containers, to feed an army for months. We'll have a very good meal this evening, and the wine cellar belongs in a good Italian restaurant."

Satisfied as to their immediate well being, Jaime turned his attention to the main exhibit: the Heinkel 111.

First, he did a walk around inspection and marveled to see the care that had been taken before the late von Lutzdorf left on his ill-fated journey. Jacks had been placed under the hard points under the wings and fuselage to take the weight off the tyres so they would not deflate and deform under the pressure. Giving them a kick, they appeared still to be fully inflated. Due to the dry atmosphere inside the sealed hangar and with little humidity, there was only a fine film of dust apparent covering the glazed cockpit area.

The entry hatch to the Heinkel was located under the belly of the aircraft which, in the standard version, was in a blister or bathtub arrangement. Due to the modifications that had removed this blister to make the fuselage more aerodynamic, the hatch was now part of the fuselage itself, albeit in the same position.

"This must bring back some memories for you, Hugo."

"Yes, although I never flew one of these on operations, I did fly in them once or twice and I remember the entry hatch was in the gunner's blister. This aircraft has been somewhat modified. However, they were not dissimilar as far as the cockpit controls and layout are concerned."

"Let's have a look inside."

Von Oppersdorf turned the handle and opened the hatch allowing it to drop down. Then he pulled down a step used to facilitate entry and, reaching up, he grasped two handles and heaved himself into the belly of the Heinkel. Directly behind him, Jaime pulled himself into the aircraft using the same technique and followed von Oppersdorf who made his way forwards to the cockpit and settled himself into the left-hand pilot's seat. To the right of the pilot's seat, there was a pull-down seat for the co-pilot which Jaime unlatched and sat next to von Oppersdorf.

"What do you think of it, Hugo?"

"I think if we started the engines, this thing would still fly."

"That's an interesting thought, though I'm sure the starting battery is quite flat and probably beyond recovery by now."

Exiting the Heinkel, Jaime and von Oppersdorf inspected the rest of the vehicles parked in the hangar. There was a five-ton Italian covered truck and a German open top half-track as well as a towing vehicle for aircraft.

"Perhaps we could use one of these," said von Oppersdorf.

"Perhaps," said Jaime, "I think I can solve the starting problem. There are some brand new batteries in the store that have never been filled with acid and never charged up. There are a number of large glass containers of acid and distilled water in the store also, so we can fill some to the right specific gravity and, charged up, they'll be like new."

"Let's do that right away," said von Oppersdorf enthusiastically.

In the store room, they put four of the empty batteries on the workbench and, checking the instructions with the batteries, they poured in the requisite amount of acid and distilled water to the right specific gravity, resealed them, connected them to a battery charger unit they found in the workshop and then left them to charge. Satisfied from the current flow on the meter that what they had done would result in four new fully charged batteries, they continued with their inspection of the hangar and its facilities.

"I've a suggestion to make, Jaime," said von Oppersdorf. "If we can get the half-track started, why don't I go back to the camp and bring the bodies back here?"

"I thought we would pick them up on the way back," said Jaime.

"What if we can get the Heinkel's engines started? We could then all fly back to Tripoli."

"We would have to give the Heinkel a really thorough inspection before we could safely think of flying her again."

"We're both experienced pilots, Jaime. We know what we need to inspect to make sure it's in good working order. I don't see why we couldn't make it airworthy again."

"Perhaps you're right. In any case, it'll be an interesting exercise to try. Let's see if these batteries take a charge and can be relied upon before deciding what to do."

"Fair enough."

"If we do get the half-track going, I think Alan should go with you back to the camp in case you run into problems."

"I don't think that would be necessary. It's only about a three-hour drive each way."

"What about loading the caskets on to the half-track? That won't be easy on your own."

Von Oppersdorf hesitated a moment before replying and Jaime had the distinct impression there was a degree of reluctance in his voice as he answered. "I expect you're right. Let's see what Alan has to say about it."

***

At the back of the hangar in the living quarters, Jaime and Hugo found Mary in the laundry store sorting out clean bedding for the sleeping accommodation.

"I hope you were careful sorting through everything," said Jaime, "You never know what could be lurking amongst those things."

"Don't worry," she said, "After my last experience and your advice, I am extremely careful and use a stick to turn everything over. So far, I've seen nothing like your scorpions or camel spiders."

"Where's Alan?"

"He's in the wine store selecting the wines for dinner this evening. You two had better go and find him before he starts sampling too much."

They found Alan in one of the store rooms which had cases of wine stacked on shelves. He had opened several of the cases and was studying the labels when they walked in.

He looked up and said, "There are some wines and vintages here which would cost a fortune in London today. That is, if you could find them."

"We'll leave the wine selection in your good hands, Alan. Meanwhile, Hugo here has suggested that, if we can get one of the vehicles started, he would go back to our camp and get the caskets. How do you feel about going with him?"

"Yes, of course. I think that's a good idea. I didn't feel good about leaving them there when we left. I'm all for it."

"That's settled then, Hugo. Let's have a look at this half-track and make sure it's in good mechanical order."

Hugo followed Jaime and together they left to inspect the vehicle. In the workshop, they found spare oil and tubs of grease for lubricating the tracks. They were surprised, however, when they started their inspection and found how clean it appeared, as if it had just undergone a complete service and refit.

"One must compliment the dedication of the maintenance personnel that were here. They certainly knew their job," said Jaime." If we had a battery, I'm sure it would start right away just like the generator."

Having satisfied himself there was little more they could do until they had the means to start the engine, Jaime went back to check on the batteries. He was pleased to find that, when he unscrewed the filler caps, the electrolyte was bubbling giving off gas indicating it was taking a charge.

While von Oppersdorf was looking at the other truck, Jaime walked back to speak to Mary who he now found was selecting things from the food store.

"I thought I would find something suitable for lunch."

"Mary, has Hugo questioned you about anything more you might know about von Lutzdorf and his mission? About what he might have been carrying for example and where it might possibly be since we found nothing in the truck?"

"No, but we haven't been alone together to give him that opportunity. Why do you ask?"

"Nothing specific, just a feeling I have about some of the things he's said recently."

"You mean you have some suspicions of him not being all he claims?"

"I can't put my finger on it but something's not quite right. I've been thinking over recent events in light of some things he's said and they've set me thinking. Perhaps I'm wrong and being overly suspicious but, under the circumstances, one cannot afford not to be overcautious. Please play it cautiously whatever he asks you and let me know what he says."

"Of course. Leave it to me: Mata Hari," she said with a grin.

"Tell Alan what I've said to you and tell him to be careful and tell him not to let Hugo know he's armed."

"That sounds serious. Careful of what?"

"Just be careful and be observant. I just have a feeling that Mueller may still be in the area."

"That must be your canny Scot's blood talking to you."

"Maybe."

Jaime found a maintenance stairway and platform in the corner which was used for easy access to aircraft engines. Wheeling it over to the 111, he placed it in position, climbed up to the platform and inspected the engine nacelles to see what tools he would need to open the inspection panels.

After collecting what he needed from the workshop, he stopped by Hugo inspecting the five-ton truck and said, "If you're finished here, can you please give me a hand removing the inspection panels on the 111?"

"I'll be right with you," said von Oppersdorf, as he closed the bonnet of the engine space.

"I think first we need to do an all-round visual inspection to see if they are any obvious leaks from perished seals and then check the fluid levels. After that, if we can turn the engines over manually a few turns with the propellers and to ensure the pistons are not seized in the cylinders, we could try starting them."

"There's a ground starting trolley over in that corner. I've looked at the connectors and it has several different adapters for connecting to the external ground electrical input for an aircraft. One of which I am sure will fit the 111," said von Oppersdorf.

"That sounds promising," said Jaime.

They set to work removing the panels and checking over the engines. They were surprised to find, like the half-track, it appeared as if the engines had just had a full service and inspection. There were no leaks of any sort and the seals looked as good as the day they were fitted.

Replacing the panels on both engines, they wheeled the stairway back from the aircraft and looked at the jacks that held the tyres free, off the ground.

They were mechanical geared all-metal types that had been manually raised with a gearwheel handle and held in place with a locking pin. All that was required was to remove the pins and unwind the handles lowering the fuselage and wheels until the tyres touched the ground and gradually took the weight as the oleo pneumatic hydraulic landing struts compressed to their normal ground position.

"Those tyres look as good as the day they were pumped up," said Hugo.

"The whole aircraft looks like it's just come out from the maintenance shop," replied Jaime. "Let's put our weight on these propellers to see if we can turn the engines over."

With the leverage of the blade and with one pulling and one pushing, they managed to turn the engine over a couple of times.

"Seems like we could be in business," said Jaime, "But first we must tow the aircraft out of the hangar before we try to start an engine, so we'll need to get the tug working."

"The next job on the list."

Just then, Mary called them and announced lunch was ready.

The sight that greeted them as they walked back to the living quarters was like something from a good restaurant.

Mary had laid the table with a cloth and set out a place for each of them with china plates, cutlery and wine glasses while Alan was standing to one side with a cork screw opening a bottle of wine like a wine waiter. As the cork came out with a pop, he smiled and said, "Please be seated, gentlemen. I can recommend the wine. It's a very good year."

Mary came back and laid two platters on the table, one with very fine slices of cured ham and the other with an assortment of salamis together with a large bowl of preserved olives.

"Something to start with while I bring in the main dish."

"Mary, this looks wonderful," said Jaime as he raised his glass and proposed a toast to the chef.

They sipped the wine and all agreed it was something exceptional.

"Do you know there are fifty cases of this stuff in the store and that's only the red," said Sherbourne.

Whilst they continued enjoying the hors d'oeuvres and sipping the wine, Mary went back to the kitchen with Alan and returned with a large bowl of steaming spaghetti and a bowl of tomato sauce smelling of garlic and herbs. Alan produced a large dish of grated Parmigiano cheese and said, "Voila! La pièce de résistance."

"If someone told me last night when we were marching across the desert that today we would be sitting down to a cloth-covered table eating a gourmet meal with vintage wine, I would have thought he was delirious with the sun," said Jaime. "Thank you so much, Mary. You've raised our spirits."

"Here, here!" echoed Sherbourne.

"You English still surprise me with your humour and attitude in spite of the time I spent at our embassy in London."

"Half Scottish, if you don't mind," said Jaime, "And it's true we can be quite surprising at times."

"You mean, there's more to come?" said von Oppersdorf at an attempt at humour.

"Wait and see," said Jaime with a smile.

"After that wine, I'm feeling a little sleepy," said Mary.

"Me too," said Sherbourne.

"I think we all need some sleep," said Jaime, "Remember, we've not slept since yesterday. I think a siesta will do us all good."

They all agreed and helped clear up the dishes. Then they proceeded to pick out their various beds in the quarters. There were two separate rooms for officers with two beds each and a larger room with eight beds for enlisted men. Mary was allocated one of the officers' rooms and Jaime and Sherbourne decided to share the other officers' room leaving the larger room for von Oppersdorf with a choice of beds.

Unaccustomed to sleeping during the day and in spite of not sleeping the previous night together with feeling the effects of the wine, Jaime managed only a couple of hours sleep. Those two hours of deep sleep, however, fully refreshed him.

He sat up and looked over at Sherbourne who stirred and opened his eyes and asked, "What time is it?"

Looking at his watch, Jaime said, "Four o'clock. How do you feel?"

"Fine. That was just what I needed."

As they were alone and out of earshot of von Oppersdorf, Jaime took the opportunity to express his suspicions about him.

At first, Sherbourne was surprised but as Jaime elaborated on the events following the incident with Mueller, he began to see the logic of Jaime's deductions.

"You remember when Mueller left following the explosion? It was von Oppersdorf who volunteered to follow and see which direction he was taking and was gone for some time."

"He did say he watched them until they disappeared over the next line of dunes."

"Maybe so, but then when we got back to camp, it was he who went up to the ridge and checked on the transceiver radio. He came back and told us they had just removed the battery. A strange thing to do when they smashed everything else."

"Perhaps."

"And then earlier today, he suggested that he go back to the camp in the half-track to collect the caskets. He was reluctant for you to accompany him when I suggested it, almost as if he did not want you around. Individually, they don't seem like very much but taken together, they begin to form a pattern."

"Don't forget, he was very indignant when Mueller appeared and questioned his actions."

"That could have been a set-up, designed to put von Oppersdorf firmly in our camp above suspicion."

"You know, Jaime, you missed your calling. With a suspicious deductive mind like yours, you should be with my firm."

"That's been mentioned before but I can't overcome this feeling that Mueller is still somewhere nearby. It's not like these fanatics to give up so easily after an initial setback."

"I can't disagree with that. What do you have in mind?"

"We'll have to devise a plan to draw him out but be prepared if our suspicions prove to be correct. Do you still have your pistol concealed about you?"

"Yes, of course."

"Don't let von Oppersdorf know about it and keep up your facade of being a representative from the War Graves Commission. I have some things in mind which I'll put in place. I think you'll have to accompany him back to the camp tomorrow but be on your guard at all times. I'll ensure he takes the Luger with him but I will remove the firing pin, just in case."

"What if he wants to take the MP 40 with him?"

"Don't worry. I'll insist it's needed here to defend the base while you're both away. He won't be able to argue against that without it appearing suspicious. I'll swop it for the Luger."

"What's your plan to draw him out?"

"I've not finalized it yet but just follow my lead. When I start, it'll all become clear."

"In this matter, you are the boss. Are you sure you don't want to consider a change of profession? My chief in London would be very pleased to meet you."

Jaime laughed and said, "All in good time. Let's complete this mission first. Now let's get up. I want to check on the batteries and see about starting the tug so we can tow the aircraft outside."

Mary's and von Oppersdorf's doors were still closed as they left their bedroom, so assuming they were still sleeping, they made their way quietly into the hangar.

Jaime checked on the batteries and was pleased to find the charger was indicating a strong steady current flow and, on opening the cells, he could see the electrolyte bubbling as gas was released.

Satisfied all was as it should be, they walked to the front of the open hangar and Jamie gave the landscape before them a complete one-hundred-and-eighty-degree scan with the binoculars.

"Still think they're out there somewhere?" asked Alan.

"With all these sand dunes and hollows, they could be hiding but a few miles from here. It's best to be safe."

"If von Oppersdorf is what you suspect then I think it's very likely you're right."

"The day after tomorrow we'll know for sure if my plan works out. We must be patient until you go with him to the camp. I want you to be away all day so I can prepare what I have to do tomorrow in his absence."

"I'll do my best to delay our return until just before sunset. That should give you ample time to do whatever it is you have planned."

"Yes, but don't give von Oppersdorf any reason to suspect you of subterfuge or that you in any way doubt his support for us."

"Don't worry. I'll play the part of a naive civil servant just doing his job."

"Be sure to bring the radio transceiver Mueller supplied and keep an eye on von Oppersdorf. I'm still not convinced about his story that Mueller's men only removed the battery. He may have removed it himself and buried it on the ridge to be retrieved later."

***

They were sitting in two chairs they had placed in the hangar entrance enjoying the sunset when they heard movement behind them. As they turned, Mary appeared bearing a tray with a coffee pot and cups.

"I thought you both might like a coffee before I start preparing the evening meal."

Jaime and Sherbourne both jumped to their feet as Jaime said, "You don't have to wait on us like this, Mary, but thank you anyway."

"It's the least I can do. I know you guys have much to do and plan today if we're to get back to Tripoli safely. Things I cannot help with."

"Don't be too sure of that, Mary. Your input will be essential. Where's von Oppersdorf?"

"I think I heard him stirring as I passed his door. I expect he'll be here in a moment. That's why I brought three cups."

Just then von Oppersdorf appeared and joined them.

"Mary has just made some coffee. Please join us, Hugo."

Mary poured three cups and passed them around. "I'll leave you three together. I must get back to my kitchen, sir," she said with a laugh and a mock bow.

Von Oppersdorf stood there with his coffee cup in hand and looked after the departing Mary as he said seriously, "You English, I'll never understand your sense of humour."

"Half Scottish," corrected Jaime, with a smile.

The evening passed convivially enough as Mary produced a very presentable meal saying, "It's basically another pasta dish. It's difficult to do anything else without fresh meat and vegetables but I've used what preserved herbs and vegetables I have to make it at least tasty."

"It's delicious, Mary. What fresh food we don't have is more than made up for by the quality of the wine," said Sherbourne as he poured them all generous glasses of the vintage Barolo.

As they prepared to turn in again, Jaime spoke to von Oppersdorf. "Hugo, I think the batteries will be fully charged by the morning and that you should get an early start back to the camp for the caskets."

"I agree. I shall be ready soon after sun up."

"I've prepared a chart for you and you can take my hand compass but I don't think you'll have any difficulty as our tracks will probably still be visible."

"You're right. I don't expect any difficulty. It should be just a straightforward trip there and back."

***

The next morning, they were all up and breakfasted just after sunrise. Between them, Jaime and von Oppersdorf carried one of the heavy batteries to the half-track and replaced the old one.

Sitting in the driver's seat, Jaime switched on the ignition and pressed the starter. They were rewarded by the sound of the starter motor engaging and the engine turning over. It did not immediately start so Jaime released the starter button for a few seconds before trying again.

"After all this time, there won't be any fuel in the line from the tank. We must give it a chance for the fuel pump to fill up the line to the carburettor."

On the third try, the engine coughed and started with a satisfying rumble and settled into a steady tick over.

"Well done, Jaime. That all seems to be in order," said von Oppersdorf.

Sherbourne, who was standing to one side with a small rucksack containing a water bottle and some food, said, "Sounds good to me, Hugo. I'm ready when you are."

"Let's go then," said von Oppersdorf with the MP 40 in one hand, about to climb into the driver's seat.

"Please leave the Schmeisser with me, Hugo," said Jaime, "I'll feel safer with it here in case Mueller is still in the area."

Von Oppersdorf laughed as he handed the weapon over without objection and said, "I think you are worrying about nothing. Mueller is long gone from here the way he was heading when I last saw him."

"Perhaps you're right, Hugo, but nevertheless I feel better playing it safe. Here, you take the Luger with you."

"As you wish, Jaime," said von Oppersdorf taking the pistol and putting it in his jacket pocket.

"We don't know how far this will go on a tank of fuel, so we've put three twenty-five-litre cans of fuel on board as well as a twenty-five-litre can of water," said Jaime. As he said that, Mary appeared and handed over a package of food she had prepared for them.

"Thanks," said Sherbourne as he accepted the package. "All being well, we'll see you back here late this afternoon."

With that, von Oppersdorf engaged the gear and drove slowly out of the hangar; the track making a grinding noise on the concrete surface which soon subsided as it drove on to the soft sand and headed off back to their previous camp site.

Chapter 68

❖

Jaime and Mary watched them as they drove off towards an area of low sand dunes at about twenty miles per hour.

"It's no racing machine," said Jaime, "But it's reliable and good in soft sand. It should take them about three hours each way, plus a couple of hours at the camp which gives us about eight hours to get done what we must do before they return."

"What do you want to do first?"

"We must locate the site where von Lutzdorf buried the documents and recover everything buried there and get it stored and concealed on board the aircraft."

"The directions are written in the log book. As I remember, the site is quite close to the cleft in the cliff face where the opening lever is located. Shouldn't be too difficult to find. Let me have a look at the log book again to check those directions."

Jaime produced the log book from his flight bag and gave it to Mary.

"Yes, it's as I remembered. Just in front of the cleft, there should be a small pile of rocks under which should be the documents. He says they buried them about a metre below the surface."

Collecting two spades with pointed blades from the workshop, they walked along the cliff face until they reached the cleft. Clearly evident just to one side was a small pile of rocks.

First clearing the rocks, Jaime set to work with the spade and dug a hole about one metre square piling the sand up to one side. At two feet depth, his spade blade struck something solid.

"I think we're there," said Jaime as he widened the area around the buried object which appeared to be a steel-bound box with leather handles at each end. Kneeling down, they each grasped hold of a handle and, after a bit of heaving, managed to loosen the box from the grip of the sand. With an extra concerted effort, they managed to lift the box clear from the hole.

Once the box was removed, it revealed the corners of four other boxes, that the first one had been placed on, that had been buried below. They set about widening the hole which eventually revealed five other boxes in total. Attached to each handle was a length of coiled rope. Although all slightly smaller than the first, four of them were much heavier.

As they struggled to lift them out, Jaime said, "These ones obviously contain the gold mentioned in the log book."

Looking down into the hole, it was clear there was nothing else to be found there so Jaime said, "Let's fill this hole in first and get the boxes back inside where we can inspect them."

Back in the workshop, Jaime found a four-wheeled trolley which was obviously used for carrying the heavy batteries.

"This will do nicely. Let's get it back to the boxes."

Even with the trolley, they had to make three journeys to get all six boxes back to the workshop.

"Let's open the first one we dug up. I suspect that one contains the documents everyone is so anxious about," said Jaime.

"It has a very strong-looking padlock and we don't have a key," said Mary.

"I'll soon take care of that," said Jaime as he walked over to the workbench and came back with a big pair of bolt cutters which made short work of the lock.

As expected, the box contained a number of file boxes and sealed packages which obviously contained all the documentation.

"Now, can we open one of the heavy boxes? I can't wait to see all that gold," said Mary.

Using the bolt cutter once again, they opened one of the heavy boxes and found it contained what appeared to be twelve ingots of the yellow metal on top of which was a small canvas sack.

"Can I feel one please, Jaime? I've never seen so much gold."

Jaime lifted one of the ingots out and placed it on the bench. Mary grasped it and, with some difficulty, managed to lift it.

"My God, it's so heavy," she said as she dropped it back on the bench. "I wonder how much that's worth?"

"More than either of us would make in a year, I suspect."

They stared at the ingot which had an eagle above a swastika stamped into the surface.

"There's no doubt about that being Nazi gold. Probably from all the gold teeth fillings they extracted from those poor Jewish prisoners before they burnt them in the crematorium."

"Oh! How dreadful," exclaimed Mary as she put her hands to her face. "And to think I just touched it. Quick, please put it back in the box, Jaime."

Jaime withdrew the canvas sack and replaced the ingot back in the box with the others.

"I wonder what we have in here…" he said as he pulled the string to open the neck of the sack. Tipping it, he poured some of the contents onto the bench.

"They look like the uncut industrial diamonds mentioned in the log book," said Mary.

"I do believe you're right. And probably worth more than the gold."

"Quite a little treasure trove. Pity we can't keep it."

"Perhaps we can claim a finder's fee," said Jaime with a laugh.

"Not so silly, Jaime. You should be able to as you first found the truck and you're a civilian not bound by the conventions of government service."

"Maybe. Anyway, let's not get distracted by conjecture. Let's look inside this other one and then reseal them and get them in the aircraft."

When they opened the larger box, it too had some surprises as, besides more files of banking and company documents, they found a separate box containing a large amount of English currency in various denominations from five to fifty pound notes.

"What a pity they've stopped issuing the old white five and ten pound notes. We could have had a good time spending these," laughed Mary.

"And probably ended up in jail. They're most likely all counterfeit. The Germans flooded the country with fake British currency during the war to try to destabilize the economy."

Jaime refastened the boxes by the simple expediency of replacing the padlocks with a nut and bolt which he tightened in place with a spanner.

Between them using the trolley, they moved the boxes out to the aircraft and, with some difficulty, lifted the heavy gold boxes up through the access hatch and placed them inside. Conscious of the weight of the gold, Jaime put those boxes forwards in the cabin space behind the cockpit so as to not affect the centre of gravity adversely. The others he placed in the rear cargo area behind the bulkhead door.

Returning to the workshop, he put one of the fully charged high-capacity batteries onto a trolley. He transported it to the ground start unit which was mounted on wheels and consisted of a diesel generator and a battery which he now replaced with the fully charged one. He pressed the starter and, after two or three revolutions, the motor burst into life. Satisfied he now had the means to start the Heinkel's engines, he switched off and, placing the old battery on the trolley, he returned it to the workshop.

Filling two more of the new batteries with acid, he connected them to the charger so they would be ready for use the following morning.

Since the chances of Mueller attempting anything without von Oppersdorf being present was extremely unlikely, Jaime felt confident in his next move which was to disassemble the MP 40 and remove the firing pin.

The more he ruminated over his suspicions about von Oppersdorf, the more convinced he became that he presented a real and present danger. He regularly scanned the surrounding landscape with his binoculars until such time that he spotted a cloud of dust in the distance which proved to be Sherbourne and von Oppersdorf returning.

Chapter 69

❖

It was almost exactly eight hours since they had departed that morning with still an hour to go before sunset. As the half-track, with von Oppersdorf driving, came to a halt in front of the hangar, Jaime walked up to them and said, "You made good time. Did you have any problems?"

Sherbourne was the first to answer. "No problems, Jaime. It went just as you expected." He gave a thumbs up and, out of von Oppersdorf's line of sight, winked at Jaime.

"Excellent. Well done, both of you. I expect you're ready to relax with a drink before enjoying another great meal from Mary."

Von Oppersdorf, who smiled and appeared to be in good spirits, said, "I would just like to clean off the dust and sand and then have a glass or two of that excellent schnapps you found in the store."

"Good idea, Hugo," said Sherbourne, "I think I'll do the same."

As von Oppersdorf walked back to his bedroom, Jaime accompanied Sherbourne to their shared accommodation. Confident Hugo was out of earshot, he whispered to Sherbourne. "What happened?"

"As you predicted, von Oppersdorf went up to the ridge on the pretext of having a look around. He took with him, however, his rucksack which definitely appeared heavier when he returned. I pretended to be busy and not notice as he placed it behind the driver's seat. How did you get on today?"

"All done. We dug up all the documents and more and they're now safely aboard the Heinkel. I also fixed the starting trolley and put batteries in the plane for the radio ready to be connected as well as the aerial. I've also fixed the MP 40 and put it on that side table in the kitchen in full view. Did von Oppersdorf do anything suspicious on your way back?"

"Well, not particularly suspicious but something at the time I thought was unnecessary and unusual. About half an hour before we arrived back here, there's a wadi like a small ravine. He asked me to stop there as he claimed he needed to respond to a call of nature and couldn't wait until we arrived back here. He went off into the ravine and seemed to be gone for rather a long time just to relieve himself."

"I must agree that does seem to have been unnecessary with so short a time to go. Whatever the reason, we must keep up the appearance of innocence this evening and just talk of what we will do when we get home and off the subject of Mueller."

"A few glasses of schnapps and vintage Barolo should see to that."

***

Having refreshed themselves, Sherbourne and von Oppersdorf, at the insistence of Mary who stated she wished to be left alone in the kitchen, joined Jaime at the table where they indulged in several glasses of the fiery schnapps before it was announced that dinner would shortly be served. This time, Mary had surpassed herself with the limited variety of preserved foodstuffs available and, although still a pasta dish, she produced a tagliatelle with a spiced creamy cheese sauce with finely chopped strips of Parma ham to add to the flavour.

Sherbourne ensured the wine flowed freely while Jaime, and Mary who had also been briefed, kept the conversation to the more mundane subjects of their family life and what they were planning to do when they returned home. Von Oppersdorf, mellowed by the freely flowing alcohol, joined in with stories about his family. Jaime almost began to doubt his suspicions such was his portrayal of himself as an ordinary civil servant in the diplomatic service with a normal family life.

Finally, they all professed to feeling tired after a long day and retired to their rooms.

***

Jaime and Sherbourne rose at their usual early hour and opened the doors of the hangar which habitually they closed at night for security reasons and to keep out any unwanted creatures of the night.

Working according to their prearranged plan, Jaime started up the tug and attached it to the tail fitting on the aircraft and, after a few false starts, mastered the operation of the tug. He gingerly towed the Heinkel outside aligning it at a right angle to the hangar entrance to avoid clouds of dust and sand being blown into it when they started the engines.

Disconnecting the tug, Jaime returned it to its place inside and then wheeled the ground starting trolley outside, plugging in the cable to the external power socket ready to try an engine start.

Returning to the hangar, they found Mary, who also had risen early, had made coffee and produced some rolls she had baked the previous day. As they sat down at the table, von Oppersdorf joined them as they ate an enjoyable breakfast of rolls with tinned butter and preserves.

"Who would think there would be such a good restaurant all this way down in the desert?" said Sherbourne.

"Thanks to Mary," added Jaime.

"I see you've towed the aircraft out, Jaime. What's your plan?" asked von Oppersdorf.

"I thought we would just try to see if we can get the engines to start and, if successful, we can then decide what to do."

"I think that's a sensible idea. I would rather fly back than drive all the way in that old truck," said Mary.

"I don't suppose it'll do any harm to try to start the engines," said von Oppersdorf in a strangely unenthusiastic tone of voice which did not go unnoticed by everyone.

"You don't sound too enthusiastic, Hugo. Anything wrong?"

Realizing he had made a mistake, he quickly said, "Oh no, sorry. I was just thinking about something else. Yes, of course, we should definitely try to start the engines. As you say, it would be better than walking home."

They all got up from the table and walked out through the hangar to the aircraft.

"I'll get in the cockpit and go through the starting procedure the way you showed me, Hugo, if you'll stand by the ground trolley. Alan, you and Mary stand back from the propellers and watch."

"You sure you don't want me to start the engines?" said von Oppersdorf.

Jaime was ready for that and said, "No, I don't think so. I'll be flying the aircraft so I must get familiar with the starting procedure and engine controls."

"As you wish, Jaime."

Jaime bent down under the belly of the fuselage and pulled himself up inside. He switched on the power and was pleased to see the engine instruments come alive. He opened the side cockpit window and gave von Oppersdorf a thumbs up signal to start the ground trolley generator to give the starting batteries the extra boost required to turn the engines over. He set the throttles and pitch controls and went through the standard procedure of calling out of the window for them to keep clear of the props as he pressed the starter button for the port left-hand engine. The propeller turned over and, after a couple of revolutions, the engine fired and caught as the revolutions increased to the tick over speed which Jaime adjusted with the throttle at eight hundred revolutions per minute. Satisfied the port engine was running smoothly, he followed the same procedure for the starboard engine and soon had them both running smoothly together.

With the parking brakes on, Jaime left the cockpit and climbed out of the aircraft and joined the others.

"I'm perfectly satisfied that the aircraft is fit to fly so I see no reason why we can't put our things on board, close up shop here and fly back to Tripoli. What do you all say?"

Mary and Sherbourne, keeping to the plan, both expressed their enthusiasm to leave as soon as possible.

"I thought you were keen to recover whatever it was that von Lutzdorf was transporting and we have not yet made any attempt to search this place for them," said von Oppersdorf.

"I have a confession to make, Hugo. Whilst you and Alan were off yesterday recovering the caskets, Mary and I located everything and it's all now safely loaded aboard the aircraft. What we didn't disclose to you before was that we knew where to find them from the cryptic message von Lutzdorf wrote in his log book."

"How very clever of you. Why did you not tell me about that before?"

"Security, Hugo. It was on a need-to-know basis."

"I see."

"Now that you know the situation, are you ready to leave with us?"

"Yes, of course. I'll just have to get some of my things together."

As von Oppersdorf walked off into the hangar, the three of them remained together in a group by the port wing tip, out of the blast from the rotating propeller.

"What do you think he's going to do, Jaime?"

"Let's wait and see if our suspicions are correct. It won't take long. Just act normal."

As if on cue, von Oppersdorf appeared from around the front of the aircraft but, instead of carrying his personal belongings, he was holding the MP 40 pointed at them.

Looking at von Oppersdorf, Jaime said, "What's the meaning of this, Hugo?"

"I'm afraid there's going to be a change in plans. I cannot allow you to leave."

"What on earth are you saying and why are you pointing that gun at us?"

"Please don't continue to take us for fools. It was obvious from the beginning that this expedition was more important to the British government than just recovering the bodies of two long dead war casualties. Why would their embassy charter an aircraft and send two representatives to recover two German nationals? Herr Sherbourne here is certainly no lowly civil servant from the War Graves Commission. Probably from MI6, am I right?"

"What you say is very interesting, but precisely who are you referring to when you say 'us'?"

"I see you're going to persist in pretending you don't know who you are dealing with."

"Please enlighten us."

"You must now realize that I am referring to Oberst-Gruppenfuehrer Mueller and ODESSA."

"Do I understand from what you've just said that you are a member of that organisation?"

"Precisely so, my dear Wing Commander."

"So, we're reverting to our former military ranks as a form of address?"

"Under the circumstances, I think we should dispense with our former, rather insincere, familiarity."

"That being so, how should we address a former major in the Luftwaffe?"

"I prefer that you address me using my now substantive ODESSA rank of Standartenfuehrer."

"That represents a considerable promotion from major to colonel."

"A reflection of my current standing in the organization."

"Since it appears you are ready to use force to stop us leaving, these documents you refer to must be more important to you to recover than for us," said Sherbourne.

"Not quite correct. What is important to us is that they do not fall into the wrong hands."

"If they are so important, why did you risk them being transported back from South America at all with the possibility of them being captured?" asked Jaime.

"An unfortunate mistake brought about by the ego of our then illustrious Reichsmarschall Goering. He was one of the originators of the ODESSA project and insisted that he have a complete copy of all documents from their concept to enable him to keep control."

"What is it about them that makes them so important to you that we do not see them?"

"They would cause my organization some embarrassment and considerable disruption and the need to substantially change our plans."

"And what plans would they be? Since you appear to be holding all the cards, there's no reason why you cannot reveal them to us."

"Why, the establishment of the new Fourth Reich, of course."

"Don't you people ever have enough? Twice this century you've tried to impose your will on Europe and failed at the cost of millions of lives and untold misery."

"It is the destiny of Germany to be the dominant power in Europe and ultimately the world."

As he said this, the look on his face changed from a sneer to that of a fanatic with a gleam in his eyes and his voice rose to a more strident level.

Sherbourne decided it was time to say something. "And just how do you propose to achieve that this time, Colonel? By the way, you may address me as 'Major', my former rank in the Intelligence Corps."

Fired now with the fervour of a fanatic, von Oppersdorf looked at Sherbourne and said, "So, Major, you are not just the civil servant from the War Graves Commission after all."

Filled with the need to provoke and deflate von Oppersdorf somewhat, Alan said, "Indeed not, Colonel. As you surmised, I'm from MI6. My department has a large file on von Lutzdorf and indeed ODESSA and it may interest you to know that von Lutzdorf was in contact with British Intelligence throughout and revealed to us the purpose of his mission. He would have delivered the documents we now have back then had it not been for his unfortunate disappearance."

"So, he was just another traitor after all."

"Not a traitor. A patriot and anti-Nazi who did not want to see them re-emerge after the war. It was you, the Nazis, who betrayed Germany and heaped shame on the country which will take generations of young Germans years to eradicate, if ever. They will never tolerate the establishment of a Nazi Fourth Reich."

"They won't even be aware of it happening until it is accomplished."

"You intrigue me, Colonel. How do you propose to pull the wool over the German people's eyes this time?"

"It will be quite simple really and with their complete and willing cooperation."

"Now you really intrigue me. Please explain this new master plan."

"The last war taught us quite a lot. Our beloved leader, the Fuehrer, was a great visionary and a man of courage but he was surrounded by fools who did not give him the right support and advice. For the most part, they were sycophants who misled him by telling him what he wanted to hear.

"We came to rely on the power of arms alone to achieve our objectives and underestimated the power of international finance and banking. As the war progressed, in spite of our technological superiority, we found it difficult to obtain strategic materials because we could not finance their acquisition. In spite of England being a beleaguered island, its empire was rich in natural resources and controlled much of the world's banking.

"When America joined in, they overwhelmed us with their financial and industrial strength. From 1942, with America entering the war, to the fall of Stalingrad and the loss of North Africa in 1943, it was obvious to the more enlightened of us that the war was lost. We set about, therefore, acquiring all the gold and valuables from the occupied territories that we could."

"You mean stealing it."

"We prefer to call it the spoils of war."

"A war that you started."

"That statement is somewhat moot. From then until the war's end, we deposited all the gold in Swiss banks who, as you know, worship gold and wealth and never question the origin and whose secrecy laws are inviolate."

"So, you amassed tons of stolen gold in the vaults of Zurich. What then?"

"We had them issue certificates of deposit, guarantees and other negotiable securities based on the then value of the gold. Then, through nominees, we formed Swiss companies and opened other accounts in friendly South American banks and, with established lines of credit, bought shares in the world's largest and most successful industries especially in America and the UK.

"The dividends which flowed from these investments were sent back to our Swiss bank accounts to increase our growing financial base. This reinvestment cycle continued to grow over the years to staggering amounts. So much so that it is more than many smaller countries' gross income."

"So, ODESSA is a wealthy organization. How does that help to establish a Nazi Fourth Reich?" asked Sherbourne.

"I see you need a lesson in economics, my dear Major."

"Please continue. Economics was not one of my strongest subjects."

"After the war, Europe, particularly Germany, was devastated and in ruins. With the rise in communism, the west, especially America, became paranoid and rather belatedly recognized the USSR as the real enemy. The only real bulwark against this growing threat was a strong Germany in alliance with America, Britain and France as the main partners.

"The Americans, now the strongest and most powerful economy in the world, came up with the Marshall Plan to finance the rebuilding of Europe. In spite of the devastation and loss of manpower, Germany, with its sense of discipline and work ethic, soon began to recover taking advantage of the funds from the Marshall Plan. Before long, its economy was outstripping those of its neighbours."

"I would have thought that a booming economy was not a fertile ground for Nazism to flourish," interjected Sherbourne.

"Let me explain something else which you may already agree with. At the end of the war, the allies had different objectives and goals. Russia just sought to increase its territory and influence. Britain sought to capture those they deemed responsible for the war and so-called war crimes.

"America's priority, on the other hand, was to capture German technology and its scientists and engineers. So much so that they overlooked any association these people may have had with war crimes and allegiance to the Nazi Party. Many former Gestapo members, whose knowledge of communist agents ended up working for the American security service, the CIA, were protected."

"I agree with that. The Americans did not always cooperate with us on those matters."

"To continue, apart from the Marshall Plan funds, ODESSA provided financial support to all of Germany's major industrial companies many of whose executives were former Nazi Party members. ODESSA also provided new identities and clean records for some of these as well as for those of local and national politicians. So, you see, our influence will continue to grow with the economy and the new government. People like our new leader, Oberst-Gruppenfuehrer Mueller, will remain in his covert position influencing policy with the strength of ODESSA behind him."

"Once we expose him and his organization, I think your dreams will begin to crumble, my dear Colonel."

"I don't see how you're in a position to do him any harm. I seem to have the upper hand here," said von Oppersdorf as he waved the Schmeisser at them.

"I would agree," said Jaime, "If your MP 40 still had its firing pin."

As he spoke, Jaime opened his hand and displayed the removed firing pin in his palm.

With a look of anger and frustration on his face, von Oppersdorf pulled the trigger which resulted in a loud click.

Throwing the weapon to the ground, he pulled out the Luger and pointed it at them. "Not so fast, Wing Commander. I still have your Luger."

"Same problem, I'm afraid," said Jaime as he opened his other hand and revealed the Luger firing pin.

"Very clever, Wing Commander, but not clever enough." As he spoke, von Oppersdorf pulled out a flare pistol. "Oberst-Gruppenfuehrer Mueller and Schmitt are watching us through binoculars waiting for my signal as arranged yesterday when we stopped at that wadi, which I'm sure you recall, Major. They will be here before you can refit the firing pins. In any case, with two MP 40s and ample ammunition, their firepower will soon overwhelm you and a few bursts of fire will render the Heinkel unable to fly."

All the time they had been talking, Jaime and the others were standing just forwards of the port wing tip with von Oppersdorf between them and the port engine which continued to tick over.

"Alan, if you please," Jaime said.

Sherbourne pulled out his automatic and, pointing it at von Oppersdorf, said, "This has a firing pin, I assure you, Colonel. Now put down that flare pistol."

Jaime and Sherbourne advanced towards von Oppersdorf who, seemingly oblivious of the spinning blades behind him, retreated backwards and said, "Too late, Major. My colleagues will be here in twenty minutes."

As he spoke, he raised his arm and fired the pistol. The act of raising his arm and looking upwards at the flare streaking skywards caused him to bend his head back at an angle of forty-five degrees to his body. It was just enough that the tip of the spinning blade sliced through the back of his skull which exploded like a ripe melon spraying blood and brains all over the underside of the wing. Everything happened in a split second, too fast almost to follow, as the blades continued to slice into his upper torso. The impact was sufficient to lift up the headless body and fling it over their heads to land with a sickening thump on the sand behind them.

"Oh my God," exclaimed Mary, "How dreadful."

Jaime was the first to react. "Quickly, both of you, we don't have long. Alan, get the radio transceiver on board. I'll shut down the generator and close the doors."

As Mary and Sherbourne did as they were bid, Jaime rushed into the hangar, pulled the fuel shut-off valve which stopped the generator and, from the workshop, he came out with a long steel crow bar.

Checking Mary and Sherbourne were safely on board, he walked along to the cleft in the cliff face, moved the operating lever and waited until the doors were fully closed. He then inserted the crow bar behind the lever and, with a hefty tug, he snapped off the cast bronze lever where it joined the shaft. Picking it up, he jogged back to the aircraft and, giving the broken lever to Sherbourne, he said, "At least we can deny them the use of the facilities so they won't be able to replenish their stores."

Mary was already strapped into what was formerly the radio operator's seat as they clambered aboard with Jaime leading the way. Sherbourne, who after raising and securing the boarding hatch, followed squeezing into the somewhat restricted co-pilot's seat as Jaime settled in the captain's left-hand position.

"I wouldn't like to try to get out of here in a hurry," said Sherbourne.

"In an emergency, we go out through the escape hatch in the roof."

"Let's hope it doesn't come to that."

A quick scan of the instruments satisfied Jaime that the engines were operating at the correct temperatures and oil pressures.

They had all plugged in their headsets to the internal intercom system so Jaime pressed the microphone switch on the control column and said, "Right, if you're all ready, let's go."

As he said it, Sherbourne pressed his button and said, "Look, Jaime. There's Mueller coming over that dune at the end of the take-off area."

Opening the throttles, Jaime quickly taxied the Heinkel to the take-off position and, not bothering with any checks, opened the throttles to take-off power. Slowly accelerating at first, they watched as Mueller's truck came straight towards the end of the runway.

"Looks like he's going to try and stop us by blocking the runway," said Sherbourne.

As they watched, the truck approached the end of the runway and then stopped.

"It's bogged down in that soft sand area," said Jaime.

By this time, they were halfway down the runway and still not at flying speed when Jaime realized the stranded truck posed a real hazard as they might not have enough power and speed to climb over it. As the distance between them decreased at a now alarming rate, Jaime, reacting quickly to the impending danger, thrust forwards the two boost system control levers to the fully open position. The effect was as instantaneous as it was spectacular. With the sudden application of an extra twenty-five percent in power, Jaime felt an enormous kick in his back as the Heinkel literally leaped into the sky and cleared the truck by fifty feet.

As they passed over it, Jaime looked down and caught a fleeting glance of two upturned faces, one of them appearing to be pointing something at them which proved to be correct as there was a sudden crack as two bullets penetrated the glazed nose making two neat holes in one of the plexiglass panels. The force of the impact reduced the bullet's momentum as they entered the cockpit. Just missing Jaime, they hit the roof above his head and dropped to the floor behind him with a clunk. Fortunately the MP 40 sub-machine gun fired low velocity lead bullets and not the high penetration steel jacket projectile of a more powerful heavier weapon.

Sherbourne leaned down into the nose and plugged the holes with some torn strips of cloth to stop the draft and the whistling sound.

"That was close, Jaime."

"They've got a big problem on their hands now if they can't get out of that soft sand."

Chapter 70

❖

Now they were climbing comfortably, Jaime closed the boost levers and leveled off at five thousand feet on a heading towards Tripoli. Taking a prepared note from his pocket, he passed it to Sherbourne and said, "Alan, these are the daytime frequencies for the radio station in Tripoli that provides an HF SSB communications service to the oil companies. Their call sign is Mike Able. See if you can get through to them with the transceiver, use Hotel One as our call sign, it's as good as any. They'll be able to give you a link call to the embassy. Get the ambassador to get us permission to land at the American Air Force base at Wheelus just outside Tripoli. With this aircraft and what we have on board, I think it would be wiser to land there. Give them our ETA and tell them also that we do not have a compatible air to ground radio so if they agree, tell them to give us a green flare to land. Have you got all that?"

"Yes, that's all clear. I'll go and connect up the transceiver."

Sherbourne called Jaime on the intercom and told him he had managed to get power onto the set and that he could hear Mike Able communicating with other stations based in the desert so he would try to raise them as soon as there was a break in those calls.

Sherbourne raised Mike Able and explained he wanted a confidential link call to the embassy and was allocated a discreet frequency on which to call back. When re-established on the discreet frequency, Sherbourne was connected to the British ambassador.

Pleased to hear from him, the ambassador listened to all he had to say and said he would call him back when he had spoken to the American ambassador and received permission for them to land at Wheelus.

Sherbourne signed off and was instructed to listen out on the discreet frequency for Mike Able to call him back. After what seemed like ages but was in fact only half an hour, he was reconnected to the British ambassador who informed him all had been approved and that the control tower at Wheelus would suspend all air traffic for thirty minutes either side of their ETA to avoid any conflict and would either fire a green flare or have another aircraft lead them in for a landing.

Relaxed now that all had been arranged and the Heinkel seemed to be performing well, Jaime switched on the autopilot and marveled at the thought of flying this museum piece from the past and the events that had so recently led to their miraculous escape.

With the autopilot functioning perfectly, Jaime got out of his seat and went back to check on Mary and Sherbourne who had informed her that their new destination would be the USAF base at Wheelus.

"Seems like we'll be getting some VIP treatment. You can come and sit up front with me for a bit if you like. Alan will stay near the radio for a bit, in case they call back."

"It's funny," said Mary after she was seated in the co-pilot's position, "I remember these flying over during the war when I was a little girl. I never thought I would get to fly in one."

"Nor me," laughed Jaime.

Fifteen minutes before their ETA, Tripoli was clearly in sight ahead of them on the horizon. Keeping to the west of the city and its international airport to avoid traffic coming from the oil fields, they crossed the coast and followed the coastline east towards Wheelus. As they did so, two T-33 jet trainers in USAF markings flew up and took position on each wing.

"I hope they've been told we're friendly," said Jaime.

Both pilots stared across and each gave a friendly wave and, as they drew ahead, they rocked their wings and lowered their wheels to signify the internationally accepted instruction to an aircraft to lower their own undercarriage in acknowledgement and follow the aircraft ahead to land. Jaime did as instructed and prepared the aircraft configuration to join the circuit for landing.

"Would you look at the length of that runway..." said Sherbourne.

"It was designed to handle their biggest bombers like the B-36 and B-47 of Strategic Air Command," commented Jaime.

Jaime joined a left-hand downwind landing pattern and, with the undercarriage and flaps lowered, he turned on to the final approach with the T-33s ahead and to each side still in formation as all three landed neatly together on the long wide runway with ample room to spare. After touchdown, they remained in formation gradually slowing down as a follow me vehicle drove out from a taxi way further down and took up the lead. The T-33 on the starboard side slowed and turned off at the same taxi way while the T-33 on the port side allowed

Jaime to pull level. As he did so, the pilot gave him a salute and a hand gesture which Jaime understood to indicate "after you", allowing him to take the lead after the follow me vehicle. As he pulled clear, the pilot turned behind him and followed the first T-33, taxiing to their regular parking area.

About halfway down the runway, the follow me vehicle turned off and led Jaime to an area close to the control tower and its administration buildings where a group of people, some in uniform and some civilians, were gathered around a number of parked vehicles.

"Looks like quite a reception committee," said Sherbourne. "I can see the ambassador. Anyone there you know, Jaime?"

"I recognize the base commander. I met him there once as a guest at the officers' club. He's a one-star general called Paul Townsend."

A marshal with raised batons took over from the follow me vehicle and guided them to a spot directly in front of the tower and, when satisfied, he crossed his batons to indicate they could stop and shut down engines.

Mary was the first to exit the aircraft and was greeted by the ambassador who said, "Welcome back, Mary. It seems you've had something of an interesting adventure."

"Thank you, Ambassador. Interesting is not quite the word I would use to describe the events of the last few days but I am happy to be back safe and sound thanks to Jaime and Alan."

He turned and introduced her to the base commander and the American ambassador who were both standing next to him. Jaime and Alan exchanged greetings with all three and the base commander said, "It's good to see you again, Wing Commander. Where on earth did you find this World War Two relic?"

"It's a long story, General, which I shall be glad to tell you about when we get the formalities dealt with."

"Your ambassador has given me a brief outline of the recent events. I suggest, therefore, that my men will secure the aircraft and we can all go to my office for a debriefing. The facilities of the base are all available to you."

"Thank you, General."

Amongst the other people waiting, Jaime espied von Lutzdorf's widow and daughter who were with a representative from the German Embassy. Excusing himself from the general, he walked over to Frau von Lutzdorf and said, "We have your husband's body on board. Come with us to the general's office and we will organize how you would like to proceed."

Thanking Jaime, she and her daughter joined the party heading for the base commander's office.

Jaime had a word with the ambassador and suggested they first deal with the matter of the caskets so von Lutzdorf's widow and daughter could leave as there was much he would reveal that was not for their ears. Also, he suggested they put diplomatic seals on the boxes he recovered and that they should be transported straight away back to the embassy.

The ambassador agreed and spoke to his counterpart from the American Embassy who approved of the priorities.

Before they moved off, Jaime was suddenly confronted by an RAF officer of the rank of group captain displaying several rows of wartime decorations below his wings.

"Wing Commander, it's good to see you again." He smiled at the look of puzzlement and then the smile as recognition took over.

"Group Captain Lucas? My God, David, what are you doing here?"

"I'm the RAF liaison officer attached to Wheelus. You'll be shocked to know that I've seen that Heinkel 111 before. You'll never guess where."

"You might be surprised there," said Jaime as he recalled the incident with a Mosquito in von Lutzdorf's log book. "Listen, we can't talk here. Are you coming to the commander's office with us?"

"If you wish."

"Right. just tag along and we can catch up later."

The base commander had a conference room attached to his office which was used for staff briefings. It was into this room that his adjutant led everyone since it had the facilities to accommodate a party of this size. When everyone was seated around the conference table, Jaime, who had effectively become the leader and spokesman for the group, addressed the base commander.

"General, if I may suggest that we first deal with the bodies of von Lutzdorf and Steinberg so his widow and daughter can leave to see they are properly dealt with."

"Of course." The general then addressed Frau von Lutzdorf and asked her what religion her husband was to which she informed him Protestant Lutheran.

He gave instructions to his adjutant to take her and her daughter to the base's Protestant chaplain and arrange for a party of men to transfer the caskets to the Lutheran chapel on the base to await there for arrangements to be made to transfer them back to Germany.

Thanking the general, von Lutzdorf's widow and her daughter left the room.

The British ambassador then addressed the general and said he and Sherbourne had to offload some diplomatic boxes and return to the embassy so Sherbourne could contact his London office and report.

"I'll remain here with Mary and give you as much of a briefing as I can," said Jaime, as he continued, "I would also like Group Captain Lucas to remain."

Since the party was now reduced to three, the general said, "Why don't we go to my office where we can make ourselves comfortable? I have a feeling this is going to be a long story."

As they entered the general's office, his adjutant returned and they all made themselves comfortable around a low coffee table.

Jaime started. "What I have to tell you, General, is currently being reported back to my government via MI6 of which department Mary here is their representative in Libya. This information will no doubt be shared with your CIA at Langley so I know this will all be treated as highly confidential. I, as you are aware, am not part of MI6 but Mary has asked me to take the lead in explaining the recent events."

"Of course, Wing Commander. Please, carry on. I'm completely intrigued to hear the story."

Jaime began from the time he first discovered the bodies in the abandoned truck and what followed when he led the expedition to recover them. He explained the reaction to the discovery in London and how MI6 became involved which Mary confirmed by disclosing how and why they had a file on von Lutzdorf. She informed them that von Lutzdorf and his family were ardent anti-Nazis and how he was collaborating with British Intelligence up until the time of his disappearance.

"Jaime's discovery partly explained a twenty-year-old mystery but the story did not end there," said Mary.

She went on to explain what von Lutzdorf's mission was and why he was found so far off the main area of the fighting in North Africa.

"How he was shot up is still a mystery because neither we nor you Americans reported any activity in the area," said Mary.

"I think you should now explain about ODESSA and its involvement in von Lutzdorf's mission," said Jaime.

Mary nodded and said, "Have you ever heard of the name ODESSA, General?"

Like Jaime's initial response to the question, he mentioned the name of the port in the Crimea but admitted he had not heard of any organization by that name.

Mary then explained it was an acronym and what the letters stood for and how they believed it was still active but completely covert and almost impossible to penetrate.

"I must admit," said the general, "You have me completely bemused. First, you turn up at my air base in a World War Two Heinkel bomber and then, you tell me it's all involved with a clandestine former Nazi organization of the SS and Gestapo."

"I know, General," said Jaime, "It's difficult to believe but it gets more unbelievable yet."

"You know, of course," said Mary, "The outcome of the Nuremberg war crimes trials and I'm sure you know of those that either escaped justice by committing suicide or just escaped and disappeared. To this day, the most wanted war criminal remains Heinrich Mueller, the head of the Gestapo and, after Himmler and Reinhard Heydrich, was the most powerful member of the SS."

"Yes, he just disappeared and no trace of him has ever been found," said the general.

"Well, General, it may surprise you to know that the last time we saw him alive and well was this morning in the desert just as we were taking off," said Jaime.

The look of shock on the general's face was comic if it had not been for the serious nature of what had just been revealed to him.

"You're quite right, Wing Commander. This tale gets more unbelievable as you tell it."

"I think both our governments will shortly be discussing a joint operation to take this opportunity to try to capture him. His circumstances at the moment are dire. Unless he can dig his truck out of the sand, he is stranded in one of the most remote and inhospitable parts of the Sahara."

"I can supply a C-47 aircraft and a couple of armed men. What about the RAF, Group Captain?"

"I can supply a couple of members of the RAF regiment. Jaime, are you ready to lead the team back to the place you described?"

"Of course, I would like nothing better than to capture that man."

"We won't be able to do anything until I get orders to go ahead, so I think we won't be able to leave until tomorrow morning," said the general.

Jaime related the rest of the story up until their arrival and then it was agreed they would be ready to leave the next morning once they had all received orders.

"I must get back to the embassy," said Mary, "We still have a car outside. Why don't you come with us, Group Captain?"

All three said their goodbyes until the next morning and left in the awaiting embassy car.

Chapter 71

❖

Back at the British Embassy, they re-joined the ambassador in his office and Alan Sherbourne explained he had made a full report about Heinrich Mueller to London and was awaiting a reply to his same suggestion that they should immediately mount an operation to capture him.

Opening his flight bag, Jaime took out von Lutzdorf's log book and handed it to Mary.

"Mary, please find the entry about being intercepted by a Mosquito. I think Group Captain Lucas will be very interested to hear it as he has a special interest in the incident."

Mary found the entry and read it, translating from the German as she did.

"That was definitely me in that Mosquito," said Group Captain Lucas. "If I had my log book here, I could confirm the date but I'm sure it's right. I was the only Mosquito photo reconnaissance pilot operating out of Malta at that time and I still have some air-to-air photographs my navigator took showing von Lutzdorf waving back to us. I must get a copy for his widow."

"I'm sure she would appreciate that, David," said Jaime.

It was agreed that Group Captain Lucas and two RAF regiment members would be ready to join the operation to try to capture Heinrich Mueller as soon as they received orders from London. Mary, Jaime and Sherbourne then all expressed a desire to return to their apartments to clean up as none of them had had a proper shower, bath or change of clothes for several days. Transport was arranged for Group Captain Lucas to take him back to the officers' quarters he occupied at the base.

Mary and Jaime decided to walk to their apartments which were not far from the embassy as Alan Sherbourne returned to his guest apartment.

***

Jaime had just finished showering and dressing in fresh clothes when his telephone rang. He was pleasantly surprised to hear Magda von Lutzdorf's voice as he picked up the handset.

"Jaime, I have someone here who is anxious to meet you. Let me introduce you to Count Mario Gratziani." Jaime heard her say, "Mario, here, speak to Jaime St Clair."

"Hello," said the count, "May I call you Jaime?"

"Of course."

"Please call me Mario," said the count. "Magda has told me all about you and how you found her husband Walter after all these years. It is quite an astonishing story. Your MI6 contacted me a few days ago seeking information on the old Italian air base down near the Chad border. I see, however, you managed to locate it anyway."

"Yes, we were fortunate that von Lutzdorf left coded directions in his log book which we were able to decode."

"I understand that recovering the bodies has been quite an adventure. I would like to hear about it, if you have the time. I became quite good friends with Walter and there is much I can tell you about that period. I am staying at the Uaddan Hotel. Why don't you and your colleague Mary from the embassy, and also your friend Alan from MI6, do me the honour of joining us here for dinner?"

"I'll look forward to that. I'll call them and see you there." As an afterthought, before he rang off, Jaime said, "May I also invite Group Captain Lucas, my old commanding officer who is here in Tripoli? I think you'll have something in common with him."

"Of course, it'll be my pleasure to meet him."

***

At the appointed hour, Jaime, and Mary who he had collected on his way, entered the residents' lounge of the hotel and found von Lutzdorf's widow and daughter Alexis already seated in a corner area with a number of suitably arranged easy chairs to accommodate the seven people expected. As they approached, a handsome figure in his late forties stood up and said, "Hello, I am Mario," first stretching out his hand to Mary and then Jaime.

With the formalities over, they sat down to await the others while a waiter poured them all a glass of champagne. A few minutes later, they were joined by Sherbourne and the group captain.

Jaime took the lead since he knew everyone and the reason for the gathering was to bring Mario, Magda and her daughter up-to-date.

Magda had already explained details of the finding of the bodies and the subsequent expedition to recover them to Mario so Jaime cut straight to the episode where Captain Hartmann revealed himself to be Heinrich Mueller.

"My God!" gasped Magda, "I thought he was dead."

"Most decidedly not, I assure you," said Jaime.

"So, where is he now?" asked Mario.

"As of earlier this morning, stranded in some soft sand at the end of the airstrip at the old Italian base you know about."

"I remember that area. Several trucks and aircraft got bogged down there to my knowledge. Do you think he's still there?"

"Tomorrow morning, we'll find out. We're just waiting for orders to mount a joint operation with the Americans to see if we can capture him."

"The operation is on, Jaime," said Sherbourne, "Just before I left the embassy, approval came through from London."

Magda, who had recovered from the shock about Mueller, said, "To think he was here in Tripoli just a few days ago. That was taking a chance, I might have recognized him."

"He knew you were here. He was told by von Oppersdorf and kept well out of your way."

"How was von Oppersdorf involved?" asked Magda. "I thought he was a respectable official attached to the German Embassy."

"I'm afraid he fooled us all, Magda," said Jaime. "He was a clandestine member of ODESSA and supporter of Mueller."

"You said 'was'. What does that mean?"

"I'm afraid he perished out in the desert as did one of Mueller's assistants by the name of Neumann."

"What is this ODESSA?"

Jaime then went on to explain the meaning of ODESSA and what they knew about the organization.

"You mean, Walter was in some way involved in this Nazi organization?" asked Magda in a somewhat shocked tone.

"No, not at all, Magda. ODESSA only came into being after your husband's death. He was only involved in the Luftwaffe operation couriering documents that happened to be associated with the initial setting up of the organization. In fact, your husband was working with us to ensure the Nazis never came to power again. He was a true patriot."

"It seems you had a very tough time of it out there, Jaime. What happened to von Oppersdorf and this assistant of Mueller's?" asked Mario.

Jaime described what had happened following the disclosure by Mueller of who he was, how he fooled them into believing von Oppersdorf was genuine and on their side, how he crippled the aircraft and destroyed their stores and water intending to leave them to their fate in the desert. He went on to relate how, by an accident of fate, they blew up one of Mueller's trucks and Neumann with it and then their epic trek over two nights to sanctuary at the former Italian air base. Finally, he described the incident where von Oppersdorf met with his demise.

"An incredible story," said the group captain. "What fascinates me is the discovery of the Heinkel 111 and how it was still airworthy after all these years."

"Mario, tell David the incident involving the Mosquito interception," said Jaime, using the group captain's Christian name since they were now all on first name terms having dropped any previous references to rank. "I think, David, you and Mario have had a previous close encounter which bears telling."

Mario started to explain how he was with von Lutzdorf on the first survey flight with the Heinkel when they were intercepted by a Mosquito.

"You mean, you were in this very same Heinkel which I intercepted near Sicily?"

"You were the pilot of that Mosquito?"

"I was indeed. We even took some photos of you."

They both laughed as Mario went on to describe the incident.

"I must admit you gave us all a fright. I was the first to spot you as I was looking astern from the navigation blister. I saw your contrail about five thousand feet above and about five miles behind us. When you spotted us and dove down on us, I managed to identify you with the binoculars and knew we had no chance of evading you, so you can imagine our surprise when instead of a hail of bullets and cannon shells, you flew up alongside and started taking pictures."

"That was my job. Taking pictures."

"Lucky for us," laughed Mario.

"I still have the photos in my log book. I will get some copies made for you and Magda."

On that more light-hearted note, they all felt better but there still remained the question of Heinrich Mueller, the most wanted war criminal still at large. Mueller: once thought dead but now proved to be alive and within the grasp of the authorities and justice.

"What does he look like now?" asked Magda. "I used to meet up with him in Berlin at official functions and sometimes at the Adlon Hotel which was one of his favourite places. Not that he was seen out socializing very often; he was a very secretive person. The thing I remember most about him was his piercing grey eyes."

"Well, he still has those, but they were well-disguised. He wore an eye patch to simulate the loss of one eye and a pair of dark glasses to obscure the other one."

"He was a most odious person. He had a very sinister and intimidating air about him like the epitome of evil."

"I can certainly agree with that description of him. He disguised it well when we first met him but I must admit, there was always something about him that made me feel uncomfortable."

"I met him a couple of times and, like you, I always felt uncomfortable in his company. May I ask you a favour, Jaime?" said Mario.

"What can I do for you, Mario?"

"Since it seems that you and David here will be leading this attempt tomorrow to capture him, could I possibly accompany you on this trip? It would be very interesting to return to one of my old operational bases."

"I think that would be a very good idea. You know that part of the desert well and if we don't find him bogged down in the sand, we'll have to search the immediate surrounding area."

"Excellent, Jaime. Thank you so much."

"I have a photograph of him with myself and my husband Walter taken at the Adlon Hotel. I could send you a copy when I get back to Germany, if it would be any help?" said Magda.

"We already have a copy of that photograph in our files in London which we looked at recently," said Sherbourne.

"How on earth did you get a copy of that?" exclaimed Magda.

"The photographer was one of our contacts in Berlin at that time. He passed a copy on to one of our agents who had orders to always send photographs of high-ranking Nazis back to London. It was that which first drew our attention to your husband and his attachment to Goering's personal staff. From then on, we kept tabs on all his movements and eventually he agreed to help us."

"I am always amazed at the extent of these secret operations. After what you have told me, I am glad Walter was able to do something to thwart the Nazis who he hated so much."

Looking at his watch, the count stood up and said, "I think it is just about time for dinner. I have booked a table on the terrace as it's such a pleasantly warm evening. Shall we go through?"

They passed through the lounge to the terrace to be greeted by Pasquale who recognized Jaime and Mary as well as Magda and her daughter from their previous visit and, assuming he was the host, said, "Captain St Clair, how nice to see you."

Jaime smiled to himself, knowing how the Italians still respected the old nobility, and said, "May I introduce our host for this evening: Count Mario Gratziani."

Pasquale put on his most welcoming smile and, addressing the count, he said, "*Benvenuto, Conte. Ho un tavolo molto bello per voi.*"

He led them to their table and, fussing about the ladies, he snapped his fingers to another waiter to assist them being seated.

***

During the course of the evening, it emerged that Mario had returned to Italy shortly after von Lutzdorf's disappearance but kept in touch with Magda. Following Italy's capitulation, he supported the allied forces until the end of the war when he retired to his estate. He married and had two children: a boy and a girl. His wife and Magda became friends and remained so until her death in a driving accident.

When he was contacted by MI6 and learned that Magda and her daughter were in Tripoli, he decided to join them to give what support he could.

Chapter 72

❖

Jaime and Mario met at the British Embassy early the following morning where it had been arranged for an embassy car to take them to Wheelus. Sherbourne had to return urgently to London to report to C at SIS headquarters while Mary resumed her normal duties at the embassy.

At Wheelus, they joined Group Captain Lucas and his two men from the RAF regiment and two marines and their commanding officer, a lieutenant colonel who would make up the American contingent for the operation. In addition, they would be accompanied by a Libyan army officer to represent the Libyan government since they were to be operating in the sovereign state of Libya.

Jaime was introduced to the C-47 crew of the captain and co-pilot to whom he gave a prepared flight plan with the navigational details for their intended destination. He also gave them a verbal briefing of the approach procedure and what to look out for.

***

The distance to their destination was approximately five hundred and fifty miles. With a cruising speed of two hundred miles per hour, the DC-3 would get them there in around two and a half hours. Fifteen minutes before their ETA, Jaime joined the crew in the cockpit to help them recognize the terrain features to assist them with their approach and landing. Once they had their landing strip in sight, it was decided they would make one pass down the runway at one thousand feet to see if Mueller's truck was still bogged down in the sand. The first pass showed the truck was no longer there so they flew a larger circle of the area to see if they could locate it but to no avail.

The crew then completed the landing and, under Jaime's guidance, taxied back to the hidden hangar.

First out of the aircraft were the marines and RAF regiment men to secure the area as a matter of routine rather than in expectation of any trouble. Jaime was the next out and the first thing he spotted was the body of von Oppersdorf left exactly where it had landed. Mueller had made no effort to bury his former colleague's body and had left it to be devoured by the elements and creatures of the desert. As he and the others approached the remains of von Oppersdorf which was lying face down exposing the gaping wounds where the rotating propeller blades had slashed open the torso and the back of what remained of the skull the sound of hundreds of flies swarming all over it attracted by the smell of blood was overpowering. Startled by their approach several large camel spiders feasting off the swarm of flies scuttled off at high speed disappearing under rocks or burying themselves in the sand. Jaime turned to the others who had followed him and said, "That's all that remains of von Oppersdorf. We must do something about it."

The group captain turned to his men who immediately volunteered and said, "Don't worry about it, sir. We'll take care of it."

"There are shovels inside the hangar. You'll find everything you need in the workshop in just a moment," said Jaime pleased at the immediate response of the men.

He led the others to the cleft in the cliff face and, producing a suitable wrench from the bag of tools he had brought with him, Jaime clamped it to the shaft from which he had snapped off the operating lever. Telling them to stand back, he said, "Watch this!"

The wrench functioned perfectly well in place of the lever and, as the others watched, the cliff face started to move accompanied by the hissing sound of escaping air.

The whole party, save for Mario who had a smile on his face, stood back and watched in amazement as the doors opened.

"Mario, if you remember how to do it, why don't you start the generator?"

"It will be a pleasure," said Mario.

As the generator started and Mario threw the main breaker switches, the interior lights came on to illuminate the darker recesses and rooms at the back. Even though Jaime and Mario had experienced it before, they both still marveled at the ingenuity of the pre-war Italian engineers who had designed and equipped the base.

The rest of the party were suitably impressed and wandered around inside exploring the equipment and stores.

"The first thing I must do is to sample that marvellous Barolo wine that I remember," said Mario.

"I can confirm it is drinking well as of two days ago," said Jaime with a smile, "But I think the men have the right priority."

The two RAF men, who had been joined by the marines, came out of the workshop carrying shovels, a rolled-up sheet of tarpaulin and a length of rope. Between them, they spread out the tarpaulin next to the body of von Oppersdorf and, using the spades, gently rolled the body onto it and folded part of the tarpaulin over it. Then they rolled the body up in the rest of the tarpaulin like a carpet totally securing it tightly inside.

Using his knife, one of the marines cut the rope into two lengths which they then used to tightly secure the two ends of the tarpaulin. Hefting the rope over their shoulders, the marines hoisted the body off the ground and carried it along the cliff face a suitable distance away from the hangar doors where they selected a spot and started digging. Taking it in turns, the four men soon had dug a hole six feet by two and a half feet and six feet deep. By use of the attached ropes, they lowered the corpse in its tarpaulin shroud down into the grave. As they did so, one of the marines, a burly staff sergeant, murmured some words customary when burying the dead to which the others, who had now been joined by Jaime and Gratziani, quietly added amen.

Throwing the loose rope ends down on top of the corpse, they set to and soon refilled the hole, tapping down the mound as much as they could and then spreading the surplus sand around so that no sign of a grave could be detected. Since there would be nobody to mourn him, they did not see the point in putting a marker on the spot.

***

Back in the hangar, they gathered around the table and the group captain and the marine commander, as the two de facto leaders, addressed the party. The lieutenant colonel started by stating the obvious that their quarry had managed to free their vehicle from the sand and were now trying to evade capture. Having failed to prevent Jaime and the others from escaping, it was obvious they could not return to Tripoli now Mueller's identity was known. Since they would naturally have expected an effort to be made to apprehend them they would have wasted no time once they had freed themselves from the sand in putting as much distance as possible between them and the base.

"The question is," said the marine commander, "Which way did they go?"

"What do you think?" asked the group captain, addressing his question to Jaime, Gratziani and the Libyan officer, "You know this area better than most."

The Libyan officer admitted he had never served in this part of Libya and was not that familiar with the desert.

"In my opinion," said Gratziani, "They would have headed west towards the border with Niger. Directly south of here, there are the Tibesti Mountains and very difficult terrain. They need to get to the west coast of Africa as their best means of escape. Their route would be through Niger to the Ivory Coast or Liberia and a boat to South America."

"That makes sense," said Jaime.

The others concurred and it was decided that they would fly in that direction for about two hours before returning to Tripoli.

"The big problem we have," said the group captain, "Is that even if we spot them, we probably won't be able to land and if we could, we will be on foot and unable to pursue them."

"All that you say is true," said the lieutenant colonel, "But at least we'll know where they're headed and perhaps we can try to intercept them at the coast."

They all agreed they had missed their opportunity but at least the authorities knew Mueller was alive and on the run.

They shut down the base, secured the hangar doors back in place but not before loading the vintage wine on board. After take-off, they flew along the surmised route but saw no sign of the truck or any other life in that very sparely populated area and, after two hours, reluctantly turned back to Tripoli.

Chapter 73

❖

The day after their return to Tripoli, Gratziani telephoned Jaime and told him the Wheelus base commander had arranged for von Lutzdorf's and Steinberg's bodies to be transported to one of their bases in Germany with permission for his widow, daughter and himself to accompany the bodies on the flight. Once in Germany, Magda would make the arrangements for her husband to be taken to the family estate and for Steinberg to be returned to his sister and mother. They gave each other their contact details and promised to keep in touch.

***

Jaime returned to his flying duties until three weeks later when he had a message from the embassy saying the ambassador would like to see him.

"Good to see you again, Jaime. I trust you have recovered from your adventurous ordeal," said the ambassador as he shook hands.

"Yes, thank you, Ambassador. Do you have any news regarding Mueller?"

"I haven't been informed of anything but I have received a message from London requesting your presence at MI6 as soon as it's convenient for you."

"Did they say what it was they wanted to see me for?"

"No, but that's not unusual. Those people always play things close to their chests."

"I'm due a few days' leave so I'll make the arrangements. Will they pay my expenses?"

"You can ask but it depends on whether your visit is to their advantage or yours. You know what governments are like. Always budget conscious and notoriously mean when it comes to expenses."

The ambassador handed Jaime a slip of paper with the address of SIS headquarters and the name of the agent to ask for and said, "Good luck. I hope you have a good visit."

Jaime thanked the ambassador and left his office. Now familiar with the layout of the embassy, he walked down one flight and walked along to Mary's office where he found her going through some files.

"Hello darling," she said, "I hear that you're off on a jolly to London."

"Is there nothing secret here? I thought embassies were security conscious."

"You know what office gossip machines are like. They know about everything first. You're quite a celebrity and a topic of gossip amongst the secretaries after your recent adventure."

"Our adventure."

"I'm only teasing. Seriously though, the ambassador confided in me only this morning as he knew it would also concern me to some extent."

"If that's so, can you get some time off and come with me?"

"I'd like that. I can ask the ambassador. I'm sure he'll be okay with it."

"There's a BOAC flight tomorrow. Ask him now and I'll book the flights."

Mary smiled, picked up her handset and dialed the ambassador's office extension and was put through straight away.

After explaining what she wanted, the ambassador, knowing of her close relationship with Jaime, agreed at once and wished her a pleasant visit.

"There you are. All done. Now let me get on. I must finish up what I'm doing before I leave."

Jaime kissed her on the cheek and said, "See you tonight."

From the embassy, he went straight to his company's office in the middle of the town and explained he had been summoned to London by the Foreign Office and would need to take some leave. Aware of his situation, his boss grumbled a bit but agreed, muttering about having to rewrite all the rosters for the coming week at such short notice.

At the BOAC office, Jaime booked their flights and, being aircrew, he always got a fifty percent discount which was a decent perk of the job.

***

Jaime had booked them a room at the RAF Club in Piccadilly which was close to St James and SIS headquarters. The day after their arrival in London, Jaime took a taxi to 54 Broadway, St James where MI6 was located and, on giving the name of the agent the ambassador had written on the slip of paper, he was escorted into the inner sanctum of the British SIS.

The agent who received him apologized that Alan Sherbourne was not there to meet him personally as he was out of the country following up some leads uncovered from the documents they had recovered from Libya.

"The director himself wants to see you, so I shall take you to him now."

Jaime was shown to the office of the director, who had formerly been the head of MI5 before taking up his present position.

After being introduced, the agent left and the director, still known to all as C, said, "Welcome to MI6. My name is Dick White but everyone calls me C. How should I address you? As James or Captain St Clair?"

"Please call me Jaime."

"Well, Jaime, I understand from Alan Sherbourne that you two have had quite an adventure."

"Yes, I suppose it was something of an adventure. I think we were quite lucky that it ended as it did."

"A fascinating story, especially you finding that old Heinkel and flying it back to Tripoli."

"As a matter of interest, what's going to happen to that aircraft?"

"I believe arrangements are being made by the RAF to bring it back to put in their museum at Biggin Hill, which brings me back to the reason I asked you to come here."

"You want me to fly it to England?"

"No need, Jaime. The RAF are fighting amongst themselves for the privilege of who gets to fly it. I believe your old commanding officer, Group Captain Lucas, is organizing it. What I wanted to discuss with you is what you brought back."

"You mean the documents?"

"No, much more interesting than that. The gold and the diamonds."

"I assumed that would disappear into the Treasury somehow."

"Not at all. There are certain rules and protocols to do with recovered funds. The gold is easy since it bore the stamp of the wartime Bank of Germany with the eagle and the swastika and has been declared to have originated as stolen from the occupied territories or private Jewish funds to say nothing of the gold teeth extractions at the death camps. Therefore, it will be donated to the relief fund for death camp survivors."

"That sounds very reasonable to me," said Jaime.

"On the other hand, the diamonds are a completely different matter. They have no provenance and cannot be attributed to any legitimate ownership therefore they come under the heading of treasure trove. That is, finders keepers. The government have decreed that since you found them, they should be given to you. Was that worth coming to London to hear?" said the director with a huge smile on his face.

"Give me a minute to absorb that. I'm lost for words."

"I haven't finished with the good news yet. You are also eligible for a ten percent commission on the value of the gold."

Jaime had recovered enough to make a small joke. "I suppose that will rule out any claim I might have for expenses."

The director laughed and said, "You can put in for them and see what happens. The accounts department will not know of the other arrangements."

"I don't think it would be the gentlemanly thing to do under the circumstances."

"As you wish, Jaime. It's not often the treasury accountants find themselves dealing with gentlemen. They only recognize the bottom line."

"What about the Libyan government? Don't they have a say in this?"

"We have good relations with the Libyan government and they have declared that they have no interest in the matter as the provenance of the gold is quite clear and the diamonds did not originate in Libya."

"That sounds fair enough."

"And finally, there's one more thing. The counterfeit British currency amounting to fifty thousand pounds. As you know, it is no longer legal tender and therefore it isn't a crime to own it, so you can have that also. You can't spend it but, who knows, it might become worth something in the future to collectors."

"Well, sir, or can I call you Dick? C somehow seems inappropriate except within your organization."

"By all means."

"As a matter of interest, did the documentation we brought back give you any good information on ODESSA and its present situation? I understand Alan is in Europe following up some leads."

"It gave us many very valuable leads and an insight as to their post-war plans but it will take months, perhaps years, to discover how far their tentacles reach into business and politics. We have to deal with the laws of many countries who are not always cooperative."

"Have you had any news of Mueller?"

"We've had some information in from the Bank of England. They've had inquiries coming in from the central banks in Niger, Ghana and Liberia of the appearance of some of the old British white five, ten and twenty pound notes. If they are genuine, they are still redeemable if presented through the banks but we suspect they might be from that counterfeit cache Mueller had with him. If that proves to be so, then we can expect that he successfully made his way to South America."

"What about his false identity as Captain Hartmann?"

"Now there we were able, with the help of the German authorities, to uncover a real nest of Nazi sympathizers. There was, in fact, a real Captain Hartmann who was wounded and invalided out and went back to live with his elderly parents on their remote farm in Bavaria. Mueller, who of course had absolute access to the records of all military personnel, picked him out and prepared a genuine set of identity papers taking his identity.

"At the end of the war, he just moved in with Hartmann and his parents who were ardent Nazis and hid in plain sight. Apparently, the real Hartmann died of his wounds not long after the war and the parents kept up the facade until they too died. Mueller then inherited the farm. He set up the veterans' help organization and recruited former SS personnel to work on the farm and build up their network keeping the place secure and inaccessible to outsiders."

"Very clever. No wonder he was able to just disappear into thin air unlike the other leading Nazis who had always sought the limelight. I wonder how many other identities he manufactured. He had plenty of time and was well-prepared long before the war ended."

"On that point, I must agree with you. He is no doubt using another equally genuine new identity right now in some South American country."

"Well, Dick, it's been a most interesting meeting and regarding the money aspect, it has been the most unexpected and fantastic news anyone could hear. I feel like celebrating. Could I invite you to lunch with my fiancée Mary who is waiting for me at the RAF Club?"

"Why don't you and your fiancée join me for lunch at my club? I feel I owe it to you for the important documents you found for us."

"That's most kind of you. What time should we meet you and which is your club?"

"Why, Whites, of course," said the director with a grin. "It always gives me a kick to say that."

Whites, as Jaime knew, was the oldest and most exclusive gentlemen's club in London.

"I thought that under the rules of Whites women were forbidden from entering the hallowed premises?"

"Under normal circumstances you are quite right Jaime but under pressure from some of these growing female rights organizations we have made a little concession that members may invite female guests to lunch in a private dining room separate from the main club area."

"The way women are they won't leave it at that, they will keep on pushing."

"I do believe you are right Jaime but for the foreseeable future I think our bastion is secure."

The director pushed down a lever switch on his intercom and asked his secretary to recall the agent to safely see Jaime out of the building. A moment later, there was a knock on the door which opened and, as the agent entered, the director rose, shook Jaime's hand and said, "Until one o'clock then."

***

Jaime could barely wait to get back to the RAF Club and tell Mary of his good fortune which had started all sorts of plans for their future buzzing around in his head.

He found Mary sitting in the lounge reading the morning papers. Before sitting down, he found one of the stewards and ordered a bottle of champagne. When it came, Mary looked at him and said, "It's a little early for that, isn't it, darling?"

"Not for what I have to say."

"Well?"

Jaime poured them each a glass and said, "Will you marry me, darling?"

Mary looked at Jaime with a big smile on her face and said, "This is all a bit sudden. Where will we live?"

"Don't worry about that. Will you?"

"Well, since you put it so nicely, yes, of course."

"Now that's settled. Where would you like to live?"

"Are you sure you're feeling all right, Jaime?"

"Never felt better in my life. How would the south of France suit you?"

"What have you been up to since you left here this morning? Let me smell your breath. You've not been drinking already, have you?"

Jaime could not contain his news any longer and told her all about his meeting with the head of SIS.

"You see," said Jaime with a huge grin, "I had to ask you to marry me first to be sure you were not marrying me for my money."

"We don't know yet how much you'll get for the diamonds. I might have to change my mind if it's not enough," laughed Mary.

"I think it'll be enough to buy something nice on the Côte d'Azur and live quite comfortably if we invest the rest wisely."

Epilogue

❖

Jaime was sitting on the terrace of their villa on Cap d'Antibes under a sunshade looking across the Golfe-Juan towards Juan-les-Pins and Cannes occasionally pecking at a portable typewriter when Mary appeared.

"Guess what, darling? We've just received an invitation from Mario and Magda to their wedding next month."

"That's great. I always said those two should get married. You realize that after all these years, she will be a contessa. That outranks a baroness by a long way."

"I'm sure she's not marrying Mario just to outrank her daughter when she eventually inherits the barony."

"Just joking, darling."

"They've asked us to try to get in touch with Alan and extend the invitation to him also."

"Do you know where he is?"

"I'll call London and find out. He's always off somewhere doing what agents do. Last time I spoke to him, he was off to South America following up some lead he had received from Simon Wiesenthal."

Simon Wiesenthal, a death camp survivor, was the head of the Jewish Documentation Centre in Austria, dedicated to tracking down Nazi war criminals.

"It'll be good to see him again," said Jaime.

"Mario particularly asked if we would get in touch with your old commanding officer, David Lucas. He says he's told so many friends about the encounter with him and the Mosquito that he needs him to confirm he's not been shooting a line."

"I heard from him recently. He finished his posting to the USAF and is now back in England in line for promotion to air vice marshal on the HQ staff."

"If we get them both to come here first, they can fly to Mario's estate with us. He's laid out an airstrip on his estate where he keeps his plane since he started flying again."

Jaime had recently taken delivery of the latest model Cessna 310, a very sleek, six-seat twin engine light aircraft which he kept at Cannes Mandelieu Airport just twenty minutes from the villa.

"How are you getting on with your novel?" Mary asked.

Jaime had started writing a book based on the contents of von Lutzdorf's log book.

"Quite well but I'm having some trouble with a title. What do you think of 'Return of the Heinkel' or 'Discovery in the Desert'?"

"I don't know. They need working on. You need a ring to a title. It has to grab the reader's attention. A title is as important as the contents."

"I'll keep trying. I've thought about a sequel to the book already. What do you think about 'The ODESSA Legacy'?"

"Now that's got a ring to it. That'll grab people's attention. What's it about?"

"It's a follow up on Heinrich Mueller and his whereabouts since he disappeared again."

"Well, if your first novel is a success, your sequel will be very readable. I wonder where he is now?"

"Somewhere in South America with a new identity still plotting the re-emergence of the Fourth Reich."

"You'll be careful, won't you, darling? You know what Alan said. Now that you have exposed him, he'll be out for vengeance. If what we have been told about ODESSA is true, they have unlimited resources and could be very dangerous."

***

"Thank you so much, Herr Mueller, for looking after our son. You are most kind sending him back to Germany for treatment. We could never afford it."

"Your son is a good German and deserves the best treatment the Brotherhood can provide. They have the best anti-cancer treatments in the world in Germany."

"We don't know what we shall do without him. We're no longer as young and strong as we once were."

"Don't worry. I will stay here with you while he is away and ensure that you need for nothing. I will arrange for you to have two of my men to help you on the farm."

The loss of Neumann was of no great consequence as it was soon made up from the hundreds of loyal followers Mueller could call upon.

Mueller was sitting on the veranda of a farmhouse in the countryside in a province in Paraguay. Since losing his false identity of Hartmann, Mueller had taken up one of a number of others he had prepared long ago for just such a contingency.

As with Hartmann, he had chosen his present identity of their son with no other siblings and with an established position and history to just blend in and disappear once again. The remote farm had few visitors and, in any event, the area had many old established families of German descent who would ask no questions. Mueller had created a number of similar identities all based on duplicating real members of the armed forces loyal to the SS of similar build and age as himself. With these identities, he was free to travel anywhere in the world even to England and America which he frequently did checking on the secret network and their investments.

In more recent years, ODESSA had all but disappeared in the quest to disassociate the SS from the new order that largely replaced it. During the Nazi period, the head of the SS, Heinrich Himmler, was obsessed with creating a new order of Teutonic Knights. The German Order of Teutonic Knights first created during the crusades, instead of being suppressed by Himmler as widely believed, was in fact seduced by him with offers of unlimited funds to support their ideals of Help, Defend and Heal. The reason being that what he really wanted was to recreate the Order to incorporate the Nazi aims and ideals. The original order was created under the Holy See of the Catholic Church and Himmler, recognizing the benefit of the support which the Vatican could give to the new Order, allowed it to continue and flourish in Germany whilst using and controlling it covertly for the Nazis' own ends. This accounted for the support given by the Vatican to fleeing SS members after the defeat in 1945.

The new clandestine order, which was called the Brotherhood of the Blood, manipulated the German Order of Teutonic Knights and caused it to bestow knighthoods on all those politicians, both in allied and axis countries, and heads of international corporations who did business with Nazi Germany and profited from the war. This organization grew in influence and power after the war and each newly created knight was bound by an oath of secrecy to defend the Order and each other, broken on pain of exposure and death to himself and all his family. With the death of Himmler, responsibility and control of the Brotherhood passed to Mueller, who with his vast resources and organizational ability unencumbered by the notoriety and obsessions of Himmler, grew and developed the Brotherhood into the most powerful secret society the world had ever known.

As he sat there, he was thinking about the events that had led him to relocate to Paraguay and the inconvenience of having had to quickly transfer many assets around the world to different accounts to avoid exposure, as well as providing dozens of new identities for many of the nominees who managed the companies under the control of the members of the Brotherhood which formerly funded ODESSA and now the Brotherhood. He was also aware some of the information contained in the documentation had found its way to Simon Wiesenthal who would be zealously following up any leads and passing them on to Mossad, the Israeli Intelligence Agency. It was agents from Mossad, based on a tip from Wiesenthal, who were responsible for the capture a few years ago of Adolf Eichmann, one of his most valued associates.

Dieser verfluchte Jude, Wiesenthal. Ich muss etwas gegen ihn und die Briten tun die dieses Problem verursacht haben, he thought. *That accursed Jew, Wiesenthal. I will have to do something about him and those Britishers who caused this problem.*

Foreword

❖

James St. Clair returns with his new found ally, Mossad agent Matt Layman. Together they face the sinister secret Nazi organization, The Brotherhood of the Blood, led by Heinrich Mueller, the former head of the Gestapo. Mueller who evaded capture at the end of world war two had been presumed dead for nearly twenty years until discovered living under a false identity in the heart of Germany.

The architect of his discovery and exposure of his secret organization had been James St Clair due to a chance find in the Sahara desert of documentation relating back to world war two and the Nazi plans to establish a new Fourth Reich in the event that they lost the war.

Now operating under another new identity, Mueller had sworn vengeance on St. Clair and all associated with him for his exposure and costly disruption to his plans. Following his exposure Mueller was forced to flee to South America where the Brotherhood had established an extensive network in several countries sympathetic to the Nazi ideology. Safe there using one of his many false identities he repaired the damage caused to the organization and planned his return to Europe back into the heart of the Brotherhood's secret headquarters from where he would continue to guide it's agenda of infiltration into government and control of industry with the long term aim of reuniting east and west Germany as the Fourth Reich and the destruction of communism.

Unaware that the highly effective and powerful Israeli intelligence service, known as Mossad, had taken an interest in the Brotherhood with the aim of capturing Mueller, as they had Adolf Eichmann two years earlier, had St Clair under constant protective surveillance. St Clair himself was equally unaware of Mossad's presence or that he was unknowingly being used as bait to draw out Mueller into the open. Following an attempt on St Clair's life, the Mossad team's leader, Matt Layman reveals their surveillance and they agree to cooperate in an attempt to capture Mueller.

Brotherhood of the Blood

❖

CHAPTER 1

A passenger from the recently arrived Lufthansa flight from Lisbon to Munich made his way through immigration. In a light raincoat over a dark business suit wearing a homburg hat and dark glasses, the man carried just a briefcase. He looked like any other businessman amongst the queue of passengers eager to get through the entry formalities. As he stepped forward to present his passport to the immigration officer, he removed his dark glasses and averted his eyes which were a piercing steely grey. This action diverted the officer's attention sufficiently so that, with just a casual glance at the man, the immigration official handed back the passport and nodded him through without a word.

Once through immigration, the man walked leisurely through baggage reclaim without stopping and out into the arrivals hall of the airport where friends and relatives were waiting to meet the incoming passengers.

At the back of a small crowd waiting at the entrance to the arrivals hall, the man caught sight of a placard bearing the name Herr Liebermann being held by a man in perhaps his mid-thirties wearing a dark chauffeur's uniform and cap.

Walking up to him, he just nodded as the young man reached forwards and took the briefcase, turned on his heel and walked towards the exit. As they exited the building, the young man turned and said, "Welcome to Munich, Herr Oberst-Gruppenfuehrer. Please follow me."

The arrival looked straight at the young man and, without saying a word, followed him to a parking area where a black Mercedes limousine awaited and stood back for the passenger door to be opened. As he settled himself into one of the comfortable rear passenger seats of the spacious compartment, the driver handed back the briefcase which he placed on the seat beside him.

Travelling on a German passport in the name of Helmut Liebermann, he had flown first from Paraguay to Rio de Janeiro in Brazil and then to Lisbon in Portugal where he changed to a Lufthansa flight to Munich. Posing as a businessman for a German manufacturing company, he kept a low profile at all times travelling in economy class even though it was tiring over such a long journey. Now the journey was almost over, he relaxed in the comparative luxury of the Mercedes and contemplated the mission ahead that had brought him to Europe.

As head of the Brotherhood of the Blood, the clandestine organization that had emerged from what was formerly ODESSA, his real identity was that of Heinrich Mueller the former head of the Gestapo of Nazi Germany. He was to meet with the group which managed the vast resources of the Brotherhood and implemented its policies. Made up of a number of former Nazis and devoted followers, the meeting would take place in a remote part of the Bavarian mountains at the Brotherhood's headquarters established as a sanatorium for former military personnel.

The sanatorium, ostensibly sponsored and funded by a number of respectable and prominent companies in the armaments industry, associated industries and financial institutions, was in fact funded by the Brotherhood through a number of those companies' shareholders who were nominee companies covertly owned by the Brotherhood. Through this method of control, the sanatorium was above any suspicion as anything other than a highly respected institution as all the members of the board of governors were also directors or senior executives of the sponsoring companies.

Security at the sanatorium was extensive and well-organized. Situated in a prominent position on high ground with a back drop of steep mountain slopes and a view down towards a mountain lake called Spitzingsee, it was surrounded by a tall wire fence. The area, noted for its clear mountain air, made it an ideal location for the sanatorium which was named after the lake. The approach was through electrically controlled gates with a military-style guardhouse and attendant security personnel.

The reason given for this level of security was that some of the patients suffered from mental illnesses and, unless kept under close surveillance, might wander off into the mountains. This ensured that not only was it difficult to get out of the grounds but no unwelcome visitors could gain access.

The driver stopped at the guardhouse and spoke briefly to the attendant who, after looking in at the passenger, called back into the guardhouse and the metal gates started to swing open silently on well-oiled mountings. Once though the gates, the car wound up a sweeping paved road to the sanatorium on the crest of the high ground.

As they drew to a stop at the entrance, a figure in a white doctor's coat appeared and waited at the bottom of the steps to greet the arrival.

The passenger waited for the driver to open the door for him, emerged with his briefcase in his left hand and stepped forwards.

"Welcome, Herr Liebermann. It's good to see you again," said the tall, white-haired, distinguished-looking figure.

"Thank you, Doctor Silvermann. It's good to be back," said the arrival as he shook the outstretched hand.

Doctor Silvermann was the sanatorium director, a well-respected psychiatrist who knew Herr Liebermann as the chairman of the board of governors.

The whole of the medical staff at the sanatorium, doctors and nurses alike, were all genuine members of the medical profession who had no knowledge of the actual covert ownership or its links to former Nazis. They, and most of the maintenance and catering staff, were all employed from, or lived in, the nearest towns or villages. The senior staff mostly had their own transport but the sanatorium ran a very efficient private transport system which catered for the local staff to accommodate the need for twenty-four-hour shift duties.

In comparison, all of the security personnel and some of the maintenance staff were all former SS prison guards or members of the Gestapo who lived on the premises in accommodation scattered around the grounds and bound by an oath of silence to the Brotherhood.

As well as being a sanatorium in the normal sense, it also offered itself as a health spa where private individuals could come for periods ranging from a few days to a week or more to restore their health following an illness or to lose weight on a fitness course. This provided a very legitimate cover for various politicians or members of industry who owed their allegiance to the Brotherhood to meet with their masters to discuss policy and ways to increase the Brotherhood's influence in government and the economy. To this end, the Brotherhood maintained a whole wing separate from the main building containing accommodation for governors and their apostles to meet.

It was to this wing which Mueller was conducted and he was shown into a suite reserved for the chairman.

"How long will you be staying this time, Herr Liebermann?" asked Doctor Silvermann.

"Have all the other governors arrived?"

"Yes, the last one arrived yesterday. All eight of them are now settled in their rooms."

"Very good. We have much to discuss since our last meeting so I expect to be here for at least three more days, Herr Doctor."

"I hope you will have time for me to report on the situation here at the sanatorium, which I must say right away is in very good shape and the staff are very happy. There is some new equipment which is available which I believe would greatly enhance our performance and profitability which I would like to discuss with you."

"I am very pleased with the way you run the sanatorium and am sure there will be no difficulty concerning new equipment. It is in all our interests to ensure we maintain our high reputation for the latest and best treatments available. When I have had the opportunity to look through my schedule, we will speak again on this subject."

"Thank you, Herr Liebermann. I will leave you now and look forward to hearing from you."

After the doctor had left, Mueller took off his raincoat and hat. He placed his briefcase on the desk in the corner of the suite's sitting room and sat back in the chair behind the desk. Picking up the telephone, he pressed a button on the instrument labelled "security" which was answered almost immediately.

"Schroeder, security."

"Gerhardt, please come to my suite immediately."

"At once, sir," was the curt reply.

A few minutes later, there was a knock at the door.

"Come in," said Mueller, loud enough for it to be heard outside in the hallway.

The door opened and a medium height, middle-aged man of muscular build, with blond close-cropped hair and blue eyes wearing a quasi-military style uniform but no insignia or badges of rank, entered. He closed the door behind him, walked smartly to the front of the desk where he stopped, snapped to attention and raised his right hand in the Nazi salute and said, "*Ich erwarte Ihre Befehle, Herr Oberst-Gruppenfuehrer.*"

Mueller, did not return the salute but instead stood up and stretched out his hand which, his visitor with a sigh of relief, took and shook warmly.

"How are you, Gerhardt?"

"I am very well, thank you, sir."

Gerhardt Schroeder had been a Sturmbannfuehrer *(Major)* on Heinrich Mueller's staff as his aide. He owed his survival at the war's end and his present secure and well-paid position entirely to his former chief and was intensely loyal to him. In return, Mueller looked on Schroeder as the closest thing to a friend he ever had and he was the only person to which he ever displayed any degree of intimacy or familiarity and was the only person he could truly trust.

In spite of this, however, Schroeder could never overlook a lifetime of discipline and take advantage of this and always recognized their difference in former rank and gave Mueller the respect required by this relationship.

"There is no need to stand to attention, Gerhardt, we are alone. Please take a seat," said Mueller, indicating the chair in front of the desk. "There is a matter which I wish to discuss with you concerning a gross breach in security."

Schroeder sat upright in his chair with a look of surprise and concern on his face. "Indeed, sir, and what might that be?"

"That young man, the driver who collected me from the airport, he is new. Where did he come from and what happened to our older driver?"

"I'm afraid our previous driver and mechanic died of cancer about six months ago and I had to find a replacement. This new driver came highly recommended through our network."

"What is this man's background? I take it you did a thorough security check on him."

"Indeed I did, sir. He served with the Hitler Youth before joining the SS where he served as a driver mechanic in a Waffen SS division."

"That probably accounts for it. The Waffen SS were never as disciplined as those that served in the security services."

"What exactly did this man do to cause such a gross breach in security?"

"He addressed me openly in public as Herr Oberst-Gruppenfuehrer."

"My God. Was it within the hearing of any members of the public?"

"Thankfully not but that is not the issue. How did he know to address me in that form in the first place? Only you and a few trusted associates know me by my real name and position. All the other security personnel here are bound by an oath of silence to the Brotherhood and know of its aims and policy but are not privy to the identity of its principals, especially mine. How could he have come into that information after such a short time here?"

"The only thing I can think of, sir, is that it was the result of some idle speculation and loose tongues amongst the security staff. But I even find that difficult to believe as all the others have been with me a long time and I trust them."

"Whatever the cause, we cannot afford this sort of breach of security. You must deal with it immediately in such a way that it sends a message that any future breaches will be dealt with the utmost severity. You understand my meaning, Gerhardt?"

"Yes, sir. If you will permit me, I will leave now and take care of the matter personally."

"Very good, Gerhardt. Please carry on."

Schroeder rose from his chair and, resisting the urge to salute, turned on his heel and walked quickly to the door and opened it. He turned back in the open doorway and, with a feeling of shame at letting down his chief, he said, "Leave it to me, sir. It will never happen again."

With that, he pulled the door closed and hurried off intent on repairing the damage to his security, of which he was so proud, in such a manner that would leave no doubt in the minds of others that such breaches would result in extreme consequences.

***

A few hours after his meeting with Schroeder, Mueller was looking out from his sitting room window overlooking the approach to the sanatorium when he saw a police car and an ambulance coming up the driveway. As they drew to a stop at the front of the building, his telephone extension rang. Walking quickly to his desk, he picked up the handset and said, "Liebermann."

"This is Doctor Silvermann, sir. In case you happened to have noticed the arrival of a police car, I am afraid I have to report to you that there has been a serious accident involving one of our staff. In fact, it is the driver who recently drove you here from the airport."

"Indeed. And what was the nature of the accident?"

"It appears he was working underneath one of the cars and the jack holding it up slipped and the back of his skull was crushed, killing him instantly."

"How unfortunate. He seemed like a very pleasant young man. Did he have a family or relatives that should be informed?"

"Not according to our records, sir. After the formalities, he will be buried in the local town cemetery."

"Very good. Thank you for letting me know." As he put the phone down, he reflected on his recent meeting with Schroeder and was satisfied with how quickly and efficiently he had dealt with the matter.